I0666341

INDEBTED

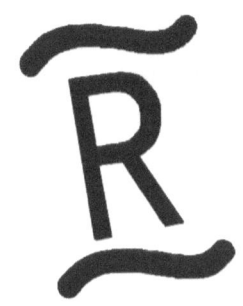

Natalie Jayne

Two Square Books Publishing
Hangtown, USA

Long May She Wave

All characters, locations and events presented in this novel are
products of the author's imagination or are used fictitiously.
Any resemblance to real events or people, whether living or
dead, is entirely coincidental.

INDEBTED

Published by Two Square Books Publishing
Hangtown, USA
twosquarebooks.com

SECOND EDITION

ISBN 978-0989076494

The boys and I would like to thank
Mrs. Connie Miller and her bathtub of chickens.

Most especially we would like to thank the author's mother for sharing a legacy of language, unbreakable love, and unwavering confidence.

Aspen

CASWELL CROSSING

Established: somewhere, somewhen

Population:

~~Horses~~ — long gone

baked — Cattle

Chickens — fried

Pigs

barking — 1 Dog

Horses

Unruly — 1 Goat

People — +2

Elevation: Don't look down

CHAPTER 1
Lost Nuts
On The Dodge
Hunting
Unkind Morning
100 doors
Harmony
Efficient Visitor

N<small>UTS!</small> A bovine at a spit roast could not have been more vexed. All the same, that was as profane, and nearly as profound, as J.E. Haverston ever became. He scurried about his study shifting nicks, nacks, brics and brac with an indiscriminant fervor. Periodically he stopped, stared about the cluttered study, gave a helpless flap, and resumed his frantic search. It was here. It must be! Haverston had held it in his very own fingers not two minutes ago. If he didn't find it, he was going to have more in common with that cow than he cared to consider.

"Think where you were last," his wife suggested from the sitting room, in that feminine way she had of attending to one thing with half her brain, whilst completely engaged in a thoroughly unrelated endeavor with the other half. The problem with that, Haverston felt, was neither venture ever achieved more than half-steam.

"Wouldn't think I had thought of that one," he said to himself, followed by self-congratulations for managing a passable 'yes, dear' that proved, between them, it was he with the better upstairs boiler.

Hadn't he done everything sensible? Backtracked every step? Backtracked places he hadn't even been? Of course it made no sense, but that's what people did who knew darn well a thing should be somewhere, despite the fact it wasn't. Somehow it twisted around to logic that if, after looking in every place reasonable, one were to look in all places **un**reasnable it would naturally **become** reasonable.

The notion went hand in hand with looking in the selfsame place one has already looked, as if by Lady Luck's fickle whim the missing item will have fortuitously appeared. Unfortunately, a lady does not keep company with a married man. Oh, dear.

C ASWELL Crossing almost didn't exist. Partly because its founding father almost hadn't arrived. It was also because, in the fine year of 18-ot, there existed an almighty stretch of territory in which one modest collection of buildings could become quite lost without much fuss. If a rider were to ask had anybody seen a town nearby, the most likely answer would have been: A what? That is, if anyone could have been found to ask.

Despite the odds, Caswell Crossing had indeed been founded. Several buildings camped in a slightly crooked row that angled, more or less, northwest to southeast. Construction had been accomplished by use of rough lumber, rock— possibly the region's greatest resource– and stout timber. Most of the buildings were greeted by a stretch of boardwalk to keep prospective customers up out of the muck which, in its various forms, proved a real problem one month out of the year and provided a considerable measure of amusement for another seven. If it wasn't boot sucking, wheel jamming mud, it was swirling windblown dust, or packed ice which, after the wind had its way, was slicker than a greased watermelon.

Gideon Fletcher walked through this modest representation of civilization as if he belonged there. It generally worked. People were inclined to take notice of someone running. The trick, the way to go unnoticed, was to act as if you belonged where you, in point of fact, had no decent business whatsoever. Unfortunately for Gideon, he was not exactly a stranger. How he had ever ended up in this predicament, he would never know.

Sure ya do, boyo.

He did. It had all started with William E. Tarlston and it was nothing Gideon talked about. The upshot was he had been pinned with a three year sentence for a crime he hadn't committed. Several crimes actually. Quite unaccountably, the town's make-shift circuit judge had skipped over the notion of a jail cell in favor of shackling Gideon with his very own court appointed guard, a well-to-do gentleman determined to reform him.

Oh well, a man had to do what he could with what he had– even if it was a reputation as a purveyor of geographically misdirected livestock of a questionably secondhand nature.

Not long ago it had been almighty close to grave sizing time— not long before that had been rope sizing time— and yet here Gideon stood, still on his own two feet. Not in his own boots though, he had no idea where they were. He'd blithely annexed everything he wore and, by and large, his gaunt frame resembled a scarecrow who only maintained employment because the crows were too busy cracking up to bother with the corn.

The apparition of his reflection appraised him from a shop window. Gideon had to allow the crows would be justified. In his experience, clothes without patches, holes, or stains from sources no one dared investigate counted for goin'-to-picnic finery. If a man had a second shirt to put on after his autumn scrubbing he was living well indeed. The borrowed duds hanging on him shaped up to a pretty penny and were washing line clean. A solid foot taller, and twice himself thicker, maybe Gideon wouldn't cut too bad a figure. As it stood, thank goodness for braces or keeping his britches up would have been a job. He had already rolled up or tied down all the extra yardage he could, like a man lashing down for a squall.

The funny side took a broader hold; there was a worse sight he could imagine. When his do-gooding guard awoke and thought to dress– now there would be one heck of a fine sight. Gideon savored the vision and continued on his way, aiding and abetting a grin that reached to his toes without much touching his face.

The first merchants began arriving to start the predictable pattern of another mundane day. Good mornings were given, welcome signs turned, doors propped open in silent celebration of the agreeable weather. Would any of these sleepy-eyed, peace-living townspeople suspect they had a man on the dodge amongst their number? If Gideon was careful, they would remain blissfully ignorant.

Alongside a saloon, empty of customers at this hour of propriety, he drew up. Through the swinging doors came noises of furniture being scraped against the rough floor, followed by footsteps of someone in no hurry. Concealed by the brim of his tattered hat, one item he could at least claim for his own, Gideon peered out at the wide street. No one peered back. A middle-aged Chinaman came out, offered a courteous nod and added an infinitesimal shake of his head, broom never pausing as he worked it along the boardwalk. The exchange was little enough for a witness to observe. What could they say? Two people nodded good morning? There was a capital crime if ever one had been committed.

Gideon set off again, lest the non-existent witness wonder why he lingered. Between one step and the next, everything blurred, as if the world had turned and left him behind. He slumped against a post, head swimming, and told himself to pull it together.

An aroma insinuated itself upon the cool morning breeze. Like a fish on a line, Gideon let it lure him along. Through the watery distortion of a shop window he spotted a woman, her pleasant oval face gone red from the heat of an oven. She transferred loaves of golden brown, oat sprinkled tastiness to the counter and spared him a moment's affable wave.

Hey! Boyo!

Gideon shook himself up. He was right; standing there gawking like a guppy was an attitude he could not well afford. Nice and easy like, he scanned the street. The mercantile remained closed, the warehouse beside it as well. At the livery stable, a horse nickered excitedly at the arrival of her breakfast. A body couldn't ask for anything more normal.

Bear sign! That woman had made bear sign! Come to think on it, maybe that mare had her a thought worth thinking. Did he have– Gideon dug for the means and came up with a quarter eagle, a veritable treasury to someone whose pockets seldom held even a three cent piece. It wasn't his, and it was barely the wish of a drop in the very large barrel of what he was due, but handing over that coin gave Gideon an unrestrained, childish satisfaction.

The first donut was gone before he left the shop and it made an excellent breakfast. Then again, he had skipped last night's supper and wasn't too sure about lunch, so maybe this was yesterday's breakfast today.

Outside, a bench invited him to linger. Gideon eyed it with no small inclination, but ducked around into the cover of an alley instead.

There was a game he played, sometimes for fun and sometimes despite himself. When the miles stretched out, he'd dust off the crates of memory, check the labels and play a few rounds of 'When Was'. When was the last time he'd owned five dollars of his very own? When was the last time he'd slept without a gun to hand? When was the last time he'd had a proper bedroll? When was the first?

What Gideon wondered now was when had the bright morning, heretofore a comfort, become too much? A stack of overturned half-barrels steadied him whilst he willed the strange feeling washing over him to wash itself away. He told himself firmly it would pass and wondered if he lied.

"You mind telling me what in tarnation you think you're doing?"

Gideon sprang from the barrels, staggered and, thanks to Sheriff Luke Gandy, failed to fall flat over.

"Gggff!" he protested, cheeks stuffed with the last of his breakfast.

"Never mind. No call to ruin a promising day," and with a relaxed inexorableness, Gandy escorted his prisoner around the corner and down the street.

The lawman was a neat, clean shaven gentleman in his early thirties. Where he was forced to look up to many a man physically speaking, it was many another who looked to him when it really counted. Gandy wondered at times if his unremarkable five foot nine might be an advantage for him as a lawman. A big shouldered brute was naturally set up to discourage a certain amount of mischief before it even got its teeth in, but there were those who felt challenging such a man, provided they came out the better, would set their ego up a treat. To some, having bragging rights was worth the risk of getting their fool head blown off.

That was one worry Gandy never had to contend with, for him it was the presumption he could be walked over with impunity. A misguided unfortunate, who did not have the knack of recognizing where impunity left off and recklessness took up, might be foolish enough to take him for insubstantial. It usually took them quite by surprise to discover his lean frame was pure compact muscle backed by a personality that knew exactly where it stood. This fact had certainly come as a surprise to many an intractable Saturday night good-timer. The smart ones took a short lesson in stepping back. The slower learners were given a few days of quiet solitude, compliments of Caswell Crossing, to reflect upon the error of their ways.

"Ya can't lock me up," opinioned his current pupil.

"Can't I?" Gandy contradicted tolerantly.

A lawman could lock a man up for right about anything, or right about nothing. It all sort of depended on their mood and, to Gideon's figuring, who was payrolling them. Although he did not resist the hand on his elbow, as it at least was steady whilst the ground was not, sheer habit drove Gideon to pursue his objection with the present embodiment of institutionalized authority.

"What's the charge?"

"'Excessive Use Of Stupidity In Public' sounds about right. In you go."

Sheriff Gandy went through his office to the cells beyond and deposited his catch on a narrow cot. Normally, he would be the first to instill the notion being arrested was not akin to checking in at the Marion Hotel. His cells held to the bare necessities and did not feature room service, hot water, nor soft feather-down beds. In this case, he decided to make an exception.

"Aspen's going to have words for you, boy," Gandy called out, as he collected a stack of blankets from the room he over glorified as quarters. Returning to the lock-up, he frowned. His prisoner sat, slumped against the wall, precisely as he'd been left. "And mighty strong words at that."

"He ain't my brother," Gideon objected, a flash of spark jumping to grey eyes gone dull.

"Did I say it? Call him an officer of the court if you like, but Aspen will still have something to say about this."

Gandy charitably chalked Gideon's stubborn refusal to acknowledge his situation up to an overwrought brain and began spreading out the extra bedding.

"What were you thinking?" he said, resuming his scolding. "No, forget I asked. Untangling your explanations makes my head hurt. Budge up, that'll do. Now let me get this shirt off you– Aspen's I suppose? —and we'll see what harm you've done yourself."

Three bullets. Three slugs of metal had ripped through this boy leaving him with a hole clean through his side, another in his right shoulder and a nearly healed furrow along his left arm.

Any rational person would take that as sufficient cause to keep still. It would make sense if the person in question had some pressing business that demanded he remain on his feet– such as if whomever had done the shooting was still on **his** feet. Gideon had no such excuse. Shot three times and here he was gallivanting around town. Aspen rivers would have something to say about that, until then the sheriff was willing and able to stand proxy.

"Stay put. Not one foot, not one toe, off that cot. Do I make myself understood?" Placing restrictions on Gideon required circling the words until he was thoroughly surrounded. "**Stay put**. You so much as think about moving and, so help me, I will handcuff you to the wall."

"Ya favor my comp'ny that much?" Gideon mumbled, in a pale attempt at humor as Gandy pulled off his boots.

Pale, that was an apt word. Gandy had helped old ladies across the street with more effort than it had taken to bring Gideon in. A thick bush of unruly hair was the only thing about him with an ounce of gumption. As usual, it was a patchwork of color that hinted towards brown with a hold out on red and no decision whatsoever as to wavy or straight. The only thing every last strand had in common was a complete commitment to chaos. Appropriate really.

Gandy rubbed the back of his neck and wished Doctor Connell were there— not that Gandy couldn't handle it, he could and had before this. It was simply that he felt more at home with the brute force and ignorance method of problem solving: kick it, shoot it or play dumb until it talked.

About to repeat his injunction, Gandy shook his head and harrumphed softly. Gideon was already asleep. The sheriff started the Arbuckle's brewing; looked like he was going to be there awhile.

A breeze twined its way through the pine trees, causing a soft rustling. It wasn't precisely cold, but it sure wasn't warm either. It usually wasn't at such an elevation; mountains were good at chilly nights no matter where they were or what name men had given them.

On this mountain there was a secluded nook of a space, sheltered from wind, cold, prying eyes and all. In this nook hunkered a man cooking his supper. His judiciously small fire burned low and what smoke escaped quickly became lost in the thick screen of pine branches overhead. More familiar with a poker table than a mountainside he might be, he'd not deny it, however he was a man with a strong desire for a long and prosperous future. Leaving the welcome light blazing for all and sundry ran directly counter to that hankering.

As he crowded close, enjoying the flames, an overly excited spark snapped up and lit upon the brim of his hat. He shook it off without bother, brushed back a lock of dark hair, and resettled the hat. Then the man adjusted the rifle cradled across his lap and listened closely, though his horse made it clear everything was as it should be. Animal or man, if something approached, that horse would go from aimless munching to instant ears-pricked attention.

The traveler sipped his coffee and pulled out a bowie knife to check the potato buried in the coals. Red heat danced and shimmered along the blade. Whilst he waited for his supper, the man considered on where he had been putting his own attention.

It had all happened years ago, but that made no difference. There were some things nothing could alter, not time, nor distance, nor whatever may have occurred in between.

He had been following bits and pieces and best guesses. It had been a fruitless search to say the least. Just when it looked like he'd found something, by the time he arrived there would be nothing but the proverbial cold soot and old tracks. It was worse than searching for a needle in a haystack. Then serendipity had delivered a discarded, out of date newspaper and, like a compass swinging around, his search had finally taken a solid direction.

AUGUSTUS Thacker, who wisely went by Gus, had been keeping an eye on the office of Doctor Tadhg Connell– pronounced Tige not 'Tag' nor 'Tad'— and for the most part the locals had been thus educated. The man himself had been called away before the rooster cockled its first doodle-do. Since Gus's barbershop was to hand, and until Tadhg's arrival Gus had been the nearest thing to a physician, it was a common favor.

It was not so common for the very patient he was supposed to be watching to slip away without him knowing and Gus had to admit to a certain amount of guilty conscience. It was this that had caused him to hold the morning coffee for ransom.

His neighbor of one door down came, as he did every morning, to share a pot and had even brought doughnuts from the new bakery, only to have his much anticipated ritual denied. Entirely focused on the delicious black ambrosia, the man heard not a word Gus said until the barber smacked his hand and levered his capacious body between mortal man and liquid heaven. Only then did Gus's urgency get through and would he mind watching— attentively— for Aspen to emerge from the doctor's office whilst Gus went to look for someone or other and he didn't care whom just give him the coffee and yes, yes he would watch and no he wouldn't leave and yes he promised.

The coffee pot was now empty, the doughnuts a happy memory, and Silas Cooper still reclined in a chair outside the barbershop. His legs were stretched out comfortably and absentmindedly he rubbed the toe of one shoe against the back of a trouser leg to remove an imagined scuff. He was well suited, though less expensively than many another lawyer, and his genial features danced as if he were forever enjoying some small and private joke upon the world. On the whole, Silas measured up handsome enough to turn the head of the average woman.

With the woman across the street he hadn't a chance. She was far too busy gawking at Aspen Rivers. Her hands flew to her mouth and her delicate young face blushed exquisitely.

"Hey, Gus! You better get out here."

The barber came to the door at a trot and stopped on a dime as the petite woman scuttled off, leaving Aspen– son of a prominent citizen— standing in the middle of the street as if forcefully expelled from the doctor's office. Locks of golden-brown hair stood up haphazardly and his chest boasted no covering but summer weight unmentionables. Aspen's feet were naked, and a pair of britches– clearly not to his measure– climbed up his shins whilst the braces dangled unproductively at the knee. Clearly the morning was not being kind; the orderly Aspen Rivers was desperately out of order.

The only thought on Aspen's mind, however, was not his state of appearance, but his charge's disappearance.

He spotted Gus and called out, "Have you seen—"

"Gandy has him– Aspen, wait! You can't parade around like that!"

Even as Gus spoke, another woman drew up sharply, this one in her fifties with every pin in perfect place, gasping and sputtering, unable to believe what she was seeing right there on the public street.

The sight of Mrs. Driscoll, scandalized and appalled as she stomped away, made Augustus Thacker crack up. He roared so loudly it took his breath and that made Silas, heretofore content to smirk, lose it as well, though he at least had the decency to do so with less volume.

Despite debilitating laughter, Gus waved Aspen over and pulled him into the shelter of the barbershop. Silas followed along and took a seat on one of the official chairs where he tried to pull himself together and failed. Gus did not even try. Aspen Rivers glared at them both.

"This is no time—" he began sternly, trying valiantly to gain some fragment of control.

"Gideon's. . . fine. . . honest," Silas gasped out, wiping away a tear.

Gus could do no more than lean against the counter, hands wrapped around his prodigious belly, and fight to draw breath.

"Will you two be serious!" Aspen scolded. "Do I look

like a man in a humorous mood?"

They examined him afresh and their laughter burst anew and that young thing blushing the deepest of reds clean to her toes and Mrs. Driscoll— that gossiping busybody of all people— it was more than they could stand.

"Aw, knock it off," Aspen tried again. "That boy could be in twelve kinds of mischief by now."

Manifestly incapable of speech, Gus gestured for Aspen to wait and went upstairs. His barrel laughter accompanied him as he left and preceded him as he returned.

Even the most generous of descriptions could not claim the clothes he handed over had even the whisper of a hope of fitting Aspen's trim 6'4". Gus was significantly shorter and, bluntly, rounder. The overall result was a distinctly hodgepodge collection that looked like it had been gathered from the depths of numerous forgotten closets. Aspen stood, if not a man of fashion, at least a man of modesty.

Though there were not many women in town to be offended at the sight of his disreputable self, for Aspen, the sight of Mrs. Driscoll had been more than sufficient. That woman had an absolute talent for being exactly where you would really rather she was not, exactly when you did not want her to be there. Why her?! He would never, ever, hear the end of this. He really wouldn't.

Gales of laughter erupted once again from his barely controlled friends. Aspen shook an impotent finger at them, searching for something, anything, he could say to make this embarrassing episode one shaved penny better.

He gave up.

The expression on Mrs. Driscoll's face would stay with him forever— his brothers would make sure of it and Gus would be sure to tell them. In a rare state, Aspen Rivers turned on his heal and aimed himself towards the sheriff's office.

Harmony squeaked like a startled child and clung to her husband, skirts rippling out around her. It had been an imp that made him swing her down from their wagon like that. Fredrick Harmon was quite sure heaven stopped in that moment and he couldn't blame the angels for staring, he couldn't help himself either.

The angel of his very own left her hands on his shoulders slightly longer than needful, favoring him with a twinkle meant for him alone. Then his young wife gave him a tiny shove that clearly said 'that'll be enough out of you, sir' and turned for the boardinghouse. Impulsively, Fredrick caught her by the arm and planted a kiss on her cheek— right there in public. It took no more than the blink of an eye, hardly worthy of mention in the monthly gazette, but Mr. Harmon was particularly pleased with his mischief. He picked up the reins— and paused. From the concealment of the boardinghouse doorway, his wife touched delicate fingers to rosy lips. Harmon tipped his hat, debonair as you please, and clucked to the horses. He could not have been one measure happier.

Sheriff Gandy could not miss the clucking of the women as, some minutes later, he drew abreast of the boardinghouse. Mrs. Harmon stepped onto the walk, still talking to her unseen companion who was commenting on how quickly infants grew.

What was it about a baby that set even the most sensible women to fussing like hens? Maybe it was something in the species– women, not hens– though it was sometimes hard to tell the difference.

"I wouldn't be surprised to see him up and walking by the time we arrive. Thank you again, Lovina. They're truly lovely," Mrs. Harmon said, pressing her new nephew's clothes against her chest. "Afternoon, Sheriff."

Gandy touched a finger to his hat. "Mrs. Harmon."

He had a feeling the young woman had something on her mind and, sure enough, she stayed at his elbow. The woman kept her peace, though, until they were well away from prying ears.

"Could I. . . that is. . ."

"Yes, ma'am?"

"I don't want to impose but, you see. . . ," Harmony's hand nervously caressed the lace trimmed baby clothes Lovina had given her. "Well, my husband and I will be gone for a couple of days and, if it isn't too much trouble, I wondered if you might. . ."

"I'd be happy to keep an eye on your place, Mrs. Harmon."

The woman's concern dissipated on the instant and brightness returned to her springtime features. "Thank you, Sheriff. You have set my mind at ease."

"Glad to oblige, ma'am."

Up ahead, Fredrick stepped out of the mercantile and the expression that flashed across Harmony's face made it clear their arrangement was not something she wanted her husband in on. Gandy winked at her.

"That's a mighty load you have there, Fredrick," he said, peering over the side of the wagon and peek-a-booing at a box overflowing with supplies. "Way you're set, a body would think that new boy was yours."

"Near enough," the new uncle beamed paternal pride once removed.

"I found your wife up the way," Gandy said, courteously handing said woman up to the wagon's seat. "Thought you might be missing her."

"Not so as to risk the women talk, Sheriff."

"Coward."

"When it comes to having the life chattered clean out of

me, yessir," Fredrick Harmon cheerfully admitted, snugging a rope around his cargo.

Gandy gave him a friendly clap on the shoulder. "Give my best to your family."

"Thank you, Sheriff."

Up on the wagon, Mrs. Harmon flashed a grateful smile. Running into the sheriff had not been intentional, but she was immensely relieved. Now she could focus on her family instead of the dented tin in her kitchen.

Harmony thought of the abundant supplies her husband had purchased. They would have to be careful through the winter, but her in-laws, with their new baby, would have everything they needed.

Should she have told Sheriff Gandy about the theft? Harmony decided not. Money was a private matter and she would never dream of speaking of it in public, particularly if it might embarrass her husband. They had counted and recounted with no change to the truth. Some of the money that should have been in their savings tin was not.

TYPICALLY, consciousness came to Gideon at the drop of a hat. The slightest out of place noise, a footstep, an unfamiliar voice– all were an instant trigger for a man who valued his hide. It was peculiar indeed for him to lay there in a muddled stupor.

Certain facts began to present themselves for consideration. He was breathing and nothing ached– at least, not more than had become customary. He had not awoken to handcuffs, ropes, or flying bullets. So: alive, not under attack, and not under arrest. A fine start by anyone's standards.

He rubbed his eyes and a wall fuzzed into existence, the paint neither yellow nor peach and certainly not white no matter what crazy moniker people tried to hang on it. Why did they do that? White was white, not eggshell nor bleached linen. Did they never stop to think how embarrassing it could be? White had quiet dignity. It held itself neutral and got on with every color in the rainbow regardless of tint, hue or prismatic position. And what did it get for thanks? Being called 'lady's lace' behind its back. Rotten tomatoes would have been less insulting.

Gideon wondered what he had been thinking about and what paint had to do with anything anyway?

You're lucky ya ain't a-askin' that from t'other side-a the grave, boyo.

Huh? That'd be a perty trick, wouldn't it?

Wake up!

The wall snapped into a sensible shape. He was in the doc's back room. That was an unduly generous description. The narrow bed upon which Gideon lay, and the small table beside him, vied for square footage. It was closer to a closet than a room and had in fact been used for storage until being converted for its current occupant. The sunlight, which sauntered in boldly of a morning and spread a wide, warm square across the patchwork quilt, was now the general indeterminate shade of afternoon.

Shtch. Shtch.

Gideon realized he had been hearing the faint noise for some time. He turned and, as usual, found Aspen Rivers. The man sat on the floor, square shoulders braced against the bed and long legs drawn up.

"What're ya doin'?"

Aspen glanced around. "Feeling better?"

"You gonna answer me?"

Aspen tapped his pencil on the broad, much used book propped upon his knees. "Ledgers, for the store. You'd know that if you could read."

"I meant," Gideon clarified, ignoring the jibe meant to inspire him, "why here?"

If Aspen was going to persist in guarding him like this, how was he ever going to get loose? The free, open out-there -ness beckoned from right beyond the window, whilst Gideon remained trapped within these infernal walls— right where he had been for ages.

"Efficiency," came Aspen's laconic reply.

That was Aspen all over: ten dollar words came to him at a dime a dozen. It wasn't as if the deuced man had to use such fancified lingo, he did it to prove Gideon could not. And Gideon flat refused to beg the meaning. To do so would have been tantamount to admitting he was at a deficit, which would have played smack bang into Aspen's hand.

He was dead set on making Gideon into a proper gentleman. Trouble was, racehorses were racehorses and mules were mules. No matter how much fancy gear you threw on a mule, or how much you kicked it, all you'd end up with was a mule. Possibly a rather vexed mule, or perhaps one with a complicated personality disorder, but a mule nonetheless.

Gideon didn't figure to need expensive trappings all spit and polished. Being himself, even if he were a mule, was plenty—

You can say that again.

—some days it was more than plenty.

Gideon supposed he had his injuries to thank for the subject ever coming up. If not for those dang bullet holes he would have been up and doing, and who cares about the proper etiquette of someone swinging an axe? As it stood, his days were filled with a whole lot of nothing.

Convalescence came easy to some folks. They read, they drifted off into the depths and turnings of their own thoughts, they contemplated the nature of the universe, content as a bird in its nest. With the territory inside his own skull as the destination, there were almighty few places Gideon Fletcher felt inclined to travel.

The terrible unknown regions cartographers surveyed from– and this is important– a discrete distance, then sat in their dusty, paper stuffed offices amusing themselves with ominous labels of 'Here Be Monsters', were nothing in comparison to the places Gideon had personally trudged through and determinedly fenced off.

With long, sharp spikes.

And deep trenches.

And bear traps.

Adding a sign in neat, cramped script warning passersby not to trespass would have been pandering to the incurably dense and inherently short lived.

The suspicious creeks and muffled cries from these regions had, of late, been muffled by Aspen Rivers. Hour after hour he had read aloud, filling the room with stories of the past and philosophies of the present. His coffee cup would click on the table, a page would rustle and the steady voice would flow ever on. In all his life Gideon could recall only two people who had ever stayed by him like that.

Efficiency.

What was he supposed to do with that? As if reading his thoughts, Aspen gave a tip of his head and a rather smug lift of his brow. It was meant to provoke and served its function with flying colors.

"Hush up, you. I done telled ya I ain't some green kid. I know my way 'round, I do."

"Indeed?" Aspen twisted around to regard Gideon directly. "Exactly what part of Rydel did you think out? When he came at you, did you take a say in the place and time or did you walk straight into him?"

The only reason Gideon had been anywhere near town

to get himself aerated was because he had slipped loose from the Rivers, smack into Chase Rydel— the biggest bully Caswell Crossing had to offer. The two of them had waltzed some and, though it wasn't how he had been shot, one thing led to another as life usually did.

"Walked into 'im," Gideon admitted grudgingly.

"More the fool you," said Aspen. "Next time, think."

"Rydel weren't a-wantin' no quiet parlay."

"How kind of you to give him exactly what he did want."

Gideon scowled. He usually did when Aspen was right. That miserable good-for-nothing had gotten precisely what he wanted, a piece of Gideon's hide. Still, there was no sense in admitting that to the likes of Aspen Rivers.

"Ain't none-a that's got nothin' to do with the price-a flour nohow."

"True," Aspen agreed. "We were discussing your lack of education, which you continue to demonstrate admirably."

Gideon knew there was no possible reply to the assertion. Besides, Aspen had turned an otherwise innocent word into a challenge. He should ignore it. He really should. There was no earthly reason to satisfy the man.

Efficiency.

Tentatively, Gideon tasted the word. He sniffed at it. He gave it an experimental tap, and then pried it apart as if cracking a stubborn walnut to get at the nut of meaning within. What he came up with, mostly, were shells.

"It'll be better come dark," he offered. "You still ain't got no kind-a needcessity to be a-writin' that right here."

Aspen's pencil stopped. He stared blankly ahead.

"What's better come dark?"

"Fish," said Gideon.

"What fish?"

"Your fish."

"When did I get fish?"

"That there scriblin' done mucked up your brain," Gideon tapped a finger against Aspen's skull, the way a farmer tests a melon for ripeness. "You don't even know what ya done said."

"What I said?" and then the penny fell.

Ee-fish-antsy. Suddenly, Aspen could see with perfect clarity where Gideon had gone. The boy spoke at least three languages, two with apparently passing fluency. His own native English he handled with the grace of a moose on a mudslide.

"I swear," Gideon was saying, "it's you should be abed."

"Mind your elders," Aspen admonished, more amused than annoyed.

"You ain't no elder."

It was an invitation to a brawl and Gideon knew it. Aspen had proven before now which of them was older. All the same, that was no reason to go believing in limitations. They might exist, but that was no call to give them the satisfaction of justifying them– nor the man who tried to impose them.

"Who dragged you off that mountain?" said Aspen, tallying his accounts.

"Disremember," Gideon answered peevishly.

"Well, I will be happy to remind you, anytime you feel the need."

"Wadda you know."

"The meaning of efficiency for one."

What did that matter? Fancy words, who needed them? Gideon snuck a peek over Aspen's shoulder, but the long, neat columns of writing kept their secrets to themselves.

Aspen felt himself being watched and smiled inwardly. One day Gideon would not be able to stand it. His resistance would crack and then he would demand, with the same vehemence he now refused, to know everything Aspen could teach him.

"Aspen? He awake?"

The hushed, pleasing brogue of Dr. Tadhg Connell grew louder as he approached. He was in his mid-thirties, a broad man, but not a big man. Gideon had seen the same sort by the hundreds when he'd been growing up, men who looked ordinary enough in a suit– if they owned one– yet could lift half a coal car if they took a mind to. He wouldn't put his pay packet on Doc Connell pulling it off now, but there-was-a-day or someday, the build was lurking under signs of steady meals. A few random strands of white had begun to edge in on his thatch of black hair, hinting at a future stateliness without any degree of arrogance.

"Ah, so you are," the doctor answered himself. "You've a visitor, Peter's here. And don't look like that Aspen, it'll do him more good than harm."

Connell moved aside to allow the young man behind him to enter, giving him a meaningful expression as they passed one another.

Awkwardly, the lanky visitor stood on the tiny patch of floor just inside the door. His trousers were brown, his shirt a sun-bleached reminder of brown. Even his untrimmed hair, curling industrially at the ends, was brown. His attention drifted nervously about and stuck on Gideon's injured shoulder. His arm had been splinted right up against his chest. Peter realized he was staring and looked away, only to have his attention drift back again.

"Hello, Peter," said Aspen.

A polite reply slipped automatically from Peter's lips, a tribute to his upbringing.

"Take your ee-fish-antsy elsewheres," Gideon told his guard.

The way Aspen saw it, Peter and Gideon had plenty to

discuss. Then, like everything else in his life, Gideon would shove the entire incident away. How did he do it? How did he direct every ounce of determination towards a single goal, invest every waking moment in the execution of that goal and then, upon achieving it, simply set the whole life consuming affair aside?

William E. Tarlston had been the most recent recipient of Gideon's attentions. It had turned out to be more than that particular claim jumper could handle. It had nearly been more than Gideon and Peter could handle. Fortunately, life gets a kick out of irony and seldom misses an opportunity. The unmourned Tarlston had burned the Harris ranch, ambushed its riders and destroyed Gideon's world. Then, in his last act of revenge, Tarlston had been the unwitting catalyst to something incredibly rare: genuine friendship. Reasoning that only a fool interfered with providence, Aspen let himself be nudged aside.

Alone in the room, neither young man budged. A slight breeze stirred the claustrophobic air. A wagon rattled by, creaks and clopping, stirring up the dust and the dry, tickling smell of it taunted Gideon's lungs.

"Gimme that pillow, will ya?"

He scootched himself up to lean against the wall and the quilt shifted, revealing more bandages wrapped around his middle. Peter forced himself to quit gawking and handed over the pillow. He searched for something, anything, to save him from his own awkwardness. There wasn't much of help in the barren room. Not a chest, wardrobe or hook adorned a single wall. Absence being the only thing to hand, he asked after Gideon's belongings.

"Ain't got much," Gideon replied.

"You have clothes don't you?" Peter persisted.

"They tooked 'em."

"Why?"

"Fig'red as I wouldn't go nowheres without 'em," Gideon explained, with the verbal equivalent of a shrug, followed by a single harrumph of satisfaction. "Learnt 'em somethin' there."

Peter stared uncomprehendingly.

"They say 's they're ruin'd," Gideon elaborated, "but I know they tooked 'em, so I tooked Aspen's."

"Where were you going?"

"Nowheres. Gettin' shut-a this cell's all," Gideon equivocated comfortably.

Silence fell again, a heavy blanket, thick and uncomfortable. Peter found himself thinking it might be nice to have someone like Aspen around. It could have its good points and he wondered if he ought to share this perspective with Gideon. A thread in Peter's shirt was coming loose and, as he stared at it, he noticed a button was nigh to popping off too. Perhaps it was a sister he needed.

"Aw, si'down," Gideon suggested, shattering the silence. "We ain't a-gettin' nowheres this a-way."

Peter perched on the edge of the bed, his hands, folded on his knees, apparently of deep interest. He would have never guessed, when he had thrown in with Gideon, that he would come so close to getting them both killed.

"You wouldn't be here if it weren't for me," he blurted out wretchedly.

"Forget it. If'n ya hadn't-a done what ya done, I wouldn't be here a'tall."

"Didn't exactly have a choice, did I?"

"You did."

Ya could-a left me to die. Same as—

Gideon stared out the window. Folks were always saying mud-dumb things like 'you ain't got no choice'. But there was always a choice, not always a good one, not one you actually wanted to swallow, but there was a choice. The trick was to make the one you could live with.

Peter had chosen to stick around. He had chosen to haul Gideon, bleeding and unconscious, to a doctor who knew a scalpel from forceps. That was a choice Gideon could certainly live with.

The afterthought of a room, its breath held anxiously, felt unnaturally still. Gideon rubbed at his shoulder. Peter examined a pinky sized knothole at his feet.

"Say, what were ya doin' under that buildin' nohow?" Gideon piped up suddenly.

They hadn't even known each other when Peter had come sliding into Gideon's hidey-hole, like to outrun the devil himself, and promptly launched himself head first into Gideon's troubles.

"I'm not supposed to tire you," Peter evaded, springing to his feet.

Gideon grabbed him by the sleeve, pulled him back down, and eyeballed him suspiciously.

"Out with it."

"It's nothing."

"Talk, afore you waste my poor, frail strength a-makin' me drag it out-a ya."

"Look where getting involved landed you!" Peter exclaimed.

"Savin' your hide's where," Gideon prodded, "an' I'm a-thinkin' I got it to do again."

"What? Who hauled you out? Me! That's who."

"You'd-a been buzzard grub without me. Talk!"

Peter wanted to tell. How could he though, especially now? Only. . . only what a relief it would be to have someone on his side. For all that he barely knew Gideon—his junior by roughly two years and at least thirty pounds—it never occurred to him to question if Gideon would be on his side.

"My father," Peter began, "he started a place. It isn't much, but it's good and it's his. There's a couple of men been hanging around lately. They want the deed."

Nothin' changes.

In years Gideon may have been young, in cynicism he was due for retirement and a hefty pension.

"Where is it?" he asked.

"I've been looking," Peter sighed his frustration. "So have they. I figured it had to be around the home place. Pa always kept his business to himself. Danged if I can find it though. Maybe he stowed it in the courthouse."

"Well? It's your pa's. He can walk in an– what?"

"I. . . I haven't told him."

Where Peter evidently held this as something of a failure, Gideon never batted an eye.

"So we fetch it."

"Us?" said Peter.

"You got you some other 'we'?"

"Why would anyone give it to us?"

"Who said we're askin'?"

Peter's eyes widened at the suggestion he couldn't believe he was hearing. Break into the courthouse? The official rooms of an official government appointed judge? With an official government appointed sheriff one shout away who would put them in a very official jail? Impossible. Completely impossible.

"It's simple," the sound of a cell door clanging shut obscured Gideon's hushed voice. "Hardest part'll be springin' me out-a here."

Peter snapped out of it and stared at the invalid before him. Gideon looked so. . . so much less.

"You can't go."

"You can pick a lock?" Gideon challenged.

"No, but you can't just waltz into a courthouse."

"'Course not. I can handle a lock in jig time."

"Be serious!" Peter admonished.

Gideon's need to get out of that room clawed against his insides. Some men could stand being cooped up. Not him. From the moment the pain had ebbed sufficiently for Gideon to care about such things as a sun rising and setting, every single day had been a week. He had finally begun to understand the phrase 'a month of Sundays' because it had been a month of Sundays and, mercy help him, it was still Sunday. Besides, he owed Peter. It was as simple as that.

"You been chased afore," he coaxed.

"Yeah, when the sheriff thought I was you, not when he thought I was me and knew I'd broken into a government building. He's government too you know. He might not take kindly to your plan."

"Weren't figurin' to run it by 'im none."

"You are serious," Peter realized. He chewed on his lower lip and considered the possibilities. Those men could not be allowed to win. They might anyway, but it wouldn't be because Peter had failed to try– not if he had anything to say about it. "You really figure we could do it?"

"Try me."

"Kind of a big hole in your plan," Peter pointed out.

"What's that?"

"You don't have any britches."

Gideon's face lit up, guilty as sin and twice as pleased. "Is that all?"

CHAPTER 2
Unfit Company
Court Date
Driscoll & Words Of Advice
Absentminded
Dodging The Rain
The Egg & The Bench

W HAT do you hear, Sam?"

The stagecoach driver twisted in his seat. From behind him a modest looking fellow sauntered up and stood in complete contrapposto ease, thumbs hooked over his gun belt. He was lean, square and his nary-a-care face was deceptively youthful. If he wanted to be taken for his true years he would have to grow a beard, and even then there would remain some question.

Dark hair peeked out from under a sun bleached hat and blue eyes suggested they too had been bleached of natural pigment. It was as if an artist had rendered them with far more water to hand than lapis. Dust clung to rough, store bought clothes, more serviceable than fashionable, and yet they suited him so perfectly one could not easily imagine him in anything else. Some folks had seen no further than this outer packaging and laid their bets against him. They had lost.

"Well, I'll be!" the driver exclaimed cheerfully. "Where in tarnation you been hidin' yourself? Reckon it's been five months if a day."

"Near six, if I use my fingers. You stoppin', Sam?"

"This late? You better believe it," the driver replied, with abundant feeling. "You?"

"Could be."

"Better be. It's your turn to buy, you reprobate."

"Climb down here and say that. I bought last time. It was steak, Little Rock."

"Sante Fe, day old bread an' week old stew," Sam corrected.

"And I should thank you for that?"

The driver hefted saddlebags and rifle, hopped down nimble as a mountain goat, and led off to the town's only semblance of a restaurant. With an arm draped over his companion he leaned in close.

"Considering you were half a jump in front of a posse and it was me who hauled you out of there. . ."

"Alright," the word bubbled with mirth, "no need to put too fine a point on it. I take your meaning."

"Knew you would. Say, what are you going by these days?"

"Matt."

"A good honest name," the driver said approvingly. "Of course, not after you've had it awhile. Here we are. Avoid the beans, coffee's middlin', don't miss the biscuits."

A stage driver transported more than cargo and letters to sweethearts back home. He ferried people, and thereby talk, because people on a long, monotonous journey had a tendency to forget they were strangers. A man in that position could come by a heap of information if he knew how to listen. Sam could have given lessons. Get them started, give the occasional prod and he heard everything from politics to crop rotation to Paris fashions. Much of what he picked up, he now passed along to his companion.

After whiling away an hour or more that felt like no time at all, they agreed to share a room for the night. It wasn't uncommon for rooms to be shared and a proprietor might feel justified in demanding a double fee to keep a room private. This way they both saved a coin along with their peace of mind.

They were in various stages of settling in by the time Matt announced he was looking for someone.

"If it's a girl," Sam replied, scrubbing his face, "you can forget it. I ain't talkin'."

"Don't figure me for fit company?"

"There's that, but I don't aim to give a leg up to a man as don't need it."

"From what I hear," Matt countered, "girls don't care for a man who looks like a riled up porcupine."

Sam examined his reflection in the looking-glass.

"I suppose I could shave," he allowed. "Trouble is, once a fellow starts, he has to make a habit of it."

"And a beard is easier to keep than a woman?"

Sam chuckled, plopped onto the bed and dragged off his shirt. It had been a long day. At the rate Matt was going, it was looking to be a long night too. Some folks needed coaxing, others would clam up at the slightest nudge. Experience had taught Sam the difference and his friend was a mollusk of the highest order.

Matt stood beside the window and tweaked the faded curtains aside a bare inch. Sam was cautious himself, but Matt– there was a man who was cautious not from intent, but from force of habit so ingrained as to be natural as breathing. He scanned the street and, finding nothing amiss, sat down on the bed to remove his boots.

"I lost track of someone."

"They owe you?" wondered Sam.

"Nope," Matt looped his gun belt over the bed post. "I owe them."

P ETER shifted his weight from foot to foot. There they stood, exposed to the world, whilst Gideon tinkered with his homemade picks. That had compounded their crime; in order to break into the courthouse they had first to break into the blacksmith's.

Shoulder blades pressed against the courthouse masonry, Peter searched the darkness. To the right loomed Zeek's livery and, beyond that, the southern side of town. Out in front lay open country skirted by mountains that sprouted up as if a crop of that fertile grassland. To the left ran the road out of town. Peter put this last item on his list of things to remember, directly after 'Don't get caught'.

"Hurry up will you?"

"Shhh," Gideon shushed, "ain't been a minute."

Peter knew it hadn't. It had been a year at least.

"You sure you know what you're doing?" he fretted.

"Sure I'm sure."

Sure he was sure. Why wouldn't Gideon be sure? After all, when they had first met, Gideon had been packing a .44 and running from the law. Certainly seemed like the kind of person who would be sure about picking a lock.

On the other side of the courthouse, out of sight yet hardly out of mind, stood the jailhouse. Someone had been thinking when they'd built it. What a prisoner wants is a nice, long stretch of the legs before he stands in a court where they will argue the law and its right to stretch his neck. For preference, he would like a nice long stretch to raise the odds of stretching his legs for Mexico.

Caswell Crossing's founding fathers had put some thought into placing that jail so near the courthouse. Perhaps the court had followed the jail. Not that it would matter, if they were caught, which came first since they would be issued an irrefusable invitation to visit both institutions.

The door quietly clicked open.

Peter fairly jumped out of his skin.

Great stampedin' bison, how'd he get to be such a

great lout of an innocent?

Devil if'n I know.

It wasn't possible and yet there Peter was, white as a sheet and twice as flappable. Gideon hustled him inside, closed the door and latched it shut against prying eyes.

"Where ya goin'?" he whispered, as Peter tip-toed along the ground floor corridor.

"Looking for the right room," Peter hissed back, clearly thinking this should be incredibly obvious.

Gideon latched onto Peter's wrist and pulled him up a flight of stairs to the second floor. At the last door on the left, he knelt down and pulled out his picks.

"How'd you know?" Peter wondered.

"Ain't my first swaray," Gideon replied absently, his attention already on the lock.

Each required its own persuasion and would not parlay with anyone who did not negotiate on its terms. It was an enjoyable task. The challenge of—

"Knock it off, will you?"

Gideon turned curiously, his hands continuing to mind their own business, as sure in their touch as if the lock were dismantled and sitting on a workbench.

"Thought you wanted in?"

"The humming," Peter clarified, his voice rough with nervousness. "You'll get us caught."

Gideon hadn't realized. The law dodger who'd taught him said humming helped him focus. Perhaps—

Click.

Peter froze. Gideon gently turned the knob.

No details could be made out, only vague shapes and shadows filled with deeper shadows. No matter, this room was no stranger to Gideon. To the right was a window covered in lace curtains to afford some privacy whilst letting in the light. On this moonless night all that filtered through was more dark. Heavy bookshelves held sentry against the far wall. On the left, across from the window, hunkered a large oak desk and, behind it, four tall filing cabinets stood like soldiers keeping silent vigil.

Peter tried a drawer and stood aside. Twelve seconds later it was unlocked.

"What would you do without me?" Gideon boasted.

Peter considered living a long, uneventful life free from the threat of apoplexy would not be a bad thing.

"Open the others," he said, picking up a lamp.

"What're ya doin?" Gideon hissed.

"You don't expect me to read in the dark, do you?" Peter lit the wick, trimmed it to its very dimmest and tucked the lamp behind the desk for good measure. "Go on, open the others."

"Ain't your deed in there?" Gideon demanded, pointing to the open drawer.

"How should I know?"

"You picked that there drawer!"

"So what?"

A thought took hold of Gideon: inept. Utterly, completely inept. That's what Peter was. He hadn't one single half notion where his flaming papers were. They were supposed to grab the deed and skadaddle. Now it had turned into a flaming blind hunt with Peter fixing to read every last blasted scrap of writing every darned yokel ever shoved into a filing cabinet.

Three years Gideon had been pinned with the last time he stood in this room— three years with those confounded Rivers. Sure, he'd be gone as soon as he healed up some, but that wasn't the point. Instead of getting in and getting gone, now they would be there for who knew how long rummaging through who knew how many files. The town no longer boasted a judge, but it did have a sheriff. And if they were caught. . .

"Hurry up," Peter ordered, shifting another document through frantic fingers.

"Are you kiddin' me?!" Gideon said, maximum vexation filling every barely hushed syllable. "An' you thought you'd do this by your onesy? A-jumpin' at shadows, don't know where you're a-goin', an' now—"

Gideon's outburst turned to muted mumbling as Peter clamped a hand over his mouth.

"Shhh! This was **your** idea. I said you were off your rocker."

"Mmm?! Mmm mm mmm!" Gideon protested.

"Can we please just finish this and get out of here?"

Peter may have been pathetically, inexcusably inept but, as far as Gideon was concerned, a better idea there could not be. He nodded, and Peter turned him loose.

"So what're we a-lookin' for?" he asked.

"Papers—"

"Thems is full-a papers," Gideon snapped, pointing to the huge cabinets.

"Shhhh!!" Frantically Peter returned his hand to its duty. "The deed'll have my father's name on it and probably a land description."

"Mmfff?" said Gideon and, after Peter shifted his hand, asked, "In official curly writin'?"

"Yes, that sort of thing."

"This land description, likely a map?"

"Doubt it."

"So. . . just fancy law talk?"

"Yes! It is a **legal** document. Now quit wasting time," Peter pushed Gideon towards a filing cabinet and dove back into his own.

"Um."

The word hung there all lonely and small.

"What?" Peter demanded.

"I—" Gideon tried again. "I can't help."

"What?!" Peter gaped at him, the file in his hand forgotten. "What do you mean you can't help?"

"Listen—"

"This was your idea!"

"Shhhh!!" Gideon chivied Peter against the wall and used his good hand to stifle the building tirade. "Listen. It's me as got ya here an' it's me'll get ya out. My hand on it. But you gotta find them papers your ownself."

Peter pulled Gideon's hand away.

"Why?" he said, eyes drilling into his new partner.

Gideon grimaced and slid his hand back. Prudence was a virtue, or so he had been told. He hadn't much firsthand knowledge.

"'Cause. . . I can't read."

Whatever the muffled response, Gideon was pretty sure Peter's own dear mother would not have wanted to hear it. Peter snatched up a pencil from the desk, scrawled his father's name on a note pad and thrust it at Gideon.

"Anything looks like that, show me."

Peter's mind raced. They were dead. Deader than dead. They were deader than dead had ever been or thought to be. Any minute Gandy or one of his deputies would come crashing in on them— and then they would be cooked.

Peter squinted at the page in his hand and shoved it back into the drawer. Illiterate! This was a fine time to find that out. And these files! Who organized them? There was no system. 'R' followed 'T', tripped over an 'A' then showed up again after 'W'.

Midnight rolled around, gave a nod and moseyed on its way. The rustling of papers and sliding of drawers were the only sounds, as foreboding as footsteps in a graveyard. Beyond the curtained window, the world slumbered on, blissfully unaware.

A racket shattered the darkness and both boys jumped, their hearts in their throats, breath caught fast. Torn between ducking and running, they did neither and, in the next moment— when the law failed to burst through the door and haul them off— the sound of their wits falling to a million infinitesimal pieces rivaled the clamor of a dog barking itself stupid.

A dog!

Sidelong glances were furtively exchanged, throats cleared and filing cabinets readdressed. The episode was emphatically not remarked upon.

The minutes gathered themselves up and dragged on, every one at least eight times longer than nature designed. Only darkness marked their passing.

"I've got it," Peter gasped, paper held before him.

"You sure?"

"Sure I'm sure. I can read."

"We all got our nat'ral bent," Gideon replied, fishing out his picks.

He reset the locks, whilst Peter returned everything to the way they found it and blew out the lamp. They left the courthouse, the room, and the file shy one deed.

Out on the street, they tucked themselves into a handy corner. The barest hint of a moon crept over the horizon and Gideon felt a considerable injustice at such rotten timing. He cradled is right arm, trying to ease his aching shoulder and burning side simultaneously. Perhaps freeing his arm from its prison of bandages had been less than wise, but sometimes need outweighs wisdom.

Gideon shrugged it off, stepped out and staggered.

"You alright?" Peter asked, catching him, shadowed face full of concern.

"Yeah, c'mon."

Peter obeyed and once again they were moving. He never should have let Gideon come. What had he been thinking? Not good sense, that was for sure.

"Quit feelin' guilty," Gideon muttered. "I comed. My idea. There's an' end. Hey, where ya goin'?"

By necessity Peter held up, trying to reason with the unreasonable. "How am I supposed to get you through Doc's window? You're barely standing as it is. We'll have to use the front door."

He had meant it as refusal so why was he fetching the crate they had passed and why was he putting it under the window? What exactly did Gideon have in mind? He couldn't climb.

"Pour you through?"

"Yeah. The box is tall 'nough."

"Pour you through?" Peter said again, giving space to each word as if this might aid in comprehension. Of all the hair-brained, plain dumb ideas.

"You hard-a hearin'? Aspen catches us, I'm done for. He'll lock me up, throw 'way the key an' forget it ever done existed. You gonna do that to me? After the favor I done did you?" Gideon watched Peter mulling it over. "A friend—"

"A friend would use the front," Peter argued.

"So be an' enemy."

Gideon climbed up on the box, bare feet making hardly a sound, and levered his good arm onto the window sill. Peter gave in. It did not occur to him, had he made his own decision and stuck with it, Gideon would have had little choice but to go along with things– just as he, Peter, was now doing.

They had several precarious moments between ground, sill, and bed— one more painful than Gideon cared to admit— before they were both safely inside. Gideon shimmied out of his borrowed clothes, and then came the hard part. Aspen slept right outside Gideon's room and he always left the door cracked open. If they wanted to avoid suspicion, they would have to return the door to this state.

Very slowly, Peter eased the latch. The hinges gave a small, high pitched squeak and the boys held their breath. On his cot, Aspen stirred in his sleep. A long moment later, the midnight malefactors gave a collective sigh of relief.

Peter dropped his extra clothes out the window and promptly followed them. Perched on the overturned box, he turned back and what he saw did not please him. He called out, waited until he heard movement, and then took off.

Gideon groaned.

That dirty, no-good, miserable. . .

. . .and then Aspen was by his side.

LUKE Gandy groaned inwardly. It was entirely within the scope of his office to hear and, as appropriate, act upon the complaints of the town citizenry. Poking his nose into other people's squabbles could well prevent a petty grievance from becoming a petty crime.

To Gandy's mind most crime was petty, not that it wasn't important, but rather it stemmed from petty intentions. Sure there were serious crimes, committed by people with very serious intentions, the kind of people who as children had needed a firm hand and a few choice words from their mother and, for one reason or another, still needed it as an adult. Of course, by then, what they would get was the firm hand of the law and a few choice words from a preacher.

The sort of crime Gandy dealt with most days was the other kind. The petty kind. The sort of crime born not from a complete disregard for one's fellow man, or a complete regard for one's own self-interest, but was really only bickering taken to extremes. Been a long day, let's have a drink, then Jimmy A. says the wrong thing about Jimmy B. and the next thing you know Jimmy's friends— doesn't matter which— are venting their frustrations.

Then there were the pigs that had broken into Mr. Mitchum's garden. Gandy had never seen a man more putout over the loss of geraniums. Daffodils? Petunias? It had gone into the report as 'assorted flowers'. Never mind the loss of the edible plants, which at least would make sense, it was the flowers that sent Mr. Mitchum clean over the edge and straight to his neighbor's where the two men commenced to dredge up every minute offense ever dealt them by the other man. Gandy had wanted to clip them both alongside the ear and tell them to behave.

The sheriff's face lit up with a crooked half grin. He had told them and they had ground to a dumbfounded halt. He further told them that if they didn't knock it off and play nicely, they would feel even dumber when he locked them both up.

Sometimes Gandy fancied effort would be saved all around if he installed a 'complaints and issues' box. He could peruse them at his leisure, feet kicked up beside the stove, and throw them in as he went. Mrs. Driscoll, that's where he should put the box: right on her front gate so she could see every poor soul who endeavored to have a brain of their own and read first hand their scandalous acts of independence. Maybe then she'd get her stories straight.

Seeing her on a B-line for his door made Gandy contemplate criminal acts. Or would they count as a public service? He thumped his forehead on the wall of his quarters. He'd not even had his coffee yet. Did the woman have no compassion? No sympathy? No common sense?

He gave his straight razor one last run at his cheek, cleaned the blade, made use of the towel and— the bell on the door sang out like an overly excited mouse in a perpetual state of perky.

"Mrs. Driscoll," Gandy greeted, stepping into the main room with something approximating friendly tolerance plastered stoically across his face.

"I am here to lodge a complaint," the woman informed him stiffly.

Yep, front gate. It would save her the continual exercise of walking to his office. Mrs. Driscoll was almighty thin already, if she kept this up she would be no more than a skeleton in calico.

"As I've explained before, ma'am," he explained again, "owning a dog is not against the law and they have agreed to keep him inside at night."

"I am not here about the dog." Mrs. Driscoll scowled imperiously and her gruff voice would have petrified small children. "Nor that deplorable incident concerning Aspen Rivers."

Gandy noticed the lack of title, not Mister Rivers as his twenty-odd years would properly allow for– and Mrs. Driscoll was first in line for 'proper'— but merely the familiar 'Aspen'. Gandy questioned her tactic and precisely what she hoped to gain. Certainly not his favor, not with that attitude. This was a 'fine upstanding citizen' on the right track for a strong word.

"I am loath to admit," she continued, "I owe the miserable creature some small credit, however I will give credit where credit is due."

Gandy elbowed around his first thought of 'How magnanimous' and said, "Would that be the dog or Mr. Rivers?"

"The dog!" Mrs. Driscoll snapped. "Were it not for that beast's infernal barking I would not have been awakened in the middle of the night."

"Which turned out to be a good thing?" Gandy prompted unnecessarily; the woman would carry on with or without him.

"Indeed. Had I not been so rudely awakened I would not have felt the need for a glass of water and would therefore not have passed by the window."

"Where you saw. . ." Gandy coaxed, trying to herd her towards the point.

"A vile miscreant lurking in the darkness."

It was a profound declaration imbued with evident distaste. The woman was practically scandalized. She was good at scandalized.

Gandy had learned not to say the first thing that came to him, often not the first three. It had taken years of pulled ears and hissed reprimands, but eventually he managed to censor the offerings from the incredibly active corners of his mind where the incongruencies of 'reality' and 'facts' were closely examined, cross examined, names filed and notes duly taken for future reference.

He censored them. He never ignored them.

What came to him now was 'where else should a man lurk?' That's what lurking **was**. Anyone trying it in the daylight would look ridiculous. Gandy stopped himself following the thought any further lest he commit the unforgivable sin of showing humor in front of Mrs. Driscoll.

"And what was the miscreant doing?" he queried, duty bound to ask foolish questions wise men left alone.

"Doing? Doing?" Driscoll huffed, despite lacking the proper stature for the task. "What do you mean '**doing**'? He was **lurking**. Must we wait for him to do something before proper action is taken? Must our homes be violated, our property stolen– or worse– before the law takes the necessary measures?"

Necessary measures. Good grief. She sounded like that

hyped up, two-bit political propaganda article that found its way into town last month. The sheriff considered the possibility anyone breaking into Mrs. Driscoll's house would most certainly get what they deserved and then some. It would be a mercy for Gandy to arrest him. The trespasser might even thank him. . . profoundly.

"Mrs. Driscoll, I understand your concern and I assure you I will look into it." Seeing the woman stiffen her shoulders for another round of self-righteous hauteur Gandy continued hastily, "And we'll make some extra rounds. Don't worry, if anyone is up to no good," that was a Driscoll phrase, "the boys and I will apprehend them."

"If?"

Too late Gandy saw his mistake.

"If??" Mrs. Driscoll fairly resonated indignation. "I tell you there **is**. I saw him myself."

"I believe you, ma'am. I only meant if they should return. Now, if you will excuse me, I need to inform Mark I'll be needing an extra deputy."

Gandy prayed the dodge worked, thanked heaven when it did, and made his escape with as much haste as could be decently excused. The better part of caution was to have a look around, the better part of sanity was to do so whilst Mrs. Driscoll was not. Could be she had seen something. Those boys from the camps were coming around more often and, where Gandy preferred to know a man before passing judgment, they were starting to work up a reputation for themselves. The only thing he found lurking about was Tadhg Connell, who caught him up as he regained the main street.

"How are you this fine morning?" the doctor inquired pleasantly.

"Hey, Connell," said Gandy, less the other man's cheer.

Connell eyeballed his friend. Luke Gandy could have

been used as a textbook case of a man suffering from an acute loss of good humor, signs, symptoms and autographed page. Fortunately, Connell had the cure and he did not intend to take no for an answer.

"Just you come along with me," he said, giving Gandy a nudge.

"I'd like to," Gandy declined politely, "but I still have to deal with the town council."

"Reschedule the meeting did they?"

Stumbling into Gideon the other day had given the sheriff a plausible excuse to miss another council meeting, an excuse he had jumped on with both feet and grabbed with both hands. Could he be blamed if his real work so often got in the way of those dratted council meetings?

Gandy had sent his deputy to the last one, his part-time deputy to the one before that. He would have to stop by Addison's place, a respected council member and solid confederate to his absenteeism, and pass along a few facts to appease the town officials for another month.

Blasted council! Caswell Crossing should have been an untidy pile of soot, or a bunch of half felled trees with a certain confusion about their future. It should not have been a functioning town a hundred miles from lost and due west of nowhere. Probability, however, had not counted on the sort of men who comprised the town council. Gandy had nothing to say against good solid democracy, and far be it from him to criticize proper law and order. He simply could not abide the tangled skein of bureaucracy which seemed to exist for the sole purpose of making his life difficult.

Did he look like a member of the town council? Well, did he? Where on his badge did it say 'mayor'? It certainly did not say 'treasurer', not if they wanted someone who could add two column sums without using their fingers. If Gandy had wanted to sit around some table in an

insufferably stuffy room with insufferably stuffy men in
starched suits he would have—

"I take it they have not rescheduled?" Connell said,
stepping squarely in the path of Gandy's wandering
thoughts.

He would have bet a month's chicken wages on the
answer— mostly from experience, but also because Gandy
had the look of a little boy who had been caught out.

"Not as such, no," Gandy admitted.

"If there's no set time, then the council will never know
you're not there," Connell reasoned, taking his friend by the
arm.

"Hey, I do the arresting, you do the doctoring," Gandy
offered by way of objection, but his heart wasn't in it and he
allowed himself to be pulled along.

"Indeed," Connell agreed, "and you, sir, are in
desperate need of my professional services."

"I am?"

"You are. My word on it."

"Tadhg, I know your word. You're the biggest—"

"Storyteller."

"Bold faced liar," Gandy amended, "in the whole
territory. You only came here because your own country
threw you out on account of your—"

"Colorful   embellishments,"   Connell   interjected
helpfully.

"They're called lies."

"It's wounded I am. Truly wounded. But, if that is how
you feel, then you'd not want to be sharing a pot of fresh,
black coffee with the likes of me."

"Connell—"

"No. No need to explain. I quite understand and
wouldn't dream of asking a respectable gentleman, such as
yourself, to lower his fine standards. You're quite right—"

"Connell, shut up!" Gandy wedged a crowbar into the doctor's show of wounded pride. "If there's coffee in it you can say whatever you like. I'll sign it. I'll swear to it."

The doctor laughed the easy sound of a man who knew how to laugh at himself as much as he found cause in others. Life, he felt, was too full of hurts and losses and wicked twists for him to go adding any more. A heavy heart gave the melancholy aspects of life a place to fester, like an infection. A light heart kept melancholy searching for a way in until it threw up its hands and gave up.

When Connell and his willing captive entered the clinic there was no alluring aroma of coffee on the brew, no sound or sense of anyone about. Aspen had all but moved in. Now that Connell thought about it, Aspen really had taken up residence and, as a committed early riser, he usually had the coffee ready when Connell arrived. This morning's echoing silence begged investigation.

Motioning Gandy to the kitchen, Connell went through to the back. Watcher and watched were both sound asleep. He returned to the kitchen and found the sheriff helping himself to a plate of golden cookies, coffee warming on the stove and two empty cups waiting on the table in eager anticipation.

"Eddie would smack your hand," Connell observed, as he sat down across from Gandy.

Eddie Miller was aunt to Aspen, sister to his father, and considered them, that is Gandy and Connell, to be 'one of hers'. As such, her sisterly I-Know-What's-Best-For-You attitude extended to them. Cookies would not be on her list of appropriate breakfast fare.

"You telling?" Gandy asked around a mouthful of perfection.

He scootched the plate across the table because, when one is mutually culpable, one is likewise mutually silent.

Connell slid a cookie from the plate and slouched down comfortably in his chair. A bit of wood thunked within the stove, crackling as it settled. The day promised fair, but the predawn hours brought a chill that liked to linger to the edge of its welcome. The little, unadorned stove served its purpose admirably and had already warmed the kitchen nicely. The minutes meandered by and, on his fifth cookie, Gandy spoke softly, his voice low and easy.

"Wearing himself out, isn't he?"

Connell nodded and filled their cups. The sheriff clutched his to his chest as if he held the very substance of his being. Perhaps he did.

Connell thought about Aspen, about how completely dedicated he had become in regards to his foundling. Once, Connell had even felt compelled to. . . induce Aspen to sleep so the man could catch up on himself. Not nice perhaps, but needful. What good if he had two patients on his hands instead of one? And what good was Connell if he stood by and let it happen?

"Mother hen," he said. "Blames himself for that boy getting shot and nothing I say changes his mind one bit. Mule-stubborn, that one."

"Say the word and I'll lock him up for you. Nothing to do in a cell but rant or rest," replied Gandy.

Connell's eyes danced behind the fragrant steam from his cup. "I can tell you which one he will do."

"He's welcome to lodge a complaint."

Not that it would move Gandy one inch towards letting him loose and Amos, Aspen's father, would be first in line with a handshake and a thank you. Looking after the Rivers– all four boys, two cousins, aunt, uncle, father and uncle by adoption– was something Gandy had done for years. He wasn't sure he could stop even if he wanted to, which he didn't.

And now there was Gideon. At current he was the sort of nuisance that kept the job interesting. Given his own say and a bit of time, he would become the sort who inspired the construction of a gallows. Hopefully the Rivers would sort him out, and the sooner the better, because he sure wasn't standing first in line to help himself. When character traits were handed out Gideon had kicked 'compliance' in the shins, knocked 'passive' to the ground and hit 'obedience' a right smart one on the nose. Of 'reckless determination' he'd annexed a second helping and run for it. The kid was born ten jumps ahead of a posse.

"It'll go cold."

"Hmm? What?" Gandy stammered, and then chuckled at himself as he noticed the oatmeal that was indeed going cold in front of him. "Guess I was thinking."

"Mm," Connell said, washing down oatmeal with coffee. "I could see the effort it cost you."

Aspen appeared in the kitchen doorway, bleary eyed and barefoot. They pressed coffee into his hands. He muttered something about taking some to Gideon. They sat him down and told him to eat. He said Gideon had not slept well. They said obviously neither had he.

Gandy dished up another bowl of oatmeal and left Aspen, elbows on the table and shoulders slumped, a man still asleep, dully sipping coffee. Connell would see to him. Gandy suspected Gideon needed his own seeing to.

He helped himself to the edge of the bed and had a word with the boy about footprints under windows and the distinctive marks a box leaves in the dirt and how a young man, as clever as he, would surely see the wisdom in taking friendly advice. So much for Mrs. Driscoll's miscreant.

EDDIE'S current customer upended her purse to

tally her coins. Shifting them inside their cloth sack was a frustration, whilst spilling them across the counter made life ever so much easier. Two bits, a penny. . .a half-dime. . .

"How about stockings?" Eddie suggested.

"No, this is special. A birthday," the older woman declined, still counting.

"Oh, I see. Special indeed. Have you seen the broaches? Arrived yesterday."

The older woman forgot her coins and followed Eddie to the glass case where she oohed and ogled to her heart's content. To Eddie's content she selected a lovely broach and matching pin. It was hardly the most expensive set, but that didn't bother Eddie. Her customer was satisfied, thereby so was she.

"Do you have a box, dear?"

Eddie rummaged about under the counter as her customer once again slid coins with a vengeance. It was like this every time. There would be no frivolous use of large coins, all the small pieces had to be used up first.

"Here we are," Eddie said, producing a stiff paper box.

"And here you are, dear."

Money was exchanged for purchase, friendly parting words spoken, and the new owner of the broach would arrive home much distracted by contemplation over her coin collection, in particular if there weren't one or two gone missing. She had probably miscounted. That was it. Or maybe she had spent a bit more than she recalled on last week's groceries. The woman brushed concern aside; with her absentmindedness if she worried over everything she forgot she would soon forget what had her worried in the first place.

R AIN poured in a torrent, flowed over the packed

earth and, summarily rejected, instantly pooled in every available depression. Tiny rivulets partnered up, became streams that twisted and pulled more drops into their current the moment they thunked to the ground. Every swollen, wind-driven pellet stung the skin even through coarse work clothes. Peter was going to get soaked.

"Hey! Get in here!"

The authoritative shout made Peter flinch and he spun around searching for the source.

"Peter!" came the voice again.

Though the rest of the words were drowned out by bone rattling thunder, Peter realized he was being waved over to the jail. There was no avoiding it, because standing in the middle of the street with the rain beginning to run down his collar and drip off his ears was plain suspicious. Obediently, Peter kicked up his feet and ducked inside.

Deputy Wilson offered to stir up a fire, but Peter was merely damp; he had missed the worst of it. As if hearing this sentiment, and taking it for an insult, the pounding rain redoubled its efforts and the sky crashed fit to shake the jail to its foundations.

"About time we had a decent gully-washer." Wilson opinioned. "Your pa out in this?"

Peter pushed at his dripping hair. "No, sir."

Wilson had seen the same careful blankness before, in any number of guests they had temporarily housed. It was a shield, a slight suggestion that here was not a welcome topic. Why now? He had asked an innocent enough question meant only as courteous conversation. Wilson fetched his guest a towel and mulled it over because, in his profession, he found it a solid bet to listen very carefully to the things others did not want you to hear.

"Do you play darts?" he asked.

It was an invitation and one always given in the eager

hope of finding someone who shared his addiction. Peter stood there as if waiting for a preacher's jeremiad. With a visible effort he suggested a shrug and attempted a shake of his head, all of which was meant to convey the idea that where he had never thrown a dart and, where he did not wish to seem overly willing, he would in fact give in if adequately nudged and was inclined to suspect he might possibly rather enjoy the game and would very definitely enjoy it more than standing there fidgeting like a half-wit to no purpose.

"Here," Wilson nudged, exchanging towel for darts. "Stand behind this mark, hold the dart so, and. . ."

Several inches of slim, fletched accuracy thunked into the center of an upturned bucket hung on the opposite wall. Peter put his first dart into the wooden shutters doing double duty as a backboard. A word of technique and his next hit the outer ring of chalked circles.

"There you go! Try again," Wilson praised. "This storm won't last; we might as well enjoy the time. Visited Gideon lately?"

Peter's throw snicked into the outermost edge of the boards, wobbled loose and fell like a smacked mosquito onto the deputy's rope-frame bed.

"You hit the wall and I will have to shoot you," Wilson ribbed. Stone did nothing good for sharp tips. He took a turn of his own, his movements so practiced as to be free of thought, which was good because his thoughts were becoming increasingly otherwise occupied. "Well?"

"Nice throw," Peter deflected.

"Did you?" Wilson pressed, as he effortlessly scored a bull's-eye.

"Did I what?" Peter asked in the tone of one denying all guilt assumed, implied, or otherwise and yet would like you to believe he was in fact doing nothing of the sort by reason of there being nothing to deny. Really.

"Did you visit Gov? Was he awake this time?"

Wilson noticed Peter's attention flick to the window and out to the rain waterfalling off the roofs and making the street appear, by casual examination, to be a lake. The storm would be over in twenty minutes, forty at the outside; thunder, rain, wind and all. In all likelihood the sun would then edge its way out, chagrined it had ever disappeared, and dry up most of the mud within a couple of hours.

Wilson's boss liked a good storm. People were inclined to hole up he said, keep themselves to themselves and out of other people's business— which meant he could stay out of theirs. Wilson agreed, however the reason he liked a storm was because it left the world refreshed, like it had taken a deep breath and was ready for another go.

Peter had his own reasons not to like this storm. First and foremost was being penned up with Wilson. He had nothing against lawman in general, only they tended to take poorly to people who committed crimes. And Peter was half sure, if he opened his mouth, he would blurt out some dirt dumb thing like: 'Well, yes, Gov was doing so well we committed two acts of breaking and entering followed by petty larceny. Thanks for asking.' He fiddled with a dart and then made a measured throw.

"Yes, sir," he answered.

Wilson figured that was about as neutrally uninformative as a body could manage whilst still linking consonants to vowels. It could mean anything or nothing. Only Wilson was a lawman. Not the kind whose role was defined by means of pinning on a badge every morning and dropping it in a desk drawer every night, he was the kind who had been born with a badge pinned on his soul. The one on his shirt was merely a civil caution to the general public that he could not help himself and shooting him for being nosey would get you in a whole heap of trouble.

What he figured 'yes, sir' meant, in this case, ran along the lines of 'There's something I'm not saying and would rather you did not know and would therefore like to tell you to butt out. Only you are my elder, and a lawman to boot, and my folks'd give me seven kinds of grief if I give you any kind of grief, so I'll go on and stick to the defensive 'yes, sir' if it's all the same to you.'

That's what the lawman heard. The man understood a bit more. Like how a fellow, having been at handshaking proximity to death and having been fished out, might feel indebted. And how he might have some contrary feelings when he realized the man who had done the fishing was the same one who had got him two-stepping with death in the first place. And how, after then saving the life of the man who had saved yours, a reasonable person might feel they were up one save– having never committed a push. After all that, would it be any wonder if Peter decided 'to blazes with it', called things square and saw no need to carry on? It made perfect sense to Wilson. Perfect sense. Provided that was how Peter saw matters.

"I suppose Gov was as ornery as ever?" Wilson asked, letting Peter have another try.

Peter wished the deputy would entertain another topic. Not that the current one was in any way unexpected only, in Peter's overactive and momentarily paranoid state, it felt not so much a line of conversation as a line of questioning. Still, hedging around the subject was apt to make the very official deputy overly curious in all the wrong ways. Peter would just have to feed himself a little more rope and hope he didn't trip.

"Can't say he's as able as he would like, but more so than they'd like. Is he always so. . ."

"Full of vinegar?" Wilson supplied. "Haven't known

Gov long, but I'd say so."

Peter chewed his lower lip. Rain continued to batter the roof and the air smelled of wet earth, lively and anticipatory.

"He likely to hold a grudge?" Peter asked, surprised to realize it was himself doing the asking.

"I'd say so," Wilson replied, leaning over the bed to collect his darts. "If he had a reason."

Wilson's statement held a suggestion of inquiry to which Peter felt compelled to respond. In the general direction of the floor he admitted to inadvertently causing Gideon's injuries.

"You are not responsible for Tarlston's actions," Wilson said firmly, and then squared up to the target. "How about Gov? Does he say you're even?"

"Yes, sir."

"You holding a grudge on him?"

"No, sir."

Wilson's shot sailed with the grace of a hawk and landed with a thunk. "There you go then."

Peter thought about this as he sunk a few darts into the backside of Wilson's council authorized water bucket. According to Gandy, no better metaphor existed.

"You trust him?" Peter said, with greater ease and genuine curiosity.

"To tell the truth? The whole truth and nothing but the truth?" The deputy gave an indulgent sort of snigger. "No. To watch my back? I'd say so. And Gov'll keep his word. You can take that to the bank. Well, if we had one. You know, since you seem set on hanging around, you might do me a favor– heck all of us really. Maybe you could sort of stick with Gov, ya know?"

Peter's face underwent several rapid shifts until finally settling on what Wilson took for a variant on the theme of self-doubt.

"Don't worry," the deputy added. "You're up to it. Thing is, don't let him pull you in. You do the pulling."

"Yes, sir," Peter's lips agreed all on their own.

Him? Influence Gideon? The deputy was off his rocker. He hadn't been able to say no to Gideon even once. Look at that whole pouring him through the window nonsense. Foolish from start to finish, but Gideon said this is what we're going to do and somehow that's what Peter found himself doing. Some influence he was.

To Peter's profound relief the rain stopped a few minutes later, allowing him to retreat into the safety of the outdoors where the sun was indeed presenting its startlingly bright self to a dripping world.

S HAGGY beard and shaggier hair of an unassuming brown marginally touched by a washed out suggestion of dull rust red. Considered short by most men and unattractive by even the most generous of descriptions. From the front, or back, he looked like he had been pressed out by a rolling pin, an egg shape in only two dimensions. That was Harvey Wilcox.

Harvey did not care about Peter. He did not care about money either, which made him fairly unique. He did care about himself which, rather than making him narcissistic, only made him fairly common. What Harvey really cared about, what motivated him and told him everything he did leveled out to acceptable, was a fundamental need for life to go on happening. Not in the sense of fireworks and monuments cast in bronze inscribed with his immortal name. Harvey didn't think like that.

When he thought of life 'happening' what he really meant was that it was not happening to him, in practically every way. He certainly did not look for adventure or opportunities to broaden himself. He was what he was and he did what he did and if this continued into tomorrow then all was well. If it continued for the next thirty years, he could go to his grave content.

Harvey Wilcox should have stayed in Ducket's Hollow.

He'd had about enough of his partner. The man had absolutely no sense of how to let things be and, the way he permitted the unpleasantries of the world to get to him, he was apt to cause himself an apoplectic fit.

Harvey soothed himself with thoughts of how, once this was done, he could be rid of Nick Pultrie. Well, not exactly **this**. It would take more than picking a lock, but when this whole big-picture job was done he would no longer be committed to Pultrie's company and good riddance.

Harvey didn't hate his partner, that would have required energy– and passion– which Harvey did not possess. The man simply grated on him, a slow continual irritation like a rough patch on a smooth bench one wished to sand away. Establishing this partnership had not been his idea, and he would be loath to call it such. It was more accurately described as two men acting in parallel to a common goal, like railroad tracks leading to the same place yet never did, or would, the twain rails meet.

"Will you get out of the light!" Pultrie snarled.

Harvey shifted slightly and mumbled how it hardly mattered since there wasn't enough moonlight to see by anyway. He let Pultrie fail for a few more minutes and then repeated, with the arrogance of the narrow sighted that, had his own suggestion been taken, they would have been in, and subsequently out, long ago.

Pultrie silenced him with unconcealed contempt. "Smashing a window or breaking down this door would hardly be overlooked, would it? Now shut up."

Harvey obliged because doing so made life easier. If Pultrie wanted to make his own life hard, what did Harvey care? Even if the sheriff happened by, what would he see? Pultrie industriously, and thus far uselessly, attempting to pick the lock of the town's courthouse. The very next thing the law would see was the intruder being seized by a two-dimensional egg who just happened to be passing by. You're welcome officer and would there be a reward in this for a fine upstanding citizen who knows his duty?

Eventually the mechanisms within the lock decided to cooperate. Pultrie would have been quite put out to know Gideon had managed the task in less than half the time. All the same, they were in, up the stairs, down the hall, and straight to the filing cabinets. They knew for what they searched.

CHAPTER 3
Nothing To Brag About
Baiting The Hook & Ties To The Past
Butcher, Baker
Even Five
The Nature Of Law, The Ways Of Sheep, & A Big Man

F OUR small fingers curled themselves around the edge of Doc Connell's front door. They were followed by corn silk hair, sharp features and round eyes bluer than the sky on a summer's day. The young boy— eight, maybe nine years old— frantically beckoned Gideon out to the porch.

The alternative being to stare down the walls, which had won the last three matches, Gideon hitched up his gravity minded trousers and shuffled across the painted floorboards. Most houses he had been in boasted only packed dirt, sometimes loose stones cobbled edge by edge. Doc's was about the sparkliest place Gideon had ever seen. From swabbed floors, to glass cabinets, to polished metal, everything that could shine did shine.

The thin, leggy child waiting for him, and clearly making a job of it, grabbed Gideon by the sleeve and pulled him to a bench with the enthusiasm of a whirling dervish.

Gideon sat and leaned his shoulders against the thick glass of the clinic's window. The outside air felt lighter, the world more real than a world should be. He gave the town a slow looking-over. Everything within sight remained work-a-day ordinary.

"They said I was to stay out and not bother you," the child rattled out, his excitement palpable. He turned sideways on the bench and leaned in, all but sitting on Gideon's lap. "I don't bother you, do I?"

His concern was obviously more for being sent away

than for Gideon's health, which suited Gideon and no complaint. He shook his head agreeably and the sprite gave an overly dramatic burst of a sigh.

"Told them!" he exclaimed.

Don't this kid belong to that Eddie woman?

Gideon ventured an unsteady guess, "Ain't you Gabe?"

Deaf and blind to anything but Gideon's shoulder, the child sat gaping as though he could force his sight through shirt, bandage and all.

"Does it hurt?" he asked, with unmistakable awe.

Gideon dismissed the truth of pain, as much to spare himself as the boy. Halfway to saying more, Gideon was beaten to the draw; when it came to talking, he had met his overmatch.

"Why're you in Aspen's clothes?" the child burbled, rambling right along. Stopping for neither breath nor pause, he went on, "Fred lets me use his stuff if I'm real nice or if he wants to hush me up about something. Last time I made him give me a licorice rope too on account-a it was worth it to keep me shut. So why're you?"

"Aspen lent 'em me."

"Does he know that?" Gabe asked, with the hard earned wisdom of one who had been told borrowing what was not lent went by a different name.

Gideon smirked. "We got us an' un'erstandin'."

Which amounted to: 'He ain't here so what he don't know, he don't mind'.

Why're we a-humorin' this here junior member-a the enemy camp? That Rivers woman sure ain't got no love for us.

Some-a her kinfolk ain't so bad.

That's as may be, but we're a-ridin' for a diff'rent brand an' headed for a whole diff'rent corral— an' I sure as blazes ain't gonna be turned.

There were things that had to be done. Things the Rivers wouldn't understand. And where Gideon had to go, it plain would not be neighborly to drag another man along.

Gideon had been on his own his whole life. Well, not actually all-by-his-onesy. . . but. . . that wasn't quite the point was trying to make.

Yeah, an' you're right. Only you're dead wrong too. Ya din't know what 'lone were 'til. . . 'til then.

I knowed what 'lone were. Were lonely I din't never knowed.

Gideon reflected on this and decided his new grasp of the inner depths and shades of lonely had been somewhat enhanced of late, revealing facets he had never thought possible. Ignorance certainly had advantages. It didn't hurt for one thing.

The grown-ups would tell Gabe nothing, but he had picked up snippets of for-real-and-true that wove a mystery around the newcomer more enticing than putting a lizard in Penelope Lynn's pocket, and she could scream nobody's business.

"Did you bleed? Did you? I mean then?"

Gideon could see that day over again, always, in his mind, in the dark. The body beneath him. The blood spreading. Himself pushing against the tide. Acrid gun smoke—

"Did you?" begged the sweetly innocent Gabe.

Gideon blinked.

This was not then and then— that unspeakable, unforgettable then— was not what Gabe meant. Of that, he knew nothing. Ignorance had its advantages.

"Wanna see?" Gideon offered.

Pure blue eyes widened in pure thrilled shock. Gabe couldn't offer words to answer but, when the human enigma before him unfolded and took himself inside, he drafted along with no inclination to protest. Protest? It would have been sheer unspeakable disgrace to shy from the magnificent horror of battle wounds.

His inchoate manhood on the line, Gabe helped Gideon out of his capacious shirt and loosened the bandages. Laid bare were the insufficiently healed bullet holes, incontrovertible evidence there was indeed a story here worth hearing.

Gideon remained stoic throughout the process of tending and rebinding his wounds, making not a peep or flinch. Gabe decided then and there, the next time he skinned his knees or slivered his hands, he wouldn't flinch either.

All the same, his fascination did a tug of war with reality. Gideon had lived an adventure, had lived through it, and yet seeing someone who had been shot for real and true hinted at an uncomfortable reality which Gabe's youth, in its idealism, was ill prepared to fully comprehend.

"I'm impressed," Connell allowed, when the boy had gone. He leaned against the surgery doorway, arms folded and tongue flowing happily in its native vernacular. "You make a lousy patient, but a decent mentor."

Gideon did not deign to reply. He did however, at a gesture from Connell, latch the medicine cabinet and lever himself reluctantly onto an examination table.

"Gabe's young," Connell continued, his expert fingers untying inexpertly applied bandages, "his world is still twinkling with stardust."

Was that criticism? He had to know though, didn't he? At some point Gabe had to know life left bruises and the hero always making it to ever-after was best left to fairytales.

Mebbe stardust is better.

Mebbe. Only if'n ya let it blind ya, one day, someday,

blindsided is what you'll be.

Connell leaned back from his work and gave his patient a long, measuring study. On the basis that he needed no one to point out his many shortcomings, Gideon refrained from imagining what the doctor saw. The scrutiny went on considerably longer than comfortable and he was relieved when Connell finally gave up and fetched a medicine bottle from the cabinet. The glass container was smaller than the usual one and the contents reeked twice as badly.

Gideon grimaced. "I keep tellin' you, I don't– aahh!"

If the colorful profanity that followed was any indication, the liquid stung twice as badly too.

"It was no gentleman taught you Irish," Connell observed, holding a damp cloth against Gideon's shoulder.

"Nor you medicine."

"Next time go easier," Connell advised, with a slant to his tone that amounted to 'it's your own fault'. "Or better yet, don't have a next time. And, yes, I know your sins, and, no, I'll not be informing Aspen."

Gideon did not sputter protests. He did not babble excuses or forgive-me's. Connell couldn't know. There was no possible way he could. Sure Gideon had slipped out, and likely the sheriff had told the doctor as much, but he couldn't **know**. If Connell, or anyone, actually knew what they thought they knew, Gideon wouldn't be sitting in the doc's office— he'd be in a cell with a lawman for company.

That jail cell's always in sight, ain't it?

What Gideon had done or not done was not a topic he wished to encourage. He floundered about for something to throw out for distraction, but Connell beat him to it.

"Do you regret killing Tarlston?"

"What kind-a question's that?" Gideon demanded sharply.

"A straightforward one. Hold still."

Gideon shifted uneasily, though whether from the doctor's inquiry or his ministrations only Gideon could tell and never would. Connell elected not to take the hint on either score.

"Well?" he said, pressing the cloth to Gideon's side.

"You tryin' to finish me?" Gideon gasped.

"It's you keeps shoveling your own grave. If you will recall, it's me who keeps trying to take the spade away. So, do you regret it?"

"Oww! Will you quit? Look, it isn't anything I dwell on," Gideon lied. "Tarlston's dead, Peter's alive. I'd not swap that for a big jar-a tea. I did what I had to. Simple as that."

But it ain't that simple, is it?

No, it wasn't and it wasn't over. Nothing to do with that sorry waste of skin would ever be over. He had stolen every meaningful thing in Gideon's life.

"Some men might take pride in such a thing," Connell pointed out mildly.

Some men had their manhood all tangled up with their ability to handle a gun and thought killing a fine reason for bragging. They'd think themselves big men and walk mighty hard, men like William Tarlston.

"I said hold still, lad," Connell chastised, dabbing more medicine onto his cloth.

"Well, go easy," Gideon replied peevishly.

The turmoil he usually kept banked was feeling frisky what with Connell's poking about. He didn't like it, not the feeling nor the poking. It was none of Connell's business why he had shot Tarlston or how he felt about it. Heck, Gideon didn't even know how he felt. It wasn't pride, that was for sure. It wasn't pleasure either.

That was wrong, he knew. He was supposed to feel more than a queasy knot in the pit of his stomach. Those men in the saloon had sure held feelings on the subject. Their words came back to him, clear as spring water.

"A man's got no choice," the big one had said.

His companion had rubbed a grubby hand down a coat oiled more from wear than proofing and pronounced his agreement like a juryman turned judge.

"Man kills one-a yourn, ya gotta settle up."

There had been others, different places, different faces, same inescapable verdict: a man stood for his own or he was no kind of man.

Gideon had meant to kill Tarlston. In the beginning it had been his every waking thought— and most of his sleeping ones. Then he found another way, a better way, and at that Gideon would have left it. He truly would have.

Tarlston's death did not mean there would be no more graves. Of that there was very little doubt and absolutely no choice. The time would come and Gideon would handle what had been put in front of him. But not for pride and never for pleasure. Thinking of that impending day twisted another knot in his already twisted belly.

"Why did you bring Gabe in here?"

"What?" said Gideon.

Connell stood re-rolling bandages and waiting expectantly. Why had he humored that kid? To keep him out of harm. To shake some sense into him before he grew up and got the sense knocked out of him. This— gun fighting and 'glorious battles'— it was nothing to flirt with. Gabe had a future, a chance.

Gideon avoided the doctor's intense scrutiny, and his judgment. There was no reason to satisfy the man's curiosity and Gideon's jaw went rigid as he struggled to frame a prevarication to stand proxy for the answer he did not wish to give.

Connell began to wrap clean linen around Gideon's

middle. "Gabe is up to his ears in people who will watch out for him. Right now – Is this too tight?— right now our Gabe is too young for real life. He wants a champion, a man in the gap to beat all odds. It's called hope, lad, everyone needs a good dose."

"If he's aiming to look up to me, he's aiming the wrong way, Doc."

"Why's that?"

Why? Because of all the things Gideon had not done and half the things he had.

"Got caught didn't I?" he evaded. "And I didn't even do anything."

"Give me your arm," Connell directed, positioning the limb across Gideon's chest.

Gideon shoved him off impatiently. "I don't—"

"I said give me your arm, not your cheek," Connell deftly interrupted in English, and then shifted smoothly back to Irish. "You think Gabe left here disillusioned? Don't you believe it. By the time he snuggles down to sleep tonight, you will be more god-like to him than ever. My hand on it, boyo."

"But—"

"You can fight the whole world, Gideon, but you fight that boy and you will break his heart, so you will. And you're not that mean. Stay put."

Connell left Gideon to stare morosely at his lap, fidget with his bandages and jig with his conscience. Nobody had ever looked at him the way that kid had, like he was the best thing since tinned peaches. Gideon knew, in the very deepest part of his conflicted soul, here was something both of him could agree on: looking up to him was a long step in the wrong direction.

Connell returned holding a pair of worn-out, all-in, rag -tag boots. Gideon lit up like a kid with his first pony, then swiftly shuttered the unguarded reaction.

"Where's the rest?" he said stiffly, accepting his boots.

"You want to call Aspen a liar, you take it up with him. Come away out of that now." Connell distracted his patient from unraveling his lovely handiwork by tossing over Aspen's shirt. "How would you like to go out?"

"Out?" Gideon echoed, brow furrowed.

"I swear, you'd question a newly minted coin if it was given you by your own mother. Out, boy, as in 'not in' and give over."

Gideon gave another tug to the cloth around his lashed up arm, quite ready to rip himself loose entirely. A babe in swaddling clothes would have more room.

"I can't stand—" he began.

"You'll stand it or you'll stand a clip 'round the ear."

"Sons of mothers."

Tadhg Connell was a man much gifted with tolerance. A happy coincidence, since his clients were much gifted with a great many idiosyncrasies in amusing variety. In this Connell delighted. There were some things, however, he felt it well in accordance with his position not to tolerate. He was, after all, a doctor, not some tonic wielding wagon quack peddling goods to the chronically unaware.

"That talk won't pass muster around here. Don't push your luck."

Gideon slid to his feet. "Only way to get her attention, I've found. We done?"

His stormy gray pupils stood in strong contrast to the sparkle in Connell's, who squinted and nodded as if he had come to a conclusion.

"I'd say you've given yourself just about enough rope. Now untangle yourself and come along. I've to check on a few people and, though some would thank you for keeping me, others would not." The doctor adjusted Gideon's shirt, fastening the metal buttons over bandaged arm and all. "Out with you and mind your manners. It should be an easy task, considering how few you have."

Connell was of the view that, were Aspen to let Gideon move more than three feet, his charge might not feel the need for midnight excursions. Aspen had cause for caution, however there was more to healing a patient than merely treating the body. An easy, sanctioned stroll to see a few agreeable people would do Gideon no harm.

As for Aspen, once that man was well and truly set, not much could change his mind. And what he had set his mind to was protecting Gideon. Against this Connell knew only two people who could prevail: Aspen's father and his aunt Eddie. Faced with her stronghold of determination, Aspen's towering height and remarkable skills of reason were useless. Eddie simply did not back down. Accordingly, Connell had set her as a battering ram against Aspen's immovable line of duty— and off he had gone with her, like it or not.

Gideon, frankly, didn't give buffalo spit for sanctioned or otherwise. He would do as needed and all the best to whomever got in his way. If that was Aspen, or Connell, or the entire compliment of Texas Rangers— it made little difference. Only, until Gideon healed up more, that would have to smoke its pipe and wait.

Peter now. There was a situation that deserved his intentional a-ttention.

Reckon they comed yet?

Beats me, but they will. Sure as shootin'.

With any luck, Peter's friends were currently tracking him down and shaking him out. Not that they would gain anything except the accidental mention of one Gideon Fletcher. If Peter played possum well enough, his two admirers ought to pay Gideon a social call pretty soon.

Better get you a plan, boyo.

That was true, only strategy had never answered to Gideon's whistle. Whatever he did would have to work though or Peter was going to be in a passel of grief. For now, all he could do was wait. Thus much they had planned and agreed upon. Peter would come by sundown. What Gideon would do then, there was really no telling, not until the time came and he saw how things laid out.

Aspen'd know.

No.

But—

No!

Gideon clamped down on the thought, crumpled it up, wadded it tight and drop kicked it into the current of life stretching out behind him, where it bobbed twice, swirled into an eddy in a last ditch effort to be heard, and drifted forlornly away.

P ETER'S father had never been a great woodworker. The roof of their cabin didn't leak and the walls stayed where they had been put. That that was about the end of his craftsmanship. It might be less than some folks could claim, but it was more than others. Peter could not honestly say he had never wished for more, he had. But, without ever a word being asked or said, there had never been any question his father had always done his best. No man could do more.

The breakfast dishes had been cleared. The floor swept clean. The beds neatly made. Peter scanned the bones of his home, mentally checking off what he would take and what must be left. On the table the salt still sat in its close-woven sack. He returned it to the kitchen shelf and his hand brushed against a tin box. It had nothing to do with the kitchen and yet had lived there for the last year.

Peter concentrated on the simple act of breathing, drawing air into lungs that seemed to have forgotten their purpose. The box was not his. Sometimes his father would sit on the bed, shoulder to shoulder in the flickering lamplight, open the lid and they would spend a few perfect minutes living in the past.

There was no time for that now, but nothing could stop the memory from flooding in. It was a good memory. It had made a far better present, but it still made for a good past. Peter had no regrets, only wishes.

He placed the box carefully in his rucksack, beneath the protection of his shirts. There was no sense packing anything more until after Pultrie and his fat friend came calling because a packed bag might well lead them to ask the wrong sorts of questions. What Peter needed was to be followed, not stopped.

He thought of the tin. It contained nothing essential. There was no useful reason to take it. All the same, the thought of anyone else touching it felt wrong in every way. He would take it. Just in case. You never knew.

Impulsively, Peter reached into his rucksack, plucked something out, and nestled the box back into hiding.

The next few hours were spent knocking about doing needless chores simply to insure he would be seen. Mostly he kept to the river and worked the rocker box as would be expected. He kept his father's rifle handy, also as expected. Everyone knew trouble and prospecting went hand in hand.

Peter dumped another shovelful of dirt into the box and came up empty. This did not bother him. It had happened before. Every time before, in fact. His father had not chosen this place with expectations of finding any color beyond those provided by nature. Wildflowers, sunsets, green grass, these were worth having– gold was a whimsy bound to empty a man's pockets and drive him insane.

Peter reached into his pocket and felt the treasure secreted there: a thin bracelet, braided from hair dark and rich as walnut, and designed such that the ends locked one around the other, an eternity circle.

Movement caught his attention and he shoved the bracelet safely away. His unwelcome guests had arrived. Peter told himself to relax. After all, how hard could it be to convince them he was intimidated by their greater size, numbers, general meanness and loaded weaponry?

CONNELL stopped at a narrow frontage. It made no pretense to distinctive personality, as if born of the same architect who had granted life to a hundred other buildings in a hundred other towns. The same flat façade, the same multiple panes of window glass all joined up because anything larger never survived the tribulations of travel. A false peak reached vainly for grandness— a box roof is a box roof no matter how you wrapped it up. Predictably, the function of the building had been painted in broad, clear strokes for all to read. In a daring run for uniqueness, this had been done in a lively green whilst the building itself boasted a coat of screaming bright yellow.

Within the shop, at ceiling height, a single vine of hand painted, violet flowers ran along every wall. To one side stood a stuffed mannequin, all chest and hips with no arms or legs. It was a strange parody and Gideon suppressed the urge to check his own body for its properly issued limbs.

Along one wall a few bolts of cloth partially filled long shelves. Another shelf housed stacks of mixed clothing, crisply folded corner to corner and edge to edge. These were the products of the 'back-room' as Mary called it. This contained the laundry and bathhouse, much needed services certain members of Caswell Crossing could stand to use more often in her professional estimation.

The 'front-room' business was a tailor's. Mary would be the first to admit it fell pointedly short of being a dressmaker's, which suited her, and her personality, perfectly. This way she saw a wider range of clients and, though her work would never be called finery, it had the dependability of providing a much needed service.

Despite being the only show in town, Mary had the business sense to never leave a customer standing. Well, for a given value of never; some people were due a good wait. When Dr. Connell came in, Mary had a happy greeting ready before the door could even close.

"Morning, Doc! Wasn't expecting you. All the same, it's pressed and ready."

Mary may not have been expecting Connell, but he had been expecting her– specifically to not show up at his office. There were days the woman worked from can to can't and never stopped. Connell was almost sure if Death himself came calling, she would tell him to wait until the washing was done— and he'd do it too.

Draping the dress she had been mending over a chair, Mary picked up a crisp, pale blue shirt from the shelves. Gideon stood quietly by whilst Connell did a proper job of admiring the immaculate garment.

"Aw, now, just the stain would have been alright, so it would. You needn't have—"

"Alright? Do I do anything to 'alright'? I should hope not. A body doesn't run a business on 'alright'. It's proper or nothing as well you know."

Connell let himself be rebuked, knowing it for altogether the opposite. Mary was one of those people whose kind-hearted nature was surpassed only by her desire to feign rejection of the self-same. She was a big woman, not obese, merely big, and so was her personality. Mary elbowed her way through life and nobody, but nobody, told her no, she simply wouldn't hear it.

"How are you today?" Connell inquired politely, letting his gaze shift subtly to her forearms.

"Here, have a look," the laundress rolled up her cotton sleeves, not the least shy for Gideon's presence.

Beneath the slightly too pink skin lurked round, solid muscles. In a saloon brawl Gideon reckoned he wouldn't want her on any side but his own.

"Had the worst of rashes and it never occurred to me it was from the washing. Been using the same soap for ages and never a thing, but Doc here guessed right off. He was right too. See? Good as gone."

"Nearly so," Connell agreed, inspecting the faint blemishes. "Give it a day or three more."

"Shall I keep with the salve?"

"Aye, do. I'll come around again to check."

"No need to dote. It'll clear a treat."

Which meant Mary would once again do her best to ignore the problem and get on with pressing forty-eight hours of work into twenty-four hours' worth of day.

"Doting is one of the benefits of my profession." Connell said, and then lowered his voice. "Only I'd take it as a favor if you didn't let on you're my favorite."

If Mary were the blushing kind, she would have. Connell's charm was fit to melt a woman's heart, even one as windblown as hers. She shifted her attention to Gideon, giving him a quick, sunshine beam of a glance, and planted both hands on her square hips.

"Looks like I could serve you better as a tailor than a laundress, boy. 'Fraid your things were altogether too far gone for washing. How all that blood found enough thread to cling to is beyond me. One more go 'round in those and you'd have been a sight. Of course, no need to fret now you're with the Rivers, they'll see you straight. Can't begin to tell you how much they done for me. They taken a shine to you. I can tell. Mercy, here's me blabbering away and you with work to do, Doc. Here, take your shirt, thanks again and out you go." Another flicker of golden summer graced Gideon, "Good to see you up and about."

He gave a polite nod and Connell offered a good-day, but Mary had already returned to her labors. The two men took themselves out, her affable nature clinging to them like the iridescent bubbles in her wash basins. In a way, they felt as scrubbed as the laundry. It wasn't a bad feeling.

A man toting a shipping crate passed them and they sidestepped to make room. Gideon subjected the towny to the same brief but searching study he gave everyone. He hardly expected to recognize anyone here, but checking had become as natural as breathing.

Another behavior become habit was taking note of horses. A horse had a lot to say for itself and the man who rode it. For all the horse flesh in the west, a noticing man had no difficulty keeping a personal list. None of those hitched about town stood out, not as friend nor enemy.

So, your clothes really were ruin'd.

Looked like Connell hadn't lied after all, and neither had Aspen. Why all this fuss over clothes anyway? They were just things.

Thems nearly all I had left.

An' now theys just one more thing on the list-a what's done been lost. Ain't the first, ain't the last.

It was a pathetic sort of claim, even if it were true. Last or first, Gideon's kit had never been much. The washer lady had been correct; what his clothes had consisted of mostly were holes. Rather like his life.

It was getting to where the only thing Gideon had left

were memories and a promise to a bunch of men long past holding him accountable. Then again, they did not have to; he held himself accountable to the very last tally.

Connell's next stop took them to the blacksmith's. Caswell Crossing's smith live up to the archetype of his profession. He was not double broad at the shoulder and narrow at the hip, a man-bull wielding a thirty pound hammer over a fiery furnace of red-hot heat no mortal man could endure. At first glance he leaned more to the archetype of average. The second, lingering glance revealed the smith's frame had indeed bulked out in every particular relevant to the trade he had learned from his grandfather.

Not the sort-a fellah ya want at t'other end of-a tug-a war.

True for you. Ya reckon Mary's some relation?

"I see you have your hands full, Doc," the smith offered in a neighborly way.

"No more than you, I'm thinking," Connell returned.

Caught fast in the smith's grip, a rather displeased little man struggled for freedom. He was nearly bald, like the great rocks that jutted out from the mountains, yet possessed none of their impressive majesty. He looked more like a thin blade of grama grass at the far end of a long summer— thoroughly washed out. Thing was, grass like that could survive. It could do more than that, it could sink its roots into the rocky soil and flourish. It had no brilliant blossoms, no blazing spring colors to herald its existence. It simply was and kept on being.

The sun wrinkled, whisper of a man was like that. Unremarkable but steady beyond common expectation, he had rooted to Caswell Crossing so seamlessly he was as much a part of the town as the buildings. At present he was doing his level best to uproot himself as quickly as possible.

"It'll take more than him, Doc," said the smithy, his

arm as still and unmovable as the iron he forged, despite the tugging and twisting of the little man in his grip. He nodded at Gideon, "Don't reckon you'll recall, I'm Jim Smyth and this here is Zeek. If he has a surname I've never heard it. Reckon he got disowned for being mule-stubborn."

The man pronounced his name like his profession. His captive gave another tug, woefully insufficient to the need, and had to settle for crossing his arms defiantly.

"Zeek?" Gideon recognized the name. "The hostler?"

"Ever since there were a stable," the captive grumbled, sullen for his predicament.

Gideon thought of his run in with Rydel, the one Aspen liked to hold up as Exhibit A against his intelligence. If it hadn't been for Zeek that day. . . Aspen might have been right to point out Gideon's folly, but nobody needed to tell him when to be grateful.

"Then it's you I owe a thanks," he said.

"T'weren't nothin'."

"Obliged, all the same."

"Get this brute to lemme go 'n we'll call 'er square."

"Forget it," Smyth declared firmly, and tipped his head towards the doctor. "Tell him."

Zeek scowled like a child refusing a dose of caster oil. Gideon had to pass a hand over his mouth and Connell felt a distinct need to clear his throat.

"Oh, for the love of Pete," Smyth exclaimed. He hauled Zeek over to an anvil and one armed him to a seat. "One of the horses stepped on him, Doc."

Zeek clamped his arms tightly in front of him like a shield. If a man is going to get injured, he at least wants a glory story to go with it. He does not want to admit he tripped over his own two feet. Smyth stood beside him and rocked from heel to toe, brows lifted, and made a rather expressive coughing noise.

"Don't say it, Jim," Zeek threatened. "Don't ya say it! I tain't no chicken. You wipe that there smirk off-a yer face. Ya hear me?"

Smyth turned up the intensity of his smugness and Connell struggled to maintain a professional demeanor.

"If'n I were afeared a-nothin' t'wouldn't be no sawbones – no insult to ya, Doc," Zeek continued, working himself into a lather. "I done fit me Injuns from perdition 'n back ag'in. Great blue blazes, even had me a wife onc't, 'n she were worse'n the Injuns. Seein' 's I still got m'hair, you got no call callin' me no scaredy. Ya hear? Go on, Doc. Tell this dirty she'pherder there tain't nothin' wrong with me. Go on, have ya a lookie-see."

Zeek stuck out his foot. There was no refusing him, to try would have been to invite full-scale, open battle. Smyth raised his hands in mock surrender, having achieved precisely what he wanted, and Connell gave a surreptitious wink of approval for a job well done.

"Gideon, take pew, lad," Connell directed, and knelt down to inspect Zeek's injured foot through boot and all. "When did this happen, Zeek?"

"Yesty'day," Zeek pronounced, as if squaring up for a fight.

"Have you taken your boot off since?"

"Had me a peek. T'wern't bleedin'."

"Well, your foot's so swollen I'll have to cut it off."

Zeek went ghost pale. His eyes widened to the size of saucers, his jaw fell open, and his vision blurred with thoughts of blunt saws and rusty tools. One strangled gulp later, he scrambled for the most immediate exit route– straight backwards– and all but fell off the anvil in his haste. Smyth deftly caught him up and held fast.

"Your boot, Zeek," Connell explained over the smith's guffawing. "I'll have to cut your boot, not your foot."

Zeek quit pinwheeling for dear life. "My. . . ?"

Connell gestured to the anvil. "If you wouldn't mind."

Tempered by embarrassment, the hostler resumed his seat. Connell opened his bag and set to work revealing the badly bruised foot. His gently exploring fingers caused Zeek to yelp and jerk involuntarily.

"Sorry about that. Stay put a minute," the doctor said, standing up. "Jim, how's that hand of yours?"

The smith willingly held out his sprained fingers for examination. He had no difficulty reading the words Connell's lips shaped nor grasping the doctor's meaning.

"It's fine, Doc," Smyth answered both questions, spoken and otherwise.

"Gives you no trouble?"

"None at all."

"What 'bout my foot?" Zeek interrupted.

"You, Zeek, will be fine too— if you do as I say. That foot of yours is broken. Broken," Connell repeated over Zeek's contradictions. The stubborn man could probably feel the fractured bone scraping together for pity's sake. "I want you to stay off your foot. Understand? Stay off it completely. One misstep and you could break that bone worse than it already is. For the time being, you can stay with Jim."

"But—"

"I know you, Zeek. The moment I turn my back you'll be cleaning stalls. When I return tomorrow I expect to find you right here with your foot up."

"But—" Zeek tried again.

"Right here, on your backside, Zeek, or I will put you there myself."

With that pronouncement hanging in the air, Connell collected Gideon and took his leave. They could hear the hostler arguing with Smyth, clearly at first, then muffled to indiscernible complaint. That was one man who would not make a complacent invalid.

Gideon squirmed against his own bandages and smothered a wince at the injudicious movement. Connell smacked him on the back of the head and regarded his patient sidelong, a silent dare against objection.

"Ow!" Gideon exclaimed, more from surprise than pain. "I ain't thick, ya know."

"Oh?"

"Alright. I admit I been actin' a mite thick, but don't you 'oh' me like you don't know what I'm a-sayin', 'cause ya do, an' I know it an' it's me admittin' it." Connell's rounds had been very coincidental indeed. Gideon continued with the confidence of an equal, "It's sorry I am to've called ya a liar, Dr. Connell. I'm obliged to ya for pointin' out Zeek."

"Good man," Connell beamed, giving Gideon's sound shoulder a pat. "I've another call to make. It's out of town, so I'll leave you with Sheriff Gandy 'til I get back."

He had promised to deliver a new stove one of his clients ordered, which meant the call would require the use of a wagon that would be jolted by every rock, root and hole on the several mile track. There was no road. There was barely the track. It was no trip for Gideon.

But Gideon had his own plans. With Connell out of the way, and Aspen off with his aunt, he and Peter could sort out their next move. All Gideon had to do was shake that bit about the sheriff.

"You g'wan," he said. "I'll manage my ownself."

"Aye, like Hephaestus's Pandora."

They came abreast of the café where young Miss Sally Calder worked. Not long ago, Gideon helped her snare Billy Nevans— her future husband of choice. This had left them, that is Sally and Gideon, on friendly terms.

Sure is a comfort to meet someone now an' again what ain't a-tryin' to shade ya by whatever means possible.

You're right funny.

Abruptly, Gideon realized he was walking alone. Connell stood two paces back, a victim of culinary temptation, vision filled with heavenly images to match the incredible savoryness drifting seductively out of the open café door. Gideon plucked a kerchief from the doctor's own pocket and offered the white linen up with the barest suggestion of humor tugging at the corner of his lips.

"All but drooling from the smell alone, aren't I?" Connell admitted, without the least measure of shame. "I'm starved, and don't tell your aunt Eddie, but Mathers makes the best beef stew in this or any other territory."

"She ain't my aunt," Gideon objected, following Connell inside.

"That's not what Eddie Rivers would say."

Between eager spoonfuls Connell cajoled and threatened his patient to eat. It was a wonder Gideon's bones stayed together for what little meat remained on them. Connell wondered if his patient had ever eaten well or regularly. He certainly leaned towards the runty side. Not that Gideon seemed to realize this; an awful lot of men twice his size weren't half so bold. And yet there was something distinctly reserved about Gideon Fletcher. It was like looking at someone who moved and acted completely well, yet the burn of fever still lingered in their eyes. In more ways than one, and more ways than fair, the melancholy aspects of life had infected Gideon. Well, he was in the right place to find a cure, of that Connell had no doubt. Funny thing is, sometimes a man pushes away the very medicine that can save him.

Connell carried their empty dishes into the back and left them with the cook, who nodded his thanks and heartily welcomed the doctor back any time he felt like forsaking medicine to become a dishwasher.

"You're out of luck, Mathers. Doctoring pays better."

"Don't give me that, I've seen your pay."

Connell's pay rarely came in the form of standard coinage. Whilst many of his clients did alright for themselves, more often than not they hadn't two actual made-at-the-mint silver half-dimes to rub together. His services were usually provided on a barter system— which had formed a local economic system all its own. Many options were available, however common methods of payment included produce, baked goods, mason jars of mystery or, lately, chickens.

"I don't even like to cook," Connell confessed.

"Bring the birds here," said Mathers. "I'll cook, you wash."

"Deal!"

Completely stuffed and immensely satisfied, Connell turned for the sheriff's office where he could safely leave his charge.

"Hey, Doc! Doc!"

A handful of children pounded towards Connell, the clatter of their feet stirred up the dust and their high pitched gabble flowing nineteen to the dozen.

Nonchalantly, Gideon took a weight shift of a step backwards. Without so much as turning, Connell reached out and blindly grabbed hold. He headed for the youngsters, bag in hand and Gideon in tow.

The two parties met and, for a moment, it was nothing but a voluble swarm of half-sized bodies all jumping, pulling and shoving for the doctor's attention.

"Hold on. Hold on. I can't– **That will do!** Simon. You. Speak."

With great difficulty the children fell silent whilst the

designated boy explained how their classmate had hurt himself playing ball and would the doctor mind having a look. Naturally, Connell obliged. As they drew up near the schoolyard, he sent the flock of children back inside.

A small hand latched onto Gideon's and Gabe Miller tugged away, arm straight out behind him and body angled forward like a horse in harness. The effect was more like a yearling colt trying to pull a loaded wagon.

"Gabe, I—" Gideon tried, but the exuberant little boy paid no mind.

"Go on. I'll only be a minute," Connell said, with a meaningful look that added a footnote of warning should Gideon get any clever ideas.

An exclamation of excitement drowned out Gideon's protests and Gabe redoubled his tugging. Gideon shot the doctor a dirty look, but permitted himself to be dragged into the school.

The single room held two straight columns of unadorned pews, scratched from use and shiny from polish. The preacher's podium had been respectfully moved aside. A chalkboard stood against one wall– though whether it ought to be called the front or the back wall Gideon wasn't familiar enough with churches or schoolrooms to know. Lunch buckets, a small kite and a jump rope lined the entry area. A dusty pile of firewood and a black stove hunkered in one corner waiting to be needed.

The children milled and chattered, voices high with excitement from the events of their abbreviated recess. How many stitches might Ethan need? Wasn't it an amazing dive? You should have seen. . .

Gideon's only thought was to get to Peter.

Liar.

Alright, his second thought had been for Peter. His first had ignobly been for himself and the possibility of escape from the doctor, the Rivers, the town with its ridiculous notions of justice– the whole crazy lot.

Nothin' doin'. Peter's a-countin' on us.

Yeah? Well ignorin' our own problems the sort-a thing don't nobody do less'n they're a fellah what ain't got no enemies. An' we def'nitely got enemies.

Ya reckon as they're a-goin' nowheres?

Nope.

Then we stick with Peter.

"Gabe, look—" Gideon tried to extricate his hand.

Gabe tightened his grip and aimed for a bench at the back of the room. Some of the children all but vanished as they sat, the pews being taller than their spring sprout size. Others were nothing but pigtails. A few were fully head and shoulders above the backs of the pews, incongruous for their height. Gideon could barely scratch up a memory from when he was as small as the littlest in this room. What he did recall only reinforced the maxim that some things are best left alone. As for the elder students, by the time he was their age. . . Gideon wasn't entirely sure he had ever been their age. Sometimes it seemed as if he had jumped those years in long strides, two or three at a time, like most boys would jump stepping stones to cross a river. He could not, at the moment, recall ever having been surrounded by so much youth all at once.

"Sit down. Amelia, leave him be. Rodger, knock it off." Simon came up the aisle and with him came order born not only from the fact no one wanted to tangle with his greater size, but also because it was the natural effect he had on others. He was a born leader. If he called his classmates to revolt and rebellion they would lift up the battle cry, pitch forks, torches and all. "Gabe, front and center."

"Couldn't I—"

"You know you squirm too much in the back."

"Aw, shucks!" Gabe protested, but he got himself up and moved to the indicated front row.

Here's our chance to vamoose.

Simon's very solid hand landed on Gideon's shoulder.

"Doc says stay put or else," he whispered for Gideon alone, and then proceeded to the front of the room where he began to read aloud from a book on the teacher's desk.

Whoall does he think he is?

A kid what's fifty pounds heavier'n you.

Man, oh man, he is that.

Then again, just now, who ain't?

True for you. Great stampedin' bison, the size-a that boy just ain't nat'ral. All the same, if'n Connell thinks some slip of-a kid–

A slip?

Alright, a great bull of-a kid, is gonna stand in our way, he's got 'im a real stop an' think comin'.

The state Gideon was in, if it came to anybody getting read from the book, it would probably be him— and the pressure Simon had applied to his shoulder promised a fire and brimstone service. Never one to be over vexed by details, Gideon levered himself up as quietly as an impenitent parishioner avoiding confession. The junior bull destined to grow into a blue ox continued to read.

Mebbe he ain't so tough—

Gideon stopped. He had no choice. He had come face to face with a dark gray city suit, less the coat. On inspection, he found the suit held a clean shaven man with curly blond hair and a poker table countenance. People would see what they were meant to see, no less and certainly no more. In the general direction of the man's brown ribbon necktie, Gideon mumbled a 'scuse me' and made to shift by.

"Sit," the schoolmaster whispered.

A few heads turned and Simon's voice grew minutely

louder. The snoopers returned to their own business, ears stretched to hear what was none of their business.

"Doc—" Gideon began.

"Dr. Connell will be here shortly. Sit down."

A peculiar harmonic in the man's voice vibrated through Gideon's ears, zigged around his instincts and, to his own befuddlement, he sat. Confoundit! The last thing he needed was another random body thinking they should call the tune when it was him paying the piper. Weren't the Rivers bad enough? Had he been taken prisoner by the whole blasted town? Maybe that was the last thing he needed– an entire town watching his every move. How could he help Peter that way?

Just you be glad it ain't ever' livin' soul.

No, only 'nough to make things complicated.

When ain't it?

Gideon was danged if he knew. His life had been complicated for about one hundred and fifty years.

There had been a less complicated time once. All traces of it had been relegated to the shadowy, canvas covered basement of memory and piled over with a million bits of everyday so he could get on with the task of waking and breathing. It worked about as well as hiding a bull moose under a bed sheet.

What about when his promises caught up with him? Or rather, when **he** caught up with **them**? If not for that dusty moose there wouldn't even be a promise. No. If it weren't for Tarlston there would be no promise; the memories were simply all that remained.

Good men lay dead. The man who had bankrolled that state of affairs was dead too. The ones who had done the actual killing still remained. What would Gideon do when he caught up with them? It was a question he would never, ever voice aloud and one which, in the privacy of his own thoughts, he could not avoid.

Gideon sat and fumed and plotted and kicked himself for sitting there. It was the bullet holes. They were doing him no good, just no good at all. The sound of Simon's reading flowed on, without finding the smallest foothold in Gideon's spinning thoughts. The room was still and warm. Somewhere a fly buzzed, stopped, and took wing again.

What about Peter? That would have to be done carefully.

Then ya'd best get some other fellah to do it, boyo.

Gideon sniggered. He was right, neither 'careful' nor 'thought out' were the proper adjectives to attach to any plan of his. No matter what he planned though, nothing would get done whilst he idled in that schoolhouse.

Hey! Look 'round, boyo.

It's a bunch-a kids. So what?

So that's how ya help Peter.

Gideon turned the flash of inspiration end for end and decided he just might be a genius. He could hardly wait to put the thought into action and consequently did not think before he moved. He particularly did not think about the gentleman sitting on the bench behind him.

"Don't believe I introduced myself," the schoolmaster leaned in close to whisper in Gideon's ear. "Name's Cooper. You've probably deduced I'm the teacher around here. Interesting thing is, I'm also the only attorney for a long, long ways. You might like to think on that before committing yourself to any creatively anti-social endeavors. From what I hear, you might want to stay on my good side."

G ANDY wondered if the packages stacked on the mercantile's counter added up to provisions for a long trip or a long stay. Their new owners, a small, neat family, poked about selecting their last items. Natural human curiosity perked up the sheriff's ears to listen for clues. Meanwhile, seeing as he was in no hurry. . .

The lawman draped himself bodily over the counter, one foot tip-toe to the floorboards, and reached for one of the large glass jars that maintained residence behind the glass. He felt a slight brush against his leg and his distorted vision filled with sage green calico. The blur became a girl, upside-down to his view, with hands pressed against the glass counter front.

Gandy returned the lid to the jar and himself to his feet. Before him, thick blond braids tied with green bows framed an angelic face. Delicate freckles graced round cheeks and long lashes batted over two huge, green eyes. The little girl stared boldly and Gandy felt as if heaven itself were questioning his intentions.

Blink. Blink.

The sheriff held out several pieces of brightly colored candy. The emerald eyes flicked to the bare counter and back again. Amused, he fished out a coin, pressed it purposefully onto the counter and repeated his offer. This time the child accepted. When he popped a sweet into his mouth and leant against the counter, the little girl mirrored the movement right down to propping her tiny boot heel on the wooden lip of the display window.

"Make a new friend?" her father asked, coming over to complete his transaction. Half in paternal pride and half to Gandy in conversation he added, "She always does, you know. My Fineas has never met a stranger yet."

"Must you call her that?" the man's wife complained, as if this were an old and much repeated argument.

"You named her, woman," he said, taking up the refrain.

"Yes, Priscilla, as I promised my grandmother. Not

Fineas. What nice young man is going to marry a 'Fineas'? Suppose they want to name their first born after her?"

"Fineas is a fine name for a son."

"Who says they'll have a boy?" the wife reasoned. "Suppose it's a girl, Lorne Spencer. Then where are we?"

"Then you'd best hope she marries a Francis or a Julian. They can name a girl child after him!"

This elicited a laugh from all present except Mrs. Spencer, who smacked her husband on the arm with long practiced and affectionate exasperation. Mr. Spencer flinched obligingly and scooped up an armful of supplies. His young daughter hefted a sizeable gunny sack to her shoulder with a confidence obviously born of practice, and followed after her father.

"Safe travels," Gandy told the handsome family.

Mr. Spencer paused at the door. "Thank you, sir, but I don't hold with traveling after a man's arrived and we've been plenty long arriving."

Gandy wished them welcome instead, thinking Connell was very much going to enjoy these new neighbors.

"I came before you, Sheriff. That means you come after."

Gandy backed up melodramatically, hands spread in surrender as he yielded his place in line to Mathers.

The café owner nodded once, a lighthearted so-there's-you-in-your-place. He was a big man, particularly in comparison to Gandy, at least half again as heavy and a hand's width taller. He had a bit of a paunch from eating his own cooking, hands the size of skillets and arms beefier than. . . than. . . well, suffice it to say Mathers rarely had to deal with rowdy customers and never had to ask twice.

He ordered his needs and pulled out his funds.

"Where's your purse, Mathers?" Gandy had never known the man to carry money loose about himself.

"Stolen."

"Stolen?"

"Yep. They must've sneaked it right out of my pocket. For the life of me I can't think when or how."

"Much in it?" asked the sheriff.

"Five dollars even."

"I'll keep an eye out."

"I'd take it kindly, Luke," Mathers replied. "Although you'd be doing the thief a favor, because if I catch them they'll be needing Gus's services, not yours."

Aside from being the barber, Gus also served as the town undertaker.

P ETER was dang near about to cut his blasted losses. He had looked everywhere and finally come around again to Doc's. There sat Gideon, kicked back on the front porch, a loafer taking his leisure. The fading summer sun spread its glow over him and dared his manic hair to flaunt its erratic copper streaks. Something there was that hinted his apparent serenity was a ruse, though what exactly skittered away before Peter could give it a name. It was not Gideon's body, as that reclined lazily between bench and building, shoulders slumped and feet spread. Perhaps that was why Peter's first words came out as an accusation.

"Where have you been?"

"Don't ask," Gideon replied.

Peter lifted a foot to the edge of the porch, crossed his arms over his bent knee, and waited.

"Aw, it weren't nothin'," Gideon relented. "I couldn't get shut-a the doc an' then I got stuck in that. . . school."

The word was spit out as if Gideon would rather eat maggots.

"What do you have against schools?" Peter wondered,

derailed from his angst.

"So what happened?" Gideon evaded.

Peter decided he had asked a question. He was in no confusion about this and, after the effort he had gone to, he was in no mood to be mucked about. He threw another log on his stare.

"Well?" he said.

"Well?" said Gideon, who figured Peter should know better.

Some things were not good etiquette. You didn't bring up politics with strangers, you didn't swear in mixed company, and you did not ask a man about his past.

Don't be tetchy, he don't mean nothin'.

"Doc were a-lookin' over my shoulder all dang day. Then that Cooper fellah done stuck his nose in. An'—"

Gideon hesitated to remark upon his brief encounter with Simon. Somehow, admitting that a kid had any hand in nailing him down did not line up with the thug-fighting image he wished to portray.

"I couldn't hardly go nowheres," he added awkwardly, with rough edged grace. "Now will ya get up here?"

Peter settled beside Gideon and leaned in close. "They came, like you said, then I came straight here."

"They follow ya?"

"I didn't see anyone."

"Did ya make it look good?"

"Of course," Peter bristled.

Acting intimidated in front of two large men apparently employed with the sole mission of lightening him of everything he owned, his life not necessarily withstanding, was not what one might call difficult. Peter knew he had done well and exactly as they had discussed.

"Then your friends followed," Gideon declared. "Put your arm over my shoulders."

"How can you be sure?"

"'Cause I am. Now, put your arm 'round me."

"What? Why?"

"If'n they're a-watchin', I want us to look worried an' me to look as young as they're like to b'lieve."

That was Gideon's flash of clarity in the schoolhouse: the best way to help was to appear as if he couldn't possibly be any help at all. So he nestled against Peter and endeavored to appear cherubic, the type who might— at least metaphorically— sleep with a teddy bear and leave a lamp burning. This was a stretch. Anyone who knew Gideon for more than five minutes would have keeled over laughing at the improbability. For Peter's sake, he was going to have to be a very good actor indeed.

"How does bringing them here get us anywhere?" Peter fretted. "Suppose they—"

"We could drown in s'posin'," Gideon interrupted. "Try'n map ever'thing out, start to finish, an' you're lost. S'posin' they don't do as ya fig'red? All your thinkin's on its ear an' you're up the creek. Trust me. We'll come out alright – just so as it's us a-doin' the leadin'."

It may have been Gideon talking, but it was Deputy Wilson's voice Peter heard. 'You do the leading,' the lawman had said, 'don't get pulled in.' Well, what was this if not being pulled in? Only. . . what Gideon said made sense. It was the risk that made Peter nervous. Putting himself in in harm's way was one thing, but this could be dangerous for Gideon too.

"Ya gotta keep close awhile," Gideon was saying. He emptied his borrowed pockets of their borrowed money. "I'd say stay here, only we might need us a man on the outside. Anybody gonna miss ya none?"

"Keep it, and no, nobody will miss me."

"You sure you got you the funds?" Peter denied need of

the coins and Gideon backed off. "Alright. Get a room at the hotel— 'lone, ya hear?"

"What about you?"

"I been a-thinkin'. When them friends-a yourn come they'll be lookin' to use me as lev'rage, only it's me'll do the lev'ragin'."

"You sure?" Peter brought himself to ask. "You don't have to do this, you know."

"You din't have to help me neither, but ya did."

This caused a silence to fall in which neither knew what to say. There was nothing to say, it was simply how it was. Who knew why? It just was. Life or fate or whatever had thrown them in with each other and, for the time being, they would each do what they could. That's all there was really, the time being, because nothing ever lasted. Nothing is permanent. Things you never thought of losing, one day were gone. A sock, your way, a person— it was all the same, easily lost and not so easily regained.

The distant clouds, a moment before streaked in vibrant Indian paintbrush hues, once again became ordinary gray-white smudges. A rhythmic banging echoed on the evening air; someone close to hand was hammering industriously.

"The window?" Peter stated more than asked.

"Yep, but don't fret none. Never been a window shut without 'nother 'n bein' blasted open."

"I don't think that's quite how the quote goes."

"Always worked for me," Gideon asserted playfully. "Now, g'wan. They willn't come 'til I'm by my lonesome."

At the bottom of the porch Peter hesitated as if he would say something. Whatever it was, he bit the words back and instead promised to return first thing in the morning. Gideon gave a weak wave and watched him walk away down the street, the classic picture of worry.

Think it'll work?

Sure, now. Peter's men willn't be able to resist.

Gideon only had to present the proper opportunity. Since they had achieved nothing thus far, why not try another angle, particularly one as unthreatening as manipulating a skinny kid?

Ain't them I meant, boyo.

Aw, don't be an old woman. Ain't nothin' to it.

Though his insides knew he was a man grown, Gideon's outsides had not entirely received the message. He had no beard, his voice, if he wanted, could still be made shrill and his limbs consisted mostly of knees and elbows. Being shot had taken pounds off, and he had not started out with many to spare. He would look plenty scrawny.

Gideon hadn't told Peter what else he planned. What Peter did not know he could not be made to tell, nor need he contrive to play his part.

It would have to be done tonight, before Aspen returned. That man could complicate the most simple of intentions. Doing so seemed to be a habit of his. Even with him around, Gideon could manage, only lately Aspen had become. . . overbearing, stifling, a right pain in the—

Ya mean protective?

Protection wasn't the word. Gideon was a prisoner, plain and simple, compliments of that blasted judge. Frankly, he was still not convinced of that particular official's legitimacy. Caswell Crossing was not within the states united. What they had was a town council who had woken up one day and decided having a judge sounded like a capital idea. It was undoubtedly how they had gone about getting a sheriff too. Other men might wake with the urge to light for distant parts or be struck with the inspiration for intricate blueprints of magnificent architectural feats. The leading men of Caswell Crossing had decided to try their luck with 'law'.

The trouble with that was, whose law was it? Theirs? Did they hunt it down, hire it up and buy it off? Did the town council then feel they ought to have final vote and say as to what the law should be?

Did the sheriff lay claim to the law? He had the gun to back it, but if the law belonged to him you had best pray you hired a good man– a very good man— or you were chin deep without a ladder.

Was it the judge who dictated law? Did the law listen to mere men like a servant, humble and meek? Was it even biddable or was it a rigid statute, written down and indifferent to men's whishes? Was it, in fact, nothing but the whims of men imposed upon other men?

That at least could not be true. Were law nothing but idle happenstance of whim, that would be utter chaos and, foolish as mankind was, it did pretend to a sort of order. Mankind had to live with itself, sometimes in very close quarters, and the only way to do so without everyone going stark raving mad was to establish a set of expectations.

Sometimes a person went too far, stepped over the line of what could be tolerated, and somebody had to set him straight. A fellow should, for example, reasonably expect other men to keep out of his gear. If his gear were pinched, the offending man should reasonably expect to be nailed to the barn wall.

What ended up as law, in Gideon's experience, was whatever the biggest man dictated. It could be someone rich, or strong, or fast with a gun— which breed in particular really did not matter— they all walked hard and talked big. People gave way to them without thinking, or at least without thinking very much. After 'He could kill me and they would never, ever find the body', what was left? Right and wrong got pushed aside until a hundred little sheep of men went through life keeping their heads down. They said things like 'It's complicated' and the age old favorite 'It's not my place'.

But there were things you could not sit by and let happen. Every now and then a man is born knowing this and is thereby incapable of bowing his head. This sort of man looks up– **all the time**. He can't help it. He does not need to examine the sheep trodden grass at his feet to know where he stands. Where the dust devil of trouble starts is that he also knows **who** he is and exactly how much he will take. A looking-up man gets mighty suspicious of anyone trying to do his thinking for him.

He also knows there are times when you have to stand up— definitely not the sort of behavior the aforesaid 'big men' appreciate. All the same, if it's not your place to speak for the voiceless, if it's not your place to champion the liberty and dignity of your neighbor, whose is it?

But if I lift my head up, it could get knocked off, said the sheep.

What'd be the loss? Ain't like you're a-usin' it nohow.

"You still there?" Connell's voice drifted out to the twilit porch.

What was the point of promising to do something, or not do something, if folks were going to keep asking whether or not you had done the thing you said you were going to do, or not do? Gideon nearly barked an answer, and then recalled how the doctor had given him a chance to draw free breath without having to black an eye or slip out the back window.

"Yeah, Doc," he said. "I'm here."

Connell came outside and eased onto the porch swing beside Gideon. He seemed content. Content with himself, the night, with life in general. The two of them sat, sharing the silence, and the minutes strolled by without hurry.

Gideon sighed gently and felt himself grow a small measure heavier, as if his bones were not quite his own. Connell's placidity was contagious. It was also no good. Gideon had an appointment to keep.

"Going in?" Connell inquired.

"The ne'ssary. Don't worry, I willn't take myself nowhere's."

Gideon wished he weren't, it was pleasant there in the quiet. Oh well, it was dark, Peter's men could come without being seen. Gideon made his way behind the clinic. He did not look into the shadows. He certainly did not look over his shoulder. He did listen to every leaf, every blade of grass, every tiny sound.

It was impressive then that he did not hear them. A hand fell over his mouth, an arm went around his body, and Gideon was hustled behind the outhouse. No need to pretend his racing heart.

Square features confronted him, with two days' of stubble and what was probably a permanent sneer. The upper lip was marred by a thin white scar and a slight crook bent an otherwise unblemished nose. For all his latest captor bore the marks of a fight or two, and he sure trotted out a well-practiced 'glare of intimidation', he was no fighter, not professionally speaking. The cut of him was more ruffian than athlete. Gideon supposed the hired thug in his late thirties.

Of the partner, what could be said? Broad hands, pudgy fingers and fat arms. That's all Gideon could see.

"I don't have time for games, boy," the ruffian in front hissed. "Where is it?"

"W-where's what?" Gideon stammered and, purely for show, tugged against the man holding him.

"Don't play with me," Pultrie warned, drawing a slim knife.

This was no working man's weapon. It was meant to be hidden away, concealed until its owner invited you to see it. It was a knife meant for the encouragement of its victim's imagination.

Pultrie felt a tingle of satisfaction. This was going to be easy. He was finally going to finish the job. The fact that he would thereby be finished with Harvey Wilcox was a bonus beyond measure.

"You want to keep Peter safe, boy, you tell me where the deed is."

"C-c-courthouse," said Gideon, wide eyed.

The sharp steel followed as he tried to turn away. The most infinitesimal twist would turn the blade from flat to blood drawing edge.

"What's your name?" Pultrie demanded, with the pleasantness of last week's fish oil.

"Gi-Gideon."

"Mighty warrior are you?" A smile lacking all warmth contorted Pultrie's scruffy features, then vanished entirely. "We've been to the courthouse, boy."

Several possibilities came to Gideon as the knife began to turn. Most of them would have been particularly unpleasant to Pultrie. Some would have been downright unwelcome.

Easy, boyo. You're s'posed to be a no account kid.

"I dunno nothin'!" Gideon babbled. "Honest!"

Harvey heard the youthful squeak and shook his head. It was not meant in sympathy, what happened to Gideon was no concern of his, but why waste time? If the kid had any knowledge of the papers, or any hint of their location, he would have confessed and been happy for his life.

The knife left Gideon's cheek and began to dance across his vision. Left, right, left, right– smooth as a rattler.

"You wouldn't want anything to. . . happen to your

little friend now, would you?" Pultrie suggested darkly.

Gideon figured, of everyone present, Pultrie was the one who really did not want anything to happen to Peter. Firstly, Peter was the most direct route to getting what he wanted. Secondly, and far more importantly, because harming Peter would leave Gideon no reason whatsoever to refrain from making sure something incredibly worse happened to Pultrie.

Eh-eh. Nancy boy. 'Member?

Harvey smacked his mute prisoner on the ear and Gideon managed a trembling shake of his head.

"Then you listen to me." Pultrie's words took on the hiss of hot iron. "You're going to find the deed and then you're going to give it to me. Because, if you don't, something bad **will** happen— to your friend and to you."

Gideon's jaw moved, but no sound came out. The knife tip lifted his chin, elucidating a meaning already remarkably clear.

"If you're thinking about telling anyone," Pultrie locked eye to eye with his victim, "don't. Understand?"

Gideon nodded minutely whilst one of the aforesaid possibilities made a return visit and introduced a few cousins as well.

"What's that?" Pultrie prompted.

"Y-yessir," Gideon stammered, in mock obedience.

Pultrie patted his cheek, a belittling counting of coup, and then both men were gone. In the name of verisimilitude, Gideon leaned against the outhouse like a runner gasping for breath.

Sure I un'erstand you, mister. Better'n ya think.

Wing ripper.

Probably true. Pultrie looked exactly the sort who'd spent his junior years plucking wings off insects, pushing smaller boys into the mud and generally terrorizing the neighborhood. Clearly he had grown into his occupation.

Gideon wondered if Pultrie had ever taken his chances with someone more formidable.

CHAPTER 4
Gaily Bedightly
Patching Peter
Tells
Making Friends
The Many Sons Of Nichodemus Rivers
Influencing People

O NE empty street. One Gideon Fletcher. No moon. No witnesses. So far, so good. He took a deep draught of the night air into his lungs. A man had come to a sorry pass when merely standing alone could be exhilarating.

Best get on with it.

Certain necessary preparations needed to be seen to as insurance against a capricious future, which at best held itself indifferent and at worst delighted in malevolence.

It don't stop, do it?

Some folks claimed every man had a fixed quantity of grief allotted to his lifetime. No matter what he did, it would never be more or less than his set ration. Thing was, if that were true, a man could see his grief sprinkled lightly throughout his years, so thinly it hardly vexed him. Then again, it could pile up into one long miserable excuse for a year until he found himself wishing he had never been born. In theory, if he survived, his remaining years would thereby be trouble free. Where nothing in the later proposition promised blue skies and pockets full of gold, it at least had the courtesy to leave a man well enough alone.

Gideon was pretty sure he had not outdistanced his share of allotted grief— not by a good long spell.

Well, seein' as you got you plen'y to go 'round. . .

It was a dark, marvelous, heart-lifting thought and Gideon allowed himself to savor it like a connoisseur sips of an elegant wine. They had pulled a knife on him and threatened his friend. No one could say they hadn't earned his attention.

A tinny melody danced on the air, its toes stepped on by the less able accompaniment of a pitch challenged vocalist. The saloon doors squeaked, rattling back and forth on their hinges, and an unsteady gentleman joined the darkness. Gideon wondered why anyone would deliberately put themselves in such a state and, moreover, why on earth they would actually pay for the privilege. Shooting yourself in the foot was faster, cheaper and more sensible.

It was amazing how the average good-timer could order another, long after every shred of intelligence had abandoned them. They didn't know who **they** were, but the bartender they could peg at fifty paces. He wasn't a man, a companion to while away the hours with. He wasn't Bob, or Jim, or Sam. He was Barkeep, and he spoke the unique dialect of the alcoholic swimmer. He was the only man— ever— to throw a drowning man another glass of what ailed him and be thanked for it.

If his customers ever became lost and inadvertently slogged onto the shores of potential sobriety, they might wonder where they were. The floor was a solid start, but the more upwardly mobile eventually stumbled onto the keen idea of going home. The brave, or unmarried, would haul themselves up and, after a few false starts, realize properly functioning legs would be a cracker idea.

Since their own legs were well and truly out of the reckoning, they needed a oresh. For preference their own resho, as self-inflicted confusion is rarely an acceptable excuse when presented to a lynch mob. The challenge, once one has located their srohe, is to identify one end from the other. Difficult to do when one is in fact a significant part of the equation.

This particular conundrum of equestrian anatomy did not bother Gideon. Odds were, folks cutting loose at this hour would have a firmer grasp on a whiskey bottle than the finer points of riding. His footsteps crunched lightly over the ground as he detoured away from the saloon, darted across the street, snuggled up to the livery, cut behind and continued on his way without so much as a neigh or a nicker to announce his passing. Horses— always a better bet than men.

At a locked door, Gideon pulled out his picks and deftly twirled them between his fingers. Humming under his breath, he made himself to home, committed several offenses and at least two chargeable infractions. Then, with alarming efficiency and nearly criminal pleasure, Gideon slipped back outside. The jaunty tune continued to play in his head, adding a bounce to his step. Peter's shadows were messing with the wrong gent entirely.

Hey, genius, pay 'tention.

Right. No need to get cocky; just because nobody knew what he was up to didn't mean they couldn't find out. Yielding to his better sense, Gideon peered over his shoulder. His attention thus diverted, he promptly bumped into the corner of the bathhouse. It moved– not an oddity he would have heretofore associated with solid buildings. He spun around, fist raised, and met a flat hand going the other way. The impact rattled his teeth. Gideon squared himself, heard a squeak and was slapped again. A well-placed forearm blocked the next assault.

"Hey! You're a girl!" he exclaimed.

"Hey! You're a boy!" the architectural impersonator countered, rather belatedly.

The battle halted whilst both parties regrouped and somewhat sheepishly lowered their respective arms.

"What are you—" they both said.

"I—" they tried again.

A sharp ray of lamplight invaded the night, whereupon the girl put a warning finger to her lips and pushed Gideon farther into the darkness of the alley. His heels caught against an overturned wash barrel and he fell amongst the stack with a thud. The girl squashed down beside him until all Gideon could see was bold orange hair and not enough gray satin. Her mother would have told her to get a coat–and the rest of her dress for that matter.

He was about to tell her to give over when the smell of soap and lemon verbena struck him nearly as forcefully as her hand had done. Smells could do that. In one brief whiff they could incite an entire panoply of memories. It had for Gideon. He sat there, shocked dumb entirely.

When the girl finally turned to consider him, her oval face creased thoughtfully. "I know you. You're Gideon. The sheriff caught you with those rustlers. The ones they hung."

Was the clarification actually necessary? Had there been any other rustlers lately? Maybe some who were not stretched? 'Begging your pardon, we didn't mean it, honest'? Not likely. It occurred to Gideon he was thinking quite a lot about ropes lately.

Hmm, now why'd that be?

Shutup.

"I ain't no thief," Gideon objected.

The girl put a hand on her hip. "Did I say you were?"

"No, ma'am," he relented. "I oughtta go."

"Wait! I mean. . ." she floundered for a reason and landed on his arm. "Oh, you're hurt."

"Yes'm. If'n ya knowed my name, ya knowed that too."

The girl had the wit to realize she was caught and the grace to be embarrassed. "Well, there's. . . I mean. . ."

"You alright, ma'am?"

"It's Isi. You should wait, that's all."

Whatever had her so all-fired jumpy, beyond his own unexpected appearance, Gideon did not wish to make matters any worse for her. Besides, the only escape route was to clamber over her, something he did not favor.

"Anything I can do for ya?"

Isi gave a charming look, offered to a thousand men before ever he came along, and Gideon was certain his offer was about to be tossed aside like last year's dirty socks. There came a shift, a sort of clouding that dimmed her for the barest instant.

"Will you tell me something?" Isi asked, as if the cloud had never existed.

Gideon shrugged acceptance of the possibility.

"They say you killed him, the man who shot you."

"Seemed the likely way 'round, ma'am."

"Why?"

"Well, it's a pure awful habit, but I got me an' uncurable a-diction to breathin'."

Isi gave Gideon a playful nudge. "You are sassy, rumor has you there."

"Talk-a the town'm I?"

Isi pursed her painted lips and batted her long lashes.

"Aw, c'mon. Ya can't not tell me nothin'."

Isi winced. "Didn't nobody learn you about talkin'?"

"No, ma'am," Gideon said, with a politeness gone stiff around the edges. "Don't reckon as nobody never did."

"I'm sorry. I shouldn't have said that. Forgive me?"

Some folks could say the self-same words without imbuing them with a single ounce of sincerity. They would be forgiven, in a passing sort of way, only to unthinkingly commit the same discourtesy again and again. Isi's world hardly hung in the balance, and yet she was sincere. It seemed to Gideon sincerity from her was preciously guarded and rarely permitted.

C'mon, boyo.

"Aspen, his kinfolk run the mercantile," Gideon confided, "he's been a-tryin' to shove his fancy talk on me. Can't say it's done me no good."

"Well, he certainly taught you some fine manners," Isi offered as reconciliation.

"No, ma'am, weren't 'im."

"Your ma?"

"Only woman ever learnt me nothin' were a lady like yourself."

Isi bowed her head and turned away. There in the anonymity of the darkness it was easier to admit to a stranger what would have remained steadfastly unsaid to any by daylight.

"I'm no lady, Gideon Rivers."

"It's Fletcher, ma'am," Gideon amended and moved on. "That friend-a mine, she said ever' woman were a lady, an' to treat 'em so, less'n they gived me good cause not to."

"You know what I am. Everyone here does."

The statement held no future, only a present full of condemnation. But, just below the bitter acknowledgement, Gideon heard something else entirely. It told him Isi's occupation went so far and no further, an intrusion into her life that had been meticulously demarcated. It was not her in any measurable sense.

"Yes'm," he agreed. "You're a lady with a helluv'n arm on ya. Ain't much else matters. That friend-a mine, she said to see what were really there, not dumbly swallow what folks 'spected. She b'lieved a fellah oughtta be civil to womenfolk, on a'count-a they'd 'preciate such behavior."

Gideon gave his tongue a rest. It wasn't accustomed to so much work, not with a stranger and certainly not with a stranger of the female persuasion. It was the orange hair. She'd had orange hair too, that lady of his. Frizzy, rebellious strands brushed every night with an ivory comb.

For all she had lurked in the back corners, Gideon hadn't really thought of his friend in ages. It wasn't that he'd forgotten. How could he? Only sometimes, the world was a mighty rough place and if a fellow figured to keep himself whole and hale, he could not afford to be sidetracked by the greener grasses growing along memory lane. Even when you wished with all your heart you could go back and have things different, sometimes life gave you little choice but to cinch up and ride on.

There was no discarding his red-haired angel though. He had simply tucked her away, a porcelain figurine carefully wrapped and boxed for safe keeping. Perfume and soap. It had brought it all back.

Blast.

Today's redhead stirred beside him.

"Your friend was right," Isi confessed, somewhat reluctantly but entirely truthfully.

"Yep," Gideon nodded. "So, you owe me."

"For what?"

"For this handprint a-dec'ratin' my cheek."

"I am sorry," Isi said, with a giggle that stole nothing from the truth.

"Uh-huh, well I'm owed," Gideon repeated dryly.

"You startled me," she demurred.

"That were startled? I'd hate to see afeared."

"You were going to hit me."

"Ya did hit me," Gideon asserted. "I could take the ev'dence to the sheriff, ya know."

"I suppose you could. . . provided you have an explanation for why you're sneaking about at this hour."

"D'you?"

"I don't need one," the lady of the evening countered.

Well, that shut Gideon up. He did not have an

explanation, at least none he cared to give. So much for the 'I'm telling' method of leverage.

"Tell you what," Isi offered companionably, "I'll do you two favors, one for each time I hit you. First, I won't tell anyone I saw you. And second, the next time I have the opportunity, I won't hit you. Truce?"

She stuck out her hand, generosity itself now that she had won. That was a woman for you.

She's funny.

Who's askin'?

Well, she is.

She was. Gideon gave Isi's hand a firm shake. Who knew what allies he might need? When it came to enemies, his dance card was right about full up.

S ORRY to put you out, Dr. Connell."

Connell sat at Peter's feet, needle in hand, and waved away the apology. "I've done a fair few stitches in my time."

Peter had shown up that morning with a rip in the knee of his britches. Not so long ago his mother would have mended it, and a fine hand she had too. She could sew anything– for anyone else that is. She used to say she could sew for herself anytime; her son, however, grew faster than she could cut a pattern.

Connell had offered his services and, though Peter naturally turned him down, Connell had refused the refusal. Peter had given in, mostly from years of well ingrained civility. He sat on the porch swing, patiently watching Connell tucking and pulling with the agile fingers of a surgeon and using a surgeon's stitch.

"No harm to your mother," Connell suggested, "but she might have taught you to do this yourself."

"I wouldn't let her," replied Peter.

"Why ever not?"

"Sewing is women's work. Oww!"

"Hold still," said Connell.

"I think you mistook my hide for cloth."

"A mere doctor can hardly be expected to manage as adroitly as a woman," Connell excused himself eloquently, tied off the thread and snipped it. "There. If that doesn't outlive your growing, I'll eat my license."

For a moment, the past superseded the present and Peter's fingers drifted to the bracelet on his wrist. His father loved to see that warm, walnut hair shimmer in the sunlight.

"Your turn," said a distant voice.

The doctor waited expectantly, but all Peter could do was gape vacantly as the clouds of memory milled about.

"Don't take a seizure, boy. It's a needle I'm handing you, not a scorpion."

"But sewing's—" Peter stopped all by himself.

"You're a quick learner. And, for your information, there is nothing masculine about a man who cannot so much as sew a button. It's pathetic."

"But—"

"Pathetic," Connell repeated, tossing Peter the thread.

Peter caught the spool and followed the doctor's instructions to mend the loose button on his shirt.

"Aren't you two pretty as a picture?"

Peter's head snapped up and his entire face flushed bright red. He hadn't heard Aspen approaching, but then, Aspen hadn't meant to be heard.

"Whew," Aspen whistled. "I've known girls who don't blush half so well."

Peter turned an even deeper red. He could feel it clear to his toes. Like a man closing the barn door after the cow's out, he ducked his head back to his work, hoping to hide the reaction— and promptly stabbed himself. He stuck the injured finger in his mouth with a scowl, which amused Aspen all the more.

"You leave him be, and you keep working," Connell addressed giver and getter. "I've been trying to convince Peter that knowing a few of the presumably feminine tasks would be to his advantage."

"You're right," Aspen agreed, leaning against an awning post, "but if either of you come calling, I'll clobber you both. Where's Gov?"

"That took remarkable restraint on your part, waiting so long," Connell replied. "Staying with your aunt must have done you some good."

"That, Peter, was me being chastised. Which I concede **might** be deserved," Aspen acknowledged lightly. "I am not, however, completely reformed and would appreciate knowing where my recalcitrant ward is hiding and what mischief he has perpetrated in my absence. If it's not too much of an inconvenience that is."

"Gideon's still asleep. And," Connell added with due anticipation, "yes, I'm sure, and no he has not run off."

"And I thought only a jail cell could achieve that."

"And I thought only a cell could restore your good humor."

"That, Peter, was me being chastised again," Aspen pointed out, in full possession of his good humor. "If it is also a subtle hint for an apology, Connell, you have it."

Connell waved away the offer. There was nothing he had done or put up with that went beyond the bounds of friendship. He turned to Peter and showed him how to tie off the thread. The workmanship would never rate a blue ribbon but, in the more-is-better technique of the amateur, the button had been secured for dear life.

"May I ask you something, Mr. Rivers?" said Peter.

Aspen leaned his aptly named self more comfortably against the post and slid his hands into his pockets. "So long as it's not for a stroll in the moonlight."

"Is Gideon your ward because of the cattle or from before?" Peter asked, tucking in his mended shirt and trying to ignore the ribbing. "I mean, if I'm not butting in."

"I'm not surprised he hasn't told you; hieroglyphs are more forthcoming. Fact is, it's something I wanted to speak to you about."

There was everything about Aspen that said joviality had been set aside; whatever was on Aspen's mind was for serious. It was cousin to the feeling that came over Peter when his father had taken Ma into town.

"Gov's had a rough time," Aspen explained. "He could use. . . well, he could use a wagon load of a lot of things, but mostly he could use a friend to steer him straight."

Peter swallowed and found it an effort. Naturally, this would not include someone like himself who spent his leisure time breaking into courthouses. That was not the kind of positive influence one wanted to encourage and, clearly, Gideon could get into enough trouble on his own.

"Did he. . . the rustling. . . was it bad luck?" Peter asked. "You know: wrong place, wrong time?"

"Gov hasn't had much of anything you'd want to call luck. Not until Judge Forsythe put him with us– and I don't think Gov would call that luck."

"Doesn't he have any family?"

"Not that he would confess to," Aspen replied, but his body language indicated he was not entirely sure if this should stand for a yes or a no.

Peter wondered why anyone wouldn't want to admit to having a family. Especially in Gideon's case? They could have spoken up for him or posted bail. That's what families were for. They were the first recourse and last stand. When everyone else walked off or gave up, family stepped in.

"Do you think you could do that?" Aspen said.

Peter suddenly realized he had not been listening and gave a hurried 'yessir' to cover the lapse.

"I'd understand if you'd rather not. What are you sniggering at, Connell?"

"Is it any wonder Peter sounds so exasperated?" the doctor replied. "I asked him the selfsame thing not ten minutes ago."

"Then why did you let me blather on?" Aspen demanded, hands flapping in frustration at the inefficiency of repetition.

Connell feigned innocence and radiated guilt. "You, actually allowing– no, asking– for someone's help? I was struck dumb with the shock. Truly dumb entirely."

Aspen frowned, though more from recognition of the accuracy of Connell's accusation than indignation. Aunt Eddie had recently handed him remarkably similar words.

"So, will you stick with Gov?" he asked, turning back to Peter. "I know you fetched him out of it already, and I do thank you, but Gov is very good at making himself about as friendly as a prickly cactus."

Peter executed a mental about-face and legged it for Aspen's train of thought. He wasn't caught and he wasn't being told to back off. Dual relief flooded in. Mr. Rivers didn't know, he couldn't, or he wouldn't be asking.

"I'll keep with him, Mr. Rivers."

"Good," Aspen declared and meant it. "And there's no need for the 'mister'. I leave that to my father. Now, could you do with a job? Don't tell me Connell."

The doctor beamed happily. "That's right, I've gone before you there too. Zeek needs a hand around the livery."

"You could work for my uncle," Aspen countered. "He runs the mercantile. Pay's good and if you can do sums he's guaranteed to love you."

"Eh-eh," Connell objected, holding up a hand. "Don't you trespass. We shook hands, so we did. The lad's mine."

"Plannin' your life for ya, are they?" Gideon remarked, padding barefoot onto the porch.

Aspen looked his ward over. Upon cursory examination he seemed in reasonable order– meaning, no new injuries and lacking handcuffs. On the grounds that asking even the most innocent question might cause him to hear things guaranteed to blast the momentarily idyllic image to smithereens, Aspen refrained from interrogation.

"Not everyone minds a little direction," he pointed out instead.

"Some do," Gideon parried.

"There are some who could do with it."

"There's some as got no say."

Peter verbally edged in between them. "Mr. Rivers is only trying to help."

"I'm so buried in help I'm like to drown," Gideon complained.

"You don't take half what's offered," Aspen replied.

"I take 'nough."

"You say enough too," the doctor stepped in, recognizing the signs of one who feels they have taken enough squaring themselves to give enough. "If Peter wants to listen to his elders, that's his business. And now that you are up, I can see to my business. Inside with you. Go on."

Gideon made to offer protests, which fell on ears made deaf by the clamor of their forefathers.

"Does he really expect Dr. Connell to give in?" Peter mused.

He had been coddled and nursed and medicined in his time and never had those well-meaning angels possessed an ounce of mercy for him.

"I suspect he does it to convince himself more than Connell," Aspen replied, with remarkable tolerance and a touch of amusement.

When it came to Gov's reasons, Aspen figured he just about had a corner on the market. After all, he'd been knocked around enough by them. Half the time why Gov did what he did only made sense to himself, and even then it sometimes made less sense after he'd done it. In this case, Aspen figured Gov did not want to owe anyone for anything so, if he objected to Connell, he could keep the slate clean. There was no need, but just try to tell him that.

"Since you'll be working in town, Peter, you're welcome to stay at my aunt's. She loves guests. I imagine you could sleep at the livery, but I'm afraid you would never hear the end of it." It occurred to Aspen he was talking mostly to himself. "Peter?"

"Hmm? Oh. Um. Thank you."

Aspen casually shifted his position to allow a wider view of the street and found nothing to warrant Peter's fixed attention. The only thing of any note was two strangers moseying along the south side of town. This hardly struck as unusual. Drifters came, drifters went. Something about them did catch the eye but, given that one of them was shaped like an egg, this was understandable.

Of far more interest to Aspen himself was the young lady on a direct line for the doctor's office. He judged her tall for a woman and her pale green dress covered a slender, shapely body no amount of modesty could conceal. Her hair was pulled up fashionably with little wisps, having escaped their morning confinement, shimmering a deep strawberry-blond.

Aspen caught a glimpse of her ankles as she strode forward with steps meant to defy the hem of her skirts. The young woman scaled the porch steps, practically at a bound, and Aspen politely stepped aside. He was right, she was tall and she stood to every inch.

"Mr. Rivers," she greeted crisply, and propelled herself inside.

Aspen stared. The door swung shut. Still he stared.

"Know her?" Peter asked.

Aspen shook his head. He was quite certain, had he met her, this woman he would have remembered.

"Your loss. Wonder if she takes to younger men?"

The spell broke and Aspen dropped onto the swing, where he knuckled Peter's head as he was known to do to his little brothers, regardless of size, age or retribution.

"I see you have one in hand," Connell observed from the doorway. "Introduce him to Zeek for me, will you? Take this other side of the coin with you. I've endured enough of his whingeing for a while."

Was that Connell teasing– and Gov not biting his head off? More than that, Gideon was trying hard not to grin. Well, wonders truly did not cease.

Aspen herded up his ducklings and headed them out, a niggling worry fluttering more to the front of his thoughts than the back. He would simply have to keep an eye on Gov; obviously Connell wanted privacy for his latest visitor.

Who was she and why had she known his name? Perhaps someone had spoken of him. In this town, gossip was the greatest, most abundant, most re-circulated commodity ever traded. Perhaps she had been to the mercantile. She would have to eventually, if she lived in town. Now there was a happy thought.

MATT LaConner picked up his cards. Nearly a straight flush. Three others shared his table and had for the last two hours. One was a quiet man of about thirty.

Under a light layer of travel dust he was trim, tidy, and well mannered. His soft speech more than hinted of the deep south. If Matt was any judge at all, and he prided himself on being a good one, the young man was more than passing familiar with the outlying edges of polite society. The other two at the table were cousins by their own confession and obvious strong resemblance.

"What happened to him?"

"Got his neck stretched."

The words rang like chimed crystal from amongst the cluttered noise of so many voices in constant chatter. The cousins placed their bets and called for more whiskey. Of the firm belief liquor and cards did not mix, Matt retained his original glass of typically watered down beer.

"Never thought nobody'd get him."

"Well, they did," said the other voice. "Out Kansas Territory, could be New Mexico. Somewhere out there."

"They hang 'em all?"

"All as let themselves be caught. Weren't no lynching neither. Can you believe it? Folks out there have themselves a judge and sheriff and all. It were legal, though I don't suppose that's any comfort to them."

The second voice cackled, "Reckon not. Hung's hung, legal or lynched. Not too smart, rustlin' so near hired law. Plenty-a easier pickins."

The drinks arrived and once again Matt slid the cards across the table into neat piles of five. No need for fancy tricks here, the effort would be lost on the cousins and the quiet one read more as the type to see through such showmanship than be overawed by it.

"Who'd've guessed?" the first voice offered as excuse for folly. "There's hardly nothin' down there but a handful of buildings set up next to the best crossing for fifty miles any direction, as I hear it."

"A crossing? Over the Black? Ya don't mean Caswell Crossin', do ya? Why that there's Rivers country."

"Don't know as there's many rivers. Didn't nobody say," the gossiper admitted ignorance of the distant region.

"Not rivers the crick, Rivers the man. He were the first out there an' he'll be the very last one in the ground, I can promise ya that. If them fellers runned into him, it ain't no wonder they's stretched. Rivers don't take to their kind, 'specially not on his land."

The noise from a nearby table grew louder, making further eavesdropping impossible. No matter, Matt had raked in sufficient information. Somewhat sidelong, he considered his quiet tablemate. Why not? Surreptitiously he made a discrete signal. To an innocent man it would mean nothing, to a knowing man Matt had just announced himself as a cardsharp.

"Your move, friend."

"So it is." The southerner played with his coins and peered at the unsteady cousins. For half a fraction of a second he clearly understood what was being suggested, then his face was once again a mask of affable serenity. His money clinked into the pot. "I'm in."

IT could've been superstition, or perhaps an overdeveloped awareness of life's twisted sense of humor, either way the back of Gideon's neck tingled.

Or it might could be ya run kind-a short on trust.

It's earned.

It was. Some mighty determined men had chosen to become his enemies. Having a suspicious streak five miles wide seemed a likely way to stay alive.

He tagged along with Aspen and Peter, far more interested in surveying his surroundings than in listening

to them carry on about some girl. As far as he was
concerned, crossing paths with a female was no reason to
get cross-eyed nor starry eyed. Some brands of trouble no
man should court, and a girl was definitely among them.

Gideon wasn't against women. As social elitism and
general prejudice went, Gideon was virtually
indiscriminant. When a body held permanent residence at
the bottom of the hierarchical heap they had no call looking
down on anybody else. Well, provided the 'anybody else' did
not go out of their way to wedge themselves into the muck
congealed beneath the strata of humanity.

Where Gideon had met one or two women who opted
for this latter category, by and large this was not the case
and therefore not a motivating factor of his reticence. It was
simply that womenfolk, in the sense of walking out
together, were an unpredictable complication best left out of
his increasingly complicated life.

A guest leaned against the railing of the hotel balcony,
contentedly gazing out at nothing. Gideon did not know the
man, but he did know the type. A riding sort of fellow who,
having reached his fill of chicory coffee, baked beans and
stone pillows, had decided to spoil himself with a night of
sybaritic comfort.

Gideon had lived that way. In his turn he had been
soaked through, half starved, frozen to the bone and hot to
misery. No mistaking it, there had been some downright
unpleasant days. Both of him sighed. What he would give to
be there now.

"Mornin', Miss Mary," he said, hoping the laundress
wouldn't mind being addressed in the familiar as he did not
know her surname.

"Gideon! On your feet again, I see," Mary stepped up to
the boardwalk, radiating sunshine.

Arms full of crumpled sheets, she fumbled with the key

to her shop and Gideon immediately obliged her.

"My thanks," she beamed. "I usually go in through the back, but somehow I went and locked it and for the life of me I can't find the darn key. Lucky for me, the front lock came secondhand and has its own key. Or maybe not. If both locks were the same, maybe I wouldn't have lost the key in the first place."

Mary was making fun of herself and enjoying the work. Her washtubs were waiting, though, and she did not permit herself to linger.

"Oh," she called, turning back. "I have something of yours. Meant to give it to you last time and plumb forgot."

Gideon followed her inside without a notion in the world what she could possibly have of his. Mary plopped her burden down and tipped her head towards the back.

"It's in the box under the counter. Help yourself."

Behind the indicated counter, Gideon knelt down and lifted a small, fairly new metal box. It rattled with the distinctive sound of mixed coinage. A larger box proved to hold seamstress's tools and notions and then, off to one side, he found a scratched up metal tin. He opened it and nearly hit the floor.

She had saved them. Why on earth would anyone save them? Gideon stared at the unremarkable collection before him. Amongst the pile of buttons cut from his clothes, a few coins of no great value, and a rusted nail, lay two small items of irreplaceable worth. He picked one up and caressed it with a thumb. They weren't lost. That's all he could think. They weren't lost. He pushed them to the very depths of a pocket, shook himself up, returned the tin to the shelf and composed his features.

"It's right kindly I'm thankin' ya," Gideon said, as he left. "You can keep what's left, ma'am."

What would possess a woman to save mismatched

buttons? For herself, he could understand. In her line of work Mary might need them. But to save them for him? Gideon was flummoxed, truly flummoxed and tipping right towards bewildered.

"Here," he said, holding a tarnished coin out to Aspen. "We're square for the doughnuts."

Aspen declined. This had to be the very last of Gideon's own funds and he had refused to accept any pay. Pay? He refused to accept anything from Pa. If the man held the last drop of water on earth, Gideon would rather suck on a dirty, sun bleached rock.

"We're square," Gideon insisted.

Aspen relented and tucked the money away. "Is that what she saved for you?"

"Yep."

"Been making friends?"

"I can," Gideon asserted. "Look at Peter."

"He was nearly shot making friends with you. What did you do to Mary?"

Gideon stammered an objection, then gave up. He could stand a bit of chaffing if it kept Aspen off his case. They passed by the bakery with its half empty racks, the siren call of warm sugar and flour entirely silent. It's seductive work had been done and dusted hours ago.

A thundering of humanity tumbled around a corner and crashed into the threesome. It had the shape of men and the loud, socially out of sync behavior commonly associated with the last rung of boyhood. They were of the age that detests being referred to as 'boy' because it points out so cutely their skin-of-the-teeth claim to the very fringes of manhood. These specimens had even less.

As they pushed and joshed, headless of any but themselves, one rough shouldered Peter into the wall. The obvious intent and blatant smugness went right up

Gideon's nose. Without thought for size, physics or consequences his foot shot out, sending the self-aggrandized nuisance sprawling cups over blessed tea kettle.

Gideon stood stock still and put whilst his opponent measured him head to toe. The other half dozen ruffians held back, making no attempt to conceal their anticipation, which was about as friendly as a vulture two-stepping on a cactus waiting for its supper to quit moving. Gideon did not care. They did not matter. If they wanted, they could be next. He let the bully get up, balled his fist and—

—his vision filled with Aspen.

He tried to step around.

Aspen tucked him back again.

"Your brother owes me an apology," an arrogant voice demanded, from somewhere on the other side of the Aspenian wall.

Gideon sidestepped again, but Aspen leaned back, pinning him like a bug against a timber frontage.

"He is clumsy," Aspen allowed. "However, if you and your friends gave a little more thought to the people around you, this sort of thing wouldn't happen."

"Hey, he tripped me!" the fool argued. "You don't make him apologize, I will."

It had the manic ring of one who knows they are backing themselves into a corner from which they cannot possibly escape and yet would very much like to. All the same, his friends were watching– he couldn't back down. Ironic really, since they didn't give two dead flies what happened to him, so long as it was entertaining to them.

"Bit of a rock and a hard place isn't it, boy?" Aspen proposed conversationally. "If I were you, I'd consider my options. Your best bet is to walk away. Your friends over there can't hear us, so you can explain things any way you like. Your other option is to remain here and discuss your attitude. I do hope I make myself clear."

Aspen began to count slowly to himself. One.

The ruffian chewed on the bitter facts. It was one thing to confront a matchstick of a kid. . .

Two.

It was quite another to contend with a 6'4" mountain whose expression had more in common with unyielding granite than easily shifted and disregarded silt.

Thr-

"Keep your baby brother away from me or next time I'll pummel him."

The ruffian took off to join his companions, leaving the threat behind him. It was pathetic and knew itself for pathetic. It scratched its head, shuffled its feet and desperately hoped it might spot somewhere to hide. It found the most likely opportunity under cover of a shouting Peter and ran for it.

"What were you thinking? He'd have killed you!"

"I'd kind of like to know the same thing," Aspen said, calmly peeking over his shoulder at the top of Gideon's unruly thatch of hair.

"You're welcome," Gideon replied with some heat, giving Aspen another shove that moved him not an inch. "Give over! You see'd what he done did."

"Yes. Where I am a little lost," Aspen replied, "is what exactly you thought **you** were doing."

"Somebody had to learn 'im," Gideon declared, an ant determined to move the world.

"And that was you, was it?"

"Why not?" said the ant, scrawny muscles flexing.

"What the blazes were you going to do?" Peter shouted, coming unglued. "Take him one handed!? Did you think he would stand around and wait whilst you fetched a deuced ladder?"

Aspen raised his eyebrows in echo of the question. Gideon was quite prepared to take offence and then noticed the glimmer. Aspen did not leave much of a trail for a body to follow, but Gideon had begun to recognize the signs. That glimmer was to Aspen what an hour's worth of tedious talking was to normal folks. It said: the boy does have a point. It also, in an indulgent sort of between the lines undertone, said: you do see how ridiculous this is, right?

Don't go a-beggin' no argument where ain't none bein' offered.

"Well," Gideon allowed reluctantly, "mebbe it weren't the most goin' prop'sition on the table."

"Just stay away from him, alright?"

"Sure, Peter, next time you can have 'im."

"Very funny."

"Come on," Aspen directed, gathering up his ducklings once more.

Would there ever come a day when Gideon could go from one end of town to the other without inciting disaster? How he had survived this long was a mystery bordering on a miracle. The angels must have gathered every morning of his few short years and flipped a coin to see who would get stuck with him. Aspen sincerely hoped there were angels looking out for him too; he could do with it.

Zeek, as it turned out, was not so eager. Smyth had taken the doctor's orders to heart and was holding to the very letter. Zeek was fit to be tied, which Smyth promised he could oblige. Zeek had his own views on this, which were discussed with some passion and no effect. In the end, he sat on a bench beside the corral, foot propped up, grudgingly instructing his temporary replacement.

With half an ear Gideon listened to the enumeration of horses kept for rental and their particular traits. This one was a biter, that one dead lazy, this one the sweetest horse ever to wear a saddle. The list drew on as if the man were speaking of his own grandchildren, part endearing and part exasperated.

Gideon felt an elbow nudge him and surreptitiously followed Peter's gaze. What was he supposed to see?

"Heard the latest?" Smyth inquired of Aspen, oblivious to the unspoken conversation going on beside him.

Aspen shook his head. Rumors took their time coming to him and, for the most part, he was disinclined to do more than nod in their general direction.

"Seems Mrs. Driscoll complained to the sheriff again," Smyth informed him.

Gideon and Peter swapped another round of nods and nudges, followed by a mutual lack of comprehension.

"Nothing new there," Aspen replied, scratching a handsome bay mare under the chin.

"True, only this time it might be real. Something set the neighbor's dog a right fit and she claims to have seen someone outside her house in the middle of the night."

Gideon tried to indicate to Peter that he had it under control. After all, the whole town could have heard that blasted dog. Whomever had set it off. . . and then Gideon knew. It could have been anybody, but he knew. That confounded dog may have scared the bejeezers out of them, but it had likely saved their necks from Peter's two friends. Who else would be running about at that time of night? Certainly not anyone up to much good.

Under control is it? Mighty close call there, boyo.

Close, not called's the point.

"I'm surprised she didn't catch whomever it was by the ear and drag them down to Gandy," Aspen was saying.

Smyth could well imagine the scene. "She may yet. Now she's going on about there being a plague of thefts and how the man she saw must be the 'miscreant', as she calls him. She's a woman on a mission."

Peter's expression shifted again, only this time Gideon was not convinced it was meant for his benefit. If Peter kept it up, it would be them caught by their ears right then and there. Gideon wanted to kick him in the shins and settled for a tight jawed twitch of his head.

"Are there?" Aspen asked.

"Thefts? Could be," Smyth allowed noncommittally. "Mitchum's lost a few dollars and Addison can't find his cufflinks. A plague? Don't know about that. More than once I've gone looking for the hammer I'm already holding."

"What does Gandy say?"

Smyth shrugged his ignorance. "Haven't heard. Where do you think you're going?"

Zeek scrunched his features into a set of intolerant creases and latched onto Peter. "Gotta show 'im the barn, don't I?"

"No, you don't. He's a smart kid. He's seen a barn."

"Doncha go tellin' me my job, mister."

"I'm telling you my job," Smyth insisted, "which is to keep you off your feet, so you can just stop right there."

"Give it up, Zeek," Aspen advised companionably. "You're a tough old buzzard, but Smyth here is too bullheaded to reason with. Peter, see you at Dr. Connell's for supper."

Peter made a show of agreeing, but underneath lurked an indecipherable suggestion of who knew what. Gideon tried to give mute assurance they had nothing to worry about and then followed Aspen. By the looks of him, if Peter got the message, he wasn't entirely convinced.

Normally Aspen had a ground eating pace to say the least, especially when he was in one of his thinking moods. Somehow his brain became so caught up in firing neurons it forgot about things as far away as feet and left them to their own devices. As they left Zeek's, Aspen fairly moseyed.

Gideon studied on the man beside him. Two arms, left and right, both in their anatomically correct locations. Remarkable, because somebody must have twisted them almighty hard. Aspen was still coddling, a sunstroked turtle could have lapped them and been home spit polishing its shell, but Gideon kept shut. At least they were out of the doc's office.

If'n ya only knowed, mister. Then again, good thing ya don't.

There were things Gideon knew though, that were making him mighty contemplative. If Peter's men hadn't been scared off the other night, things would have become quite complicated, quite fast.

Lefty, the one with the knife, he was the one to figure on. It was always like that, one to lead and the rest to follow— poor mud-dumb sheep. The other fellow, what could Gideon say? He'd been a bit pudgy with stubby fingers that had never held a plow or swung an axe. Not exactly a convicting description.

It wouldn't be long before one of them showed up to check on Gideon's progress. How unhappy would they be when he failed to present them with a deed? One armed and needing a leg up. Peter had a point. Gideon would have to be quick to keep ahead. Of course, there were ways to even the odds.

"Hey, Aspen?"

"Yes?"

"I been a-thinkin'."

"You don't say."

"I do. An' I reckon ya oughtta give back my gun."

"No."

Well, that was brief, clear and no kind of surprise.

Aspen had been dead set against Gideon having any weapons since day one. Gideon could see the point, arming a prisoner wouldn't be his first move either, but that did not alleviate the inconvenience. Still, having something to hand would make him feel a sight better. Not that running around with a revolver strapped to his hip would lend much to his innocent persona, but knowing a gun was tucked somewhere close by would sure be a comfort.

"C'mon," Gideon cajoled, "a man don't rightly feel altogether dressed if'n he ain't got him some kind-a iron."

"I'll get you a horseshoe."

Possibilities crowded in as to what Aspen could do with that horseshoe. Gideon flexed against the bandages on his arm and tried again.

"S'pose some jasper comes 'long an' I ain't kitted?"

"No," Aspen repeated evenly.

"S'pose it's my hide they're a-fixin' to nail up?"

"No."

"But s'pose—"

"In this family we look out for each other. That's what brothers do."

Gideon stopped dead and poked a finger at his guard. "Ain't you, nor none-a your brothers, no brother-a mine. Weren't my choice to be throwed in with ya an', if'n it were, an' I were, then lookin' out for you lot'd be my lot an' I'd do that a far sight better if'n I were armed."

"Do you know, Gov, there are people in this world who get up and spend the entire day— the whole day from dawn to dark— without one incident. No calamity. No adventures. And then, amazingly, they go to bed and when they get up they do it all over again. You might consider getting into the habit."

"I see'd that. I have. Cogitated on it some too, only couldn't never see how nobody managed it, so I got me 'nother habit. A Colt."

"Look how much trouble you got into when you didn't have a gun," Aspen countered.

"My point 'zactly!" Gideon rallied. "If'n I hadn't-a liberated me 'nother man's shootin' iron, I'd be a-standin' here dead right now."

Aspen cocked his head at the oxymoron, a response dancing on the tip of his tongue, begging to be said.

"Forget it," he told himself as much as Gideon.

"But what if'n—"

"But what if'n," Aspen mimicked, "you try expanding your somewhat limited supply of socially appropriate vocabulary."

Gideon stood alone on the conversational path.

"Yes, sir," Aspen enunciated carefully, and started walking again. "They're short words, quit arguing and give them a try."

"You ain't got you no right," Gideon said, standing his ground.

"Have. Have no right," Aspen corrected. "And from such utterance I surmise the finer, and I must say even the banal, significance of 'guardian' continues to elude you."

"Crazy folks got guardians."

"So do convicted criminals, at least the ones who aren't locked up until the jail rots around them."

Gideon chewed on the thick serving of words he'd been handed, trying to get them down with little success. The most he could placer was that Aspen felt disinclined to listen to reason. Well, if it was an argument he wanted—-

"C'mon," Aspen coaxed, before Gideon could draw breath. "Spending three years stuck with me can't be the worst thing that ever happened to you."

Gideon's expression showed evidence of considerable consideration, and then a mischievous spark flickered to the surface.

"W-e-e-l-l, there were oncet. . ." he began cautiously. "No, no that weren't worse. Mebbe. . . no, not that neither."

"Take your time," Aspen said, putting a hand on Gideon's shoulder. "If it hasn't happened yet, it will."

Gideon had been tackled, flattened, chased, caught, dusted off and flattened again. Fair enough and no harm. Now Aspen's hand was on his actual shoulder and no bruises were imminent on either side of the battlefield. Gideon felt like . . . like . . . he tugged a nervous sort of twitch at the bandages around his shoulder and had to bite back a sharp spasm of pain.

"Don't," Aspen cautioned.

"I ain't."

"You are."

He was. Gideon wasn't going to admit it, but he was. Being delicate with his carcass was nothing he'd ever bothered with. He was finding it tedious in the extreme.

Aspen was finding he wished Pa were there. Or Fort. He was great at keeping Emberlee in line. Not that Lee took much work, but Ember– he could be a handful. Aspen would have thought, after being a second father to three younger brothers, what was one more? Right?

B OYS, that's enough. Sit down and eat your breakfast in a civilized fashion."

The mildly issued order revealed a certain lenience, and perhaps a measure of expectation, on the part of Amos Rivers for the carrying-ons of his progeny.

Cricket, the cook of the Rolling Rivers ranch, was somewhat less tolerant when it came to the bounds of his particular domain. He hated to have his hard work sit neglected and growing cold because someone, anyone, was late. And Emberlee was late.

Father, cook, and elder brother were seated and waiting by the time the two young men came thundering through the backdoor, shoved their hats on hooks and each other out of the way. With a final heave at Ember, Lee turned to the table and became aware of the small pantheon pointedly staring at him. Contritely, he slid to his customary seat and offered Cricket an apologetic glance. To Ember, his younger brother of two minutes and thirty-one seconds, he gave a look of pure smugness, which was readily returned several degrees cooler.

Fort, the second eldest, caught Ember's attention and gave a meaningful nod towards Cricket. The brown skinned man of average build, short stature and indeterminate racial origin had been with them for so long he was as much an uncle as if they'd been blood kin. He sat at the foot of the table, an honored place one of their mothers would have occupied had either still been alive. It never occurred to them Cricket should sit anywhere else and, had someone suggested it, the boys would have been baffled as to the reason. Even were Cricket a servant Fort would have given the proverbial elbow to his brother; polite was polite and a man should conduct himself accordingly.

Ember gave his apologies which, though somewhat mumbled, were at least sincere and he paused for not so much as a breath before putting his case to his father.

"Pa, Lee—"

"Ember, I said enough. Whatever heinous offense your brother may have committed I suspect it was no worse than whatever you have done. Let it drop and let it stop. Lee, elbows off the table. Fort, put down that spoon. Ember, grace," Amos directed, rapid-fire.

He folded his long, work roughened hands and waited for his sons to assume similarly humble poses. Only then did Amos bow his head. From across the table, Cricket winked. It took a wagon load of order to keep this household operating smoothly. Thanks barely finished, the boys started the laden dishes on their circuit around the table.

Amos hoped his eldest was managing in town. He reminded himself Aspen would have everything well in hand. That's what Aspen did. He was always planning, always sorting out three possible solutions to one hiccup before most folks had even noticed the hic. And Gideon Fletcher was a hiccup in anybody's carefully laid plans.

All the same, it didn't seem right coming home without all of his boys. The two empty seats at the table felt like gaping holes. He wanted to stay in town, but had yielded to reason. Aspen's of course. The days might still be warm, but winter would soon be upon them and it did not always have the courtesy to present a calling card in advance. A wise man put his affairs in good and proper order whilst he had the opportunity.

He should take the big sorrel. Not that there was any need. There were plenty of people in Caswell Crossing who would charge the gates of Hades itself were there need.

"Pass the preserves, please," he said.

Amos spread the sticky sweetness onto a biscuit and bit generously. His sons were talking and Cricket was laughing and Amos really wasn't hearing a word.

He wondered what mischief Ember had perpetrated this early in the day. Whatever it was, Lee never gave more than his twin had coming. They were brothers. They squabbled. The definitions were interchangeable.

Amos took some satisfaction in knowing, no matter how they bickered and wore at each other's nerves, any man pushing one of his boys would find himself in the unenviable position of confronting all of his boys.

He supposed the boys would want to go to town too.

"Ember," Cricket admonished quietly, and that was all it took for the boy to pass the potatoes he had been keeping from Fort.

Now there was the big brother no one would expect. The twins were dark haired, slightly angular of feature, and still on the trailing side of average build. Neither was anything next to Fort. He was three years their senior, marginally shy of six feet and roughly the weight of a grizzly. With hair as deep red as chili powder, and a face at once powerful and affable, he could not have appeared more different than his siblings.

Ember often voiced the opinion-leaning-towards-aspersion that Fort had been adopted and his old family refused to take him back for fear of the damage he would do to their larder.

It would be a pleasure to spend the miles between the ranch and Caswell Crossing in his sons' company.

Amos sighed good-naturedly. Try as he might to keep his promise to mind his own and let Aspen mind Gideon, he'd might as well relent. He really did want to check on is absent family members. It was unnatural not to have them at his side. The dawn had bird song, the sky had stars and Amos Rivers had his sons.

Lee took the serving bowl from Ember, presumably to pass it on, and stopped it at his own plate instead.

"You want to live, you'll not consider that," Fort suggested, his fingers twitching a 'hand it over'.

Lee daringly spooned up squares of tasty fried spuds. "I could take you."

"Not without provisions, a stepstool and a nap halfway through."

"You better look again. I'm getting pretty broad in the shoulder, big brother."

"That you are, and thicker in the head."

Fort committed a boardinghouse reach and commandeered the bowl.

"You wait," Lee cautioned, around a mouthful of ill-gotten potatoes and a poorly concealed smirk. "One of these days . . ."

"One of these days is not today, baby brother," and Fort almost managed to hide his own grin, not that there was any point.

In one gulp, he downed the last of his coffee. Fort missed his father's disapproving frown, but did notice the older man's empty cup. Taking the coffeepot from the stove, he started with Pa and ended with Lee.

"Hey, you're supposed to look after me," Lee complained, when Fort dribbled a teensy drop into his cup.

"Nope. That's Aspen's job."

"Well, he ain't here and I'm a growing boy, so fill it up, big brother."

Fort decided to oblige and Lee sipped the strong, scalding liquid whilst he considered on Ember. So much silence from his voluble counterpart was not a good sign. Nine times out of ten, it meant Ember was up to something.

"The gray's about ready, Pa," Lee volunteered, in a rare preemptive strike.

"The one with the scar?" Amos's brow creased as he mentally reviewed the horses they were currently working.

"Huh-uh," Lee mumbled, and paused to swallow. "The sister."

"She's a touch small."

Lee shrugged one shoulder and nodded, his sense of equality to any man when it came to horses modestly unshakable.

"She's willing, and a quick study." With a sidelong glance at Fort, Lee added, "Better than her brother."

Fort ate his potatoes and kept his peace, but his smirk

dared Lee to prove it.

"Think she'll take to cattle?" Amos asked. They could always use more horses suited to working the burgeoning bovine population of their ranch.

"Yes, sir, if I take my time." Lee let the hint hang there, carefully judged his moment and went on, "Thought I'd work with her today. Maybe take her out, let Misery show her a thing or two."

Misery was one of their best cattle horses. It was a ridiculous name for a horse, but the man who'd named her was, to put it kindly, a poor match for her. Since he got nothing but misery so he had called her and, since according to going superstition you did not change a horse's name, so the Rivers still called her.

"But, Pa," Ember jumped in, objection at the ready.

"Good idea," said Amos, neatly overriding him.

He peered over his steepled hands and fancied he could actually see Ember working out a way to readjust the tilted scales with Lee. To Ember's preference, the only way the balance should stand was with him slightly higher, something he currently was not. Never mind whatever Lee had done was in response and retribution to his own misdeeds. No, that hardly weighed into the matter. For one slow breath Amos considered playing with the boy, savored the taste, and opted for mercy.

"I will be happy to see to it whilst you three are delivering the hay."

Ember fairly beamed. Lee wanted to kick him a right smart one under the table, but that would not erase his brother's smugness nor incline Pa to change his mind.

"She's used to me, Pa. I've been working with her and she's really coming along." Lee read his father's expression. It suggested a similarity to stone: one could go on talking for ages and the stone would not mind one way or the other, it would simply go on being stone. He pushed a lost bit of egg into a forlorn puddle of gravy. "You're going to tell me I'm not the only one who can work a horse. You've been doing it for more years than I've been alive, and wasn't it you who started me, and be sure to give your regards to Mrs. Ward."

Lee really didn't mind taking the hay out to Mrs. Ward's place. He liked her. He simply liked the idea of Ember going without him, and thereby doing twice as much work, even more. Oh well, it wasn't worth contradicting Pa. He would simply have to find some other way to make Ember's day difficult.

"And remember the apples," Amos said, as if contributing to a grocery list. He knew what prompted Lee's words, and is wasn't disobedience.

"I'll remember them, Pa," Ember promised quickly.

"He mean you remember bring apples home," Cricket clarified.

As a child, Ember had gone head first into a barrel of green apples and made himself so sick that for months afterward he had shuddered at the mention of apples, or sauce, or even fritters.

"I'll keep an eye on him, Pa," Fort half promised, half threatened.

"You weren't much use the first time, son."

"I've had practice, since then," Fort said, with a confidence intended to add to Ember's dose of ribbing.

"He wouldn't try nothing if Aspen were here."

"Anything, Lee," Amos corrected automatically, but to no avail.

Ember and Fort were eagerly setting Lee straight, one that he needed minding and the other that he couldn't assert himself sufficiently to be minded. Like any good sibling, Lee had known exactly where to push.

Cricket and Amos peered at each other from opposite ends of the ruckus and the thought between them practically took voice of its own: They're your fault, right?

"Fort," Amos spoke softly to the son nearest him, whilst his lead-heavy attention locked onto Ember. His children ground to a stuttering halt. "Eat."

Somewhat ruefully, Amos realized he would always be a busy man. The cogs in Ember's head were already whirring away, plotting what would likely be Lee's next adventure. Heaven help the boy if he was planning to give Fort any trouble.

D EPUTY Wilson? I believe this is yours."

Wilson drew up his palomino. He knew precisely what Reed wanted. It wasn't hard to work out: one disgruntled town resident in possession of one Gideon Fletcher. Not exactly a call in the Pinkerton's situation. What he could never figure was why Reed could not approach an issue from the positive side. His face reminded Wilson of pickles. Very sour pickles. In a very large jar.

"Beg pardon, Mr. Reed?"

"This town voted for law and order, if I recall correctly," Reed replied vitriolicly. "We also voted for the installment of officers to uphold that law. If you cannot manage such a simple task, I shall be forced to take the matter up with the town council."

Wilson took a gnat's breath of a heartbeat to reflect upon this. He'd heard it before. He was not surprised to be hearing it again. Simple task was it? A day in my shoes dealing with you, thought Wilson, and you'd go back to selling grain, my friend. He leant on his saddle horn, the picture of indolence.

"Which law is it I am supposed to be upholding, at the

moment?"

"Now look—" Gideon elbowed in.

Wilson raised a hand. "In a minute."

"I'll tell ya now—"

"Will you relax? I'm talking to Mr. Reed."

Gideon hushed. Not because of his amazing penchant for adhering to the constituted will of the law, but because the law, at the moment, had a suspiciously cheeky resonance about him, no matter how earnestly he appeared to be awaiting Reed's reply.

"I expect you to keep this convict away from my property henceforth," Reed bristled. "I am well acquainted with his. . . habits."

"You have the right to ask anyone to leave your establishment," Wilson agreed.

There was a certain dodging flicker on Reed's part.

"He was **in** your store, yes? No? Then what, exactly, is your issue?" Though Wilson had a number of his own suggestions, not a twitch betrayed him. He pressed on in the same unyielding tones of official helpfulness. "If you wish to enact a law preventing the public from freely using a public street, you will have to take that up with the town council. I imagine they will schedule a meeting to decide if they should arrange a meeting to discuss the issue at full length and considerable breath. Then, I reckon, they'll set up another meeting to decide if we should hold a vote. Then there'll be a meeting for the actual vote and another for the tally. All sounds a mite complicated if you ask me, I just carry 'em out I don't make 'em, but I'm sure the council will see to it at their earliest possible convenience."

Mr. Reed's expression had puckered ever more deeply until he reached what the deputy thought of as 'fully brined'. His eyes seemed to shrink, his chin to extend, his dignity swelled. It was nearly more than Gideon could stand. For the first time in his life he realized a lawman feeling his oats could actually be entertaining– at least, when it wasn't you on the receiving end.

"I want this boy arrested," Reed demanded.

The deputy shrugged helplessly. "As matters stand, there is no law preventing anyone, regardless of character, from walking on a public street."

The furrows that were Reed's face, beyond all expectation of possibility, deepened even further. He quite suspected he was being got at. That it was by an impudent hired man was no help to his mood.

"He is a menace to society."

"Is he?"

"He is a known criminal," Reed insisted stiffly.

"Let me see if I have this straight," Wilson said, scratching his jaw bone. "You want me to arrest this boy for something he's already been convicted of?"

"I want you to arrest him as a matter of public safety," Reed shot back. "That is your job, sir."

Sir.

Scorn dripped from the monosyllable. Wilson had heard men of a rougher nature use the same tone with a more colorful and select vocabulary. A man like Reed was too good for words like that, even if he did think in terms of 'people like him' and 'people like that'.

"Oh, my job is it? You should have said." Wilson swung down and tied his horse to a hitch rail. "Come along, Gideon. Mr. Reed has important business to get back to."

Sarcasm had never been so well clothed in official sincerity. The whole thing made Wilson's patience run out faster than two-penny beer on a hot August day. His job! What did Reed know about his job? He couldn't arrest a man today on suspicion of what someone thought they might do tomorrow. The cells would be packed. Men would have nowhere to stand but on top of all the other men.

And for all that, you couldn't be sure you had the right man in custody. Maybe all you had done was clear the way for someone else to stroll in and make off with the cash, because no one was left to stop them.

Wait, that was his job. So when he did arrest the real thief, where was he supposed to put him? Was he supposed to waltz up to the sardine packed cells, pick some random lucky soul and say, 'Hey you, yeah you standing on Billy Bob's toes. We caught the men who did the crime we thought you might someday commit, so you're free to go. Seein' as there were two of them, take Billy Bob there with you. Go on, and don't do it again! No Marv, you'll have to stay. You might still commit a crime.'

His job! That wasn't Wilson's job and no self-important grain peddler was going to tell him otherwise. As for the council, they may have approved his hiring, but they couldn't tell him what to do. Not that they wouldn't try, they simply would never succeed. The deputy was not, all said and done, their hired man.

His annoyance gave him due excuse and fair cause to ignore Mrs. Driscoll and the daggers she threw their way en passant. A body should only have to deal with one helpful citizen at a time and, where Wilson could have handled her, he was in no mood to guarantee his own good behavior. Sometimes he fancied the woman had a twin she let out to canvas the streets lest she miss a single whisper of happenings.

An insistent voice at Wilson's elbow reminded him he had more immediate concerns.

"How's that?" he asked.

"I ain't broke no law," Gideon repeated.

"Really? Must be a slow day for you."

"Funny, but ya still can't 'rest me."

"Who said I was?"

Gideon stared at the hand clamped on his arm.

"Why were you at the river?" Wilson asked, ignoring the none too subtle hint.

So much for amusin' lawmen.

Ya got that right.

"Who said I were?" Gideon dodged, his choice of words deliberate.

"Why no one, son. That was what we in law enforcement call a 'deduction'."

"Ya mean like takin' stuff away?" Gideon wondered, despite himself.

They had done that in the mines. A man put in a week of rock shifting, knuckle bashing, darn hard work and, after all the company deductions, what he came away with was a lung full of dirt and a half-dime. Thank you very much and see you tomorrow.

"Something like that," Wilson agreed. "Only a bit more like adding stuff up. Take your pant legs for example. Soaked. And your shirt there? Red dirt all over it. Those shiny specks on your knees? Mica, my friend. Clingy stuff mica. If I made you turn your palm up, bet it'd be there too. Now you take all that, add it up, and it comes to only one thing: you've been 'round the riverbank."

Gideon rubbed his left hand against his britches to no avail. The little shimmering flecks dancing in the sunlight refused to be dislodged.

"Evidence always snitches," Wilson remarked. "So, what were you doing?"

"If'n ya ain't a-lockin' me up, why're we headed to the jail?"

"Did I say I wasn't?"

"Don't nobody own the street!"

"True, no matter what Reed may think. At least, for

the next year anyway. The council will take that long to sort out all the meetings. Now, you can tell me or you can tell Aspen. Up to you. 'Course, if you tell me, maybe I could have a word with him before he has a word with you."

"I gotta word for ya—"

From the seat of a wagon, a woman glared down disapprovingly, her pigtailed girl tucked close to her skirt. Both men gave a courteous 'ma'am' and touched their hat brims as they passed.

"You sure know how to make an impression," Wilson observed, with a rueful shake of his head. "So what were you doing at the river?"

The question grated on Gideon. It was none of Wilson's affair. That was the thing about lawmen, they acted like everything and everyone was somehow some business of theirs. At least that's how it was with the good ones, if you could call them such. The other sort, well, the only thing worth their business was business– and who would pay the most for services rendered.

As they came abreast of the saloon, Gideon offered a casual greeting to the odd-jobber. Rag in hand, the Chinaman cleaned the dusty windows, an activity that amounted to scrubbing the grime of yesterday into the filth of today until the rag turned brown and the rinse water turned to murky soup. He rattled off what appeared to be a friendly 'hello' in his native tongue. Deputy Wilson nodded politely, without any apparent comprehension.

Lawmen, dense as rocks.

"What were you doing at the river?" the question came again, quiet and steady as if Wilson was entirely content to go on asking forever.

It was the eternal plink-plink-plink of water dripping from a roof in the middle of the night. It was the mosquito that wouldn't go away or the pinch in a new pair of boots that made you want to rip them off and blow them full of holes. It was, bluntly, infuriating.

"Fallin' in!" Gideon snapped.

"What for?"

"I'd-a felled out if'n I'd-a knowed how. You got you any t'other questions?"

It was meant to be the final whoa-up on the wagon train. What it was, in truth, was about the dumbest thing anyone in custody could ever say. How else may I be of assistance, officer? Is there anything more you'd like to know, sir? These are fine, neighborly phrases guaranteed to put you in good standing with those of the tin star persuasion. They are unlikely to suggest, in anyway, that you would appreciate spending a long night in a cold cell, followed by an even longer morning in the company of the aforesaid officer who has spent his entire evening coming up with more questions for your unique, and pointedly captive, entertainment.

"Oh, son, you and I could palaver **all** day long. Believe me. Fortunately, as fun as that sounds, I have somewhere else to be. Now get in there."

No other option presenting, Gideon stepped inside the jailhouse and proceeded to follow dumb with dumber.

"You ain't got you no charge!"

"Making An Otherwise Pleasant Day Difficult," Wilson rattled off without missing a beat, and the heavy cell door clattered shut.

For all the talk about his questionable past, Gideon hadn't spent much time behind bars. He was certainly picking up the habit lately. It was amazing how simple it was: upset a few half-way prominent folks and there you were finding out, to your own astonishment, you'd been a career criminal your whole life.

Mebbe not up-'til-now your whole life, but it's lookin'

mighty likely for the rest-a your nat'ral born life, ain't it?

Shutup.

I'm just a-sayin'.

Do I need you just a-sayin'?

Gideon heard the keys clink as they were tossed into their drawer. Wilson called out assurances he would speak with Aspen and then the front door shut. And then there was nothing. Gideon stood in the middle of the cell whilst it crowded around him, pressing for space. He looked at the floor. Stone. He looked at the walls. Stone.

What now, boyo?

Thought you were a-shuttin' up?

Gideon's inner voice shrugged and went off for a metaphysical stroll. Gideon looked out the barred window and envied himself. If he had a spoon that might be something. At least then he could scrape his way to freedom in. . . oh. . . twenty or thirty years. Oddly enough, this had not hitherto been a requisite item in his kit. Come to think on it, he didn't even own a spoon.

A gentleman would have said 'dagnabit' at this point. Gideon said something else. Followed by some more something else. Kicking something was preferable, but this would do. And then he paced. And then he stared out the window again. And then he paced some more.

He had come back around to kicking something when the bell on the front door chimed. A moment later, Aspen Rivers draped his forearms through the bars.

"Hear you've been making friends again."

"Ya might could say that."

"I make it a practice to tell the truth," Aspen said.

Gideon said nothing. What could he say? He was not known, even to himself, as a dealer in absolute truth. And the truth was he could live with that. You could play the devil's own telling the truth. Whereas, if you told enough little lies, you might squeak by without having to tell the really big ones.

One of Gideon's favorite little lies was the existence of justice. Experience told him no such creature existed, yet he clung to the idea with the passion of a drowning man to a shattered scrap of driftwood. There had to be justice or the whole thing became one of the big lies, and then what was the point?

One of the big lies, one that so many people bought into, was that justice and law were the same thing. A lie that went hand in hand with this was that men who wore a badge could inherently recognize justice and made it a practice to nurture this elusive creature. Hogswash. The average lawmen couldn't dig up an ounce of justice with both hands. You could smack them upside the head with it, in a particularly forceful and informative fashion, and still they would be locking up the wrong man or turning a blind eye where they should have the sense to see.

"You alright?" Aspen asked.

"I can handle Wilson," Gideon replied dismissively.

Aspen looked at the stone walls, the iron bars and who was behind them.

"He weren't in'erested in bein' neighborly."

"I'm sure you'll have another opportunity," Aspen suggested mildly.

"Bring 'im a plug, will I?"

"Sugar sticks."

"For real play?"

"Yep. So, what was your plan, up to here?"

The plan, up to here, hadn't included being here. Everything up to here had gone well. Right up to the point where here had become here, and then it hadn't.

"Naturally you had a plan," Aspen coaxed.

Tell 'im.

No.

He might could help.

Shutup.

"I. . ." Gideon said.

"Yes?"

"I. . . don't s'pose there's a key in my future?"

Gideon's inner self groaned. He told himself to keep out of it and tried to concentrate on the man giving him such pointedly undivided attention.

"Is there a straight answer in mine?" asked Aspen.

Ain't likely.

"Could be," Gideon allowed.

"Soon?"

Don't reckon.

"Shutup!"

The word rang in the empty nothingness of the cell. The rattling tumble of a ladder freefalling to the black depths of a mineshaft held more optimism than the sound of that word dying away.

"I beg your pardon?"

It wasn't a ladder. It was a key. A bulky key with big teeth that Gideon would never, ever see again.

"No! I were. . . I mean there ain't. . ."

"Would you like to try again?" Aspen offered helpfully.

"Yes," Gideon admitted, with no confusion whatsoever.

He had to get out of there or what good would he be to Peter? Unfortunately, that meant scrounging up a trace of compliance along with a measure of plausible explanation. Gideon was feeling a might shy on both. He rubbed the side of his jaw. He studied the random crisscrossing lines of mortar in the floor. His hand reached down to rest on the walnut grip of his revolver and, finding it not there, tapped once or twice against his leg instead.

Aspen grasped the bars in both hands and rocked idly

back and forth, not unlike a man doing push-ups. Or, perhaps, like one trying to subtly point out the immutable nature of iron.

"Whenever you're ready," he prompted.

"What were the question?"

The rocking stopped. Aspen's eyebrows rose.

"Straight up," Gideon said. "I ain't a-plannin' nothin'.'"

"Now there's something I can believe. Let's try an easier one, and we'll see if you can answer me better than you did Deputy Wilson. What were you doing at the river?"

"Weren't—"

"Ehh, that's going to be a lie."

"Well—"

"That one too. And if you are considering 'falling in' for your next answer, I strongly suggest you think again."

Gideon did think again. He thought about his picks and wished he had used them. A jailbreak would have been less than discrete but, on the up side, he would not be here now— and here and now was a good place not to be.

He thought about the river. Sometimes, without any real effort, everything sort of comes together. A moment of crystalline perfection. The look on Lefty's face, for example. For years to come Gideon would be able to take it out, blow off the dust and cherish that moment. All the same, nothing there he wanted to share with Aspen. Regrettably, one look made it plain: with the next evasion Aspen would leave him in jail. Then where would he be?

In jail.

Got that, thanks.

"Thing is," Gideon began, testing each word as he spoke them, "thing is I ain't so used to no town."

He knows that.

I know he knows!

"Well, I fig'red to stretch my legs a mite an' sort-a

ended up at the river."

With Lefty right behind ya.

"There were a tree, an' it were the only way 'cross."

Springy too. An' almighty slip'ry after you done pretended to stumble an' got it wet.

"I done slipped some," Gideon repeated aloud, "but it weren't nothin'."

Wonder if'n Lefty thought it were nothin'?

Gideon couldn't help but take a moment to reflect. It had been perfect. Lefty teetering precariously, arms flailing, until the critical second at which flailing became falling. The current had devoured the splash and yanked the thug downstream with commendable alacrity. For charity's sake Gideon had flung a few words of helpful advice at the swiftly disappearing swimmer.

"An' then," he hurried on, lest Aspen think falling in were the end of his explanation, "I were up by Reed's, an' ya know, that fellah plain don't take to me none. Ain't nothin' to me, only he wanted to exchange 'im some words. Then Wilson comed along an' Reed done exchanged 'im some more words. Mostly Wilson told 'im to go soak his shirt. Said as Reed din't got 'im no charge. Wilson din't have 'im no charge neither, but that don't never matter none nohow 'cause here I am, ain't I?"

Aspen cringed and let out a mock whistle. "He should have charged you with Willful Slaughter Of The English Language."

Gideon's native, ill-timed impatience got the better of him. "Aw, c'mon, get the key will ya!"

"Did you provoke Mr. Reed?" Aspen queried, unperturbed and unmoving.

"Huh?"

"Did you start it?" Aspen tried again, one step lower on the morphological ladder of sophistication.

"Nah, I telled ya, he just don't cotton to me."

"And these words you exchanged? Please and excuse me, were they?"

"I don't start ever'thing, ya know."

Aspen filled the following silence with more silence. It was eloquent.

"Well, I don't," Gideon insisted, without entirely feeling the need. Thus far no explosion, not even a tongue lashing. It prompted him to salt his story with a little broader truth. "Weren't neither of us leanin' towards 'I do beg your pardon, my good man', if'n ya get my drift."

Aspen stood there, arms folded. He hadn't been told the whole truth, yet he had been offered a truth of a sort. How many times did Gideon need to make the same mistake? Still, if this wasn't entirely on the barrelhead, it was a step in the right general direction.

In an overall, broad sort of way.

More or less.

Basically.

Aspen found himself wondering what he would do if Ember in front of him. Only Ember was merely young and mercurial, whereas Gideon had been knocked around so much he'd aged more than some men's grandfathers. He was also very, very angry. It burned in his every fiber with an irrepressible intensity. Some men turned inward and their anger would implode only on themselves. Gideon wouldn't. When his someday came, and he finally reached his limit, he would explode with the devastating force of a powder magazine.

"I ought to leave you here for your own good.'"

Aspen sounded more like he was thinking aloud than actually making a decision and Gideon did not say 'you wouldn't dare' because Aspen very much would dare. He stood there waiting, not realizing every line of his body shouted the words he had left unspoken. To his great relief, Aspen quit eyeballing him and went for the key.

The lock turned and Gideon fairly bolted out. He really should have anticipated the hand on his collar.

"One thing. Deputy Wilson? Sugar sticks. Right?"

Friends? With the law? There was no call for that kind of talk. Aspen knew his feelings on the subject. He knew Gideon's reasons too. Well, mostly. He certainly knew better than to ask a thing like that.

"Are we clear?" Aspen pressed.

"No! We ain't no kind-a clear– Alright! Alright!" Gideon amended, as Aspen hoisted him back towards the cell. "I get your drift!"

"Promise?"

"I got a choice?"

"Not really."

"Fine. Candy sticks. Love 'em. Wouldn't want it no other way. Downright neighborly, that's me."

The kind of neighbor who kept a shotgun handy, that Gideon could right about handle. The kind who kept a light on and tended the cow, you could stuff that.

Out on the street they walked side by side, the mountain and the scarecrow, and automatically fell into the same ambling stride.

"You could have just said 'yes sir', you know," Aspen suggested, and waited for the response he knew must come.

"Buff'lo spit."

It was good to be right, very good indeed. And if that was all there was to whatever had happened at the river, Aspen would eat his own hat.

CHAPTER 5
Athens & A Goat
Not It
Corting
Hard Work & Lost Keys
Emerging Species
Knight To Rook Three
A Random Act

G IDEON did not know where he was going. This wasn't the first time, nor was it likely to be the last. What really put the prickly cactus in it though, was this particular moment of ignorance was not his choice. Once again he had been chivied into following Aspen to who knew where for who knew why. The man had an annoying habit of doing that.

An ancient wisp of a man sitting on a bench cackled as they passed by. Obviously the old-timer felt his advanced years a fair excuse to stare at whomever he liked, because he was still doing it and possessed an air that suggested anyone who didn't like it could be clipped alongside the ear.

Gideon wondered what could be so amusing and then realized it was probably him. He must look ridiculous skulking along like some delinquent kid brother. Well, that's one thing he wasn't. Man, did he need to get out of this crazy set-up.

Reckon that'll take a double-jack.

Gideon was not opposed to making his own opportunities, forcefully if necessary. Those who sat, idly waiting for their 'someday', made him want to grab them by the shirtfront and give them a good shake. Just sitting there, taking the kicks of the world and filling the resulting gloom with complaints about the bruises– it was insufferable. Stand up for pity's sake!

Of course, that was a mite hard to do with a judge appointed shadow following your every step and breath. They reached a staircase leading to a second floor landing and Gideon promptly about-faced.

"Where do you think you're going?" Aspen asked, holding fast.

"Back to jail."

No matter how mind numbing or anxiety inducing a cell was, at its very worst, its horrors were nothing compared to the confinement of Aspen's office. A man could go stark raving mad in a cell, but an office held him prisoner whilst his entire life slipped meaninglessly away like a useless trickle of sand into an endless eternity of abysmal nothingness.

Like a badly wired marionette, Gideon was manhandled back to the stairs.

"Why here?" he said, halting on the fourth step and blocking all progress. "Whyn't Doc's?"

Aspen tried to give the sort of look his father did, the one that said continents could crumble to dust, but I have made a decision so you'd might as well concede and the sooner the better– at least for you.

A broad ray of light spread across Gideon's features, like a stranger returning to a half-remembered house.

"She done told you, din't she?" he said, fairly crowing. "You done been told by your auntie."

"Up!" Aspen said, giving his ward a nudge, but Gideon remained above him, grinning like a fool, clearly loving the view from the other side of the table.

"We had. . . a talk," Aspen admitted, with the reluctance of a man who would have preferred to avoid this particular here and now.

"An' this talk, please an' thank you were it?"

"I was raised to understand courtesy," said Aspen,

clearly suggesting Gideon might want to consider the idea.

"Aspen done been telled by his auntie," Gideon sing-songed instead, "Aspen done been telled—"

With precise movements Aspen turned Gideon about and carefully twisted his good arm behind his back. Up to the office they went, Gideon sing-songing all the way.

"Gov," Aspen said, a short while later. "Must you?"

Gideon paused, the brick of construction held inches above the floor plan of civilization. The table by the window was covered from edge to edge with books, edge on, spine up, cover down books. Two of Aspen's shelves were gaping black holes where his precious collection should have been.

"Ain't much else to do," Gideon replied.

Aspen gestured to the papers and files spread across his desk. "You could help me, well, if you could read."

"You can come away out-a that, so ya can."

"It's a better use for my books than Fort Fletcher."

"Athens."

Aspen blinked. "Excuse me?"

"Birthplace-a democracy. Plato. Aristotle."

Gov couldn't put two words together without causing a linguistic train wreck and here he was talking about classical philosophers? Oh, he was bright, no doubt. Aspen would be the first to say so. The problem was Gideon had a way of leaking intelligence in such a random way it caught a body off guard. It was like watching a horse get up and dance, then calmly go back to chewing grass as if musically coordinated equines happened every day.

"How erudite," Aspen remarked.

Gideon set a palace wall alongside a stretching rose garden. "Nah, it's Greek. Were hundreds-a years ago. Don't reckon as none-a 'em's more'n dust now."

"All Greeks?" Aspen probed, a man intrigued.

"Folks got a way-a fallin' 'part after they done been

dead an' buried that long," Gideon pointed out.

"You don't think there might be any around today?"

"Only if'n they got 'em some mighty peculiar ways."

The horse went back to picking its way through a fine selection of grasses. Aspen cleared his throat.

"Be that as it may—" A light tap on the door interrupted him and a politely hesitant Peter poked his head in. "Come in, Peter. What can I do for you?"

Peter remained on the threshold and gestured with a thumb over his shoulder. "Mr. Smyth sent me. If you have the time, he says he'd sure appreciate your help."

"Zeek?"

Peter nodded. "I think Mr. Smyth is herding cats, if you know what I mean."

Aspen glanced at Gideon. Didn't he just.

"I'll stay here, Aspen," Peter offered helpfully.

Aspen released a slow breath, one foot on either side of the decision.

"Aw, g'wan. I ain't gonna blow nothin' up."

"Only for want of dynamite, Gov, which I've no doubt you could find." Aspen pushed the cork into his ink bottle. "Alright, Peter, don't let Gov out of your sight and don't listen to anything he says."

"Yes, sir."

"You," Aspen pointed a finger at Gideon, "you can knock off the bright and shiny innocent look; it makes as much sense as ribbons on a bob-tailed cat. Peter is in charge. You listen to every word he says. I mean it. Especially the small ones, you could learn something."

"You're right funny," said Gideon.

Aspen picked up his hat and paused at the door. "He stays put. Are we clear?"

"Yes, sir," Peter agreed.

"And Gov—"

"I know, I promise or you will. Now git, will ya?"

"Behave."

"Shove off."

The moment Aspen had gone, Peter got straight to the point. "Well? What happened?"

"Weren't nothin'. One-a them friends-a yourn done fig'red as I should have the deed by now. He were minded to discuss it, so I tooked 'im down to the river." Gideon's face glimmered with mischief, "He don't swim so good."

"What does that have to do with you being in jail?" asked Peter, at a loss for the connection.

Gideon eyeballed Aspen's shelves with their shoulder to shoulder books, spines aligned like soldiers at attention. He plucked several unsuspecting volunteers from the close order ranks, leaving a rather forlorn gap.

"Well?" said Peter.

"That were Reed," Gideon replied.

"The harness man? What does he have to do with it?"

"Nothin'."

"Talk!" Peter demanded, snatching a half positioned book out of Gideon's hand. "In sentences. You know, nouny things and verby things all hitched up together."

Gideon picked up another book and added it to an ancient market. "Ya know goats? Only thing they're good for is blamin' stuff on. That's me. Reed fig'res whatever's ailin' his day's my fault. Had us a run in, but it ain't nothin' to do with nothin'. What is to do with nothin's them men-a yourn an' what we're a-gonna do 'bout 'em."

Peter picked up a couple leather bound editions of somebody or other's great moments in history and weighed them along with whatever was on his mind.

"I've been thinking," he said, putting the past back on a shelf, "if they want Pa's place so badly, why don't they just take it? There's no one out there to stop them."

"You suggestin' we run 'em off?" Gideon asked, coming around the table to reclaim a burgundy brick-to-be.

"No. I'm suggesting maybe they're after something else. I know they said deed—"

"That's what Lefty done told me," Gideon agreed.

"Lefty?"

"Got 'im that knife."

"Pultrie," Peter corrected, dismantling ancient architecture. "That's what the egg called him."

"What egg?" said Gideon, returning 'Business Law: An Essential Understanding' to its structural duties.

"You know, the other one," Peter insisted.

"Who?"

"The egg!" said Peter, plucking up another book from the table.

"Now look—" Gideon began impatiently.

"There's two of them right? Pultrie and his fat little partner." Peter dodged as Gideon grabbed for the book in his hands. "Set him on a wall and you'd have Humpty Dumpty, only I don't suppose you'd know who that is."

"'Course I do. What I ain't seen were nobody shaped like no egg," Gideon said indignantly, trying to dart around Peter's guard.

Peter placed one hand on his friend's chest and stretched the other well out of range. "He's an egg. You see him, you'll know."

"Fine!"

"Fine!"

They glared at each other, then glared a bit longer.

"That's the Parthenon ya know,' Gideon said, trying for the captive novel.

"Eh-eh! Aspen said I'm in charge."

"An' mules bray. So what?"

Peter considered on this. He wasn't precisely sure what

role Aspen Rivers held— guardian, big brother, jailer— but he was dead sure Gideon was wrong.

"'So what' is we're putting all of these books back or I'll tell Aspen you're the one being a mule and he'll kick you from here to next month. That's so what."

"What's it to you?" Gideon demanded.

"I need you in one piece."

Ain't his fault, ya know.

Gideon had to agree with himself. He was picking a fight with Peter for no good reason except his own morning had gone less than well– which was no good reason.

"Don't get your unmentionables in an uproar," he relented, perching himself on a corner of the table and accidently crashing over a garrison. "What we oughtta fig'r is what we're a-gonna do 'bout your egg men."

Peter held out a hand.

"Do-gooder," Gideon accused, handing over the wreckage of a south wall.

"Way I see it," Peter said, ignoring the remark, "what we took from the courthouse wasn't a deed."

Gideon recalled the four cabinets with their numerous files that had taken far too long to sort through.

"Then why the bejazzers did I bust into that office?"

"We did," Peter amended sharply.

"Yeah, an' then I did."

"You went back?" Peter paused between shelf and table to stare at Gideon. "What on earth for?"

"Think 'bout it. Your egg men ain't a-gonna look for nothin' where they already done been. Right back in the courthouse were the safest place to hide your deed."

"Then why'd we take it out?"

"'Cause they din't a-been there yet then."

Peter sifted through the atrocious grammar, processed the overall idea, and finally came up with, "But we didn't actually find a deed."

"What good's your readin' then?" Gideon said, handing over Shakespeare's 'Much Ado About Nothing'.

"I read better than you."

"I mean any readin'. I could-a grabbed us the wrong dang thing all by my onesy."

"I didn't find the wrong thing, that's what I'm trying to tell you."

"So we're a-playin' find-the-button, only ain't nobody got the button in the first place?" Gideon said, hands spread in incomprehension. "What were all them papers then?"

"Lots of things," Peter shrugged, squaring up the contents of the bookshelf. "I think what we took was more like an agreement. Give me that manual on surveying."

Gideon surveyed the collection on the table, but it would have helped if he could have read the manual. He picked up a candidate at random and tossed it to Peter.

"This is 'Memorable Poems and Poets'. Oh dear, volume one," Peter grimaced and put the book away. "The thing about a deed is that it's a binding contract with an established governmental authority– which we don't exactly have out here."

"A what?" Gideon said, not at all sure he'd heard English.

"Learn to read. I said we're so far out in the back of beyond lost, the law doesn't give a hoot about us."

"Ya got that right," Gideon agreed emphatically.

Caswell Crossing boasted the only lawman for several days ride in any direction, the only jail for even farther. When you're that far out, by and large, a man only has as much law as he can hold for himself.

Gideon scooped up an armload of Greek rubble and returned it to the rank and file of its stayed existence. Peter followed along behind, adjusting his work.

"What're ya doin'?" Gideon asked.

"They're upside down."

"They're square!"

"At least you know your shapes. But," Peter tapped an embossed capital, "the big letter goes on top."

"That right?"

Gideon flipped several books at random upside-down. Aspen was such a straight-buttoned stiff it would drive him clean over the edge.

"Look," Peter said, trying to pry Gideon away so he could fix the literary chaos. "If all my father had was a nodding— Will you move?—a nodding agreement with the town council, what's Pultrie after? It doesn't make sense."

"You found nothin' in Caswell Crossin' as does?" Gideon made use of an elbow and managed to upended 'Etiquette for Gentlemen'. "Mebbe your friends're morons. **They** think they're a-lookin' for a deed. Us tellin' 'em diff'rent's not gonna help none."

"But—"

"Look, seein' as they're still a-doggin' us, I'd say there's still something on their mind."

Another round of elbows were exchanged, shoulders applied and heels dug in for leverage.

"What's your point?" Peter asked with a grunt.

"Folks like them want easy pickins," Gideon replied with a grunt of his own. "More trouble we make, less they like it. Whatever they're after, it won't be worth it."

"This isn't a game," Peter said, shelves forgotten.

That depended on one's perspective, but the upshot was simple: they have it and you hunt, or you have it and they hunt. Either way, all a man had to do was use his wits better than the other fellow. It was like that blasted chess Aspen liked so much, only a whole lot simpler because real life, when you got right down to it, had fewer rules.

"Sure it is," Gideon shrugged.

"These men are dangerous."

Gideon straddled a chair and leaned against the backrest. "You quittin'?"

Peter flinched. "Course not, I just. . ."

You know he ain't no coward.

"Forget it," Gideon offered by way of apology. "Men say a lot-a things. Bigger men'n them've said the same thing. I'm still here."

"They threatened to kill you."

"When the likes-a them go a-shootin' off 'bout somethin' like that, it is my civic duty to climb their frame."

"Doesn't anything scare you?" Peter half asked, half accused.

Gideon hadn't been scared for himself in a long, long time. Being scared meant you had something to lose. All he had left to his name were saddlebags scarce of contents, an outdated revolver and a horse– all of which had been confiscated by the Rivers. Gideon had nearly lost his life and, for all practical purposes, had lost his freedom. There was nothing of himself left to be afraid for.

"'Cassional," he admitted, though more retrospectively than currently.

"And?"

Gideon swept a book from the table and flung it at Peter's middle. "I hit harder."

"Hey, watch it."

"Why? You gonna tell Aspen?"

"Yeah," Peter grinned. "I might."

"Well, if'n you're a-snitchin'," Gideon suggested companionably, "might 's well think up an' explanation too."

"For what?"

"What's this?" Gideon asked, holding up a piece of paper from Aspen's desk.

"An inventory list. But—"

"This?"

"Some kind of contract," Peter answered, moving closer so he could see. "What are you doing?"

Gideon folded the single sheet into crisp thirds. "Aspen's always a-sayin' as how I should be a-plannin'. Which, seein' as how I ain't the one sent us to annex the wrong thing entirely, I reckon I'm a-doin' a far sight better'n you. Now all you gotta do is explain why I'm gone."

"No, I don't," Peter refused.

"Well, I s'pose you ain't gotta stick 'round," Gideon allowed.

"Oh, yes I do."

"What for?"

"'Cause you're staying here," Peter declared, with a genuine effort at decisiveness.

"No, I ain't," Gideon said, with a decisiveness that required no effort at all. He poked Peter with the folded paper. "Your Mr. Dumpty's out there an' you better bet he done watched ya come up here. I go out, let 'im see this here contract an' he'll follow me."

"Then what?" asked Peter.

"Wadda ya mean then what?"

"Then what. It's what happens when you plan. There's some stuff and some more stuff— and everything doesn't all just happen. That's what 'planning' means."

"I meant there ain't no then," Gideon insisted. "You go back to work an' I hide this here deed."

"It isn't a deed!"

"Neither were the first one! They dunno know no diff'rent."

"You think Aspen won't know the difference between you here and you gone? If you think I'm going to stand here and explain it to him, you're dumber than dirt." Peter plucked the document out of Gideon's hand. "And if you think I'm going to stroll off whilst you use yourself as bait, you are plumb off your mental rocker."

A muffled voice reached them and the cheerful hale was promptly answered by the unmistakable voice of Aspen Rivers. Gideon snatched the fake deed from Peter's fingers and abandoned the desk like a rat fleeing a sinking ship. Peter followed in close pursuit, barely in time to slide between Gideon and escape.

"He'll have your hide," Peter warned, leaning against the interior office door.

Gideon tried for the handle. "Ain't likely."

"Please?" Peter leaned harder. "He'll kill me."

Gideon hesitated. Peter took advantage of the moment, seized the paper, shoved it under his shirt and leapt for the opposite side of the room.

When Aspen entered, pure instinct made him give the two young men a sharp study. Something in the air suggested this was a very sound idea, yet nothing presented itself as due cause.

"Well," he said, suspiciously, "Gov's still here, neither of you are dead and half the town's not blown up. I'm impressed."

"What's that?" Gideon demanded, ignoring the sarcasm.

"A slate. And this," Aspen continued, holding up exhibit B, "is a book of your very own."

"What for?" Gideon asked, like a man who hoped the rattlesnake he was facing was, somehow, not actually a member of the notorious Viperidae Gang.

"McGuffy Primer," Peter read, and could not have stopped himself from smirking even had he been inclined.

Gideon nailed him with a glare.

"Maybe you'll– Aw, no!" Aspen exclaimed. "No, no, no!"

"I tried, Aspen. Honest."

Aspen stared at his poor, disarrayed shelves and absently waved Peter to silence. It wasn't right. No one should put 'Desert Plants' next to 'Modern Metallurgy' or separate a four volume series over three shelves. As for upside-down, there was simply no call for that.

"Gideon Fletcher, you take one more step towards that door and I will personally see to it you spend every last second of the next three years in this office."

One foot in the air, Gideon froze. Blast those goldarned cows. He could have cussed them a blue streak. If they hadn't let themselves be relocated, the sheriff's posse wouldn't have walked in on his party, and he wouldn't have been shanghaied into this mess. Three years– and he hadn't even stolen anything! Reluctantly, Gideon lowered the offending appendage.

"I din't hurt nothin'," he pointed out, in the slightly injured tone of one who feels not separating a three volume series over four shelves was a favor worthy of recognition.

"Lucky for you," Aspen agreed, unsympathetically. "but if you think committing literary assault is sufficient distraction to facilitate your escape, you sir, are out of your mind."

Gideon did not care for being outmaneuvered, particularly by Aspen Rivers. He especially did not care for it when he had not actually thought to maneuver and realized, quite belatedly, it would have been a good idea. He liked it even less when there was a witness who saw no reason not to laugh at him.

"I take it you've already had this conversation?" Aspen inquired of Peter.

"Something like it, yes."

"Once is enough for any man. See you at supper."

"Thank you, but I wouldn't want to put anyone out."

"Good. See you at supper."

"Yes, sir."

"See how easy that was, Gov? Two words, and he didn't even choke himself."

"Peter's very sweet. Bet he always does what he's telled an' never gets in no kind-a trouble," Gideon agreed, hoping Peter would take the double meaning.

What Gideon wanted was for Peter to fade into the background– the nice, safe background. Flashing a false deed at Humpty Dumpty put that notion flat on its ear. Flagrant harassment was a great idea for Gideon, just a lousy one for Peter.

With a discrete wink, Peter picked up his hat. Gideon had to do something, only what could he say with Aspen standing right there? Hey, Peter, don't be an idjit? Aspen had a curious streak a mile wide; handing him bait like that would make Gideon the idjit.

Blast.

There was nothing Gideon could do but watch Peter walk out, straight into danger.

R EED swept the half-dimes from the register and added their tally to that of the three cent pieces. He counted everything twice. Always.

Billy had learned never to offer help with the till. Come closing time, he stuck to sweeping the floors. It made life easier. He may have needed this job for the extra money, but he did not need the extra stress. Soon, and soon could not be soon enough, he would be speaking to Sally Calder's father. The pay might not be worth it, but Sally sure was– from her pretty blond hair right down to her charmingly mismatched feet.

"Billy, did you sell those spurs?"

"What's that, Mr. Reed?"

"The new spurs Smyth finished last week, did you sell them?"

"No, sir," Billy answered, careful not to show his exasperation. Everyday it was something, some niggling why-aren't-you-good-enough comment that robbed a man of sanity one syllable at a time. He couldn't force people to buy whatever Reed thought should be sold that day. Still, best to offer up some sort of consolation as a salve against ill-humor. "I noticed you sold the silver conches though."

Reed stopped counting. "I didn't sell them."

Billy paused, halter in hand. "I didn't sell them."

Brand new spurs and an expensive set of conches, gone. Reed did not have think very hard to figure it out. His expression grew very sour indeed.

LONG amber rays slanted between the weathered boards of the stable. The sweet smell of hay mingled with the sharp tang of cook fires. Peter filled the last of the water troughs, returned the bucket to its place by the pump and had a final look around. When you think it's done, his father used to say, take one more look. Peter felt pride at the remembered words and the orderly barn. Job done, it was time for his own supper.

He was so hungry it wouldn't have mattered if supper were pea soup. Well, provided it was at least warm. Cold was not to be thought. Of course, with Mrs. Rivers cooking, it was bound to be considerably more palatable. His brain may have agreed out of politeness, however his stomach had jumped on the wagon out of pure, unmitigated greed. Good food was good food and not to be lightly dismissed.

The tall sorrel in the first stall quit munching, strands of hay dangling haphazardly from his lips. Despite the natural confines of equine expression, he quite clearly wanted to know if there might be some grain in this for a good natured fellow.

Peter gave him a scratch along the jawbone. The horse tipped its head, leaning in appreciatively, then flipped Peter's hat to the ground and resumed munching.

"Hey, don't blame me. Oats are in the morning."

Peter reclaimed his hat and took his leave of the impudent horse. He went out, blinking in the golden sunlight, stunning after the dimness within.

"Hello, Peter."

The words may have been civil, but the tone could not possibly have been mistaken for friendly. Three young men crowded in, two more or less from behind and one in front. They were generally unkempt, taller and in possession of considerably more muscles. Their collective attitude might be delicately classified as 'displeased'.

"You aren't thinking of leaving us are you?" the front one asked, with that special edge that said, no matter what you answer, this is not going to go your way.

"Leaving?" Peter echoed, trying to sound calm. "Why would I do that?"

"Maybe you like your new friends better. Maybe you're getting funny ideas."

"Aw, come off it," Peter bluffed, trying to shoulder his way out.

The two flank men caught him by the arms.

"Thing about ideas, Peter," the brains of the outfit continued, "is they can be bad for your future."

"I told you, Cort—"

"I'm not sure you're hearing me, Peter. See, we want the kind of future that doesn't include getting caught. We'd like you to want that kind of future too."

These unprincipled thugs had nothing to do with the

kind of future Peter had imagined. How had it come to this? A thousand little things probably. There were a few events he could squarely put a finger on as life altering, but generally life takes its time, shifting by tiny increments until one day you stood there wondering what had happened. Like today.

Peter rallied as much confidence as he could and dug in. "I haven't told anyone anything, Cort."

Cort stared, long and hard, a man trying to read his opponent across a poker table. Whatever he saw, it only half convinced him.

"Maybe we should get to know your new friends," he suggested. "That skinny one could do with a lesson in manners."

Peter fought down the impulse to tell Cort to back off. It would only make him sneer in that infuriating way of his, and just might provoke him into messing with Gideon out of pure meanness. This was a test. That's what it was, Cort was testing him.

He would never believe some sop story of loyalty, but a self-interest that happened to align– for the moment– with the needs of the gang? That kind of twisted thinking Cort might understand.

"Look," Peter reasoned, "why would I talk? First word I say, I go down too. What good is that to me?"

"Aw, let it go," one of the lackeys piped up. "He ain't said nothin'. Even if he did, who'd believe him?"

"You want to take that chance?" Cort snarled.

The third committee member made a derogatory sound, like half a chuckle being strangled. His breath reeked of tobacco.

"He ain't brave enough to say nothin'."

Peter didn't like it, but he was in no position to argue. There were limits to what a man could do– and taking on three knuckle bashers at once? That was a limit. A hard one to stand there and accept, and it galled him to do it, but stand there Peter did. A thin stream of brown juice splatted near his feet.

"See? What did I tell you?" tobacco boy scoffed.

"Nothing," Cort said, watching Peter closely. "That's what you're going to say. Nothing. To nobody. Because you're right, we go down, you go down. And if that happens, I might get a notion to take a few others with me, if you get my meaning."

A dark smile crossed Cort's face. He pulled back his fist and stopped it an inch short of Peter's ribs. The smile became a sneer and in a rowdy, back slapping, gaggle of superiority the three ruffians were gone.

M ARY removed a peg from her washing line and dropped the last towel into her big wicker basket. Doing the linens and such for the hotel always seemed to take ages; towel after towel, sheet after sheet, it grew monotonous.

Not that she would ever complain, the hotel was a major customer. The boardinghouse was her other big customer, and Mary rather preferred that work. It felt more personal, more of a direct service to a specific individual rather than another great pile of identical sheets.

She carried the laundry basket up to her porch and dumped the huge wash barrel, sending suds slooshing out into the weeds. The rinse barrel followed and then both were turned upside-down on the boards.

It had been a gift from the Rivers, that porch. It would withstand the weight of her washtubs for years to come and it spanned all the way from the clotheslines to the back of the shop. No more having to walk through the mud every time a load needed to be brought in. What a shame it did little good when Mary couldn't even open the backdoor.

Where had that blasted key gone? It wasn't like her to misplace it, or anything else for that matter. Handling other people's belongings had made an otherwise natural bent for organization dang near compulsive. Mary jigged the basket onto her hip, went around front, and dwelt on the problem as she folded the towels.

The key was supposed to hang on a nail by the stove. Had it somehow gone under? Surely she would have heard it fall. All the same, best to have a peek.

Nothing but dust and. . . what was that? A bit of fumbling with a long spoon produced a stale chunk of toast. How had it ended up under there? With a frown, Mary chucked the bit of toast into the firebox.

When the work was done, the cash box tucked away and the fire smoldered low, Mary once again picked up the wicker basket. She placed a smaller basket of mending on top; buttons and patches could be seen to later that night. Then, snagging the door with a foot, she turned the lock and headed for the hotel.

H ARVEY Wilcox ladled out a glob of what, for lack of better description, must be called food– no matter how insufficient the term.

Pultrie grimaced. "Your cooking's not good enough for me to stick around any longer than necessary."

"I'm telling you," Harvey repeated for the third time, "Peter has it. That kid took you on a goose chase."

"I'm not a fool, Harvey."

On the basis all men were entitled to their opinion, Harvey Wilcox said nothing. He thunked another glob from the blackened pot onto another banged up tin plate and sat down across from Pultrie. He knew the man would rather he didn't, which was exactly why he did. Harvey would be dagnabbed if he was going to buckle to the likes of Nick Pultrie. If Pultrie didn't like it, he could move.

Dagnabbed. What kind of word was that? Harvey had been in the sticks too long. He felt a passive-aggressive tingle of satisfaction as Pultrie's face crinkled in disgust. Pultrie hated strong coffee. Accordingly, Harvey had brewed it with big, thick horseshoes in mind. The kind big, burly blacksmiths pounded onto big, thick draught horses. It was practically worthy of a spot on the great Antoine Lavoisier's 'List of Elements'. Left forgotten on the hob for a week it might even rate its own designation as an immerging species. After a month, anthropologists would have due cause to gather around with notebooks in hand to observe intricate social rituals and secret rites of passage.

Could drinking his coffee then be considered some sort of pre-genocide? Interfering with the course of natural design? They said if you tread on an ant it could change the world. If it had drank Harvey's coffee, the inconsiderate oaf who stepped on it would sure be on his ear, right along with the footprints of an irate ant.

"We'll get both of them together," Pultrie decided, around a morsel of what appeared to be pure charcoal. "They can't both lie to us at the same time."

Again Harvey said nothing. In his experience a man could lie to as many people as he liked, for as long as he liked, regardless of who stood beside him or what lies they felt like trying out themselves. It was a useful skill and one that had seen him clear on numerous occasions.

"Well?"

"No killing," said Harvey.

"You gone squeamish?" Pultrie chastised.

"I want the pay. You know what the old lady said."

It was practically their employer's only stipulation:

they were to get the papers, but they weren't to kill.

"I need the money as much as you, don't I?" Pultrie acknowledged the prohibition. "We get them together, they'll talk."

"Sure," Harvey shrugged indifferently. "They'll break."

I'M sorry, Connell. Aunt Eddie was. . . insistent."

Slouched in one of the waiting room chairs, Gideon indulged in a smirk. Aspen endeavored to ignore him, with somewhat less success.

"I told her we'd go to Mathers's for supper, but she wouldn't budge."

"I don't mind," Connell allowed graciously, since it had been him who had given Eddie the nudge. "Take Peter and enjoy yourselves."

Aspen peered at Gideon. The idea that here was a place to stay definitely found no welcome mat at Gideon's door. But, more to the point, he had made enemies. Aspen did not like leaving him unprotected. Fat lot of good he had done the last time, but he intended to do everything possible to prevent something like that from happening again— whether Gov liked it or not.

"Aspen?"

"Hmm?" Aspen answered the doctor vaguely.

"We'll be fine," Connell assured him. "Stop at Mathers's and ask him to send over a couple of plates and we won't even need to leave the clinic."

"What if someone calls?" Aspen argued.

"I haven't any immediate cases. The Harmon's baby is doing well and Zeek is in the loving hands of our smith. The only thing I expect to make demands upon my time is the dust overtaking my office. I suspect it, and I, shall be in conference for some while."

"If there should be an emergency. . ."

"I'll take Gov along or lock him up at Gandy's."

It was a simple solution and hard to refute. Aspen knew Connell would do everything he could to look after Gov. The problem was, Gov did everything in his power not to be looked after.

"G'wan," Gideon coaxed. "I done been locked up with ya long 'nough. Could use a change-a scen'ry."

He tried to look like someone thinking something mischievous who did not want to be noticed, whilst in fact wanting to be noticed.

"Why?" said Aspen.

"Wadda ya mean 'why'?"

"It's a simple question."

"'Cause I don't need ya a-guardin' me ever' minute-a the day."

Aspen's gaze narrowed.

"Why?" he asked again, suspicion rising.

"Ain't ya never wanted to be in your 'lone?"

"My what?"

"Your 'lone, without no blasted court a-pointed prison guard a-breathin' down your throat."

Aspen flinched ever so minutely.

"Gideon—"

"It's alright, Connell," Aspen interrupted. "Gideon wants a break, he can have one. I'll get your suppers and pick up Peter."

Gideon watched the retreating back of his affronted guard and then noticed Connell, leaning against his desk, arms crossed. Gideon had rarely seen a stare with more obvious meaning. He didn't need Connell's censure though, he already felt like a sorry excuse all by himself.

Ya could-a asked for his help.

No need.

You see the look in his eyes?

Shutup.

So ya did see'd.

'Course I see'd. You see, I see. Only don't think you're gonna haul me over no coals. This ain't 'bout what we like, it's 'bout what we gotta do.

Did we have to do that?

Hey, we done got us loy'lties a-plen'y. You itchin' to cross them?

This ain't 'bout that.

Ain't it? Sooner Peter's sorted, sooner we get back to our own affairs.

There were men Gideon still had to hunt down and he did not need complications. Well, he didn't need more complications. Some things just had to be done and it plain did not matter if it left him with a bitter aftertaste. He had made a promise, and it wasn't to Aspen Rivers.

His inner voice continued to elbow its way forward and, despite efforts to push it aside, Gideon ended up arguing with himself right up until Aspen returned. Unaccountably, he couldn't quite keep himself from eyeing the man, trying to judge the impact of his barbed words.

Say somethin'.

No.

Chicken.

By all appearances Aspen was the same as always: calm and virtually unflappable. He set two well laden plates on Connell's desk. Then, without word or gesture, he plucked Gideon up and led him to the tiny bedroom.

Livin' with yourself are ya?

He'll get over it.

Ya could've asked.

Why ask for help? This was exactly what Gideon wanted, and this way Aspen didn't have to know a thing.

Gideon was steered to the edge of the bed. It was done gently, yet allowed for no argument. Neither did the handcuffs Aspen secured to Gideon's wrist.

"Aw, c'mon," Gideon objected, as if truly bothered.

"I don't know what you're planning," Aspen replied, securing the other handcuff to the metal bedframe, "but you are not going to do it tonight."

"I can guard my ownself."

"The evidence is lacking," Aspen chided and, properly educated by experience, he began to pat down Gideon's pockets, boots and even his hat.

"I keep a-tellin' ya—"

"Repetition does not constitute accuracy and this would be a good time for you to hush."

Aspen gave up on Gideon's person and shifted to rifling through any and every hiding place suitable for concealing small slips of metal best employed for the unauthorized cozening of levers.

"Satisfied?" Gideon asked, in a carefully constructed tone of injury.

"Don't."

"What?"

"Don't play dumb with me."

"You done tooked ever'thing. 'Member?"

"Yeah, I remember alright," Aspen agreed, thinking of the effort it had taken to bring Gideon in, the subsequent chases and the numerous bruises this consistently provided. Finding nothing, he exchanged searching for looming. "If you give Dr. Connell any grief, I mean anything, you and I will have words, Gideon Fletcher."

"S'posin'—"

"S'posin' we have words now?"

Gideon tipped his head back. Pale gray storm clouds were building in Aspen's eyes with every promise of a gully washer should the prevailing winds continue.

How far d'ya fig'r to rile 'im?

Think he's 'bout swallowed it?

All he's gonna.

Perhaps there could have been a kinder way to go about it but, by and large, things really couldn't have gone much better. The picks hadn't been found, Aspen was safely out of the way, and promising to be nice to Connell interfered with nothing.

Gideon only had a few hours to wait before he could commit yet another act of breaking and entering followed by petty theft. Well, some folks would say theft. Gideon didn't figure it that way– after all, a man cannot steal what is already his.

"I'll be right nice," he relented, shackled hand held out in a suggestion of surrender.

"Promise?"

"Reckon."

"Good enough," Aspen permitted, turning to leave. "Oh, and Gov? Eat your supper this time."

SUPPER was a simple affair with no complications and few expectations, but it was hot and there was plenty. It certainly held more interest for Matt LaConner then the rest of the shadowy, smoke filled saloon. The place was big and, though it was practically shoulder to shoulder from wall to wall, Matt had gleaned nothing of any use whatsoever.

The yellow light from a few scattered lamps did nothing to improve his spirits, as the pall it cast over everything it touched suggested a greasy, unsavory atmosphere.

Across the room, at a table almost entirely concealed

by the press of the crowd, someone watched him. It was not his imagination and Matt would not tell himself it was. Someone was making a study, but why? Who would even know him here? Not a soul, as far as Matt knew. And yet there he sat, the object of incompetent surveillance.

Through peeks and glimpses as the crowd jostled itself, he pieced together the image of a profoundly average man. Average height, average build, average face. He was exactly the sort to use if you did not want a single witness to provide a clinching description.

Had Matt become a target by intention or opportunity? He met an uncommon number of people in his line of work, though he did his best to hold to the more salubrious end of society, drawing the line shy of thugs and cutthroats. He really couldn't recall having unduly upset anyone lately, not on either side of the line.

Tossing a coin to the proprietor, Matt shifted his way through the noise. No one deliberately made room for him, and yet somehow the tide of people ebbed and flowed out of his way without so much as an 'excuse me' being uttered even once.

He contrived to look back without appearing to do so. His watcher had pushed back from the table and was elbowing his way upriver with remarkably less success. Matt smiled. He kept to the street, as if headed for the hotel, then ducked quickly onto a side street. Through the darkness and down to the livery Matt went, his dance partner following behind.

The livery's tack room was cluttered and nearly pitch black. Matt cast about for something of use. There was always something, provided you looked at it the right way.

Two barely audible footfalls fell silent. For a long breath there was nothing, as if someone were weighing their chances. Then, very softly, the footsteps resumed.

Now, there were ways to be sociable amongst one's fellow man, and Matt LaConner did not mind abiding by them. Thing was, anyone creeping up on him in the dark clearly had nothing good on his mind. Matt thereby felt justified in helping them run into something even less good coming the other way.

When the tack room door flew open, the poor soul on the other side was introduced to the broadside of a two-by-four. He then gained a personal understanding of the term 'demon', because one had landed squarely on his chest. Grappling and swinging to no particular advantage, chance rolled the man onto his fallen gun.

"I'd leave it, friend."

It wasn't the cold, metal barrel of the Colt pressed against his skull that stopped the errant man, although this certainly offered sufficient persuasion. It was the expression on the individual behind the trigger that made him hold as still as humanly possible. He had seen similar expressions before— and it usually ended with someone becoming very, very dead.

Matt's finger strained at the trigger and his lungs heaved— whether with the exertion of the brief struggle or with the effort of not firing, the man beneath him did not care to wager. With stiff movements that suggested pulling the trigger would have been preferable, Matt reached out and flung the man's gun away. A knife followed.

Then time stretched out and several possibilities jostled for position.

Matt climbed to his feet, Dragoon still leveled.

"Get up." It was not said loudly, but the tone offered a cold promise. The demons may have receded, it said, but they could just as easily return. "Against the wall."

The man did exactly as he was told— disobeying was not a healthy option— and Matt searched him for anything to give purpose to the attack. Not surprisingly, he found nothing.

"Who are you?" he asked and, when no answer graced the simple question, he continued. "Could be you're a mite slow, friend, or maybe your just plain stupid. I'll give you one more chance and then I am going to do the world a favor by taking you out of it. Your name. Now."

"Jimmy, Jimmy Murdock."

"Who hired you?"

"Nobody. Honest, mister." Primal instincts suggested this was not an auspicious beginning. Jimmy hurried on, "I ride with the Wade gang."

So, it was nothing more than a random act of unsolicited re-disbursement of personal property. Everyone found themselves victim to such base crime at some point, but Matt LaConner did not see this as any excuse to try it on him. If Jimmy had hoped mentioning the Wade gang would tip the scales, he was very much mistaken. By the looks of it, this was a common state of affairs.

"That's kind of a rough outfit," Matt acknowledged, with a thoughtful nod. "I'd recommend you find yourself a new line of work though, because if we ever cross paths again, Jimmy Murdock, and you're still wearing a gun, I will shoot you on sight."

That said, Matt hit the misguided entrepreneur across the back of the head and then heaved the dead weight over his shoulders.

Every head in the saloon fixed on the odd pair as they burst through the swinging doors. The noise faded and the future waited for instructions. Not so much as a stray cough broke the uncertainty. Two unspoken questions hung heavily upon the air: 'Where is this going?' and, more importantly, 'Will it require anything of me?'

Unceremoniously, Matt dumped the unconscious

Jimmy onto the bar. "Barkeep, I'd like a pen, ink, and something resembling paper."

Every eye pivoted to the barman, who suddenly seemed quite small behind his polished counter. The luckless fellow dropped his rag and scuttled off to fetch the demanded items. One could not rightly call it a request, not when the man doing the asking held a loaded gun and did not seem in any kind of mood to care how he used it.

Matt switched the gun to his right hand and penned a brief note politely suggesting the Wade gang find better ways to amuse itself. He blew on the ink and then, for want of a pin, tucked the note through a button hole on Jimmy Murdock's coat.

"Whoever hired him, had better fire him," Matt informed the room at large. At the door he halted, the anger in him still evident for all to see, and jabbed a finger towards the unresponsive, blood smeared man sprawled out on the bar. "He got off easy."

When Matt had gone, the room gave a collective sigh and slowly came alive again with the eclectic buzz of several dozen people all talking at once.

CHAPTER 6
Pink Ribbons
Of Hills & Coffee
Gossip
Crispy Bacon
Brothers
About Dumpty
Watched

GIDEON grasped for a weapon and, once again, came up empty. His first reaction was one best not spoken aloud. The second was not much improved, unless it be by greater color. The underlying theme ran along the lines of how to shoot, beat or otherwise bash whomever had awoken him into an unidentifiable grease smear.

"C'mon! You'll be late!"

'Hit it' came quite easily and without any real need for brain cells to fully engage. Pinning an identity on his exuberant assailant took some thinking. Mainly because he could not imagine what on earth Gabe Rivers would be doing at his bedside or why the child would be waking him.

Gideon muttered an incomprehensible objection and, to his relief, Gabe quit with the shaking.

"Hurry up," the now muffled voice insisted, "before he gets here."

One of Gideon's boots arced through the air to land quite surprisingly near his head.

"Afore who gets here?" he inquired groggily.

"That would be me," Aspen answered from the doorway, and standing to his every considerable inch. "What did I tell you, Gabriel Miller?"

"But I wanted to show him my marbles," Gabe pleaded, from sub-bed level. "Couldn't I? Please? Just for a little while?"

Like so many others when faced with one of Gabe's plaintive arguments, Aspen felt himself crack. How did anyone face such a vibrant, good-hearted child and do anything less? But the fissure was a minor one and did not allow for a complete reversal of injunction, only a softening of approach.

"And miss school?" said Aspen.

"Gov could come too. Ple-e-a-se?"

"I'm sure he would like nothing better," Aspen said, eyeballing his ward, who cringed under the covers as imagination painted pictures across his mind. Sufficiently amused, Aspen added, "But not today."

"But I—" said Gabe, risking a peek.

"Can do as you're told," Aspen finished, gesturing with a thumb towards the waiting door.

Gabe obeyed and Aspen gave him a friendly pat.

"Oh and, Gabe," he called after his young cousin, "when Mr. Cooper scolds you for being late, don't use me as an excuse."

"Yes, sir," the boy called back.

Aspen tipped his head towards the retreating child. "See there? Even he can say it."

The slander held an unmistakable offer of reconciliation. Gideon felt a rush of relief, and then a counter flood of guilt. It didn't matter what Aspen thought or did or said. The man was a distraction, and as with all distractions, he was better kept well away.

Kind-a got 'imself a habit-a standin' right smack bang in the middle-a the road though, don't he?

Yeah, he surely does. Blast.

"Gabe don't know no better, he stands 'scused such foolishness," Gideon offered casually, and then threw down a counter charge of his own. "You're a dirty liar, you are."

Aspen grinned. "At least I am a good liar. You're about

the worst I've ever met."

"Ain't."

"Are."

"Ain't."

"So you admit you are a liar then?"

"Nope," Gideon said, and swung his legs over the edge of the bed. "Only, if'n I were, I'd be better at it than you any day."

Aspen raised an eyebrow. "That so?"

"Yep."

"So when you lied about the river, I shouldn't have taken any notice?"

"You're a-fishin'."

Aspen was, but that was beside the point. Sometimes you only had to give the appearance of knowing what you were talking about and other people would, quite obligingly, fill in the missing bits for you. It was a unique form of interrogation wherein the malefactor was made to snitch upon himself.

"Were you?" Aspen asked.

"Fishin'? After ya done told me to take it easy?"

"Right, because you always do what you're told."

"That's me," Gideon beamed, unabashed.

"Yep, that's you– big fat liar," Aspen agreed, kneeling down to remove the handcuffs from Gideon's wrist. "Thank you, by the way."

"For what?"

"Not letting Gabe see these."

Gideon shied from the praise, genuinely discomfited. "Gabe ain't so bad."

"He's had me for a role model," Aspen bragged.

"Huh, an' he's still a decent kid. Don't that just beat all. I take it back! I take it back!"

"Thought you might," Aspen smirked, and quit

pretending to re-secure the handcuffs. "Get dressed."

"What for?"

"Because you always do what you're told."

He's got ya there.

Gideon reckoned he did. If he could be accused of anything, the very last thing on the list would be following orders, anyone's. He had once. Well, when he said 'once' he didn't mean a whole once only and ever, but more in the sense of 'once upon a time'. Long ago, life had been. . . different. That was the problem with 'once upon a time'— it was always in the past tense.

Mebbe. . .

No. Not ever again. It wasn't in Gideon to go through that again, not for love, money nor a big jar of tea.

"What's wrong?"

Aspen's sincerity pulled Gideon back to the present. It also burned in a way he could not possibly describe.

"I were just wond'rin'," he bluffed, fumbling one handed with a shirt button, "how'd a nancy like you get 'way from your aunt without no frills nor pink ribbons?"

"She says I look better in burgundy."

"Can't say as I'd mind ya none in Burgundy."

"You don't mind anywhere," Aspen countered.

Gideon continued to fight with the button, frustration growing. They were only buttons for the love of Paul; he had managed the task a million times. He couldn't even blame it on his injuries, being left handed anyway.

"Blast!" he cursed, and pushed away Aspen's attempt to help. "I can—"

"Lie to me again?"

"Ain't."

Aspen raised his brows.

Gideon lowered his eyes.

"That's what I thought." Aspen did up the last of the

buttons and took a fist full of Gideon's shirtfront. "Come with me."

Immediately outside the bedroom sat Aspen's makeshift cot. Beneath this resided a small chest. Aspen retrieved a comb, shut the lid and stowed the box, all without once letting go of Gideon.

"You'll be the one with the pink ribbons if your hair gets any longer," he observed, attempting to inflict some measure of civility on his ward's manic display of hair. "Hold still."

"I ain't one-a your dollies," Gideon protested.

"Am not."

"Huh?"

"Am not," Aspen repeated, all patience and helpfulness. "It conjugates: I am not, you are not, he is not. I'm not, you aren't, he isn't."

Gideon's features scrunched up as he thought about this revelation in grammatical correctness. It occupied so much of his attention he even forgot to duck Aspen's ministrations. He stood there, transfixed in honest contemplation for a whole eleven seconds.

"Amn't," he finally declared.

"Pardon?"

"Amn't," Gideon repeated. "Am not. Only that ain't so easy off the tongue, so I reckon I'll just stick to 'ain't'."

Aspen shook his head and reminded himself Rome was not built in a day.

"I don't think there's much more we can do here without a currycomb."

"You're right funny, you are," Gideon complained, though there was no actual complaint in it.

"Keep sassing me, I'll get even funnier."

"This ain't sassin'," Gideon contradicted as Aspen steered him outside. "You just don't make no kind-a sense."

"I'll see what I can do about that."

"I'd 'preciate it."

MRS. HILLMAN answered the knock at her door and wished, rather uncharitably, that she had looked first. Mrs. Driscoll stood before her, hands clasped as if no one would notice she'd been giving her hair a quick primp.

"Ahhh," the busy-body breathed, searching for words to cover the act of vanity, "Good morning."

"What can I do for you, Mrs. Driscoll?"

"I was wondering if you could loan me some coffee. My grinder broke this morning and, well, you know how it is dear. The day wouldn't be the same without fresh coffee."

Mrs. Driscoll's affected courtesy and falsely sweet soprano instantly jumped on every nerve Mrs. Hillman owned. Of no help at all was the fact that Mrs. Driscoll was the stingiest person in Caswell Crossing. Anyone borrowing from her would be plagued until every last salt grain had been returned in full. Somehow she never applied the same standard to herself and had yet to return a single item ever borrowed.

Mrs. Hillman took a deep breath and reminded herself one should be charitable to neighbors.

"Do come in," she said, stepping aside.

Those were the last words Mrs. Hillman managed to get in. She led her visitor to the kitchen, took down the coffee grinder and dropped a handful of beans into the hopper. With every crank of the handle, she was treated to a rather vitriolic dissertation that touched on nearly everyone and everything in town. Mrs. Hillman ignored most of the diatribe on the grounds that some things weren't worth listening to. The chatter filled the kitchen whilst a happier tune filled her head like fluffy cotton, drowning out the nattering noise.

"It's beyond me what those Rivers were thinking. His kind does not change, mark my words."

Mrs. Hillman stopped. "I'm sorry?"

"Of course, with people like that, what can you expect?" Mrs. Driscoll carried on.

"Who do you mean?"

"That boy, of course!" Driscoll answered with all the frustration of one who naturally thinks you should understand exactly what she meant, no matter how little sense she actually made.

"Do you mean Gideon?" asked Mrs. Hillman, still not sure she had heard correctly.

"Who else would I be talking about? From the moment they connived to get that boy off—"

"Mrs. Driscoll, from the moment Judge Forsythe chose to put Gideon with the Rivers it has been none of your business."

"Well, I—"

"And it is still none of your business," Mrs. Hillman said, picking up her grinder. "I think you will find the coffee at Mathers's more to your liking. Or you could go and buy some. My husband— You remember Ollie? He clerks for the Rivers?— he just left for work, so I'm sure the mercantile is open now."

"Well, I never!" exclaimed Mrs. Driscoll indignantly.

"Then why don't you run along and see if you can? Good day, Mrs. Driscoll."

Mrs. Driscoll, for once at a loss, gathered her skirts and huffed out. She stomped down the path and across town, appalled at the nerve of some people. What was the world coming to when folks could exhibit such atrociously bad manners?

ASPEN entered the mercantile precisely as the pretty young woman with the strawberry-blond hair was on her way out. He tipped his hat and, once again, she brushed by with the barest of acknowledgements.

Gideon giggled.

"What did you do to her?" the store clerk asked from the top of a ladder.

"I don't know," said Aspen, smacking Gideon on the arm to hush him up. "Who is she, Ollie?"

"That is Miss Evelyn Pernell. She and her sister opened the bakery," Ollie pushed a box onto the top shelf, hooked both feet around the outside of the ladder and slid to the floor. "I'd introduce you, but it looks to me like she already has opinions about your kind."

"I swear I don't know why," Aspen asserted.

"Whatever the reason, you'll be sorry. Try this," Ollie pushed a plate of baked goods across the counter. "She made them. Now, did you come to negotiate a bride or is there something else I can do for you?"

"I'll pass on the matchmaking, thanks all the same," Aspen said, selecting a fluffy mound of sweetness from the plate. "Doc needs a pound of sugar, two pounds of coffee, a jar of honey and two bars of soap, please. Oh, and two pennyworth of peppermint."

Ollie picked up the sugar scoop, along with a jaunty tune his do-da-ing rendered completely unrecognizable.

Aspen picked up the newspaper on the counter. Due to the ancient date of the edition, justifying it as 'news' would have been a misnomer entirely. Ollie amused himself by calling the few lost papers that eventually drifted into town the 'Olds'. Sometimes they were 'Odds' because they came in fractured scraps that left the reader whiling away the hours manufacturing ludicrous replacements for the missing details. Last summer, the second half of an article from two years previously had appeared, only to have the first half wander in seven months later.

Another customer entered and, behind his paper and very much against his will, Aspen felt his clean shaven cheeks grow warm. He prayed for patience— and particularly deliverance— then turned to offer a greeting with gallantly shored up dignity and remarkable courtesy.

The granite chiseled Mrs. Driscoll imperiously pushed his existence to the outer rim of her personal universe. Her disdainful attention locked on Gideon instead, and her expression clearly said a wet dog dragged through the mud and left to sleep on a barn floor that hadn't seen a rake in a month would gain her approval long before he would.

"Obviously your. . . guardian. . . is incapable of seeing to it you are properly attired," she huffed, "but then I should hardly be surprised."

Mrs. Driscoll's lips puckered in a tight line. Her chin lifted. One shoulder gave a carefully constructed 'so there', and then she left, dripping so much hauteur it fairly puddled in her wake.

Ollie stood frozen, forgotten sugar trickling from the scoop. Aspen still clutched the counter, Gideon at his elbow. All three alike stared at the door as its ribbon of bells faded to an apologetic stop, pitifully insufficient after that magnificent display.

"She were a-starin' that hard, I should-a charged her for the priv'lege," Gideon pronounced into the awkward silence.

"Haven't you heard?" Ollie asked, face aglow.

"You'd best put that to good use before I put it to a better one," Aspen said, pointing to the sugar scoop.

"He's bound to find out," Ollie argued reasonably.

Aspen turned on the man in melodramatic warning.

"Sugar, Ollie. In the barrel. First on your right."

"What'm I bound to find out?" Gideon prompted the obviously willing clerk.

"Him and her, they had a—"

"It was nothing," Aspen interrupted sternly.

"—misunderstanding. He'd hear it from someone," Ollie offered as excuse for his flagrant gossiping.

"Heaven forefend it should come from any but you," Aspen vented sarcastically, and pointed meaningfully towards the shelves. "Will you get the sugar?"

Ollie leant his elbows conspiratorially on the countertop. Obligingly, Gideon leant in as well.

"That morning you snuck off?" Ollie began, "When the sheriff found you? Well, Aspen here came out of the doc's office and ran right into Mrs. Driscoll. And him being considerably short on clothing—"

"It wasn't that bad!" Aspen temporized. "Would it help if I offered to fire you, Ollie?"

Enjoying himself no end, Ollie pressed on, "Seems Mrs. Driscoll felt a bit put out by Aspen's less than gentlemanly appearance. To hear her tell it, he was all but jay bird—"

"It was not that bad! Sugar, Ollie! Is there any chance of it?"

Having rattled the unshakable Aspen, Ollie allowed he could indeed find such a thing as sugar. With the broad, unguarded mother of all mischievous grins, he moved to do just that. Over his shoulder he said, "Whilst I'm about it, why don't you take your ward over there to the corner and see he's properly attired."

Aspen latched onto the suggestion gratefully, even if it did come without an ounce of innocence, and gave Gideon due appraisal. The overall image definitely lacked something– like everything remotely resembling civility.

"I suppose it is about time we got you some trousers

that fit. You aren't half big enough for mine."

Gideon appraised right back, with no need to look any further than Aspen's recently flame bright cheeks.

"Ya know, your aunt's got her a point. Ya do look better in burgundy."

A groan escaped Aspen and he wrapped an arm around Gideon's neck as if to throttle him. "I am going to owe you for the rest of your life. I hope you realize that."

They addressed the shelves filled with clothing to suit the needs of any gentleman, and even some to suit Gideon. If Aspen had been prescient at all he would have selected something with wide stripes.

F OUR laden plates slid onto a table. Mathers then swept up half a china hutch of empties. He returned to his kitchen, off loaded the collection into a massive bucket, flipped half a dozen eggs, checked the biscuits and pulled the griddle cakes off the fire before catching up the coffee pot and heading back out.

"Mathers?"

"Yes, Barker?" Mathers addressed the councilman perched half in and half out of the café.

"Have you seen the sheriff?"

"No, sir," Mathers answered, coffeepot moving from mug to mug.

Sally Calder, the best waitress he ever hired, handed over a stack of order slips, smoothly took the pot and continued with the rounds.

"You sure?" Barker asked, doubt riddling his tone.

"Three eggs fried," the cook rattled off, "solid centers, two biscuits– light butter, heavy jam— four sausage, a half slab of beef— medium well— no toast and double coffee. I haven't made it 'cause he hasn't ordered it."

Mathers gathered up more dirty dishes and headed for the kitchen. He heard Barker greet someone distractedly on his way out and then Sally's warmer voice doing a better job of it.

"Good thing you didn't order the sausages or I'd be a liar," he told the kitchen at large.

Hunkered off to one side, with the upturned rinse bucket for a chair, Caswell Crossing's sheriff balanced a plate on his knees.

"Bacon's good," he said, around a mouthful of the crispy stuff.

"Your bacon was nearly cooked there," Mathers replied, plating up the next four orders.

"Hah, Barker would have never made it past you."

"Suppose he'd come through the back?"

"Of your kitchen?"

Gandy supposed he would have to endure another infernal council meeting someday, but he preferred to keep that someday as hypothetical as possible. It was strange how, when faced with a man aiming a gun, or a drunk holding a shattered bottle, he went in feet first and head on. Present him with the specter of dry, redundant, inefficient meetings in stuffy, closed up rooms and Gandy was the biggest– well his deputies called him the biggest yellow-bellied dodger they'd ever seen, though he didn't let anyone else get away with talk like that.

"You owe me dishes," Mathers reminded the sheriff.

"That was the deal, and you certainly held up your end." Gandy sucked a bit of jam off a finger and popped the last of the biscuit into his mouth. "I'll start with this one."

It was worth a few dishes to eat breakfast in peace.

EMBER Rivers crept cautiously alongside Rosie

Ward's barn. No corners had been cut or effort spared by the self-appointed mob who had so recently raised the sizeable structure. The important thing, however, was that the recent construction had trodden all the ground within a dozen feet to bare dirt. Ember's tip-toe steps were barely audible.

He peered around the front: no one there. Contrary to common instinct, he did not take this as due license to stride boldly out. A man could get killed that way. No, Ember knew his adversary and he knew better. Tucked against the protection of the wall, he scanned every foot of the yard and found nothing out of place. He crept forward, inch by measured inch. The wide double doors of the barn stood fully open and deep shadows fell within. He took a better grip on the rock in his hand— and the ground smacked into him.

"I ought to make you eat dirt, Embrey Anatole!" Lee threatened.

Ember grappled and twisted, but his doppelganger maintained the advantage. In short order Lee straddled Ember's stomach, doing his best to fulfill his promise. Ember squirmed, tugged, and finally managed to twist an arm free. Into the ensuing tussle came Fort.

"C'mon you two, we have work to do," he told them.

"But he—" two voices chorused.

"You can settle who's bigger later."

Fort would have been fine at that. Emberlee would have shoved each other once or twice more and gone back to work. Where Fort went wrong was the tone with which he muttered 'children' as he walked away. The twins' response to that required no consultation. They were up, they were on him and he was down.

A tangled downside-up knot of arms and legs followed until Fort wedged a muscled arm under Lee and peeled him bodily aside. The smaller boy hit the ground like a lion cub smacked down by its mother's paw.

Ember then gained his big brother's undivided attention. He had a fist full of hair and an awkwardly twisted arm, and try as he might, Ember remained thoroughly pinned beneath Fort's greater bulk.

"Lee!" the besieged Ember pleaded. "Whose side are you on?"

Lee blinked. Sides. Right. He got off his backside, leapt back into the fray, and within seconds found himself neatly trapped. No matter how he pushed or twisted, it came to nothing but an ineffectual scrabbling. Lee would praise the move later, with a full heart too, but doing so then would have been to encourage the wrong side entirely.

Heaving and shoving, he finally pried an arm loose, but stuck he was and stuck he stayed. If he strained, it was almost possible to get himself around to use his teeth but the thought did not even occur. Such an act was forbidden with a brother— definitely with this brother. Besides, losing terrifically or not, it wasn't for serious.

"Emberlee?" Rosie's bemused voice carried clearly from the house.

"Yes, ma'am?" came the dual reply.

Lee's heels carved another furrow into the earth.

"Quit pestering your brother," Rosie admonished, placing her bucket under the water pump.

"Yes, ma'am," came the solitary reply.

"Ember?" Rosie waited, pump handle raised.

Ember kept his mouth firmly shut. Above him loomed the promise of a handful of dirt should he be so unwise as to speak. Unfortunately, Fort seemed quite willing to wait for the inevitable.

"You hear me, Ember Rivers?"

And there it was. When Rosie Ward asked a question

like that, wise men answered. Ember stared up at his brother, who smugly stared back down at him. There was nothing for it. Ember opened his mouth and gave a muffled gurgle which might have been a 'yes, ma'am' had it not been smothered by particalized terra firma.

"That'll learn you, you little upstart."

Rosie could hear Fort's playful scolding over the creak and gurgle of the pump. She watched him release Ember, wrapped an arm around Lee and knuckle his head before letting him go too.

They were good boys. Rosie supposed she really ought to think of them as young men now, only sometimes they did make it a hard.

T WO men rode their horses right down the main street. Everyone and sundry could see their faces plain as day and identify them to any sheriff, deputy or lawman of choice. That was just it though, they didn't expect anyone to recognize them. They certainly didn't suspect Gideon or Peter had the nerve to identify them to the law.

Lucky for you, I ain't 'zactly on speakin' terms with no law.

Gideon stood outside the mercantile and tried to ignore the riders. Not entirely of course, that would have been suspicious, but just enough to suggest there was nothing there worth noticing. He really could have wished for better timing. Like any time Aspen wasn't standing right beside him.

Wadda ya think?

Think I looked more like a kid fifteen minutes ago.

Traipsing around in Aspen's clothes, it had been easy. The affect was somewhat harder to accomplish when one's clothes more closely fit one's proper measure. He had flat refused to exchange his beat up old boots, though he would have gladly exchanged blows had Aspen pushed the point. By and large, looking normal left Gideon feeling oddly exposed. He needn't have worried. First impressions could go a long way, and the two riders had already made up their minds about him.

Gideon would have known the thinner man anywhere. By daylight, Pultrie's hair was black as obsidian, yet lacked the same shine, and his jawbone still had not seen a razor.

Beside him rode an egg. An unattractive, shaggy, toss-pot of an egg. Any self-respecting chicken would have been mortified to lay claim to it. It would have packed up its feathers and hit the road for preference.

Neither of them did a thing to suggest they wanted to be noticed, yet clearly, not only did they want Gideon to see them, they wanted him to worry over it.

"Humpty Dumpty."

"What's that, Gov?" said Aspen.

"Hmm? Oh, nothing. Just something Peter told me." Gideon tugged at his new shirt. "Mebbe we should see how he's a-gettin' on."

"How come? And quit that."

"Is it suffocatin' me you're after?"

"That shirt doesn't even have a proper collar."

"So why bother butt'nin' it up to my chin? I'm a-wearin' it an' I prefer breathin'."

"Come here," Aspen said, turning Gideon towards him. "You have two fingers of room you big baby." Aspen unhooked the top button anyway. "Better? Now what were you saying about Peter?"

"Zeek din't seem happy havin' nobody 'round's all."

"Zeek's alright, just noisy. Don't worry, he'll take to Peter alright."

"I ain't worried."

Least ways not 'bout that.

Gideon followed Aspen towards the doc's, but stole a glance down the road after the two riders. He hoped they were not on their way to try another round of intimidation on Peter. Sure the kid was game, but he wasn't too savvy on the rougher edges of life. Somehow Pultrie and his egg friend would have to be kept at a respectable distance. Not too great a distance, just far enough to give Gideon room to maneuver.

There was no deed, and no way to convince them the deed didn't exist. The only option left was to convince them it did exist. Which meant convincing them not only that he and Peter knew where it was, but that they weren't going to hand the deed over. Then, after a bit of tug and pull, he would have to make it look like the deed which Pultrie thought existed, but hadn't, now really didn't. Simple.

Right after that came convincing Pultrie and company to cut their losses and go back to whatever eastern hole they'd crawled out of– preferably without venting their frustrations on anyone handy. Like, say, Peter. That part might be a bit trickier, but it was also step five or possibly seven, which put it too far down the list for current concern.

The whole problem could have been solved with a couple of bullets. A mite hasty perhaps, but solved. Well, if Gideon had a gun which, thanks to Aspen, he did not. Every living soul and their six cousins had it in mind to hunt his hide, but don't give him a gun. No, leave ol' Gideon a sitting duck. Now there's a plan. Still, it could be arranged, this was the west after all– everyone had a gun. That is, everyone but him.

Billy Nevans came alongside with a friendly nod. "Hello, Mr. Rivers, Gideon. Is the rifle in yet?"

"No, not yet. Should be any day now," Aspen assured the eager young man.

"Hope it comes before we get weather. I'd hate to have to wait until spring. 'Course, with the weather we've been having, winter's looking a ways off yet."

"How about I send a runner when it gets here?"

"That would be great! That is, if it isn't too much trouble?"

"No trouble at all."

Billy gave his thanks and shook Aspen's hand vigorously. In an excess of gratitude he then pumped Gideon's hand as well.

"Good to see you up and about," Billy gabbled in his excitement. "Some folks weren't too sure for a while. Don't think I'd want to brace you though. I'd better get to work. You know Mr. Reed. Thanks again, Mr. Rivers."

"That's nice," opinioned Aspen.

"What?" Gideon wondered.

"You two are still friends even after he stole Sally Calder from you."

"Weren't never like that an' you know it," Gideon objected, whilst Aspen enjoyed his own sense of humor.

"Come on, let's get you off the street before someone tries to have you arrested again."

"Aw, ain't nobody got nothin' on me."

"Really? Well, let's not tempt fate, hmm?"

They reached the clinic without incident and settled on the porch swing. Now and then Gideon gave it a nudge.

"I hear you met Mr. Cooper," Aspen said idly.

Gideon ignored the undercurrent of question in the statement. But it had niggled at him, that meeting.

So ask 'im.

"What's a ay-tur-nee?"

"An attorney," Aspen explained, putting the emphasis on the proper syllables, "is someone who speaks for you in court and tries to get you out of trouble."

"A lawyer? That why he's schoolmarmin'? On a'count-a there not bein' no judge in town?"

"On account of him being a respectable and well educated gentleman."

"He can read?"

"Yes indeed, very well."

"There ya are then," Gideon declared.

"There I am what?" asked Aspen.

"I ain't the sort to go bein' no lawyer nor no schoolmarm, so why bother?"

"You aren't the sort to stay out of trouble either, so why bother leaving the jailhouse?"

Several responses elbowed for first place and, whilst they were shoving, Gideon's back thoughts asked a question of their own.

"Who's Humpty Dumpty?"

"Did you ask Peter?" said Aspen.

Gideon's silence said a lot.

Aspen's smug expression said the rest: I know you didn't and I know why you didn't and you are a fool.

Sliding to Gideon's end of the swing, he held out the slate in his hands.

"Look here."

"What for?"

"Because you always do what you're told."

"An' you're a big fat liar," Gideon accused comfortably.

"Are you going to be difficult?"

Likely.

"Likely," Gideon admitted, leaning his head against the back of the swing.

He had no intention of being pulled into one of Aspen's tricks. He shifted until he was in just the right spot for the porch awning to prevent the sun from glaring into his eyes and gave the swing another idle nudge.

Aspen added a few more strokes to the slate. "You can learn to read, you know."

"So what?" said Gideon, unmoved.

"What do you mean 'so what'?"

"They's easy words. Little uns too."

"Is this you sassing me again?"

"Me? Sass a duly appointed officer of the court?" Gideon replied, with mock sincerity. "Wouldn't dream of it."

"Good, then look here—"

"You gonna tell me 'bout Mr. Dumpty?"

"Ye-e-s," Aspen drawled, "as soon as you look here."

Gideon allowed himself a sidelong suggestion of a surreptitious half peek. On the slate was a rough picture of a round, fat egg with face, limbs, britches and all. Towering behind, stood a thick wall.

"What's all them little lines?" Gideon asked curiously.

"Cracks. He fell off."

"What for?"

"I suppose he would have fallen up," said Aspen, "if he had known how."

"This you sassin' me?"

"Wouldn't dream of it."

"Good," Gideon said, straight faced. "Why'd he go climb some garden wall, if'n he's all round an' fally?"

"Fally?" Aspen echoed.

"It's a word."

"To whom? And you're one to talk. Why did you go near the river if you're all fally?"

"See there? It's a word," Gideon boasted smugly.

"Only to you. Where did you ever see a garden wall anyway?"

"Telled ya. I been 'round. Don't ya listen none?"

"I'm surprised you had time to notice a thing like that," Aspen commented, nice and easy like, and then tagged it with, "given you were probably outrunning an irate mob at the time."

Gideon inspected the slate more closely. "Ain't that perty? Ya done did put ivy on that there wall. Nancy."

"What do you know about ivy?"

"I know you go a-climbin' 'round in it, you'll be a sorry son," Gideon answered, pleased with his knowledge.

"Oh? Why's that?"

"Makes a fellah itch somethin' awful."

"How would you know?" Aspen challenged.

"'Cause I—" Gideon cut himself off. "Oh, no ya don't. Uh-uh. That were slick, but no."

Gideon figured the less Aspen, or anyone, knew about his past the better because, simply put, people who didn't know anything couldn't be questioned nor easily blamed. Ignorance had its advantages.

Wouldn't be 'cause you're a-tryin' to hide nothin'.

Ain't none-a Aspen's business, that's all.

Really?

He'd only get in the way.

Really?

Look, he'd get 'imself hurt, alright?

What's it to you?

Shutup.

"Almost had you," Aspen was saying, though bragging might have been more apt.

"That ya did," Gideon allowed equitably, "but no ya ain't."

"Since you're not going to tell me about ivy, why don't you tell me what Billy slipped you instead."

Oops.

"Huh?" said Gideon intelligently.

"You heard me."

"Don't mean I un'erstood ya none," Gideon stalled.

"Then allow me to be more clear: What did Billy Nevans slip into your hand that you hid in the left pocket of your britches and do not want me to see?"

How'd he catched that?

Beats me.

"He din't slip me nothin'," Gideon said, as innocently as he could.

"Liar," Aspen said, as plainly as he could.

"Thems is fightin' words to some folks."

"Do you intend to take me?"

Nosir.

"Could be."

"Take my advice," Aspen said, hand out. "Save yourself the embarrassment and just hand it over."

"Nosir."

Aspen leaned over, effectively pinning Gideon against the bench. "Close, but the words you wanted were 'yes sir'."

He dug into Gideon's pocket and fished out the paper. A brief moment of contention for possession followed, and then it was Aspen's.

"Give it here!" Gideon wheedled, trying to reach around the bulk splayed across him.

"I swear," Aspen said, pinning Gideon's grasping hand and shaking out the missive, "you've had this for hardly two minutes together and already it's smudged."

"It's a knack. What's it say?"

"You don't see any need for reading," Aspen demurred, reading silently. "Gideon, you stay right here."

Gideon?

"What's wrong?"

"Right here," Aspen repeated. "No games. Are we clear?"

"Sure," Gideon agreed, more curious than alarmed. "What's wrong?"

Aspen raised his voice. "Connell? I need to step over to the harness shop for a minute."

"What for?" Gideon asked again.

"A certain gentleman and I need to have a word," Aspen answered, taking the stairs in one long stride.

"'Member please an' thank you!" Gideon tossed after him.

Ya don't reckon it's Billy, do ya?

Nah, gotta be ol' pickle face.

Aspen din't looked that vexed even when we done chucked his favorite rifle off-a that there mountain.

Nor when we 'bout drowned 'im in that there lake.

He din't a had-a go an' follow us.

But he sure did.

Gideon picked up the note, squinted at it, tipped it over and stared again. Over at the harness and feed, Aspen swung open the front door. Amazingly, the hinges survived it. Aspen stepped back to let someone else leave and then disappeared inside. Who else could be that aggrieved and still think to be polite?

Mebbe he don't want no witnesses.

You fig'r Reed's got hisself in a trouble?

Ohhh, yeah.

THE mare was no great trouble. The worst of the lot was yet to come and Smyth had been putting it off until the end. Peter's father had felt it best to get the hardest part of a job done first, when a man was fresh, and everything after would seem that much simpler by comparison. Smyth went the other way around, reasoning the first task set the tone and a tired man would spend the rest of his day in no good mood. Peter wisely kept his father's advice for another day and contented himself with holding the mare.

The smith finished the last nail, dropped the mare's hoof and stood up, straightening every inch of his spine. Shoeing bent a man up on himself, especially a larger man. He fetched a bit of grain from a barrel inside the shop and let the complacent horse eat from his hand.

"Women rarely object to receiving presents," he informed Peter. "You remember that. They also tend to do things in flocks, so you'd best bring her sister over next."

Peter did as he was bid, and the sorrel Smyth had pointed out earlier came trotting over as soon as her sister had been led into the corral.

"Guess he was right about the flock," Peter remarked, giving both sisters a scratch and switching the halter from one to the other.

"What did I tell you?" Smyth said, examining a front hoof. "One shoe gone and another near to it. Women."

Smyth took the lead rope, tied it to a rail and handed Peter a large rasp. Peter set to work more confidently than he felt.

"Not bad, boy. A bit more off the outside. Here, this mare's an easy fit, this should do."

Peter stared at the horseshoe the smith held out. As many times as he had seen a horse being shod, he had never done it himself.

"We all learn sometime. Don't worry, you won't hurt her," Smyth said encouragingly. "And if you do, she'll let you know. Hell hath no fury like a woman scorned."

Peter took the shoe and picked up a hammer. Breath held, he set a nail as Smyth directed. Several hundred pounds of horse flesh leaned into him like a man leans against a fence post on a warm summer's day. If that mare got any more relaxed, they were both going to topple clean over. Peter drove the next nail with more confidence and soon had them all in, clipped and bent.

Unbeknownst to him, the lesson was not a private one. Harvey Wilcox had been watching. Over the hours his feet had grown more sore, his stomach had begun to rumble more loudly, and his patience had steadily dwindled.

Go fetch him, Pultrie had said. And don't be seen.

Don't be seen? How was Harvey supposed to do that with the smith standing right there the whole blasted time? His stomach grumbled another loud complaint. Hang it. Nick Pultrie was an idiot. The kid wasn't going anywhere, watched or not. Harvey abandoned his hiding place for a table at the café.

CHAPTER 7
Reasonable Doubt & A Low Level Buzz
Pressure
Isi
Listening
Grizzly Advice
Swapping
Desperate Measures

T HE sheriff played with the bits of shattered lock in his hand. Why had the more difficult door lock been picked and this simple one smashed to pieces? Whoever had broken into Mary's left no signs to explain their trespass. Thanks to her porch, the culprit hadn't even left any footprints, despite all the mud. They had simply broken in, emptied the cash box and gotten clean away.

Mary only kept a few dollars on hand to make change, but that was most emphatically not the point. Someone was robbing Gandy's town. Worse than that, if it kept going, someone was going to get hurt. Gandy rocked back in his chair and propped his feet on the desk. Someone sure would get hurt, just as soon as he got his hands on them.

He knew the current talk around the checkerboards and who was being put forward as the prime suspect. He couldn't really blame the townspeople, although he'd sure keep an eye on them. It was amazing how quickly average people could go from talking to doing, and with every step average became imbecilic— in exponential proportions.

Dang it all, why didn't people come to him sooner? Only after her shop had been broken into and the money taken did Mary think to report her missing key.

Well, that solved the one issue anyway— with a key, the outer door would pose no barrier. So far, the evidence did nothing to incriminate or exonerate the leading contender for blame and incarceration.

Gandy eyeballed the violated lock. It was trying to tell him something. Why smash a lock if you had the means to pick it? Picking was quieter and did not leave evidence to be found and wondered upon. Perhaps, whomever had done this, did not have the means or the little lock now resting in the hands of the law would not have presented a challenge—which it manifestly had. Reasonable doubt perhaps?

The sheriff mentally shuffled through the current gossip. The town was beginning to buzz. It was a pretty low level hum, but it wouldn't take much to stir things right up, and there were some who never left home without a spoon. As far as Gandy could tell, the prevailing wind gained more substance from fiction than fact. No matter how he turned it, he simply could not bend the evidence to fit the obvious answer. Sure it was handy, and from a distance it even made sense. It just wasn't fact.

He dropped the talkative little lock into a desk drawer and lifted his hat from its peg. There were a few people he needed to see.

P SSSTT!"

The hissing sound struck Gideon as unnecessarily dramatic. Why not poke your head around the corner, flash your gun and get on with it? Who would argue with a loaded Dragoon?

You.

Good point.

"Pssst!" Pultrie beckoned again.

Gideon peered over his shoulder as if afraid, or possibly hoping, someone would see him. Connell was inside. Aspen was still at Reed's. Pultrie's coast was clear. Gideon got up from the swing, lest the man spring a leak of an irreparable nature. Not that such an eventuality would be altogether unwelcome. It would certainly save some time and effort.

"That wasn't very smart, dumping me in the river," Pultrie whispered, hustling Gideon around the corner.

"I din't a-knowed you were clumsy, mister," Gideon offered, in his best whine. "It weren't a-purpose."

Pultrie lifted a hand– and changed his mind. He didn't need inconvenient questions about unexplained bruises.

"An accident?" he hissed. "Then where were we going?"

"I told ya, where I were gonna hide the papers."

"You have them?" Pultrie exclaimed, his eagerness palpable. "Hand them over."

Oh, for the love-a Paul. Mud's brighter'n 'im.

On that we do a-gree.

Gideon did his best imitation of a snivel. "He. . . he ain't gived 'em to me yet."

"What do you mean—" Pultrie began, and hushed as someone called out. "Who's that?"

"The doc."

"Answer him," Pultrie ordered, drawing his knife, "but don't get clever."

"I'm just goin' out back, Doc," Gideon hollered.

How many time's d'ya figure he's gonna buy that?

Just this once'd be real nice.

"Look, boy," Pultrie resumed impatiently. "Peter isn't going to **give** you the deed. You have to **take** it. It's called stealing. Are you listening to me?"

An innocent would probably find the notion of stealing rather shocking, or at least find Pultrie somewhat intimidating. Accordingly, Gideon tried to make his eyes look as if they were about to bug out of his head.

Pultrie grinned. "Way of the world, boy. You'd better get used to it. Fast."

Gideon nodded mutely and swallowed half a dozen responses that would do his persona no good. It must have read as hesitation to Pultrie, because he reached out and caught Gideon roughly by the chin.

"Remember our deal: I get those papers or you start losing friends. What are you doing here anyway?" Pultrie looked at the building to which he had pinned his prey, as if realizing for the first time it was a medical facility.

"Doc's a-fixin' my arm," Gideon answered meekly.

"Don't you have folks?"

"No, sir."

"So, if you were to disappear," Pultrie leaned in until Gideon could smell stale coffee and camp smoke, "no one would care. Or even notice. Right?"

"Nosir. I-I mean yessir. I mean. . ." Gideon faltered.

"Gideon?" the doctor's voice rang out and footsteps could clearly be heard.

Pultrie yanked Gideon off the wall, took a step left and then right, but neither direction presented the best of escape routes in broad daylight.

"Get the deed, before I lose patience," Pultrie threatened, gave Gideon one last shake, and skedaddled.

Ya know, boyo, I do b'lieve Doc done saved ya a kidnappin'.

Did sort-a seem to be on Pultrie's mind, din't it?

You gonna have to learn that boy some.

I'm open to the notion.

W ORKING girls tend to keep to their own territory, but Isi didn't mind running Gin-Bow's errand. He had been good to her and she was more than willing to return the favor by fetching the doctor for him.

Though she had gone twenty-three, thus far the years

had left no visible sign of their passing. She did not talk about the invisible signs.

Her deep green skirt covered delicate ankles and her white blouse was fastened up to her throat, with only the top most pearl daringly left undone. Her abundance of red hair curled about her head in a loose bun. Anyone would, and often had, said she was cute as a button.

Even so, some folks did not care for her kind to be on the public street. Interesting how, when those same people used the term 'public street', it came out meaning 'private domain'.

She was grateful to James Miller, and more so to his partner Amos Rivers, whom she suspected was the root of her welcome at the mercantile. Isi wasn't sure if she would go so far as to call it respect, yet not once had either man, or anyone in their employ, ever given her the social stiffness or downright scorn one of her profession typically received from the more morally starched.

If Isi were honest with herself, something she usually was but rarely lingered upon, deep down she agreed with them. She really did. What went right against the grain was their self-righteous attitude and shunning uprightness. There was no call for that in her book. She was simply doing her best to get by, same as everyone else and, unless they had a smile and some practical suggestions, how she did it was none of their concern.

Across the wide, dusty street a pin-perfect woman in modestly muted gray followed Isi's progress. She was like one of those hunting dogs that, upon homing in on the scent, locks its whole body into the effort of pointing towards its prey. As if Mrs. Driscoll were her dearest friend, Isi waved with overly dramatic girlishness and even managed to put a bounce into her knees. It only needed pigtails and ribbons. She was rewarded by a shocked, and fruitless, working of Mrs. Driscoll's jaw, and then the woman's expression underwent a tight clamping down of nearly comical proportions and the busy-body moved on.

Isi stuck her tongue out at the woman's back, which caused her a moment of genuine girlishness.

W HAT took Aspen off in such a hurry?"

Gideon gave the doctor a calculated half shrug. "Don't reckon as there's much-a nothin' I could throw down on that there a'count."

"I wonder if that might actually make sense if you told me in the Irish?" said Connell.

Gideon stepped up onto the porch. "It were plain English."

"At a stretch, perhaps. 'Plain' you'll never make stand up in court. Let's have a look at you."

"Mebbe ya oughtta see what she wants first."

Connell followed Gideon's gaze. A young woman was approaching at a decent clip, though without the frenzy normally associated with a true emergency. She had bold orange hair, a modest dress and an overall self-possessed carriage that was hard to miss. Connell had seen numerous ladies who worked of an evening, most did not take the same distinct care of their appearance as this young woman. One might almost think she was not what he knew her to be.

"Do come in, ma'am," he greeted politely. "How may I be of assistance?"

"I was hoping you could come to the saloon," Isi explained from the foot of the stairs. "Gin-Bow, the odd-job man, he woke up awfully sick this morning and doesn't seem to be getting any better."

"I'll get my bag," Connell agreed.

Isi gave Gideon a broad wink; their truce still held. It made Gideon think of the note in his pocket. He'd sure like to know what had set Aspen off, and clearly he wasn't going to hear it from Aspen.

"Shall we?" Connell said, as he returned.

"Why's he coming?" Isi asked.

Connell put a hand on Gideon's shoulder. "Well, miss, you could say he is my assistant in training. This is Gideon Fletcher."

Gideon touched his hat brim. "Ma'am."

"It's Isi," she returned.

Gideon had to hand it to her, with one simple question she had preempted any possibility Connell might suspect they knew each other.

Perhaps Gideon had found another candidate for his community of listeners. He supposed he ought to call them spies, only that had such a negative sound– like they were on the brink of treason or inciting sedition. It was all much simpler than that, if not precisely any more innocent.

From town to town, hut to shack, stage stop to hard rock mining pit, Gideon had strung together a collection of people willing to pick up information. It hadn't been intentional, not at first. It had simply formed of its own accord until one day Gideon realized, in nearly every place he had been, someone was willing to listen. Only a fool would pass up the incredible possibilities inherent in this– and Gideon did not count himself a fool.

The whole thing was really nothing more than the power of rumor put to good use. So far, it had been useful indeed, even if it had yet to provide the information Gideon most needed.

He felt a surge of anticipation as they neared the saloon. Gin-Bow had recently joined this happy union of listeners. Up until now, he'd had nothing to report. But you never knew. Whilst rumor's preferred method of travel was to fly every which way, Gideon's listeners worked like water down a flume. Truth be told, it worked a whole lot slower than that but, the point was, eventually, somebody told someone something.

Maybe Gin-Bow was playing sick so he could pass along information without drawing suspicion? In the next instant Gideon scolded himself. Chances were the man had simply twisted a gut from eating to too much.

But mebbe?

Perhaps that was the hope Connell had talked about, the thought that— despite what was likely– maybe things would turn your way. Only, if there were a lead. . .

Yeah.

Yeah.

Gideon felt pulled two ways. On the one side, he would pursue any lead with every ounce of his strength to his very last breath. On the other side, he didn't like to dwell on the day he would finally finish what Tarlston had started. He would do it, without regret, but that did not mean he had to like it.

Did that make him a coward? Did other men feel proud or pleased when another human lay dead at their feet? Gideon supposed some did– like those men in the saloon– but he also figured some of it was only show, a kind of strutting by big men with small brains.

Right, wrong, proud or not, the only one who could release Gideon from his promise was dead. If he had been alive, there would have been no need for the promise.

MATT LaConner listened very carefully. He had never ridden through the country ahead of him, details could be important. There were a million ways to die out there and folks were coming up with new ones all the time. Some went by murder, some by disease, an awful lot were self-inflicted by shear lack of planning. Then there were those who simply fell asleep at the wrong time, lost their horse, broke a leg or nicked their hand and died of blood poisoning. A million ways and counting.

A million one.

Out here, one of the best things a thinking fellow could do was listen to the advice of people who had been before him. Sometimes what they had to say came in the very fact that they never came back to give advice. In this case, Matt had stumbled upon a man of indeterminate occupation, universal age and an origin unguessable by those of a civil persuasion. Matt found himself unwilling to try.

What his informant was mostly, was fur. His boots were fur, his hat was fur, his enormous coat might once have been an entire grizzly– or quite possibly still was and it simply preferred going about piggyback rather than walking for itself. Even the man's own wild bush of hair and bristled beard added to the impression he was one massive, walking heap of matted up, unwashed fur that seriously needed a few good shakes and a couple of months airing out.

"You listen here, boy," the heap squatting down by the fire said. "Nothin' out there but cats 'n coyotes 'n bears. Even the insects'd like to kill ya, an' the snakes'd like to he'p 'em. Don't look at me like that, I ain't askin' your business. There's a stage as goes 'round there now 'n ag'in, only this ain't one-a them whens. One fella, all on his lonesome, all the way from here to there? Pack a gun. Ya hear what I'm sayin'?"

"I hear," Matt replied tolerantly.

Obviously the old– or possibly not– man took him for a newcomer. Matt allowed he had been known to have that effect on people and decided not to take offence today. His companion would share whatever information he could, he merely wanted to give a disclaimer so he could offer the advice without feeling anyone might take a notion to come back and call him on it later.

Matt refilled their coffee cups and the talked resumed.

"You still goin'?" the man asked, as he wound down.

"Yes," Matt answered quietly. "I sure am."

"Hope it's worth it."

"What is?"

"Whatever it is you're lookin' to die fer."

"I don't die so easy," Matt said, and though the words were affable, the foul smelling heap of fur squinted at him for a long moment.

"No," he finally said. "Don't reckon ya do."

Matt offered the last swallow of coffee to his informant and emptied his own cup. "Well, sir, thank you for the posting."

"I'll give ya one more piece-a advice."

Reins in hand, Matt peered over his horse's back and paid attention.

"You run inta nobody name-a Rivers, don't rile 'em. Nor no Miller neither. They're clan, them two."

"Obliged again," said Matt, and mounted up.

A N' y'all say I ain't no prisoner."

Gideon had taken a single step away from the doctor and been latched onto faster than a rattler could spit.

"You are not a prisoner," said Connell, still holding fast to a fist full of Gideon's shirtsleeve. "You are a walking one man catastrophe on a hair trigger waiting for any half plausible excuse to wreak havoc."

"It's a knack. Don't worry. I promised Aspen: no

trouble."

Connell's eyebrows rose. "And he believed you?"

"Prob'ly not," Gideon allowed easily.

Connell thought about it, resettled the black bag in his hand, and thought about it some more. "No trouble? You promise?"

The blacksmith's and the livery were elbow to elbow neighbors. Gideon could chuck a stone from one to the other. Did Connell honestly think anyone could get into any real trouble?

In your case?

Shutup.

"Would **you** b'lieve me?" Gideon grinned.

"Probably not," Connell admitted, shaking his head at such blatant cheekiness. "I suppose it wouldn't hurt. Only whilst I see to Zeek, mind."

Gideon nodded, thankful again to the doctor for not trying to hobble him completely. If only Aspen could figure that out half so well. Still, Gideon was a prisoner, no matter what Connell said, and he really couldn't expect to be treated any differently. Meantime, there was someone he needed a word with.

"What were ya a-thinkin' a-lightin' out-a that office with that there paper?"

Peter looked up from the stall he was cleaning. "Hello to you too."

"Well?" Gideon insisted, climbing onto the bottom rail and hooking an arm over the top one.

"The same thing you were when you suggested it," said Peter, working the fork in his hands.

"I never suggested you take it."

"Well, I did!"

"Yeah, ya did!"

"If want to fight about it, you had better finish

climbing over that rail. I ought to be just about done by the time you've hauled yourself in here."

Gideon supposed it took a friend to be willing to wait on him, because he sure wasn't going to launch his sorry self over that rail with any agility.

"What'd ya do?" he asked.

"Stopped in different places and then lost him. Wilcox won't even know where to begin looking."

Gideon chewed this over. "Reckon ya did alright."

"Obliged, I'm sure."

"You know what I mean."

"Yeah, you're sorry for being such an ornery mule," Peter translated, throwing a dried horse apple at Gideon.

Gideon ducked, fetched it up and threw it back. He did not miss. Peter threw another, leapt out of the stall, and commenced to manhandle his friend.

"What's this?" Peter said, plucking something up from the ground.

"You're a readin' sort-a fella. Ain't you see'd you a note afore?" Gideon replied, tucking it into his pocket.

"You want me to read it for you?"

"Nah, no need."

Thanks to Isi, who had taken a surreptitious moment to read it whilst the doc had a look at Gin-Bow— who turned out to have a sore belly and no news— Gideon knew what the note said. He even knew what to do about it.

"Suit yourself," Peter gave Gideon a playful punch, "some of us have work to do."

He went back to mucking and Gideon went back to watching. There was something infinitely calming about the smell of leather and dust and horses. It was as if time stood still, or never existed at all. No past, no future— only right then, quiet and asking no odds.

"Hey, Gov? Can you. . ." the last of Peter's question

petered out until Gideon could make nothing of it.

"Can I what?"

"You know– fix stuff, with thread."

"Ya mean sew? Sure."

"Oh."

Gideon one-armed some fresh straw and spread it over the stall floor. Peter nudged it into the bald spots with his boot, then caught up the barrow and headed out. Gideon latched the gate and trailed along.

"Say, Peter?" he ventured tentatively. "When did ya learn to read?"

"About six, I suppose. Same as most folks."

"Oh."

Gideon plucked a dullish red berry off a wild growing, scrawny bit of a bush. It stabbed him for his trouble. Unperturbed, he crunched his scavenged treasure and prized out the thorn.

"Rose hips," he explained to Peter, tossing one over. "Makes a passable tea, too."

Peter nibbled and found the unexpected edible bearable if not desirable.

"Hold your hands up," he directed.

"What?"

"I know you've heard it before: put your hands up."

Peter shaped Gideon's thumb and index fingers into a sort of spiral shape.

"That's a 'G'." he announced, dumping the barrow and heading back to the livery. "So how do you figure to annoy our friends? Misleading them is one thing, but we can only do that for so long."

"I got it fig'red," Gideon answered vaguely.

"And?"

"An' what?"

"This is my fight, Gideon Fletcher. You are not leaving

me out."

Makes sense.

But—

Would you stand for nobody a-boxin' you out?
Blast!

It was almighty hard to stand against yourself when you knew you were right.

"I can't brew a cup-a tea without bein' watched," Gideon relented. "An' them egg men a-yourn are a-watchin' us both. What we need is someone who can get 'round."

Peter parked the wheelbarrow and hung the fork on the wall. "Like who?"

"Miss Isi, over to the saloon."

"You mean. . . a . . . a. . ."

"A saloon girl," Gideon supplied comfortably.

"Why her?" Peter said, uncomfortably.

"Watch your mouth or I'll split your lip."

"Simmer down. I didn't mean anything. Only. . ."

"Don't tell me ya ain't never talked to a saloon girl?"

"You kidding? My pa would have skinned me alive."

"Miss Isi's right nice," Gideon replied, his tone edged with warning.

"I said I didn't mean anything." Peter led them to a bench by the corral. "How can she help?"

Gideon chewed on his response whilst the warm sun danced between big, fluffy white clouds.

"Ya ever stoled nothin?" he asked.

"What?!"

"Shhh! Somebody's been a-nickin' stuff 'round town—"

"What kind of stuff?"

Gideon had made a better friend in Billy than he realized. It seemed Reed had lost a few spendy items and naturally shoved the whole thing, blame and all, onto Gideon. This was no surprise, only it never happened. Once again, Gideon hadn't done it.

A certain train of logic suggested, if Gideon were going to be blamed for things he had never done, he might as well fill the void and commit the crime. The whole thing did sort of stand there in wide open invitation.

"Reed's got his nose out-a joint," Gideon explained, "an' we're gonna see it gets pinned on them friends-a yourn."

"On them?"

"Why not? They ain't no roses." Why was Peter hesitating? He should have been thrilled to get a little of his own back. "You want out?"

"You ask me that one more time," Peter warned, "and I will split your lip."

"That's plain 'nough," Gideon accepted evenly. "Think ya can?"

"What?"

"Pinch stuff."

Peter fidgeted, avoiding Gideon's eye. "Like what?"

"Nothin' folks ain't gonna get back," Gideon assured him. "A few things here an' there's all. Give 'em to Miss Isi, she'll see they get put to good use."

"How do you know she'll have the chance?"

"See'd our egg men in town today."

"That doesn't mean they'll go near her."

"You haven't seen Miss Isi."

Peter had nothing to say to that.

"You know whereall they're holed up?" Gideon asked, after the barest of sniggers.

"I think I could find it," Peter supposed.

"Good. Then tonight we go a-visitin'."

"Guess that means I'll have to bust you out again."

"If'n ya please."

"You going to pass out this time?" Peter prodded.

"Weren't fig'rin' on it. You gonna get all jitt'ry?"

"Wasn't figuring on it."

"There's Doc," Gideon said, standing up. "Don't get caught. An' don't come too early."

"I won't," Peter promised. "Hey, Gov?"

Gideon turned to face his partner in marginally illicit activities.

"Where's your kinfolk?" asked Peter.

"Where's yours?" Gideon countered, and went to meet Connell.

S HERIFF?"

"HeyMathersjustusingthebackdoormuchobliged."

Gandy had been spotted, but that did not mean he had lost, not yet. He cleared the backdoor of the café, ducked through an alley, shimmied around to Silas Cooper's office and slipped inside.

"Sheriff?" the schoolmaster greeted inquisitively.

"Uh, sorry, Mr. Cooper." Gandy tiptoed between several perplexed school children staring up at him from their places on the floor. "I'll just be going, thanks."

Out the front he went, cut left, and took a sharp sidestep into the barbershop where he spied a table piled high with Gus's blankets, ends and edges trailing to the floor. Ignoring the barber, Gandy dove under the table and tugged the bedclothes into a more helpful disarray.

"Gus?" A pin striped man poked head and shoulders into the shop, "Did the sheriff come in here?"

Gus blinked, closed his mouth and forced himself to quit ogling at his laundry pile. "Had his trim last week."

"I don't mean for a haircut," the suit complained.

Gus paused his sweeping to look squarely at the chairman of the town council. "Why else would he come in here?"

"Because he's avoiding me again."

Gus thought maybe the councilman would do well to think about that for a minute, but did not venture so far as to suggest it.

"It's hard to imagine why an intelligent man would come running in here just to play hide-and-seek with you, Barker. Where would he hide?" Gus spread his arms wide to include the entire bare shop. "Under my laundry? That would take a very desperate man, let me tell you."

"Alright," Chairman Barker bristled, "but if you do see him, you tell him I want to see him."

"Will do."

Gus worked his broom around one chair and another, into the corners and back out. Then he brushed the collection of dust and debris outside and clear off the boardwalk. He waved to the hotel manager across the street, looked both ways and went back inside.

"Coast is clear. You can come out now," he told the linen pile, and Caswell Crossing's most respected and successful lawman crawled into the open. "You mind telling me what an intelligent man is doing under my laundry?"

"Taking desperate measures," Gandy replied, pulling in a deep breath of fresh air.

"You're going to have to face them you know."

"You wouldn't say that if you'd ever been to a council meeting, Gus. The last one took so long, my prisoner died of old age. I'm giving serious consideration to arresting the whole lot of them for Interfering With An Officer In The Execution Of His Duty. They know what I do, for pity's sake. And I know what they do. Why hold a meeting when we could all being **doing** what we do instead?"

"You know what Barker would say to that," Gus suggested.

"Ever been part of a siege, Gus? The key thing is who

can hold out the longest." Gandy stood up and brushed himself off. "Speaking of siege, keep on eye an Mary's place will you? Someone made off with her petty cash."

"She alright?"

Gandy grunted bemusedly at the memory of Mary's statement. "Fit to be tied and ready to stomp the life out of them."

"Them?" Gus echoed. "So it's a gang?"

Now why had Gandy said that? There was nothing to point to more than one thief. Three different incidents. Might be only one person.

"Could be," he said, and left it at that.

"Well, I'll keep an eye out, Sheriff. I surely will. Mary's a nice gal, and the way she works, she shouldn't have to put up with something like that."

"Thank you, Gus." Gandy nodded towards the laundry. "And you might want to get that over to her."

"It suited you well enough a minute ago."

"A minute longer and I might have expired."

"I'd have taken real good care of you: a new box and everything so you'd go to your rest with the sweet perfume of fresh cut pinewood."

"That gives a man comfort," Gandy drawled, as he left. "It surely does."

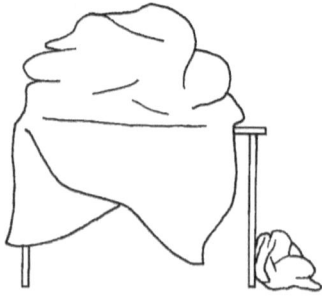

CHAPTER 8
Framed
Making Camp
Identification
Old Men & A Full House
All But One

I'M telling you, this whole thing is a set up," Pultrie insisted, as if the small time sheriff hassling them would understand better by dint of repetition.

Maybe one of those girls in the saloon had done it, maybe all of them. Maybe it had been Wilcox; he was certainly stupid enough to ruin everything for the sake of a few bobbles. If Pultrie hadn't been undergoing a financial inconvenience when that old lady had approached him. . . even so, no one should have to put up with this. The miles, the conditions, the company, and now this.

"Boots," said Gandy.

"What?"

"Take them off."

"We've been framed," Pultrie repeated, his tone shifting to one dealing— not with someone a touch slow— but someone who in fact had a great deal in common with a rather large pile of bricks.

"Being framed is better than being shot," Gandy pointed out reasonably. "'Course, you want to press the issue, we do have a doctor in town."

Gandy's prisoner turned out to be one of the quicker learners. He took off his boots. The other man, the oddly shaped one, complied without any suggestion of doing otherwise. Why anyone who looked like him would ever conceive of going into outlawry was beyond Gandy. He could have been identified twenty miles away by a blind man with his back turned.

The voices in the back of Gandy's head had already raised their red flags in regards to the talkative one. His western clothes fit, yet suggested he did not belong in them. His eastern voice was civil, for a man being arrested, yet suggested it was poorly accustomed to the habit. His words claimed innocence, yet this twanged right up against good common sense.

"Through there, back cell," Gandy directed. He locked the two men up and stepped back. "Now you can have your say and you can start with your names."

"Harry Wilson," the fat one piped up.

"Sam Bennet," said the other.

Gandy waited. Neither prisoner expounded further. Obviously this was not their first go round. Gandy hooked his thumbs into his gun belt and tisked.

"Yeah, see, I meant your real names. No? Well, you think on it a might. I'm sure it'll come to you. Meantime, I'll go let Mathers know there will be two for breakfast."

G IDEON separated from the shadows and crossed the street with a measured lack of hurry. Walk like you didn't care who saw you, and no one would; run, and every living soul would want to know why.

"They in jail?" he whispered, upon reaching Peter.

"Would I be here otherwise?" Peter replied, pulling his foot out of the stirrup.

"Froggy— that there's a sign-a bein' jitt'ry."

"You figuring to stand there insulting me all night or get up on this horse?"

Gideon's satisfaction would have been no more visible by day than it was by night. He led Peter's horse to a stump where he could more easily climb up. It was an admission of weakness, but trying it any other way would have been a bigger one.

"How'd you get out?" Peter asked, when they were well clear of the town.

"I'm a mite lighter on my feet than I were."

"Good. Maybe I won't have to carry you back."

"Ya din't last time."

"Near enough."

"Near ain't so."

They went around a low hanging branch and ducked under another. The sack Gideon had looped over the pommel of the saddle bumped against Peter's leg. Knowing Gideon, it could contain almost anything.

"What's in the sack?" he asked, to save himself guessing.

"Provisions."

"Where'd you get them?"

"Rivers."

"Thought you weren't a thief?" Peter pressed.

"I'm owed."

They were crossing a shallow rivulet of water, a tributary to the Black, and Gideon wrapped his arm around Peter as the horse nimbly levered himself up the far bank.

"Owed?" Peter picked up where they had left off.

"Why din't ya bring two horses?" Gideon asked, mostly because he wasn't going to answer.

"I only own one."

"Aspen's bay is stabled down there, ain't it?"

"Yeah."

"Well?" Gideon said, his meaning clear.

"Are you trying to get me killed?" Peter balked.

"Aw, Aspen ain't so much. We could've had that critter brushed an' lullabied, an' 'im never knowin' nothin'."

"You may not care what happens to your hide," Peter

replied, "but I like mine intact, thanks all the same."

"That's 'cause you're a—"

"You want to walk?"

Gideon chuckled and shut up.

When they reached the camp of their eastern friends, the boys drew up and gawked. Even by moonlight it clearly wasn't the work of any self-respecting westerner. No wood had been gathered for their next fire and the ashes from the last indicated a blaze larger than necessary. A clutter of dirty iron pots slouched in a disreputable pile. The bedrolls were crumpled heaps. Everywhere lay signs of waste, ignorance or flat out laziness which, out here, all amounted to the same thing— a short life span.

"It's a wonder a bear hasn't strolled through here with all this food around," Peter marveled.

"That there's a right fine idea," Gideon said, sliding down. "Glad to see you're a-gettin' into the spirit-a this."

"How on earth are you going to get a bear here?"

Gideon's eyes glittered brighter than the stars above and somehow Peter just knew he would do it. Influence Gideon? How did you influence anyone who could sweet talk a bear? And why would you even try when he was doing it for your sake?

"Forget I asked," Peter gave in. "Just don't get yourself killed."

"Why, I din't knowed ya felt that-a way," Gideon said, all honey-toned, as he unhooked the flour sack.

"What I don't feel like is explaining to Aspen why you're bear bait," Peter countered, rummaging through a pair of saddlebags left by one of the lean-tos.

"I telled ya, he ain't so much. Here," Gideon tossed over a small glass bottle. "Careful, get that stuff on ya an' ya ain't never gonna 'splain the stink off."

"Whew!" Peter whistled, popping the cork. "You aren't

kidding."

He leaned as far away as possible and sprinkled the noxious liquid over various bits of the camp. Then he tossed the bottle back to Gideon and returned his attention to the saddlebags– the contents of which he scattered hither, yon, and long far gone.

"Didn't figure he had one of these," Peter remarked, launching Pultrie's razor into the night. "Where are you going?"

"Hunting," Gideon answered, slinging the flour sack over his shoulder.

"I'll come along."

"You'll stay here."

"Gideon—"

"We ain't got us a heap-a time, an' looks to me like you got the idea here right good. I ain't a-goin' long nor far, so you ain't gonna have to 'splain nothin' to nobody."

Peter doubted that. The longer he knew Gideon the more he got the feeling he would have to explain a great deal. Probably quite fast.

Gideon jogged out of sight and Peter told himself, someday, he would win an argument with that boy. Meanwhile, he went back to wrecking the dismal attempt at a camp. It was, he had to admit, a good piece of fun turning the tables on Pultrie and Wilcox.

By the time Gideon returned, the place looked like it had been hit by a rather creative tornado.

He gave a low whistle of appreciation. "Son! You done you a job!"

Peter pointed to the squirming flour sack in Gideon's hand. "What's in there?"

"Misery," Gideon answered, and gave Peter a peek at the crawlies and slimies he had rustled up. "Help me tuck 'em 'round the place."

"I'll pass, thanks all the same."

"Nancy."

"So you do want to walk back to town?"

"Were kind-a fig'rin' to leave a mite quicker'n that."

"Why?" Peter said, suspicion rising.

"'Cause I ain't a-hankerin' to be on no first name basis with no bear."

Peter changed his mind and with due industry they bedded down the crawlies, all nice and tucked in so they wouldn't wonder off and get lost before delivering their welcome. Leaving the disaster behind them, they rode out.

No one spoke for a while. An owl hooted and a distant howl lost itself in the folds of the mountains. The susurration of pine trees ebbed and flowed with the breeze like seaweed in a gentle tide. The night air smelled faintly of good red dust and strongly of wide open country.

It had been a long time since Gideon had ridden across open ground. It had been a long time since he had ridden anywhere, and it was likely to be a long time yet. Sending his horse back to the Rolling Rivers had been a dirty trick. What could Gideon do but walk right onto the Rivers' home range? Thing was, if he tried it, he was not likely to get back out. It was an interesting life, not being a prisoner.

How many folks d'ya fig'r'd like to hunt us down an' string us up?

Includin' the townsfolk? Plen'y.

They ain't got 'em no reason.

Reason ain't got nothin' to do with nothin'.

And that was true, at least as far as people were concerned.

"About the bear?" Peter interrupted Gideon's thoughts. "Were you serious?"

"Yep."

"Kind of makes me glad you're on my side."

Gideon filed the compliment, or possibly aspersion, he wasn't really sure which but either way it would do. His thoughts slipped back to his own affairs and how to sort them out. Skipping town right then and there looked mighty inviting. Only he couldn't. Peter had saved his life, the least he could do was stick around long enough to give the kid a hand.

The creek splashed and gurgled below their feet and, though it wasn't loud, for the moment it was the only sound in the world.

"You like provoking him, don't you?" Peter asked.

The question, careening in from out of the blue, knocked Gideon out of his solitude.

"Who?"

"Who do you think?" said Peter. "Aspen."

"Ain't me as starts nothin'."

"Uh-huh."

Gideon peered around at Peter. "What?"

"Never mind. You wouldn't understand."

"Why? 'Cause I'm il-lit-rit?"

"You know a G, don't you? You know a G, you aren't illiterate."

"I ain't?"

"Not so much as you were. 'Course, there's more to it, but that's a start."

It was getting late, or rather it had been late and was now reaching the part of late that somehow became something closer to early. Some people could measure the stars or the sun and declare it some specific hour of the clock. Gideon had always felt that a bit silly. Did it matter if it was two-thirty or three-thirty? Dark was dark and would remain so until dawn, no matter what o'clock fancy men wanted to hang on it. Provided they made it back closer to dark than dawn, they'd be fine.

"Hey, Peter?"

"Yeah?"

"Can you tell time?"

"Sure. Why?"

"Must be a gen'l'mun thing," Gideon answered, without answering, and then the rigid outlines that were Caswell Crossing came into view. He fished a square nail out of his pocket, the sort one might use to seal a window, and handed it up to Peter. "Here. You're gonna need this."

ASPEN wondered what the sheriff could want. The answer had been simple once. With Gov around, the possible answers had become numerous, complex and always just a little unpredictable. When it came to calamity, Gov had Ember beat by a long country mile.

"Where's your shadow?" Gandy asked.

He leaned back in his chair, feet propped on his scratched up desk. Since Wilson occupied the only other chair, Aspen helped himself to a corner of the desk.

"Left him at Connell's," he replied, not quite innocently, "with Aunt Eddie."

The two lawmen winced.

"Gov has some chance," Aspen supposed wryly. "After all, he was asleep when I left."

"Heaven help him if he wakes up," said Wilson; he had seen Eddie in full swing, fortunately never at him.

"It was her idea," Aspen replied.

"I bet it was," Gandy allowed, and whether his tone was meant as admiration for Eddie or last thoughts for Gideon, only he could tell.

"One of them will survive it," Aspen said, with the tiniest hint of humor playing at his eyes. "So what can I do for you, Luke?"

"Have you heard the rumors?"

"About the thefts? Who hasn't?"

"Have you heard all the rumors?" Wilson nudged.

"I'm beginning to," Aspen acknowledged. "Reed and I had a word about it."

"Well, I locked up a couple of gentlemen last night," Gandy explained. "Seems they had a few things in their possession that did not exactly belong to them. Naturally, they swear up and down the girls framed them. Anyway, I've been asking folks to stop by and claim their property."

"Thank you, Luke, but I haven't lost anything."

"All the same, I have a few items no one has picked up yet. Maybe you can help me identify them."

Wilson silently asked his boss a question.

"Something else you might could do for us," Wilson said, when he got the nod. "Those men in the cells could use identifying too."

"You don't know them?" Aspen asked.

Wilson and Gandy knew every face in town. A few prospecting camps had begun to spring up, though, with populations that were more transitory and less salubrious. And less well known.

"I saw them the other day," Gandy replied, "but they weren't causing any trouble. Go have yourself a look."

Aspen obliged and returned within seconds.

"Who are they?" Gandy asked, as soon as the door to the lockup had been closed against eavesdroppers.

"I don't know. Not to name," Aspen added at their obvious disbelief. "I saw them in town recently. I wouldn't have taken any notice, except Peter seemed thoroughly distracted by them."

"Have you seen them since?"

"No, but I think Gov did. He saw something that made him think of Humpty Dumpty. Your round fellow in there sure fits the bill."

"Did you ask him about it?"

"You know Gov. He brushed it off, said it was something Peter had told him."

"You know," Wilson mused, twirling his hat by its brim, "I had Peter in here during that thunderstorm. He was about as jumpy as a cricket on a hot skillet."

The three men regarded each other and each knew what the others were thinking because they were thinking it themselves.

"Well, Boss?"

"Worth checking out," Gandy replied, in the sort of tone that suggested half the story had just slotted itself into place and the other half was not far behind.

T HEY say women are the worst gossipers, but this is not altogether accurate. Or, from another point of view, it is entirely accurate. Old men. If one wanted to hear every bit, parcel and grain of who'd done what, when and with whom, a knowing individual listened to old men. They sat on their porches or gathered in dry goods stores swapping whoppers and yammering the day away. The difference between them and women was that women used more words. Thus it seemed, to the untrained ear, women in fact said more.

Now, the argument as to which gender was the better sort for the surreptitious gleaner of information balanced greatly upon the nature of the information sought. Men were unlikely to discuss the latest fashions in silk frills—unless it was to comment upon how sufficiently complimenting said frills had steered them clear of the dog house. Women were unlikely to brag about the latest features on, say, a newly purchased Colt revolver. Both genders would discuss politics, social equality and flat out everybody else's business without reserve.

At the last shack masquerading implausibly as civilization, Matt had gone for a shave and a haircut. Presumably this was because he was beginning to look like a riverboat gambler, and in his profession it did not pay to look like what you were. In truth, what did not pay was asking questions when listening would suffice. For what he wanted to know, and given his current persona, he had opted for the barber shop.

"Ain't seen you around," said the barber. "What's your name, friend?"

Matt eased into the barber's chair and hooked a boot heel on the foot rest.

"Buford McBee." At least for now, tomorrow was a different matter. "Feel free to laugh. I'm sure my folks did."

"You kidding? William Cutter. The barber. And I'm practically bald. Shave or a cut?"

"Both."

The barber shook out an apron. Throughout the lathering, brushing and trimming, dark hair fell in snippets and talk fell around the room. Without their realizing it, supposedly-Buford-McBee had given the local bench polishers a gentle nudge, a sort of bottom deal to the gossip, and walked away with a full house.

"Him and his four boys," someone had remarked.

"It's five now. Seems Rivers took in some stray."

"Where'd you hear that?"

"Over to Littleton, couple three months back," the young man said, rocking on the back legs of his chair.

"Who was it?"

"Some maverick kid. Rustler, way I hear it."

That had been a week ago. Matt had covered a lot of ground since then.

W HEN did you first notice it missing?"

"Four days ago, Sheriff. And if my wife had known what I was looking for, I would have been a dead man. You wouldn't know much about wives, Sheriff. Let me give you some advice– keep it that way."

"Thank you, Haverston," Gandy replied, "I intend to. Wilson, you miserable cheat, get behind the line."

Wilson knew his boss could not have seen a thing with his back turned. All the same, he sheepishly scootched back to the legal throw line before tossing his next dart.

Gandy figured his deputy should know better, after all this time, than to try pulling something like that. He took the logbook from its shelf and laid it out on the desk.

"Last one am I?" J.E. Haverston said, dipping pen to ink and adding his name to the list of people who had reclaimed their property. "Lucky for us, you caught the thieves before they had time to sell anything."

"Nine times out of ten 'smart' and 'criminal' just don't hitch up. Isn't that right, Wilson?"

"Yes, sir," Wilson agreed cheerfully, redrawing the mark he had erased from Gandy's side of the tally board.

Trepidatiously, Haverston picked up his silver snuffbox and opened the lid. Everything was there: the snippet of his wife's veil, a bit of his necktie, a dried purple petal, two paper hearts folded together, the coin with its date, and a little roll of paper with the word's 'let no man put asunder' written in the preacher's curly handwriting.

"Thanks again, Sheriff," Haverston said, embarrassed to realize he had been standing there fawning over so personal an item in front of an audience.

Gandy politely refrained from commenting. "Be sure to give your wife my regards."

"Will do," Haverston replied, and took himself home enveloped in a cloud of relief.

Gandy picked up the logbook and blew on the fresh ink. Above Haverston's name ran a list of claimed items, their descriptions and the date they'd gone missing.

The sheriff handed the logbook to his deputy. It didn't take Wilson any time at all to see what his boss had already seen. All the items had been taken within the last two days, had been reasonably identifiable and basically insignificant— all but one.

CHAPTER 9
Driscoll's Rights
Reconnaissance
A Long Walk
Night Cap
Bunkmates
Only One Key
Tense Past
Wound Up

M RS. DRISCOLL stared daggers at the two men entering the livery. No matter that Deputy Wilson accompanied them every step of the way. Oh, no. That did not matter one bit. She stomped over to the jailhouse and glared at Sheriff Gandy.

"How can you let those two go?"

From up on the porch, Gandy looked down on Mrs. Driscoll, which was no inconvenience.

"Because that's what we do with innocent people," he replied simply.

"And exactly how do you know they're innocent?"

"'Fraid that's confidential, ma'am."

"If you insist," the nosy woman huffed, "I shall have no choice but to inform the ladies of this deplorable dereliction of duty."

Caswell Crossing hosted a budding woman's group, which boasted far more ambition than members. Fortunately, most of them were notably more friendly than the dear Mrs. Driscoll.

"Why not?" Gandy replied, giving his back thoughts free rein. "You tell them everything else."

Mrs. Driscoll's overall social temperature plummeted several degrees. "If you let men like that get away with this sort of thing, it will only get worse. Mark my words."

"Mrs. Driscoll, you've been throwing your words all over town trying to convince anyone who'd listen that Gideon Fletcher is the thief. Now you want me to keep these two locked up instead. Which is it?"

Mrs. Driscoll squared her narrow shoulders and lifted her chiseled chin. "Those two men being thieves doesn't cure that boy of his ills. I've said all along no good would come of it."

"Well, ma'am, I'll have to thank you to stop saying anything about this or Mr. Fletcher."

"I beg your pardon?" Mrs. Driscoll bristled.

"Because," Gandy continued smoothly, "if you persist with your hateful talk, you will leave me no choice, ma'am."

Driscoll's lips formed a tight, thin line. "Are you threatening me?"

"Informing you of your rights," Gandy corrected. "Maybe you weren't aware, but you do have the right to remain silent."

H OW did Peter react?"

Wilson tugged a kerchief from his pocket and soaked it in the water trough. No way around it, summer had decided to hold on with determination. Peter, as it turned out, had also been determined.

"Right normal," Wilson informed his boss. "The kind of normal folks act when they want you to think everything is nothing but fine."

People could get funny when they tried not to attract suspicion. They tended to give a shrill, off-pitch feeling where one expected easy harmony. Anyone acting innocent around Gandy was bound to attract his attention.

"How about our two friends?" he asked.

"Like men paid to act normal," Wilson said, running

the kerchief over his face.

"Mark's onboard?"

"Yes, sir. He's right behind them."

There might have been one or two men taller than Mark Spencer, and one or two broader, but no one could compare on both fronts at once. Bluntly, Mark Spencer was a marvel of human biology. He was also light on his feet, good with a trail, and steady under fire. A rancher by trade, he kept life interesting by working part-time as a deputy.

"Well, guess I'd better go buy some of those disgusting candies he likes," said Gandy.

Wilson moseyed along beside his boss. "What would you do if Mark ever decided to hold out for a real bribe?"

"Fire you so I could afford him."

LIFE had happened to Harvey Wilcox. He had no idea what to do about this. Normally, he did everything possible to avoid such an eventuality and therefore possessed limited coping skills. He stood. He stared.

"Move, will you?"

Harvey ogled at Pultrie. Move? Where? Everything lay in complete, irreversible disarray. Wasn't that his last pair of drawers in that pine tree? And over there was definitely his shirt, or one sleeve of it anyway. Looked like Harvey was wearing his last shirt now. And his last socks. And, apparently, he no longer owned a coat. It seemed he'd also burnt their last meal, because something had carried off the food. That was something for his partner to be glad about at any rate.

"Hey! Let's go!" Pultrie snapped, throwing a stone at Harvey along with his abuse.

"What for?"

"Because I'd like to have a place to sleep tonight."

"You can't mean here?"

"Where else would I mean?"

Harvey re-examined the wreckage spread around him. No way. No possible way could it ever be restored to anything close to an inhabitable camp. What kind of word was that anyway? Camp. He did not 'camp'. Camping was what boys did on jolly holidays. Harvey had never camped, nor was he amused at having been forced to do so now.

"We'll never fix this," he declared.

"We could if you'd move," Pultrie growled.

The path of least resistance. Harvey thought about this and, submitting the present situation for evaluation, he could feel the ground shifting. All the same, he righted a pan and picked up the only surviving utensil. It was a fork. Half the tines were bent clean over.

"This is pointless," Harvey complained, picking up the coffeepot. He jumped back with a yelp, giving Pultrie an excuse to enjoy a bitter laugh, as one more reason he did not camp slithered near his feet.

"It isn't poisonous," Pultrie judged from a safe distance, all condescending.

"How do you know?"

"You're right. Why don't you move, we'll find out."

Harvey did not move. He stayed very still indeed until the last reptilian coil left him behind. Then he scurried to the other side of the camp.

"Wilcox, you're such a– ahhh!" Pultrie yanked his hand away from the scorpion he had nearly grabbed.

"What's that?" Harvey inquired pointedly.

"Shut up," Pultrie growled.

"Why don't we just go back to town?"

"We're supposed to be quiet, not advertise ourselves to everyone in sight."

"You have a better idea?" Harvey demanded, already

convinced there was no more perfect idea.

"Yeah, we stay here."

"With one blanket, no food and no shelter?"

"That old woman sent us to do a job," Pultrie said, stomping within inches of Harvey. "I don't know about you, but I need that money and I'm not going to lose a single penny of it because of you. We're staying here."

Pultrie pointed to the ground in emphasis and something in the dirt drew his attention.

"What. . . is. . . that?" he asked, the question finally finding an escape route.

"A footprint," Harvey offered acerbically. "They're all over, if you had bothered to notice."

"You're right. We should stay in town."

Harvey did not argue. When a man saw sense, that was no time to distract him. They mounted up and headed back to town, leaving the bear tracks behind them.

Less than a mile later, Nick Pultrie looked up at the world from the flat of his back. This vexed him considerably as it was an unfamiliar perspective. Holding his aching head, he kicked angrily at the saddle tangled around his legs, righted himself, and struck a match. The billet had torn loose from his saddle.

"Someone cut this."

"You're paranoid," Harvey argued. "The stitching probably wore out. If you wanted good equipment you shouldn't have stolen from a tramp."

"It's called gear."

Way Harvey saw it, it was called rubbish.

Pultrie considered the miles to town and decided it made for a long walk. He braced his hands to vault onto his horse— and the animal obligingly shifted, dumping Pultrie on his backside. After expressing his feelings on this in fairly clear terms, Pultrie tried again. And got dumped again. That was enough and more. Nobody, but nobody, put Nick Pultrie in the dirt. He went for his gun—

"Leave it," Harvey interrupted.

Pultrie stood there, feeling the weight of the gun in his hand, then rammed it back under his coat. Explaining a dead horse was not conducive to getting the job done quietly. He grabbed the ornery creature by the reins and rigged up the saddle so he at least didn't have to carry it.

"Get your foot out of the stirrup," Pultrie ordered, giving Harvey's ankle a smack.

"What for?"

"You think I'm walking all the way to town?"

Less amused than he had been five minutes ago, Harvey grudgingly allowed his partner to climb up behind.

"You really think there's a bear around here?" he asked after a while.

"Of course not," Pultrie answered, voice thick with sarcasm. "Those were squirrel tracks running straight through our camp."

A trapper snored softly in one corner. Gandy had seen him numerous times and, though gruff and burly, the man never caused any trouble. A couple of working girls, with nothing better to do, shared a table near the back of the dimly lit saloon. Behind the bar, the owner stood engrossed in a game of solitaire. Up by the door, a rowdy handful of boys were trying to decide if they were playing poker or fixing to disturb the peace.

Gandy walked over and planted a hand firmly upon the shoulder of a young man about to make up his mind.

"Evening, gentlemen," he greeted, with a politeness that announced itself as a clear warning. "Glad to see you're enjoying yourselves."

One of the other card players started to rise, but a somewhat smarter boy grabbed him by the arm.

"There's nothing like a nice, quiet game of cards amongst friends, is there?" Gandy continued in the same sweet, hard-to-swallow tone.

A half-hearted chorus mumbled a ragged 'yes, sir'.

"Glad to hear it," Gandy said, releasing his aquiline grip.

He moved to the bar, where a large mirror allowed him an unhindered view of everyone at the table.

"Evenin', Sheriff," the owner said, his hand coming back above the counter. "On or off?"

"On. Red ten."

The barman glanced at his game of solitaire, moved the indicated card and popped a top on a sarsaparilla. He always kept a crate on hand, as Gandy never drank alcohol on duty and did not permit his deputies to do so either.

One of the girls swished up beside the lawman and pressed her slender back against the bar. She was not so close as to brush against him, but he could smell the delicate fragrance of lemon verbena perfume. The girl really was a beauty. What a shame her life had come to this, because she would have made some man a fine wife.

"Evening, Miss Isi. I was hoping to talk to you."

"Something in particular you're hoping to hear, Sheriff?" she asked, batting her lashes.

Gandy sipped his drink, unbothered. If Isi wanted to make a show of flirting, rather than let folks think she was talking to the law, he wouldn't ruin it for her.

"Tell me about the two men I arrested," he prompted.

"What more can I say?"

"Maybe nothing. Maybe something."

Isi was not going to cooperate, but she could afford to be friendly about it. It was silly, but she liked the way

Gandy nodded at her when he said hello. She sidled closer.

"Like I told you, I hadn't seen them before, but they just didn't feel right. You know?"

Gandy peeked at the poker players in the mirror. He did know.

"A girl gets to where she can read a man," Isi continued, "and those two weren't worth the dime."

"Did they say anything?"

"I'm sorry, Sheriff. Wish I could tell you more."

"Why were they here?"

The same reason most men ended up there or any place like it: a pretty girl stands just so, there's drinks, and music, things are happening, and no one asks too many questions. In this case, the pretty girl had been Isi and there were turning out to be a few questions after all.

"One of them said business," Isi answered, stealing a sip from Gandy's sarsaparilla. "But. . ."

"Yes?"

"Well, it sounded like they didn't expect it to take long, like it was something small, then they'd go back east."

"Did they say where exactly?" Gandy asked.

"No, not that I recall."

The same rowdy young man was growing loud again. Sometimes when a fellow took a certain path so far there was no coming back. This one had done just that and was dead set on butting heads with somebody. The others tried to hush him, which only succeeded in making their intoxicated friend even edgier.

This was not the first time Gandy had run into this group. They fancied themselves prospectors but, as far as Gandy could see, they preferred a night in town to a day of work. An ounce of prevention might just save him a pound of headache later on.

"Thank you, Miss Isi. If you'll excuse me?"

Isi couldn't help wondering what Gideon had become mixed up in and why the sheriff was so interested. Suppose Gideon was in over his head? Just in case, there was a little something she could do.

"Sheriff? I heard you let them go."

Gandy paused, half turned. "Is that a problem?"

"None of my concern," Isi said, but the real answer lay in her painted face.

Now what—

A raised voice pulled Gandy back to the poker table. It was brewing for a dust up and the loud mouth was itching for his gun. Gandy arrived behind him before the barrel cleared the holster.

"I wouldn't," he warned.

The words may have been easy, but they were loaded with confidence and, more importantly, the gun Gandy held was loaded with bullets.

The boy stood there, stuck halfway between trying it and giving up. His friends sat frozen, waiting. They all looked able, but facing an armed man who indisputably had the drop on you sort of has a dampening effect on a fellow's willingness. Unless, of course, he's too drunk to have the sense of a common rock.

The fingers of the loudmouth twitched near the butt of his revolver and, in a move he probably thought fast, the boy went for it. Gandy upped with the butt of his own gun and the drunk dropped, out cold.

"That goes for you too, son," Gandy said, gun leveled. He snapped his fingers and the second boy very carefully handed over his gun. "Now, pick him up. Come on, he's your friend. Pick him up."

The boy complied and Gandy made it clear to the others staying right where they were would be an excellent idea. He informed the barman he'd be back for the rest of his sarsaparilla, and ushered his two guests out the door.

Hank pulled a shotgun from under the bar, set it in plain view, and turned over an ace.

A hand tapped Gideon on the arm. Purely for fun, he ignored it.

"C'mon, shove over," Aspen whispered. "Giving Peter my bed was your idea."

"You done went 'long with it," Gideon replied, pulling the bedclothes closer about himself to emphasize the point.

"I'm bigger than you."

"Losin' man's last stand. S'pose you'll want some-a the blanket too?"

"If it's not putting you out any," Aspen parried.

"An' if'n it is?" Gideon said, already budging up to make room on the narrow bed.

"Sleep on the floor."

"Poor, frail me?"

"Poor you? Hah," Aspen tugged at his boots. "If you're breathing, boy, you're kicking."

"I oughtta kick you on the floor."

"You're welcome to try."

Gideon tucked the extra pillow up against his own. "Peter asleep?"

He had all but nodded off in his chair after supper and Gideon had persuaded Aspen to persuade Peter he should stay. Thing was, he had a feeling Pultrie and Wilcox were entirely too soft to stay out with their camp turned upside down. There was no sense leaving Peter alone in the hotel because, odds were, he would not be alone.

"Spark out," Aspen answered, settling under the covers. "You like him?"

"Peter? He's alright," Gideon supposed, "for a kid."

"You're one to talk."

"I ain't been no kid in a coon's age."

Aspen pried the spare pillow free, tucked an arm behind his head and stared at the barely discernible ceiling.

"Hey, Gov?"

"Hmm?"

"When were you?"

"What?"

"A kid."

"'Bout ten, twelve year ago. Summer I think. It were a good day," Gideon pushed at Aspen's feet. "You're on my side."

"There's more of me, I get more side," Aspen explained, reasserting his proprietary rights.

"D'ya know you're a pain?"

"You're the first to mention."

"Liar. I oughtta tell your aunt."

"Did she say much to you?"

Though Aspen had told himself not to pry, natural curiosity proved a mighty strong corrosive to discretion.

"She done said as I oughtta listen to you more."

"And?" Aspen went ahead and pried when Gideon failed to add more.

"Promised I would."

"Liar."

"Straight up," Gideon professed, turning onto his side. "Telled 'er I'd be happy to 'blige— soon as you start makin' some kind-a sense."

"It's not my fault you don't understand. I keep telling you to start with the little words."

"Go to sleep. Thems little 'nough for ya?"

"Yes, sir," said Aspen equitably.

They lay in the quiet and something rustled softly in the corner. If it was a mouse it had picked the wrong place, coming to Doc's.

Aspen nudged Gov with an elbow. "Did you see how that worked?"

"Go to sleep," Gideon told him.

"You missed it again. You were supposed—"

"Could I pay ya to shutup?"

"Hush."

"It's you been a-jabberin'," Gideon argued.

"We don't say shut up," Aspen clarified.

"Ya don't do it none neither."

"It's 'hush', or 'shoosh'," Aspen continued, "or in your case I suppose 'shove off' might be acceptable."

Gideon turned towards Aspen, disbelief compelling him to ask, "Who in tarnation'd say 'shoosh'?"

"Me, for one."

"Nancy."

"And there's Pa," Aspen added, "of course you don't much care about him. Then there's Fort and, given his size, I'd suggest you care what he thinks."

"Is ya or is ya ain't gonna shutup?"

"Shoosh," Aspen corrected.

"Shove off," Gideon said, rolling back over.

"Yeah, that's close enough."

Gideon groaned. There was no outtalking Aspen. That man had been born with more words than a dictionary and he must have swallowed an entire thesaurus on top of it. There were so many words in Aspen's head, maybe it wasn't his fault they kept spilling out. Gideon fell asleep wondering if a man could drown in words.

Aspen lay awake. Amongst other things, he wondered what Aunt Eddie had really told Gideon. She could certainly hold her own, but so could Gov. Of all the people Aspen had known, only his brother Ember would dig in half so hard. They did it on principle, Aspen figured. Of course, it could have been shear hardheadedness.

Ember had always been that way. From the time he could walk, to tell him there was something he couldn't do was to dare him to do it. It wasn't really about proving you wrong. It was about being stubborn right up to the point where he had no choice but to quit. Fortunately, Ember was getting better about reaching that point less the metaphorical bloody nose.

Had Gov ever seen that day, even once, in his whole life? Not, it seemed, where the men of the Harris ranch were concerned. He had gone after their killers with a passion most men would never possess even if they wrapped up their entire life's quota in one go. They didn't talk about it, but Aspen could spark up a pretty good mental flame without needing to be handed much in the way of kindling. Gideon was dead set on running headlong at whomever remained on his personal list of vengeance— regardless of consequences and headless of caution.

What were he and Peter up to? And what did the men in jail have to do with it? Whatever it was, he'd never hear it from Gideon.

Aspen glanced at the sleeping figure beside him. Gov had saved his life. Lee's too. Returning the favor wasn't merely a matter of keeping Gideon hale and breathing– a challenge in itself– but of altering the overall direction of his life. The real challenge, though, the thing that made the entire notion an uphill battle, was Gideon had no intention of letting Aspen succeed.

"We'll just see about that," Aspen whispered, tucking the blanket over his ward's shoulders.

D O you have any rooms?"
"Do you have any money?"

Pultrie pulled a coin from his pocket and slapped it on the hotel's guest book with a metallic thunk.

"There's two of you ain't there?" the bland little nothing of a clerk yawned.

"That's a silver dollar in front of you."

"There's two of you ain't there?" the clerk repeated, pushing up his wire rimmed spectacles.

Pultrie nearly went over the counter, but Harvey handed over a coin of his own. The clerk reached behind him without even looking and took the only key hanging on the huge, empty peg board. Pultrie snatched it and waited.

"Top of the stairs, turn right," said the clerk, as if there was nothing in the world he cared about less than the two men who had so inconveniently interrupted his year old newspaper.

"What about the other key?"

"Ain't no other key," the skinny clerk said, turning over his paper. A corner sagged and crumbled to dust.

"We paid for both of us," Pultrie grumbled darkly.

"There's two of you ain't there?" the clerk replied, with an indifference utterly bereft of the motivation to be bothered by petty questions.

"We want two rooms," Pultrie insisted.

"Ain't no other key."

"Now look, mister—"

"There ain't no other key," the clerk repeated, in the same bored monotone that threatened to transcend the ages, no matter how many of them one cared to present. "We got one room. You want it, top of the stairs, turn right. You don't, front door, turn left."

Pultrie's hand ached for his knife, but they couldn't afford trouble. Not with a nosey sheriff around who had already made their acquaintance. Once Pultrie finished the job, then he'd see about teaching this clerk some respect.

They found the room, lit a lamp that was all but out of oil, and assessed their situation. To call the accommodations remotely accommodating would have been more than an overstatement– it would have been an out and out lie. A battered trunk stood to one side, a single hook wobbled on the back of the door, and an ancient bed huddled in the corner. There was nothing more.

Pultrie scowled at Harvey. "What do you think you're doing?"

"Going to sleep," said Harvey, as if Pultrie were every bit the idiot he suspected him of being.

"Get up."

Harvey did not get up. He stretched out on the bed with no intention of doing otherwise, not for Pultrie or anyone else. They had hardly ridden a mile when his horse had thrown a shoe and flat refused to carry them any farther. Harvey had never walked so far in his entire life. His legs hurt, his feet hurt, his lungs hurt, and he was not moving from that bed.

Pultrie had walked that far before, but his feet still hurt, his bruised head ached and it was a wonder he hadn't broken his arm. What smarted most was his pride.

He really did not want to spend an entire night sleeping beside the likes of Harvey Wilcox— who didn't have any pride to be injured— but he wanted to sleep on the floor even less. Disgusted, he collapsed on the edge of the bed, levered off his boots and unceremoniously shoved Harvey over.

They lay there, letting lassitude take over.

Thirty-one and a half seconds passed.

"Get off me," Harvey mumbled.

"You get off," Pultrie countered.

Both men turned onto their sides, back to back, and tried to pretend the other did not exist. Unfortunately, neither of them were particularly imaginative.

"I said get off," Pultrie complained, giving Harvey a nasty jab with his elbow.

"I did," Harvey jabbed back.

They stopped. They looked at their respective sides of the bed. They peered at each other. They looked back at the bed. It wasn't them. The bed was slanted, rolling them inexorably into the middle. They sighed in a long suffering way and did their best to keep to their own territory.

"What is that?" Harvey demanded, sniffing the air with a nose that truly wished he wouldn't.

"Something outside," Pultrie guessed, and got up to close the window.

It stuck. Four inches from latching, the frame jammed tight as a cork in a bottle. Pultrie tugged, shoved and went back to bed wishing he could ease the horrible kink in his calf or the burning ache in his feet.

Harvey sniffed again. His nose threatened to go on permanent strike.

"It's you," he accused.

And he was right. Whatever had been on their blankets back at camp had clung to Pultrie's clothes and, in the confines of the room, had grown into a stench.

Again Pultrie got up, stripped off his outer clothing, stashed them as far away as possible, and lay down once more. Whereupon, his stomach growled fiercely.

Harvey did his best to ignore his own hunger. Lunch had been meager and mediocre— that sheriff had no idea how to feed prisoners— and supper had been impossible. He shifted his weight, trying to get comfortable, and heard a curse as Pultrie whacked a toe on the bed frame. Harvey kept his face to the wall and savored the moment.

"Quit hogging the blanket," Pultrie admonished roughly, yanking at the coarse, moth-eaten fabric.

"Hey!" Harvey objected, tugging back.

"I told—"

The bed gave a brief, agonized whine, as any bed would at being forced to host two men of less than delicate physiques who were exhibiting less than delicate natures.

CRRAACK!!!

The wafer thin mattress snapped up, devouring the two men in one enthusiastic gulp.

"OW!! That's my face!"

"Who could tell?! Ow!"

"Well then move!"

"Get off me!"

It was knees and elbows, curses and jabs that continued right through the complicated extrication process. One was up, the other down and the bed seemed to be everywhere in between, dead set on keeping hold of its midnight collation. One thug took a fist to the ribs, the other an elbow to his belly. It was only by mutual, and remarkable, restraint they failed to beat each other blue.

At last, the two men divvied up their paltry resources and retreated to opposite corners of the cramped room. Pultrie claimed the sheet as well as the capricious mattress and Harvey curled up under the blanket. Each continued to give vent to an assortment of mutters that were entirely to loud to bare such a modest label.

"Ewwww!" Harvey squealed.

"Another snake?" Pultrie sneered.

Harvey flapped his blanket frantically to be rid of the unwelcome, skitter-legged trespasser. "Something crawled on me!"

"Oh, go to sleep."

Harvey gave one more furious flap, stared about as if he could see in the dark, and hesitantly put his head down. Bears, snakes, bugs, cold, jail, far too much walking and no supper– it was intolerable. Worst of all, he was still partnered up to Pultrie and no closer to payday.

"Urrg!"

Harvey beamed from ear to ear. "Told you."

"Shut up."

Out in the corridor, the clerk tip-toed down the stairs, a hand over his mouth to muffle his amusement.

Ten minutes later, a large family of bats helped themselves to the open window.

ASPEN jolted awake. He'd no idea when he had fallen asleep, but he knew precisely why he had woken up. Now and again sleep contrived to torture Gideon. This was one of the agains.

"Gov," he whispered. "Gov, wake up."

Gideon's eyes flew open, but the dark, familiar images of the nightmare still claimed his vision. It left him enough sense to reach for a gun, but not enough to remember he didn't have one or on whom he would have been pulling it.

"Look at me," Aspen coaxed.

Gideon started, blinked, and came to himself. He almost wished he hadn't. Nightmare shifted to memory which gave way to the empty, searing ache. If only he had done more. . .

Gideon turned on his side, penned in by his own embarrassment and Aspen's compassion.

"Gov, do you—"

"No."

No, he did not want to talk about it. He did not want to explain what Aspen could not possibly understand. About things that had happened and things that still had to happen. And most especially he did not want to talk about his own unspeakable shortcomings that had cost good men their lives. Some nightmares were a private affair– even if they were born of reality.

Gideon lay very still, one foot in the real world and one still hobbled to the surreal shades that haunted him. They reached for him, taunting, calling. It hardly seemed like much to be grateful for, but at least this time he was not wracked with tremors.

Forcing an unsteady breath, Gideon decided to light the lamp. Yep, there were lucifers right there on the table and he would go right on and light one. He would sit right up and–

Aspen shifted and a moment later a pale wisp of light stung Gideon's eyes. Thoughtfully, Aspen licked his fingers to smother the match, cutting short the sulfuric residue. Even so, Gideon could smell its ghost tainting the air, overlapping the shadows of the dream.

"You know," Aspen said, adjusting his pillow, "if you could read, you could take your mind off it."

"What?!"

Was Aspen really trying to pick a fight? Now? Of all the—

"Pa taught me, he used to read to me all the time."

"You. . . had dreams?" Gideon said, the words coming reluctantly to his tongue, as if neither words nor tongue were entirely his.

"Mm-hm," Aspen answered.

Gideon couldn't ask what came to mind, because doing so would open the door to answering the same question in return and he was not about to.

"My mother died when I was young," Aspen volunteered, letting him off the hook. "I had a pretty hard time of it for a while. That's why I started reading so much, to be somewhere else— anywhere else— because I couldn't stand being where I was."

Lamplight flickered, doing its best to chase away the wraiths of memories. Gideon had about had his fill of that, but there was no stopping it. Chances were, until it was finally done, those shadows would stick right by him like a banshee wailing her warning and grief and flat out no way to sooth her.

Gideon recalled the novel on the nightstand.

G'wan.

He crawled over Aspen to fetch the book. The cover felt smooth and the crisp smell of the pages elbowed in around the sulfur. Gideon shoved it at Aspen, bunched up his pillow and turned away.

Aspen opened the book and began to read.

MARK Spencer rode up to the jailhouse and homed in on the Arbuckle's. The coffeepot practically lived on the woodstove. If he was lucky, this batch had been made by Wilson. He was filling a cup when Gandy came out of the lockup.

"Company, Boss?"

Gandy nodded and helped himself to the coffee. "Couple of those prospector boys, though I suspect the lot of them aren't after color so much as mischief. Speaking of which?"

"Humpty and Dumpty went to their camp, stayed for about ten seconds, and came back here," Mark shrugged the simplicity of the assignment, then cracked a grin. "I'll tell you something else, those boys are being wound up– and a better job has never been done."

"Do you think it's anything serious?" Gandy asked, frowning at the weak coffee in his cup.

Mark wobbled his free hand 'so-so', and refrained from pointing out that the problem was not with the coffee, but his boss's taste buds. The sheriff could do a lot of things well, but judging coffee was not one of them.

"You saw Humpty and Dumpty," Mark replied, "they're serious alright. I'd say whomever wrecked their camp is more interested in baiting than shooting. I can also tell you they have a mighty sharp sense of humor. Our friends were hoorahed all the way back to town– and the culprit was already long gone."

Gandy slanted a glance at his deputy. "Doesn't exactly sound like Peter, does it?"

"Not exactly," Mark agreed.

CHAPTER 10
Uneven Odds
A Little Cooperation
First Things
Sproinng!
Clear Signs
He's Crazy
Nearly There
Stand

SOMETIMES a body has no choice but to walk smack bang into trouble. There are healthier pastimes, and a thinking man would do best to avoid such occasions whenever possible, however, on this particular occasion, sidestepping was not an option.

Nothing anyone would want to call cover grew up near the clapboard house. A fellow could approach from any direction he liked, and he'd still be in the sightline of any son, brother or cousin who took a notion. A large rock caught Matt's attention, and twenty yards later another. It reminded him of a shooting gallery and it was not a comforting realization. Then again, it probably wasn't meant to be.

He loosened his rifle in its scabbard and unlashed his Colt, but kept to the nice sauntering gait of a man in no particular hurry wanting no particular trouble. No voice challenged him, no warning shot rang out. All the same, something suggested caution would be a salubrious idea. It was an instinct Matt had learned to heed, even when he hadn't sufficient evidence to explain it.

A couple of men near the house sawed away at a thick log, apparently still unaware of their approaching visitor. Matt wasn't buying. This must be how a fly felt inching towards a spider's web.

The nearer man sported red hair and broad shoulders that made his darker hued partner seem downright petite. And the way the little one watched, and then conveyed everything he saw to his companion without a word, bespoke a comfortable familiarity between them. Matt's senses gave him another nudge.

Right about the time a body could figure the clomping of horse's feet couldn't possibly go overlooked, that big fellow finally turned around. He wiped his brow and drifted towards a canteen which, coincidently, put him so near his gun belt he might as well have been wearing it. The little one let gravity tip the two-man saw to the ground and eased himself the other way, nearer his own Colt Dragoon.

Matt slouched in the saddle and drew up a good forty or fifty feet off, hands in plain sight. If it came to it, the big one would have to be dealt with first. The other one was younger, not even twenty yet, but the way he rubbed his hand down the side of his trouser leg was telling. The kid would make a grab for it.

"Fine day," Matt opened politely.

"It is," said the redhead. "Come far?"

"A piece. Any Indian trouble?"

It was an expected question.

"Not if you mind your own."

I bet that holds for you too Goliath, thought Matt. The giant's round face suggested a customary friendliness that was, at current, not to be relied upon.

The backdoor of the house swung open and a blond woman, slender and tall, stepped outside. She didn't come crowding up, electing instead to keep her peace on the porch. A fool would think she was holding back, only it wasn't so. That shotgun cradled in her arms was snug as a baby, and she had a clear line of fire.

An armed woman made most men jumpy, since they

could never quite predict what she might do. This one left Matt with no questions at all.

"There a town nearby?" he ventured.

"There's a watering hole that wishes it was, west and lean south," the big one answered. "Caswell Crossing's farther on, but has most things. West and north, up river."

Matt nodded and made an effort not to notice the movement on the roof. It would not do to make the rifleman up there nervous, especially when he could put a bullet right in your ear. Matt had seen men on the dodge holed up with fewer defenses. Thunderation, these people weren't taking chances.

If the aroma coming from the house was any indication, there was one gamble Matt should take.

"Ma'am?" he called out, Sunday friendly and decently humble. "I know I'm a sorry excuse with no right to ask, but I'd be obliged if you could see your way clear to sharing whatever's on the fire. Just smelling it has my stomach asking some mighty hard questions of my throat."

"Won't be ready for a while," the woman of the house spoke up, her voice carrying clearly across the yard.

Leaving was about the last thing Matt wanted to do, considering how far he had come to get there. Then again, there could be room for thought because, in point of fact, challenging these folks just might be the last thing he wanted to do. The thing about gambling, though, it's really about reading people– and there's always more than one way to play your hand.

Most decent folks had a hard time turning a man away without offering him hospitality. Matt had even known a few law dodgers who would gladly steal your horse, but would never refuse a man a meal. He tipped his head politely and turned his horse for the distant town.

"You could help the boys 'til then," the woman called,

the words coming out gruff, like she was an army sergeant chastising a delinquent private.

"Yes, ma'am. I'll do that," Matt agreed.

He hitched his horse outside the picket fence, whilst that woman stayed stock still and put on her porch. And there was no question it was her porch, just none at all.

Unbuckling his gun belt, Matt looped it over the pommel of his saddle. It was a risky move, but then, the way these people were set, they could make a mighty fine window out of him in two seconds flat— whether he held a gun or no. Besides, if he were betting right, it would be safe enough. Of course, if he was wrong, he would be too dead to care. It was a tough sometimes, being a gambler.

I don't like deceiving Aspen," Peter objected.

"You better come 'round to likin' it."

He and Gideon had squirrelled themselves away in the back of Connell's clinic and, under the guise of playing dominoes, they dickered the issue between themselves.

"But—"

"There ain't no 'but'," Gideon interrupted firmly, "You want this done an' over, you got things to do, ya hear me? Aspen ain't gonna just go 'way on a'count-a it bein' convenient for us."

"I know," Peter shot back. "But that doesn't mean we have to be deceitful."

"Mister, you already done crossed that line."

". . . only a mite."

"You're a-drawin' lines 'twixt the same things."

Gideon was right. 'Making distinctions' Peter's father would have called it. A penny or a dollar, if you were in for one you were in for the other.

"Well?" Gideon said, placing a domino.

Well. There it was, one simple word with no simple answer. Peter knew better, the same as he had known better than to go along with the mining boys. Yet he had and now here he was about to go along again– despite his better judgment.

What was he supposed to do? A man in his position couldn't exactly go to the law. And going to a man like Aspen Rivers would be a guaranteed first step on the way to the law. Peter wished he had met the Rivers before all of this happened. Then again, he desperately wished all of this had never happened.

Gideon had no idea how lucky he was. Peter would have given anything to be in his place, to have a man like Aspen on his side. Anyone who let an opportunity like that pass by was dumber than dirt and then some. A set up like that, with the son of one of Caswell Crossing's founding fathers backing your play, likely Gideon could be excused five of the seven deadly sins. Who would say otherwise?

But Peter, what was he supposed to do? He had walked himself right into a corner and nobody's fault but his own. No arguing it; he'd done himself a right good one. The only person on his side now was Gideon and, though Peter was danged if he knew why, it didn't seem like he was too all-fired set on terminating their association.

If a man was willing to stand by you, didn't you owe him something? A little cooperation at least? Wasn't that exactly what he thought Gideon should be giving Aspen? A show of faith? An ounce of gratitude?

Peter's life had become one lie twisted into another until all the strands had become one big, tangled mess. There was no way to unravel a single one, not one in itself, nor even one at all. But did that mean he should add to the growing knot? Did he have a choice? Gideon said everyone had a choice. A man might not like his choices, but he had them and he had to make them.

"Alright," Peter agreed, trampling roughshod over his own good sense. "But I go too."

"'Course. All we gotta—"

A loud thump followed a brief grunt. The implications hit Gideon like a full force brick. He didn't know how, but he knew. He ran into the waiting room, Peter hard on his heels. Aspen lay stretched out on the floor, limbs askew.

Above him stood Nick Pultrie.

All reason packed its bags and pure instinct moved in. Gideon charged. What his instincts forgot to take into account was that the body housing them was not entirely up to standard. Pultrie dodged, tripped Gideon up and sent him sprawling.

"You want to try it, boy?" Knife in hand, Pultrie turned on Peter.

Peter backed up slowly. His hand brushed the doctor's desk and found a iron paperweight. He swept it up and hurled it. Pultrie's arm came up to deflect the blow and Gideon, crouched on the floor, leant into the thug's knees. Over Pultrie went and Peter dove for Aspen's gun.

"Leave it!" Pultrie barked, his slim knife at Gideon's throat.

Peter inched his hand away from the gun.

Pultrie tipped his chin towards the door. "Let's go."

"What about him?" Peter pleaded, pointing to Aspen.

"Move, before you have two hurt friends."

Gideon's heart pounded against his chest. Dammitall, this was exactly why he hadn't wanted Aspen involved in the first place! He was so still. Gideon couldn't even see him breathing. Suppose. . .

And then Aspen made the tiniest of noises.

The world rushed back to Gideon. Pultrie holding him, the knife at his throat and Peter wondering what on earth to do next. Gideon shifted his gaze towards the door. They could go, it would be alright.

As they made their way to a think stand of trees on the edge of town, the sound of voices, loud and confused, came to them and the sharp smell of smoke tainted the air.

"Tie him," Pultrie ordered. "And do it right."

Peter took the cord shoved at him and tied Gideon's wrists. His eyes asked a silent question: Now what?

Gideon gave a broad wink. They had meant to do the luring but this way around would work just as well, maybe even better.

Pultrie stomped over, yanked Peter aside and tugged at the rope. Satisfied, he pushed Peter to the ground, told him to keep still and went back to pacing. This whole job had turned bad as far as he was concerned. It should have been simple, instead it had dragged him clear across the country to this wretched perdition on earth.

He scratched industriously at his ribs. Something in the bedclothes had given him the worst rash and he was not entirely certain he was alone in his clothes. He couldn't even remember his last decent meal. How hard was it to fry eggs? The hotel cook had been even worse than Harvey. A mouse had been trapped under Harvey's cup and somewhere, a five legged insect hobbled for cover because its sixth leg had been on Pultrie's plate.

Sitting there amongst the fallen pine needles, Gideon did his best to look intimidated, whilst inside everything was fire— red, burning, barely contained fire. He could feel it breathing, feeding on the fuel Pultrie had given it. The image of Aspen, knocked out on the floor, danced within the flames. This new element of vengeance presented itself for admission into the ranks of reasons for what he was about to do and the other reasons stepped smartly aside.

Gideon took a good look at his enemy. Pultrie was

horribly disheveled, his face blotched, his blood-shot eyes dark rimmed and his left hand swollen. Lines creased the still unshaven face. And he reeked. Nick Pultrie hadn't been living well lately.

What a shame.

Gideon latched onto the smile that tried to escape him.

"What're ya gonna do?" he pleaded, in his best pathetic tones yet.

Pultrie set the blade of his knife against Gideon's cheek. "That depends on you."

"M-me?" Gideon stammered, leaning into the tree trunk behind him.

"That's right. If you want to keep your friend here alive, you tell me what I want to hear. Where's the deed?"

"I have it," said Peter quickly.

Pultrie studied on him, and then addressed Gideon. "He's trying to protect you, boy. But if you don't start talking, he's the one who's going to need protection."

"I. . ." Gideon said, letting the confession wobble uncertainly. "I hided it."

"Now we are getting somewhere. Where?"

"Dunno."

"Don't play with me," Pultrie warned, giving Gideon a shake that rattled his teeth.

"It were dark! I dunno! I swear!" Gideon squeaked. "Wait, wait, I can take ya there!"

The shaking stopped.

"How far?"

"Over the river," Gideon mumbled, head bowed.

"That wasn't so hard now, was it?" Pultrie said, patting Gideon's cheek.

Gideon wanted to rip the hand off at the joint and ram it down Pultrie's gullet where, with any luck, he would choke on it. Instead, he stared at his lap, wrapped up the idea and added it to the fire.

Equine footsteps rattled off the trees and Pultrie reached under his rumpled coat for a gun. He waited, ears pricked, until a rider came into view with another horse in tow. Pultrie jammed the gun back into its holster.

"It's about time," he snapped acerbically, dragging Peter to his feet and shoving him up behind Harvey.

"I'm here now," Harvey snapped back. "They talk?"

"I told you they would."

Gideon mustered up a small whimper as he was hustled onto the spare horse behind Pultrie. Tucked up so close, he got a stinging lung-full of stench. It was like a blunt, rusty saw dragged across the olfactory nerves and it made Gideon's insides dance for joy.

"You don't smell so good, mister."

"Don't get smart," Pultrie growled, displeased at having been reminded of a single half second of the last few hours, the exact number of which he had completely lost count of. "Which way, kid?"

"The river," Gideon sniffled. "Near that tree I done showed ya."

You rec'lect, Nicky. Where ya done tooked a swim.

"The horses can't cross there, boy."

"Dunno no other way."

"Forget it, we'll find a crossing when we get there," Harvey declared, kicking his horse forward.

L IKE soldiers sworn to give no quarter, a splitting headache pounded against Aspen's battered skull. More significantly, the state of his vision, whilst physically undamaged, had taken a decided turn red-wards.

Gov was gone. Was there any possibility the knot on Aspen's head had appeared purely by random and unrelated happenstance? He doubted it. Gov might have run off on his own but, had that been the case, it would have been him doing the hitting and it hadn't been.

"Hold still," Connell admonished, for the umpteenth time. Aspen was right about fit to be tied and Connell was right about fit to oblige him. "I said, hold still."

"Peter and Gov could be in twelve kinds of trouble by now! Aunt Eddie, tell him," Aspen argued, as his aunt came into the clinic's waiting room.

"Gandy won't leave without you," she said, tipping her nephew's head to see the welt more clearly. "Sit still and let the good doctor finish or I won't let you leave at all."

"Ow! Take it easy, Connell," Aspen objected, hissing through his teeth. "I have to go after them, Aunt Eddie."

"You have to stop bleeding too. First things first."

"The first thing—"

"Is for you to quit backtalking your aunt."

Aspen clenched his jaw, which made his head ache all the more. He really should have foreseen this— he **had** foreseen it. Last time, Peter had been kidnapped and nearly shot. Gov had nearly been killed. Blast that boy, but he was a top hand at getting into a scrape. Aspen had to find them. Rational thought kicked in: he was not going to get one step closer to Gov or Peter by running roughshod over his aunt.

"Yes, ma'am," he sighed by way of apology.

Eddie laid a hand on her nephew's shoulder for a moment and then went into the kitchen.

"Drink this," she ordered, returning with a cup of lukewarm coffee. "I've loaded your rifle. You'll find extra ammunition, along with anything else you may need, in your saddlebags. Your father's with Gandy. I'm going to see what's keeping them. You stay put and quit giving Tadhg a hard time."

"Yes, ma'am," Aspen replied by way of gratitude.

SOME things only offered a fellow one chance. Gideon had a feeling this was one of those. If he didn't get this right, he'd be running on a wing and a hope– only he was down one wing and was hardly even at nodding acquaintance with so much as a distant cousin of hope.

You'll manage.

Probably. But if he didn't? This having people rely on you business could really wear on a man's nerves. It was one thing with– well with some people– the very idea had always fit snug as you please. It still did. With new folks, though, it was like mending a broken bowl: all the pieces weren't there anymore and patching in with broken bits never quite lined up.

Shutup an' climb.

Fortunately, Gideon had taken the liberty of restoring himself to two unbound arms because he was going to need both hands for this next bit. Levering himself over a boulder, he wondered why on earth he had taken a notion to put anything in such an inconvenient location.

'Cause we're smart.

True for you.

Humpty Dumpty sure wasn't going to haul his keester, rock by boulder, up some craggy mountainside, not on his best day. Pultrie wasn't going to put himself out either, not when a no-account kid could be intimidated into doing it for him.

That was one gent who was about to get a rather rude awakening. Not that he knew it. His type never did. After all, it was impossible. Sadly for Pultrie, Gideon knew a thing or two about doing the impossible.

He shimmied along as if scaling a mast in a gale, or like a boy who had more agility with complex physics equations than the complicated operation of putting one foot in front of the other.

Gideon had deliberately chosen this particular hidey-hole for its lack of convenience. It really wasn't all that far. If he took a notion to run they could be on him in a minute— well, if either had been anything like Aspen they could have. They sure weren't going to chase him down on horseback. Thanks to step one— AKA: the river crossing— they were all equally afoot. Pultrie and Wilcox only held authority by strength and possession of weapons. As far as Gideon was concerned, this tipped the scales slightly in his favor.

Mebbe there's somethin' to this chess thing.

Shutup.

Maybe there was though. Thus far, chivying Peter's friends around had been rather like pushing pawns to the slaughter. Gideon would not have minded if this blissful state of affairs continued. It would have been a new experience for him.

"Hurry up! I don't have all day," Pultrie hollered from his cozy spot on the ground.

Of course, technically, Gideon was at ground level too, only his ground was on better terms with the sky. He let himself slip and then swiped an arm across a nose that didn't need it. Down below, Harvey held tightly to Peter. It really made Gideon want to jump down there and explain things to Mr. Harvey Wilcox.

Easy. Theirs is a-comin'.

It surely is.

Up where wind and rain had conspired with solid rock to create a cave, Gideon had left a gunnysack. He'd tucked it, and its contents, into the narrow crevice on the night he'd tricked Aspen. Now he shimmied inside and began to make a few preparations, which included palming several lucifers, selecting a couple sheets of paper from a rather thick stack, and pocketing a few sticks of dynamite.

Some might call using explosives overkill but, the way Gideon figured it, if Wilcox and Pultrie didn't want to get blown up, they should have stayed back east.

Gideon went back out and rubbed away non-existent tears to give his vision time to adjust to the glaring brightness of day.

"Well?" Pultrie demanded roughly, contempt vying with impatience.

"Got it!" Gideon replied, holding up the crumpled papers.

"Well, get down here!"

Gideon struck a match. "Or I might could not."

Pultrie's sharp-edged retort died on his lips and he stood there blinking at the inconceivable juxtaposition of reality standing before him. Somehow, a whiney little brat of a kid had become a cocky, self-assured nuisance about to torch his meal ticket. After weeks of tedious work, Pultrie was about to kiss his pay packet sweet au revoir.

"You get down here," he growled.

"There's something you sorry idjits really need to un'erstand," Gideon countered, edging the match closer to the document in his hand. "First-a which is ya don't wanna be doin' that."

About to grab Peter, Pultrie rocked forward and stayed put at the same time, momentarily paralyzed by indecision. Where was the fear, the self-doubt? He didn't know, but there was no doubt about that match. He stepped back, hands spread.

"Well done," Gideon continued. "Now, thing is, my friend an' me's a mite particular 'bout the comp'ny we keep. If'n we give ya this here deed, we don't never wanna see the neither of ya 'gain. Am I bein' clear 'nough for ya?"

"You hand it over or neither of you will be seeing

anything again," Pultrie threatened.

"Is that anyway to be neighborly, Nicky?" Gideon said, with a shake of his head and a mocking tisk. Then his voice went hard and he let the energetic match begin to singe the highly flammable paper. "Harvey boy, you're a mite slow on the uptake."

"How do we know that is the deed?" Harvey challenged, fist still clinging to Peter's shirt.

Ya don't. That's why you, my friend, are an' idjit.

Gideon squinted at the document in his hand and recited the officious words Peter had taught him. "Whereas . . . party-a the first part. . . in consid'ration of. . . receipt wherefore is hereby ack-nowledged. . . described prop'ty. . . signed by my hand this day. All sounds mighty legal to me."

"Good," Pultrie said, drawing his gun. "Now drop the match before I drop you, boy."

If ever there were a time to put all your chips on the table, this was it. Gideon spared a quick glance— Peter was ready.

Inch by inch, Gideon lowered the match, the flame nearly burned down to his fingertips. Pultrie's expression began to suggest the sort of amusement that really isn't very funny. And then Gideon's hand reached his side and the fuse loitering in his pocket sparked eagerly to life. With no warning whatsoever, he crumpled the paper, chucked it into the crevice behind him and followed it with the fizzling dynamite. A glimpse at the fuse as it left his singed fingers suggested he might have cut it a tad close.

And then Gideon jumped.

ASPEN leapt off the doctor's porch.

"How'd you lose track of them anyway?"

"Same way you ended up out cold," Gandy replied bluntly.

"Guess I don't take too well to being given a headache," Aspen said, taking the reins Amos held out to him.

"Me neither," Gandy accepted the apology. "One of our friends started a shed on fire. How is your head?"

"No need to worry about him," Deputy Mark teased, "he's too hard-headed."

"Good thing, too," Amos agreed.

Sitting up in the saddle as he was, Amos caught Aspen by the collar and looked down at the damage to his son's head. He kept his examination brief; Connell knew his business, there was no sense questioning that judgement.

"I'm alright, Pa," Aspen told his doting father.

Amos gave Aspen a look. It said, very clearly, that he knew darn well the doozy of a headache his son must have and, yes, he probably did dote more than other fathers. Doting was his prerogative. Amos gave his eldest an understanding pat on the shoulder.

"Good," he said. "Then let's go."

An explosion rolled between the hills. The rumble was magnificently loud and the search party automatically turned towards the general direction of the blast.

"Well," said Gandy, "sounds like Gov's alive."

"For now," Aspen agreed, nudging his horse.

GIDEON felt the blast against his left side and landed about one second before the world exploded.

Mite close there, boyo.

Close, not called's the point, 'member?

Large chunks of rock ended their unexpected flight and lighter bits, which had started life as much bigger bits, drifted aimlessly on the air as if unsure what to do next. As the crashing, pattering rain of stone, soot, dirt, smoke and hastily relocated terra firma tapered off, Gideon rolled to his back, a broad smile spread across his face.

Something there is in the human male that likes a bit of harmless destruction. From the time they are knee-high to a grasshopper, block towers are toppled, bottles are smashed, and rocks are thrown. The lucky ones grow up to be explosive experts, where they can go to work every day and light up a pitch black mine with roaring fire.

This wasn't that good, but it tickled the inner block pusher all the same. As for harmless, well, everything was relative— and no relative of Gideon's had been harmed.

If profanity could be admitted as evidence, Pultrie was certainly unharmed and breathing a fair amount of air. Gideon could plainly hear his venting, and now his cussing Harvey, and now the two of them arguing. This suited Gideon fine; the more they argued, the less what stood for their minds would be on him or the business at hand.

Speakin'-a the business at hand?

Gideon ticked off the priorities. First: get Peter loose. He might have over planned some there, but how much experience did he have with planning anyway? Or explosives for that matter? Second: get mad. Pultrie and Wilcox had accomplished that with such excessive efficiency Gideon had gone clean beyond mad, past 'your butt is mine' and landed squarely on 'I am really going to enjoy this'.

So, check and check.

Yep. Reckon that's 'nough plannin' for one day.

"Not smart, boy!" Pultrie shouted, still curled up in the dirt out of a primal desire for self-preservation. "You just destroyed the only reason I had for putting up with you!"

Gideon scootched around the bolder protecting him.

That there's what a guardian oughtta be: silent an' useful.

Gideon gave the barest breath to a perky Irish tune and peeked out.

Ya reckon that there's Pultrie's knee or Dumpty's?

Don't reckon as it matters.

Twirling a stick of dynamite between his fingers, Gideon fished out a match and introduced one to the other. The fuse flared up, sparking and fizzling away the limited seconds of its life. He gauged the distance, aimed a few degrees towards 'probably harmless', and sent the explosive spinning end for end through the air.

He dove for cover. Behind him, the air shattered and the earth leapt in an industrious effort to reach the heavens. The report of Pultrie's handgun was paltry by comparison.

"I worked hard for those papers, boy!" Pultrie hollered, from somewhere amongst the rearranged landscape.

Beside him, Harvey stood up and dusted himself off.

"Where are you going?" Pultrie barked.

"He's crazy," Harvey declared, with a tip of his chin in Gideon's general direction.

No one holding a burning explosive should look that peaceful, or have a glint about them as if they'd just been given a fork and a fresh apple pie all their own.

"Hey!" Pultrie tried again.

But Harvey was a man who had come to a decision. He may have owed a few unfriendly men a few dollars, but the path of least resistance had just shifted due east. And the time to travel was now. Nick Pultrie was on his own.

"You could at least leave me your gun!"

"You find it, you can have it," Harvey replied, over his shoulder and not slowing down.

Pultrie cursed loudly and then, after a brief reflection, decided Harvey's desertion wasn't so bad. At least now he didn't have an anchor on his leg questioning his every move and bombarding him with inane suggestions. Pultrie levered himself up and checked the chambers of his gun.

Gideon hunkered on one knee, flipped an explosive in a low, graceful arc and caught it. Round about a good hard throw to his right he could see Pultrie creeping about, searching for him. He could also see blood on Pultrie's forehead. It was a good sight– Pultrie was due a few.

The lively tune in Gideon's head jigged back around to the chorus and a dark thought slipped insidiously forward. Suppose he did not miss? Suppose he settled the score all around, for Peter and Aspen, all in one go?

Gideon flipped the explosive over again and imagined how the throw would feel in his arm, how much force his muscles would need, what angle—

What happened to not likin' the killin'?

I done decided I don't take to Pultrie even more.

That ain't the way, boyo.

Ain't it?

If he had been quicker with Tarlston, a great many things would have turned out differently. There was no going back but, here and now, going forward would be so very easy.

You a-list'nin' to me?

No. Gideon was listening to the voice of angry flames and the crackle of hate. It told him how simple it would be. One throw. One throw and everything would be over.

You gonna listen or am I gonna have to haunt your every livin' moment from here to perdition?

Huh?

Ya done heard me. Are ya really this stupid or did your brain take itself a holiday?

No need to get that-a way. It were just a thought.

Is that what it were?

Yep. An' now I got me 'nother one.

"Hey, mister!" Gideon sang out, and proceeded to reflect upon Pultrie's general uselessness as a human and utter incompetence as a hired thug, all of which was offered in clear, monosyllabic terms to avoid misunderstandings. He jumped up, put his arm behind a fine throw, and dropped out of sight. Then he slithered under a clump of scrub bushes, slid over a pile of rocks and tucked behind a boulder whilst once again the air rained dirt.

Yeeehhaw!!

Gideon wasn't sure if he thought it or said it, but either way it was true. He skidded to a halt and leaned against a flat stretch of mountain to catch his breath— and did a double-take. Sure enough, he'd created the nook he was now hiding in.

Ain't that handy.

Gideon gripped his side, ribs heaving, and then forgot all about catching his breath. Down where only rock should have been, lay something metal. Of course, with him around, rock was going everywhere.

That, boyo, is a gun.

A body wouldn't think there would be any need for a gun. One would think dynamite would do the trick. Harvey had sure thought so. But Pultrie was a different breed. That one was a buzzard, not a sheep, and buzzards could get very single-minded when it came to their supper.

You still 'gainst a-shootin' the miserable son?

Yep.

Can I at least graze 'im? Shake 'im up a little?

Welll. . . s'pose it's better in your hands'n his. G'wan with ya.

Gideon listened to his better judgment and got on. It took a few minutes to shift within reach of the revolver. By then, Pultrie had changed positions and inadvertently blocked Gideon's path. But he hadn't seen the gun. If he had, he would have leaned over and picked it up.

Now what?

Pultrie would have to be lured away. If Gideon could—

And there was Peter. Had he seen the gun? Did he see Pultrie? Gideon waved. He waved again. Then he hurled a walnut sized rock. Was the boy blind?!

After a moment of searching, Peter finally turned. Gideon made a gun with his fingers and pointed to where the real one lay. Peter nodded, then shrugged. Pultrie was still in the way. Gideon made a few more gestures that made no sense and then Peter saw the match. And then he saw the dynamite. At which point, he realized he really ought to get down. Ears ringing, his chest vibrated with the force of the explosion and pebbles pattered sharply against his back. A bullet zinged and screeched somewhere to his left. Peter inched his head up and gestured at Gideon to try another throw.

In reply, Gideon turned out an empty pocket. His other hand held nothing but an ordinary firecracker.

Oh. Peter had another look and, where Pultrie had indeed moved, so had the ground. Gideon still had no clear path to the gun, but Peter did. It wasn't the best route but, one step at a time, right?

Gideon signaled Peter to stay put, but his friend was already moving. The last few feet would be right out in the open. With one eye on Peter, Gideon kept the other locked on Pultrie.

That boy's gonna get hisself planted.

Likely.

"You'll run out of dynamite eventually, boy," Pultrie called out blindly.

He may have been hunting Gideon, but he was about to find Peter. Unarmed, easy going Peter.

"Wanna bet your life on that?" Gideon hollered, good

and loud. "I got me right 'bout 'nough s'plosives up here to blow you clean into next July."

Pultrie spun towards the voice, his anger rising at the flippant tone. "You haven't managed to hit me yet."

Behind Pultrie's back, Peter inched closer.

"The law 'round here's got funny notions 'bout killin'," Gideon replied, burning time instead of fuses. "Me, I can't say as I'd mind killin' ya, an' that's the truth. Can ya count to twelve, mister?"

"Why?" Pultrie asked, and took a cautious step, anchoring on Gideon's voice. The rocks played hob with sound and Pultrie wasn't entirely sure. He wasn't entirely sure about that dynamite either.

"'Cause that's 'right 'bout how long this fuse'll burn," Gideon explained helpfully, "an' then you're gonna be one almighty untidy mess."

"You won't kill me. You don't have the guts."

"Could be," Gideon agreed cheerfully. "Then again, could be you won't. Eleven!"

"You're lying, kid."

"Ten! C'mon, Nicky boy, give it up. There ain't nothin' here for ya. Ever'thing ya done wanted done gone up in a **fine** shower-a soot! Nine!"

Gideon chivied to a new position, pulling Pultrie along with him. What would he do– chuck rocks? Gideon had no idea, but he truly hoped something would come to him, because Peter should not have to know what it felt like to shoot a man.

"Ya've lost, Nicky. Ya couldn't even get candy from a babe– oh wait," Gideon laughed outright and the mocking sound skipped amongst the rocks. "You done thought you tried that! Seven!"

Gideon lobbed another round of slanderous insults at Pultrie, ranging from comments upon his mother's footwear to his father's dubious pedigree.

Pultrie was getting close, so was Peter, and there was Gideon walking the line between them. There had to be something he could do, something he could use. And then Gideon remembered the firecracker. It was in good time too, because something had caught Pultrie's attention. He was turning and—

Gideon worked his hands as fast as he could and jumped to his feet.

"Up here, ya miserable streak-a yellow coward!"

And that did it. Every man had his trigger and that was the last straw for Nick Pultrie. No impudent half-sized no-account was going to talk to him that way and nobody, but nobody, put him in the dirt. Pultrie charged.

F INDING those Rivers boys had been downright moral building. Matt hadn't been certain, not right at first, but by the time they sat down to eat, all doubts had fled. Wrong house, and none of the talk had mentioned women, but the small militia he'd left behind were definitely Rivers. One division of them anyway.

No last name had been offered, but what need? No one else could match the big one's description and how many twins did a man meet? They had been civil, in a stiff, reserved kind of way that suited them like frost on a wildflower. Matt had a pretty good hunch he knew what– or rather who— had made them so jumpy.

He ruminated on the meeting, and on what he had come to do. And Matt was going to do it, no matter what. Caswell Crossing wasn't far now.

P ULTRIE skidded to a roaring stop.

A red stick pirouetted towards him and, quite automatically, he caught it. The explosive went off in his fingers, screaming and popping, whilst he juggled it like a hot potato until his hands finally decided his brain had shut down. They dropped the firecracker and fumbled for his fallen gun.

"Don't!"

Very slowly, Pultrie turned and met the business end of a revolver. Behind the trigger stood Peter. He did not appear particularly scared, but Pultrie knew the kid couldn't do it. Peter was one of nature's runners, he didn't have the first notion how to make a stand.

"What now?" Pultrie said, imbuing the phrase with the sort of harmonics that suggest there could not possibly be a 'what now' because you could not possibly manage it.

If Gideon could have wrapped up every ounce of brass he had been born with and gifted it to Peter in that instant, he would have done so without the least hesitation. If he could have entirely swapped places and saved Peter the unpleasantness of confronting Pultrie, he would have done that too.

Life has a way of making its own plans though. This had started as Peter's fight and now it had come around to ending with him. If Peter wanted to keep men like this from riding roughshod over his life, he was going to have to make some decisions about what could be swallowed and what plain would not go down. It was time to decide if he was a looking-up man or a sheep.

The niceties of life were all well and good when one could afford them, and when folks were inclined to be obliging, but when unscrupulous men took it into their heads to help themselves to what was yours, be it property, life or a man's proper hold on dignity, niceties could darn well be packed up and kept for later.

"Kick that gun over here," Peter directed, "real easy. Now your knife. And don't get clever, 'cause I'd dearly love an excuse to fill you with lead."

"You'd murder me?" said Pultrie. "In cold blood?"

It was a challenge, a slander meant to infuse the enemy with the crippling affliction of doubt. A sneer began to spread across Pultrie's face— and then it slinked away. Pultrie had noticed a very important fact. The gun leveled at his chest was fully cocked.

"Mister, I'd gut shoot you for a tin dollar," Peter promised, his voice dead level. "Only I don't want the inconvenience of burying your pathetic corpse. I could leave your bones for the buzzards– but even they don't deserve that. Get. Right now. Before I change my mind and pull this trigger. Move!"

Faced with a barrel full of lead, Pultrie moved. He didn't like it, but Peter wasn't backing down and, as far as Pultrie knew, a complete nutcase was still out there itching to blow his insides all over the territory. He hadn't signed on for this and nobody was paying him to take chances.

Peter watched Pultrie retreat out of sight and then hauled in deep breath. His shoulders eased and he lowered the hammer on the gun. Maybe he should have shot Pultrie. Many another man would have and never a second thought. No one would have called it anything but justified either.

Peter stared without seeing as Gideon slid carelessly down from the rocks, a shower of pebbles skipping and bouncing in his wake.

"Not bad," Gideon remarked, coming to stand beside his friend. "So what's a nouny?"

"Huh?" Peter said, snapping out of it.

"Nounies an' verbies. Ya said as I should hitch 'em up."

"Well, what we just did? That would be a verby thing. A very big verby thing."

A sensation began to trickle through Peter that made him feel about seven feet tall. If it hadn't been for Gideon though. . .

"Thanks," he said simply.

"Were you done sent 'em packin'.'"

"All the same."

"Worked out for me," Gideon admitted easily. "If'n he'd a-come up them rocks, I'd've been stuck for sure."

"What were you going to do after the firecracker?"

Gideon rocked lightly on his heels and grinned. He really didn't know. Something would have come to him.

"You're impossible," Peter declared. He eyeballed Gideon from head to toe. "You're filthy too."

"Much as I'd love to discuss my a-ttire,' Gideon replied comfortably, "I should-a lit me a shuck ages ago. Keep your powder dry."

"Hold up," Peter said, grabbing Gideon's sleeve.

"Ain't nobody 'bove snakes done missed the racket we been a-makin'," Gideon explained, not entirely believing they were having this argy-bargy. "Ever' livin' soul's gonna come a-flyin' 'round the bend any minute. I done telled ya, ain't nobody gonna blame ya none."

Who could fault anyone for loosing hold of a man with a fist full of dynamite? Not a soul could blame Peter, not even Aspen.

He's sure gonna be sore.

Don't matter. We ain't gonna be here nohow.

S'posin' he—

He were breathin'.

But—

"You aren't leaving," Peter insisted.

"You got things back to front. What I ain't a-doin' is stayin'. Look, I'm. . . kind of-a bad luck charm, ya know?"

"Not really," said Peter who was still alive, breathing,

and happy to be so.

As much as Gideon wanted Peter to understand, he simply could not stand there debating the issue. The longer he did, the less likely his chances– and they hadn't been that great to begin with. Unceremoniously, he shoved his friend off.

"Don't make me shoot you," Peter called.

Gideon waved over his shoulder. Another time, another place, maybe it could have been different, but he had to contend with this place and this time where choices were limited and the future already determined for him.

A gunshot cracked.

Gideon hit the ground with extreme alacrity and a fair measure of mind numbing shock. Hands curled protectively over his head, he peered under his arm. The gun was on the ground and Peter was coming on fast. He had bluffed! Peter, of all people, had bluffed! And Gideon had fallen for it. He gathered his wits and scrambled to his knees.

Now who's the idjit?

Shutup.

"Get off!" Gideon grunted, as Peter piled into him.

He shoved and pushed and pulled. Peter counter shoved and pushed. On a different day Gideon might have won. On a different day he might have broken free and joined the express riders, or hitched up with a freight outfit. He might have done a lot of things. On this day, he did not win.

"Ow! You ungrateful son, I done helped you!"

"And I'm trying to help you," Peter shot back, trying to both pin Gideon and not aggravate his injuries at the same time. "Hold still!"

"Help? How!? By breakin' my arm?"

"By taking you back."

"Devil ya will!" Gideon swore, regaining his knees.

"I'm not asking!" Peter insisted, pulling Gideon back down.

"I see you're learning to deal with him, Peter."

Aspen had arrived and, by the sound of things, he was not in the best of humors.

CHAPTER 11
Unanswered Questions
Fat Lot You Know
Promise #92

D O you intend to spend your entire life locked up?"
Gideon certainly had not intended to be giving explanations, that was for sure. Now, thanks to Peter, he sat in one of Gandy's cells shifting through the steamer trunk of possibilities for anything handy.

The hard part was, no one would believe what he said, no matter what he said, so it was up to him to make sure he said what nobody wanted to hear because then, when they naturally did not believe him, he could obligingly tell them what he wanted them to think– which they would never have believed had he said it in the first place.

The happy memory of rocks dancing through the air was turning out to be of considerable lift to Gideon's spirits. Thus far, he had given the sheriff a pretty good run around. There had been questions, and not many answers, and some more questions and even fewer answers.

If Peter had any sense, he had stuck to their story. Undoubtedly, Gandy had already questioned him. They'd spent the entire ride back to town together and there was nothing a lawman liked better than asking questions. You'd go blue waiting for him to answer one, but asking came easy.

You gonna see Peter clear?

After what that dirty no-good done gone an' done?

We promised.

I done promised the fellah what din't turn me in. I dunno whoall you went 'an promised.

Gideon was going to have his hands full keeping his

own bacon out of the fire. If that left him too busy to fetch Peter out too, that was no one's fault but Peter's.

Vaguely, Gideon realized the lawman was talking. Again.

"Is this what's bothering you?" Gandy asked. He unpinned the star on his vest and tucked it away. "There. Better? We're just two people having a conversation."

Gideon settled his back against the stone wall, and blinked. The tiny movement pointed out what they were, truth be told, were two people distinctly **not** having a conversation and definitely not two people who just happened to bump into each other over a cup at Mathers's. It very neatly added a postscript clarifying that he was, in point of fact, handcuffed to a big iron ring anchored to a very thick and remarkably solid wall. That this came compliments of Aspen, rather than the sheriff, made no difference whatsoever. It was a blink with a lot on its mind.

The corners of Gandy's mouth twitched minutely. "Alright, we're two people having a conversation who are not going anywhere."

Reckon he's half right, seein' as he done locked the door.

"You should thank me," Gandy suggested helpfully.

With an economical lift of brow Gideon neatly indicated he did not see why this should be so, though he would be danged if he knew what glimmer of his thoughts he had let slip.

"It's called 'protective custody'," said Gandy.

"Ain't needin' no protection," Gideon's tongue volunteered of its own accord.

Specially not from the likes-a you.

"Really? Did you see the look on Aspen's face? You don't want to talk to me, I can fetch him back here."

No one with all their bricks in one barrow said yes to

an offer like that. To say Aspen had been upset would have been akin to calling a hurricane 'a touch of rain'. He hadn't yelled or done much of anything one might associate with an angry man clearly expressing vexation. He had asked no questions, offered no threats, yet impending hazard radiated off him like heat waves in a desert.

"Do you intend to spend your entire life locked up?" Gandy tried again.

"Don't reckon as no place could hold me quite that long," Gideon replied, so drunk on the sound of dynamite, even if he had wanted to be civil, it would have been impossible.

"Yes or no?" Gandy said evenly, settling onto the cell's other cot.

"How many guards?" Gideon prodded.

"Yes or no?"

This was water dripping from a roof again. The question would keep coming, a juggernaut not to be dodged.

Gideon supposed, if he were pressed to it, there might be the off chance he had heard slightly more inviting propositions.

"Good," the sheriff opinioned blandly, "because I do occasionally have to lock up someone else, you know."

Despite Gideon's inclination to get feathered up over a lawman laughing at his expense, at the moment, giddy indifference held stronger than grievances.

"I'd 'preciate it," he allowed, as if due the favor.

Gandy cleared his throat. "You might like to know everyone reclaimed their property."

"Good for them," Gideon replied, because it was something to say that offered no commitment whatsoever to anything or anyone for any reason.

"Haverston was especially thankful. Sure got him out of a sight of trouble with the missus."

Silence seemed the most prudent response to this tidbit of flotsam information. Not knowing who Haverston was, or what he had to do with the price of flour, there really was no safe reply. Moreover, the comment made Gideon feel like a big ol' trout looking up at a big ol' tasty bug right before he became a big ol' tasty supper in some smug fellow's frying pan.

"So what did those men want?" said Gandy.

When a fellow knows his fish, he doesn't have to bait a hook. He just reaches out and nets his catch. Since Gandy wasn't, he probably didn't. Thereby anything Gideon said could clear or muddy the waters anyway he saw fit.

How nice.

Gideon's perpetually inimical features, which usually blamed the world at large and lawmen in particular, shifted to an impish grin.

"Seein' as how it ain't me a-wearin' no badge, I don't reckon as I could say what all them men done wanted."

The sheriff tisked and placed two fingers to his lips. Aspen was one room over having a word with Peter. If Gandy let out that whistle. . .

"Whoa up, mister," Gideon said, suddenly an expert on causality. "I take your meanin', I do."

"Glad to hear it," Gandy allowed agreeably, despite very much doubting Gideon had given in. It simply was not in his nature to give a straight answer, especially when asked a clear, straight question. "So tell me about those men."

Well?

Well what?

Ya want it set to music? If'n you're gonna see Peter clear, ya ain't gonna get no better invite. 'Sides, can ya think-a nothin' better'n leadin' this tin-star astray?

Gideon was glad, when it came to lawmen at any rate,

he was in complete agreement with himself. It would have been too confusing to two-step with the voices outside his head whilst simultaneously jig timing with the voice inside his head.

"Reckon they done wanted what ever'body wants, soon or late," he offered.

"Which is?"

The grin broke out again, lighting up Gideon's grimy face. "My hide."

"You knew them?"

"Not in no social goin'-to-picnic way."

"So you just happened to run into a couple of strangers and fell into a difference of opinion?" Gandy asked, with due sarcasm.

"Somethin' like that," Gideon agreed, thoroughly resolved to do everything he could to say as little as possible whilst doing his best to appear as cooperative as possible.

Gandy knew that game. He had played it before.

"How's Peter fit?" he prompted.

"He don't. I told 'im to keep out. He wouldn't listen."

"You fought with him?"

Gideon made a sniggering noise, barely more than half a harrumph.

Gandy waited.

Gideon counter waited. He stared at the ceiling. He glanced at Gandy. He stared though the bars to the bare corridor beyond. He glanced back at Gandy.

There was one thing Gideon could say with complete honesty that would be believed with complete conviction.

"I were a-fixin' to pull my freight."

"And?" Gandy prompted.

"An' it sure din't go to plan."

That's what he got for planning in the first place.

Reflection was one thing. That, at least, you could count on to guide you right. Granted it was in a distinctly hind-sight fashion, which did very little good whilst one was actually **in** their moment of need, but it did wonders for helping a body avoid that particular inconvenience the next week.

"What exactly was your plan?" Gandy wondered. "I mean, after hitting Aspen?"

"I din't hit him!"

Oops.

And it was an oops. Someone had sure done it, and they were running out of candidates for that particular nomination. He couldn't blame it on Pultrie. And he could hardly blame it on Peter. Unless they were a blood enemy, Gideon couldn't see double crossing anyone to the law, and Peter hadn't been relegated quite that low yet.

Blast.

Blast? That all ya got? Blast?

Ain't my fault you went an' messed up.

But I din't hit 'im!

An' you fig'red this were the best time for a-hitchin' your horse to the truth tellin' wagon, did ya?

Gideon didn't figure that so much. He had no idea why he'd thrown down anything that mud-dumb. Perhaps the truth could be as useful as dynamite though– at least when it came from someone like him.

"Look you here," he said, lighting the proverbial fuse. "I were a-gettin' shut-a this whole infernal, tetched prop'sition an' Peter done followed me. You see'd."

"Mhhm," Gandy nodded, tapping the heavy cell key against his palm. "I saw a lot of things. Heard some too. Dynamite, for one. Seems to me, either someone really wanted to blow up a bunch of useless rock, or they really misjudged the charge. You do realize, most people aiming to commit a crime don't stop and set off enough dynamite to blow the lid off Hades."

"I weren't committin' me no crime," Gideon objected.

"Jailbreak," Gandy clarified.

"What? That's plumb loco."

Gandy shrugged. "That's how the judge will see it."

"Ain't no judge 'roud here no more."

"Circuit judge," Gandy said, scribing a small circle with one hand. "You can argue it out with him when he comes around again."

Even this news did not pierce Gideon's euphoria. One day, he would really wish it had.

"In the meantime, you can tell me about those three explosions," Gandy continued.

"Four," Gideon corrected, holding up his fingers as a visual aid for the thinking impaired.

"The firecracker doesn't count."

"You sure 'bout that?"

Sure seemed to count to Pultrie.

The heavy door to the lock-up swung open, presenting a rather vexed Aspen Rivers. His entrance stole the bang from Gideon's calculated truth and snuffed the fizzle from the fuse.

"What were you thinking?" he demanded with a control wound up so tight the words were louder for having been merely spoken than if they had been yelled.

"Now, Aspen—"

"No, Sheriff, those men rode for Tarlston and not a word does Gideon say. Not a single, solitary word. What's worse, he pulled Peter into it— **again**. Now I want an answer and I mean straight. What in blazes were you thinking?"

"Right fine, thank ya kindly," Gideon replied, with irrepressible insubordination and a dollop of pride.

"Give me the key," Aspen demanded, squaring up to

the cell door.

"I'm sure he has some explanation," Gandy temporized helpfully. "No one could be that stupid without an almighty good reason."

Aspen stood, hands on hips and fire obscuring his vision. Gideon still sat on some cloud of giddy indifference. The sheriff straddled the line between them, the only reasonable man present. He had never seen Gideon like this, and at this rate he never would again because Gideon was going to get himself killed. The sheriff tipped his head, a suggestion that this would be an excellent time for very quick, and very clear, explanations.

"If'n them men were, or if'n they weren't, Tarlston's don't matter none," Gideon said, as if enumerating the most reasonable thing in the world. "Either way, it weren't no concern-a yourn. If'n it were, an' if'n there were somethin' as ya could-a done, an' if'n there were some needcessity for ya to do nothin' more'n what I done did my ownself, then I reckon there might could-a been some call to round ya up an' post ya up. Only, it weren't, there weren't an' there still ain't, so I din't an' I ain't."

And it was half a truth. If it really had been Tarlston's men out there, the less involved anyone else was, the better off they would be. As it was, it hadn't been Tarlston's men and thereby it was still no one else's concern. Since it was Peter's affair, it was Peter's concern and Gideon hadn't done the bringing, he had been brought, so there again— no one's concern but his own.

That Aspen had been hurt only proved to Gideon how right he was. There were enough names on his ledger, he had no need nor desire to go adding any more.

"How many times do I have to tell you, Gideon Fletcher, there is nothing about you that is not my concern? Where do you. . . "

There was more to Aspen's rant, but Gideon did not hear it. A conundrum had completely seized his butterflying attention: middle names. It sure seemed as if Aspen had been in serious want of a middle name to add to that sentence.

Funny really. When a man was on solid ground he was simply Jim. No more, no less. The deeper in it he got, the more names he acquired. Having never owned a middle name, nor known many people who would have been inclined to flog him with it if he had, Gideon wondered if a man thus burdened would sink faster than a man with only the one given name to weigh him down.

Might it be rather like being sent to cut the switch you were to be licked with? A fellow had a lot to draw back and let fly with when the one on the receiving end of the tongue lashing handed over a mile long handle. Ty or Taw, there was nothing much a man could get hold of there. Frederick Jeremiah Fitzellingsworth, on the other hand, was a man in a spot.

"Gideon Fletcher, are you listening to me?"

There it was again, still in want of more yardage.

"This here bronc done left you afoot, mister. Lemme trot her 'round again so 's ya can have 'nother go," Gideon offered, generosity itself. "There weren't nothin' more ya could-a done that I ain't already done my ownself. So ain't no need for ya to fret none. I don't make me no habit-a askin' no odds-a nobody. Ain't never have, ain't never will."

"That is **not** how we do things in this family," Aspen warned.

Gandy could feel the intensity of Aspen's glare. It would have nailed any normal culprit to the back wall so hard he'd have to be pried off with a crowbar. Not Gideon. He may have come down off his cloud, but his feet had yet to gain any appreciable acquaintance with the ground.

"What do you reckon is **your** concern, at the moment?" Gandy proposed, toying with the cell key.

He waited whilst some strain of the implications filtered through Gideon's peculiar state of mind. Even a limpet would know better than to let Aspen come through that door. Setting it up this way meant the only thing keeping Gideon whole and hale was Gandy's good will. There was a twisted streak there that really was downright good and, at the bottom of Gideon's oceanic eyes, Gandy detected understanding– and possibly a smidgeon of appreciation.

Reckon as ya done got their a-ttention, boyo.

"I take to breathin' same as the next man,' Gideon pretended to relent. "Sure them men were a-lookin' to even up for Tarlston, but that still don't mean neither of ya got nothin' to say 'bout it."

"Sheriff," Aspen repeated stiffly, "give me the key."

"Oh, shove off!" Gideon said, before even he knew he had said it.

"Excuse me?"

"You done heard me."

"I will thank you to be civil," Aspen cautioned, in the same tight control that threatened a future as grim as coal black thunderheads. "Did you even tell Peter what you were getting him into? Or did you just decide to feed him more of your half-truths? Obviously you don't give two dented pennies for your own life, but did you think about his?"

Of course Gideon had thought about Peter! Everything he had done had all been to square things with Peter. He owed him. He had even done his level best to keep Aspen out of harm's way for pity's sake. What more—

He don't know none-a that. 'Member?

Right. Right.

Gideon collected himself, once again glad he was on his

own side in this one.

"I done told Peter to keep out," he told Aspen. "Only he done followed me. Fool could-a got hisself killed."

"He's not the only one," Gandy remarked.

"I take care-a my ownself."

Both men sort of froze, like statues in one of those fancy towns that stare out at the world as if not a shred of it made any sense to their marbly little brains.

"Them bully-boys're gone, aint they?" Gideon insisted, somewhat indignantly.

"So's half the landscape," replied Gandy, somewhat more accurately.

"So I might-a got. . . watcha-call-it. . . over—" Gideon's fingers, dangling from their iron bracelet, flapped as if he could pluck the missing word from the air.

"Overzealous," Aspen supplied tersely.

"Yeah, well, they're still gone."

"Yeah, well," Aspen mimicked, "I still have more than half a mind to come in there and straighten you out."

"Aspen," Gandy suggested calmly, "why don't you go and see to Peter."

"I already talked to Peter."

"Go and talk to him some more."

"What for?"

"Because I don't want to have to arrest you for murdering this boy."

Aspen stayed stock still and put, his attention riveted on Gideon. Gideon stared right back, giving nothing.

"Out!" Gandy ordered, pointing firmly at the door.

Aspen looked as if he would press his argument, then turned and left, boots echoing on the stone floor.

"You do know he's trying to keep you alive?" the lawman pointed out.

Gideon's body language clearly said, where this might

be true, it was also, in a more fundamental way, irrelevant. It would take more than a few disgruntled former associates to make him back up, let alone run for cover.

"And you do know those men will probably come back?" Gandy added.

Gideon nodded, that was about how he figured it too. Not that they had any good reason, only someone like Pultrie would have his own reasons. Getting even would be top on the list. Harvey would be long gone, but not Pultrie.

"Well, guess I better go see if I can calm Aspen down— though why I don't let him knock some sense into you is beyond me." Halfway out, Gandy turned back. "Oh, have you ever seen one of these?"

Gideon peered at the smashed padlock. It was a lock, like a hundred other locks used in hundreds of houses and shops in every town from Sticksville to Heckangone.

"Sure," he shrugged. "Who ain't?"

"Guess you're right. They are pretty common."

"Right foolish," Gideon remarked, off-handedly.

"How's that?"

"A concussed toad could open it with two toes on his back flipper, so why's ever'body so keen on 'em?"

"Good point. You behave yourself now."

Gandy slipped the lock into his pocket, let himself out and gave the door a gentle tug to assure himself it was secured.

Gideon's story was plausible. It was also rather neatly irrefutable. After all, Tarlston was dead. What could he say one way or the other? If a man wanted to wrap up an entire story, all nice and pretty with a string, that would be a fine way to do it.

"You ever seen him like that before?" Gandy asked, sitting down on the front step next to Aspen.

Aspen plucked a long stem of grass from a wild

growing patch. "Yep. It's usually a good time for wise men to take cover."

"Glad it wasn't me out there," Gandy admitted, with some feeling.

"Me too," Aspen agreed.

"You made a decent bad guy, by the way."

"Three brothers, I've had practice."

"Well, your newest one is clear of Haverston and he didn't break into Mary's either, which she never believed of him anyway. As for setting up those two men, if I were a betting man. . ." Gandy tugged up his own blade of grass. "What does Peter say?"

"He won't be tripped up either, says just what Gideon says."

Gandy thought that an interesting way to put it– not that Gideon says what Peter says, but that Gideon set their tune. Well, he probably did at that. It was sure hard to imagine it the other way around.

"You buy it?" Gandy asked.

"Not a pennyworth," said Aspen.

D ID they buy it?" Peter asked, hands wrapped around the cell bars.

"Don't worry," Gideon replied. "I told 'em it weren't no fault-a yourn."

"I don't know about this."

"Promised ya din't I?"

"Yeah, but—"

"Ain't no but. I been a-swimmin' in one brand-a trouble or 'nother for so long, one more ain't gonna make no nevermind."

Peter looked over his shoulder for the sheriff or Aspen. He was kind of impressed Gideon had kept to their plan, seeing as how he had sure put a crimp in Gideon's.

"I did it for your own good."

"Fat lot you know," Gideon contradicted flatly.

"You mad?"

"Yeah, some."

"Well, I'm not sorry," Peter admitted.

"Ya should be. Here's me facin' all the why-fors 'bout them friends-a yourn, an' you a-turnin' me in. What kind-a thanks is that?"

Peter could not see how, or why, Gideon was so set on cutting loose. This worked out alright though, because Gideon could not see how, or why, Peter was so set on him **not** cutting loose. On this, they were at an impasse.

"It's too late, you know," Peter said, recalling the look on Gideon's face when Aspen had been knocked out. "You're already caught. If I were in your place—"

"Yeah, well ya ain't," Gideon interrupted tersely.

"Well," Peter said, letting it drop, "thanks anyway."

"I owed ya somethin'," Gideon shrugged.

Gideon may have felt squared up but, the way Peter saw it, he had owed Gideon in the first place. Now he owed him double.

T HERE were some things a man did not want to see. Eddie Rivers coming out of the sheriff's office, when you knew Gov was locked up in there, was pretty near the top of the list. Aspen quickened his pace and the doctor kept right along with him, glad he had brought his bag. You never knew.

Inside, everything was quiet. Could be good. Then again, dead men had a tendency to make very little noise.

"Gov?" Aspen called uncertainly, one hand reaching into Gandy's desk drawer for the cell key.

"You reckon I done gone somewheres?" Gideon spoke up, with more than a hint of sarcasm.

He hadn't much choice in the matter, seeing as Aspen had left him locked up and Gandy had approved the notion. Gideon reckoned he was supposed to be learning something from the experience. The only thing that came to mind were the many advantages of not getting caught.

Aspen opened the cell, trepidation mixing with curiosity, rather like when people gawk at the grotesque, both wanting to know and, at the same time, not entirely sure they really did.

"What did Aunt Eddie want?" Aspen asked, getting straight to the point.

"Don't rightly know," Gideon replied, entirely unruffled, "but she were some riled."

Connell sat on the edge of the cot and began to look Gideon over. Gideon, for his part, went ahead and let him.

"What did you say to her?" Aspen pressed, fixed on exploring the depths of horrors past and those yet to come.

"Nothin'," Gideon admitted, with the same general concern one gave the weather on the moon; it might be interesting, but it wasn't exactly relevant.

Aspen and Connell shared a doubtful glance. Since when did Gideon come face to face with a confrontation and not give his fair share? It wasn't natural. And standing crosswise to Eddie could certainly be tallied as confrontation, no matter how you looked at it. She had already given him proper warning the last time– and the time before that come to think on it.

"Nothing?" Aspen queried suspiciously.

"She were a-unburdenin' herself-a so many words, weren't no kind-a room for no more. Easy, Doc. When're ya gonna have done with that blasted bejazered stuff nohow?"

Connell dabbed more of the atrociously pungent

ointment onto Gideon's side. "As soon as you stop tearing open what I'm trying to mend. And mind your language."

"I did."

"Did she know you weren't listening?" Aspen interrupted.

"Wadda you think?" Gideon said, eyes twinkling with an echo of yesterday's cheekiness.

"Knew you had a grain of intelligence hiding in there somewhere. You ought to try using it more often."

"You got you 'nough trouble a-keepin' up. I go bein' smart all the time an' you'd be plumb lost, so ya would."

"What are you sniggering at, Connell?" Aspen said.

"He does keep you running, you have to admit."

"Don't encourage him. He keeps it up and I may take it into my head to tie him up for the rest of his natural born life."

Connell reached up and tapped Gideon alongside the head.

"What in blue blazes was that for?"

"So you don't think I'm encouraging you. Shameful it was, you not telling Aspen anything. You all but had him in an apoplectic fit worrying over you."

That was hardly Gideon's fault. He'd been telling Aspen all along to cut his losses. He couldn't have made the point any clearer if he had set it to music and whistled out the tune. Besides. . . well. . . well never mind besides. It simply wasn't his place to worry, end of palaver.

He were though.

Ain't none-a my bother.

Really?

Gideon snuck a peek at Aspen. The telling expression was gone, yet a shadow of it lingered. Aspen really had been worried. Still, given the choice between two evils, Gideon knew which he would pick— this time and every time.

Bein' worried's a far sight better'n bein' dead.

True for you.

"Like it or not, need it or not," Connell was saying, "Aspen's not going to quit you, no matter how much you fight. Might as well face it, boyo, you're stuck."

With some awkwardness Gideon and Aspen failed to quite, well, not exactly, in any sort of direct way, not entirely managed to not look at each other after this rather uncomfortably direct and embarrassing proclamation.

"What's it to him?" Gideon finally demanded.

"What's it to you?" Connell countered, more insightfully.

That shuts us up.

It sure did and no mistake because there was nothing Gideon was going to say to a question like that.

"Maybe this time you'll leave my handiwork alone," Connell said, pulling Gideon's shirt into place. "How long will you be leaving him here, Aspen?"

"Until he's ninety-two," Aspen threatened, ". . .or gives me a promise."

Again?

Every time Gideon turned around he was giving Aspen one promise or another. At this rate he was likely to run clean out.

"I realize there's no possible way you can stay out of trouble," Aspen said, arms folded. "But from now on, at least warn me before I get hit over the head with whatever idiocy you decide to perpetrate."

"I don't need nobody a-backin' my play," Gideon refused. "A man don't go runnin' for help ever' time he's got hisself a job to do."

"I didn't say anything about getting help. I said **you** are to help **me** not get clobbered again."

There was no way on this wide green earth Gideon

would promise to tip Aspen off. If he did, he'd have his hands full every living minute trying to keep the deuced man out of the way. Keeping Aspen from getting clobbered, though, there was a possibility. No harm in agreeing when that's what he had been trying to do all along.

"Reckon I can take a hand at keepin' ya unclobbered. Less'n it's me a-doin' the clobb'rin'."

"That reminds me," Aspen added, in a uniquely placid tone Gideon would learn to dread. "You recall that understanding we had awhile back?"

"What's that?"

"The one where you step out of line and I clean your clock?"

"Yeah?"

"It still stands."

CHAPTER 12
Instincts
Habits To Change
A Helping Hand
Two Questions

INSTINCTS. Equally capable of fetching one both in or out of trouble, it paid to listen to them. The Rivers knew about instincts and theirs had been set twanging. Their blue-eyed visitor hadn't asked many questions nor volunteered many answers. There was nothing inherently wrong with this set up; a man's business was his own and other men did well to leave it that way. There was just something. . .

He hadn't seemed the sort to make a life of wandering so far out, yet wandering he had been. He was quietly intense, and tried not let it show. He stepped up to the work with hands that bore no calluses. His youthful face said he knew a great deal, but also managed to indicate you would never guess how much.

"Gambler?" Lee suggested.

"Definitely," Fort concurred.

"Gunman?"

"Could be."

Lee set an armload of wood on the growing pile and watched Fort study the hills between them and town.

"Gov?" he asked.

"Ain't sure," Fort told the hills.

Instinct was edging in though, like the tingling before a storm that made cattle stampede and men jumpier than all get out.

"Big brother, are you going to keep leaning on that axe or saddle up?" Lee finally asked.

"Ember! Get Down here," Fort hollered, and headed for the barn.

T HE street stretched, the boardwalk echoed and, once again, Gideon followed. He knew he was being toyed with and thus refused to ask questions, but it irked him to be reduced to tagging along like some brainless tethered creature who hadn't the gumption to make his own way.

Baa-a-aah.

"You not tellin' me nothin's a habit you could change," Gideon accused, despite his vow of silence.

Aspen scoffed outright. "Do you really want to start a conversation about withholding information or habits that need changing?"

"Is it too much to ask whereall we're a-goin' afore we get there?"

"Is it too much to ask to get a straight answer? Is it too much for you to keep out of harm's way for a single day? Or stay out of jail? Great day in the morning, you can't even keep clean for three seconds together. Look at you."

"What?" Gideon said, peering down at himself.

"We just bought those clothes and already you've torn a sleeve and both knees. Scrubbing all that dirt out will take Mary an entire bar of soap."

"It's a knack," Gideon professed glibly.

"It's about time we taught you some new ones."

"Done tooked me my whole life to learn these ones."

"Undoubtedly," Aspen agreed sardonically.

A cackle interrupted their exchange. It came from the same ancient old man. This time he balanced his collection of matchstick bones on a dried out tree stump nearly as old as he was. Gideon couldn't imagine what he found so funny, but the man kept it up like he had nothing special in mind for the next month or so.

"Let's go to Mathers's," Gideon suggested.

"Does he deserve that?" Aspen replied.

"You're right funny, you are. C'mon, you're a-buyin'.'"

"How generous of you."

"Yep. Now get a-move on. That bump on your head's doin' ya no good. You've gone all pale, an' I'd hate for ya to suffer Connell's tender a-ttention."

"Yours is better?" Aspen marveled.

"Hey, I din't reckon on ya gettin' leveled."

"Funny, I didn't ask for it either. Of course had you told me anything, or stayed out of trouble in the first place, or bothered to—"

"Will ya c'mon?" Gideon caught Aspen by the wrist. "You can row me up over coffee."

"Fine by me, but let's go to Connell's."

The doctor was over at Zeek's, so going to his office presented no danger of falling into his care.

"Mathers'll have a pot already on," Gideon pointed out.

"Is now your best time to argue with me?"

It could not be said Gideon reflected upon anything he personally had done recently or historically, but he did reflect upon what Aspen had been through and decided to give the man a break.

"After you," he said, with the suggestion of a bow and a broad sweep of an arm.

S HERIFF Gandy headed to the livery yard. Coincidently, Cort had been about to do the same and changed his mind. If only that could be made a more permanent state of affairs. Gandy's appearance, whatever the reason, would merely serve as a delay, not a complete hindrance. Peter worked the pump handle at the corral trough and watched one problem walk away whilst the other grew nearer.

"How are you, Peter?" Gandy greeted amiably.

"Fine, Sheriff," Peter replied, trying to sound relaxed.

"Glad to hear it. I wanted to talk to you about Gideon."

"Yes, sir?"

"Thing is, he doesn't mean any harm, but when it comes to falling head first into grief. . ."

"He can't help himself," Peter finished.

"No more than a compass could up and point south," Gandy agreed. "It's good of you to help him, but those men you two ran into might not be the only ones after him. Dealing with their kind on your own is not a good idea."

Once again, Peter wondered if maybe he shouldn't have let Gideon take the blame.

"Yes, sir," he managed.

"Good," said Gandy. "Heard from your father?"

"No," Peter answered, taken aback. He stumbled to add, "I'm not really expecting to as yet."

"When did you say he would return?"

"He didn't mean to be gone long," and this wasn't exactly a lie even if it wasn't exactly the truth; Peter was drawing lines again and knew it.

"Well, you need anything in the meantime, you let me know. I'd be happy to help you out. So would Aspen Rivers, for that matter."

"Thank you, Sheriff," Peter answered politely, if somewhat distractedly.

He had lost sight of Cort. Unfortunately, there was no possible way Cort had lost sight of Gandy which meant Cort was going to have some questions of his own. Peter was torn between wanting Gandy to go away and truly hoping he would stay.

"I mean it," Gandy repeated. "You need something, you

let me know."

"Yes, sir."

"Well, I don't want to keep you, and I can hear Zeek giving the doctor a hard time, so I'll just head over there and let him know you have everything well in hand. Oh, and see if you can get some of that good character of yours to rub off on Gideon, will you?"

Peter buried a guilt inspired cringe. "Yes, sir."

The sheriff moseyed over to the blacksmith's having gained more from Peter than the boy had ever meant to tell. He loved talking to people when they had no idea they were being interrogated.

T URNING coarse, repugnant grit into an even more repugnant cup of liquid stench was not hard. A lot of people argued over the procedure and insisted on their own personal technique, but stench was stench and coffee was coffee. Gideon made it, other people drank it.

"Where'd you learn to make coffee?" Aspen asked.

Gideon put up the doc's grinder. "Around."

He had answered shorter than he'd meant, but habit was habit, and keeping himself to himself had become a strong habit indeed.

Might could be a fine time to say a bit more.

It could at that. Aspen wasn't all that far from wanting to take him apart and there hadn't been much promise of being put back together.

"Farm," Gideon elaborated, as he added a log to the stove. "Afore the Harris place. Worked there some."

"Where was this?" Aspen investigated.

Gideon thought a minute. "Beats me. Don't seem as there were no yucca, nor many pines neither. Plen'y-a heat. Plen'y-a flat too."

"How many jobs have you held?"

"Fair few," Gideon answered short, and meant it.

Not many of his former occupations could be discussed in polite society, and Aspen sure counted for polite society— at least from where Gideon stood. He'd known skinners, drovers, drifters and trappers. He'd kept company with men who rode among the willows and shunned the lawmen who hunted them. Some had been the coarsest, roughest, most unrefined specimens of humanity a man could ever wish to avoid. The intriguing thing was, when it came right down to it, some of those same rough and ready folks had turned out to be right gentlemen at heart.

None of them had been like Aspen. He was the first person Gideon had ever met who could be counted a gentleman on the inside and the outside at the same time. Even when pushed, Gideon had never heard him say a single profane thing. He kept his word and definitely made sure everyone knew where he stood. It dawned on Gideon that, in a world full of sheep, Aspen was a looking-up man.

Oh, boy.

If you hoped to maintain your own course in life, a looking-up man was not the sort you wanted to tangle with. Sheep moved out of the way. A looking-up man was more likely to plant his feet and butt heads.

He sure does.

Stubborn, that's what Aspen was. Mule stubborn. Any sensible person would have given up ages ago. There was no reasoning with a man like that. You just had to plant your own feet and butt heads right back.

Else skip out whilst he ain't a-lookin'.

"How long did you stay at the Harris place?"

Gideon stared out the kitchen window. It had rained again and everything was shiny new— everything above mud level at any rate.

Ya gonna answer 'im or butt heads?

"Thought we done did the questions," Gideon finally said, taking both options at once.

Aspen tipped back in his chair and waited. Gideon had the distinct impression he was being laughed at.

"What?"

"I was just thinking you must like having your arm twisted," Aspen replied, eyes a-twinkle.

"Don't look that a-way to me."

"It's going to in a minute."

Ya lookin' to invite the row up ya done did dodge?

"'Bout a year. Mebbe somethin' shy."

The snow had already melted when Gideon signed on with the Harris outfit, and had melted again by the time he buried his friends. Only he had not buried them. He couldn't. Tarlston had destroyed the home ranch and posted a small army of armed men. With an embittered heart, Gideon left the men of the Harris ranch behind and moved on to dealing with those who had killed them. It hadn't been about pragmatic choices, nor even prudent ones. It was about finding every last hired killer and removing them from the world— permanently.

Gideon poured a cup of black sludge and handed it to Aspen, who sipped carefully and nodded appreciatively.

"Not bad— considering you hate coffee."

Any response Gideon could have made would have acknowledged the implication that he'd only made the coffee out of the shear goodness of his otherwise pessimistic, life besmirch heart. And there was no way he was going to be roped into that. Aspen could make his own conclusions.

"You might think about using the extra water to wash up," Aspen suggested, with a nod towards the bucket.

The Rivers were about the washingest folks Gideon

had ever met. Personally, he couldn't care one iota if his face was smudged, smeared, or coal black for that matter. The thing about washing was, if you went at it like they did, you'd never stop. No matter what a man did, he'd only get dirty again and, if he tried to keep up with it, the poor fellow might find he had scrubbed himself clean away.

There was that expression again, the glimmering one that came with the arm twisting. It was very much in Gideon's mind to—

Be nice.

Gideon supposed he could manage and proved himself correct. He splashed cool water on his face and reached for a dish towel.

"Let's go out to the porch," Aspen suggested.

Gideon willingly followed and took a seat on the swing.

"Here, hold this," said Aspen.

Gideon took the cup whilst Aspen settled himself. Between trying not to spill the scalding liquid and Aspen's fingers clamping on his wrist, Gideon found himself neatly handcuffed. The other iron loop went around Aspen's wrist.

"Much obliged," he said lightly, taking back his cup.

Aunt Eddie may have counseled otherwise, and Connell and Gandy too for that matter, but so help him— letting Gideon out of his sight had reclaimed its status as a non-negotiable subject. When any reasonable person would have drawn up and decided a situation was well worth leaving alone, Gov took one miniscule half second of a peek and said: 'Weehee!'. It never occurred to him to round up a few extra hands to haul him out again– oh, no– feet first, head first and anything else he could get into the fray, that was Gov. And don't even try to tell him differently. Stubborn. That's what he was.

Whomever those two men were, Gideon had apparently vexed them a considerable degree. Gandy was right, they might well come back to even the score. Clearly they weren't anything to do with Tarlston but, if they returned, Aspen still meant to be in on the fracas.

"Hey, what's the idea?" Gideon said, feeling as if the other shoe had dropped.

"You ought to have figured that out by now," Aspen answered, "you've been handcuffed often enough."

"If'n ya din't want me a-goin' nowheres, all ya had to do were ask."

"That would get me somewhere, would it?"

Alright, that would probably get Gideon a whole lot farther than it would ever get Aspen, true enough. Some things did not merit admitting though, no matter how accurate they may have been– particularly when doing so would mean putting yourself on the bottom rung of the argument ladder.

"Might could," Gideon replied instead.

"The evidence is lacking. You can't even keep still, let alone stay put."

The prosecution's current claim lay in the fact that Gideon had already slipped loose from Connell's handiwork. He had become quite good at that.

"We're just a-sittin' here, so you ain't got you no call to go all mother hen on me," Gideon warned, in case his guard was making any plans. "Ain't like I went an' promised 'im nothin', 'cause I keep my promises."

"You surely do. To the very word," Aspen affirmed with sincerity. "It's the shades in between that worry me."

'Aw, c'mon," Gideon wheedled. "Lemme loose."

"No."

"But—"

"Is this you sassing me again?"

Gideon considered his options and recalled he had a few more to hand than Aspen realized.

"Wouldn't dream of it," he said.

They sat under a cobalt blue sky with the occasional fluffy great cloud, and an agreeable silence fell unobtrusively between them. A breeze rustled idly through the big cottonwood tree beside the clinic.

"Hey, Gov?"

"Yeah?"

"Will you answer me something?"

"You're just a-fig'rin' I'll answer on a'count-a you gettin' your melon thumped."

"Yes, sir. I am," Aspen admitted.

"Well, ya done used that up already."

"Not quite."

He's got 'im a point.

Shutup.

But Aspen did have a point, confoundit. Maybe. . . maybe answering a few of the simpler breed of questions wouldn't do any harm.

"I swear, you're worse'n a woman for askin' a man questions. I'll give ya one."

"Two," Aspen haggled, "and you promise to answer me with the truth."

Aw, g'wan.

"Reckon that balances on what ya ask. Tell ya what, if'n I answer, it'll be the truth."

Gideon waited whilst Aspen cut out two questions from amongst a possible thousand. He seemed to have dropped a loop on his favorite, then changed his mind and started again.

"How do you feel about killing Tarlston?"

"It's done. What diff'rence does it make?" Gideon countered, more statement than question. "An' why does ever'body keep askin' me that?"

"You promised me two answers."

"Wrong," Gideon corrected. "I done promised ya two questions."

"Shades in between," Aspen accused.

"I weren't 'spectin' ya to out with a doozy like that."

"All the same," Aspen said, taking nothing back. "Unless you'd like me to pick an even better one?"

"Great stampedin' buff'lo," Gideon exclaimed, "I shouldn't oughtta've gived ya the first go."

"Ah, but you did and now you're stalling."

"Give a fellah a chance to think!"

"Don't think," Aspen advised, because he knew exactly where that sort of thing could lead with Gideon. "Just answer. First thing that comes to mind."

"I dunno."

"Content? Indifferent? Guilty?"

"He's dead," Gideon explained, his words coming quickly. "I don't dwell on it none–"

'   *Truth*

"—alright some, but not for serious. It were 'im or Peter an' I'm glad it weren't Peter. He's worth more'n that miserable, excuse for– well, he's worth more. Mud's worth more."

That was an answer, and it was true, and it did not commit Gideon to being pleased or bothered or anything else. He really didn't know how he felt, or how to reconcile with how he should feel. Feelings weren't exactly anything Gideon related to on a first name basis.

"Are you—" Aspen began.

"This your second question?" Gideon interrupted.

"No."

"Then I ain't a-answerin'. What else ya got?"

To Gideon's surprise, Aspen actually squirmed like a little boy about to admit to some dereliction, the consequences of which he would rather not explore and yet knew there was nothing for it but to trudge forward and get it over with.

"Well?" Gideon prompted, curious despite himself. "You foldin' or drawin'?"

"Do you. . . I was wondering. . . do you blame me?"

"For what?"

"Everything," Aspen said. "For Tarlston shooting you, for not being there so you didn't have to shoot him, for Rydel snuffing your candle, for—"

"Whoa!" Gideon had sat in slack jawed amazement until he could finally round up that single syllable. "Is that what all this confounded motherin's 'bout? You fig'rin' to come 'twixt me an' trouble? That it?"

"I am supposed to—"

"Can't be done, mister," Gideon averred firmly. "Trouble always comes, soon or late. Best ya might could do is fish me out-a the worst now an' again, but there ain't no pre-ventin'. Not reg'lar nohow. You try that, you'll wear yourself plumb out, so ya will."

Aspen's family had known he could not prevent every ounce of calamity— no matter how hard he tried— any more than they could. They understood his feelings, yet they couldn't relieve his sense of inadequacy. Gideon's few, poorly articulated words accomplished everything all their more eloquent ones could not.

"So, you don't hold it against me?" Aspen asked.

Gideon watched a raven hopping in the road as if this triviality held some interest. Possibly it was a crow. He never could tell the difference.

"Well, I'd-a laver a-done the pummelin' than get it, but that ain't no fault-a yourn. Put the lot out-a your head an' forget it. Ya hear?"

"Yes, sir," agreed Aspen, surprised and relieved in equal measure. And then another thought occurred to him.

"Do you ever **not** get into trouble?"

"Sorry. Ill-lit-rit I might be, but count I can, an' that there were two. You, sir, are done."

So was Gideon. If having that bit of awkwardness out of the way meant Aspen would back off, all well and good, but it really did not do to have someone– anyone– worrying over him. There was no place in Gideon's life for that sort of thing and no reason to encourage it.

Truth?

Shutup.

Gideon idly rocked the swing in the warmth of the day and Aspen's eyes grew heavier until sleep finally overtook him. There wouldn't be any more questions out of him for awhile. A man had come to an interesting turn when he got along best with people who were unconscious.

That's on a-count-a your charmin' pers'nality.

That there's sarcasm, right?

Gideon continued to nudge the swing, talk to himself and keep an eye on the street. He could see from the barber's all the way down past the café, and what he saw ran to the extremely mundane. And then something drew his attention. He could barely believe it, but he had definitely seen it, and there was not one single possibility he would refrain from butting in.

Had he known where such a well meant, and seemingly innocent, decision would lead he might not have 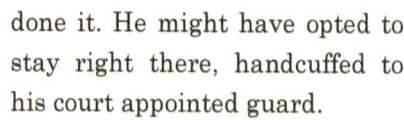 done it. He might have opted to stay right there, handcuffed to his court appointed guard.

Of course, if that's what Aspen had wanted, he should have gone with the promise. It was more binding than handcuffs.

CHAPTER 13
Peter's Transgressions
Pickle Jar
No Earthly Good
A Centipede & The USS Optimism
A Lasting Impression
Stampede

GIDEON headed across the street like a Spanish bull charging a toreador's red cape and didn't draw up until he stood chest to chest with Peter.

"Wadda ya think' you're a-doin'?"

"Nothing," Peter evaded.

Gideon knew 'nothing', he had even done it a few times. He also knew what he had seen. Where he would be the first to admit there were things a man occasionally had to do, and not all of them qualified as 'proper' in the strictest sense of the term, there were some things that should not be done. Right smack bang on the top of the list was theft. That sort of 'nothing' was exactly the right kind of something to land Peter neck deep in a whole lot of trouble.

"Give it back," Gideon demanded.

"I didn't steal it!" Peter objected, his voice strained and pitched low.

Gideon squared himself up and, despite his scrawny height, managed to give an impression of immovability like to the Great Wall of China. They glared at each other, equally resolved in opposite intents.

"She dropped it," Peter offered belligerently.

"An' this's you givin' it back?"

"You saw her."

Gideon had seen the young woman, all frills and scented soap wafting along like a breeze born wishing-puff in a field of cactus. If Peter thought that split the difference, he was sadly mistaken. What did it matter if the woman could afford to lose her broach— or the entire United States treasury for that matter? The victim's ability to endure a theft was no excuse for the crime.

"You can come away out-a that, mister," Gideon scolded. "Give it here."

"What?!"

"Give it here," Gideon repeated, iron hard.

This wasn't a bit of borrowing to good cause with everyone getting back what they hadn't known they'd loaned. This was straight up, flat out theft. And there were some lines you did not cross.

"Oh, I see," Peter spat bitterly. "Time to get even."

"This ain't 'bout you turnin' me in. It's 'bout you turnin' over that there broach."

"What's it to you?" Peter demanded.

"It's you to me."

Under cover of that baffling statement, Gideon plucked the broach out of Peter's vest pocket.

Peter reached out to snatch it back, but it was too late. Gideon was already headed for the young woman. Peter nearly followed, but he could not afford to be identified. He turned on his heel, fists clenched, and mutely cursed the whole wide world. What his self-expression lacked in craftsmanship, it made up for with a heartfelt passion that came from the toes.

It was all well and good for Gideon to get sanctimonious, he could afford to be. Some folks didn't have that kind of luxury, because life surely did give a fellow choices and sometimes they really weren't good coming or going. But you still had to make them. And you still had to live with them. Right there was where Peter figured Gideon's theory went astray. 'Living' with your choices wasn't simply about accepting them, it was about staying alive long enough to have the chance to accept them.

Gideon had the whole dadblamed Rivers clan on his side and was too mud-dumb to know it. If Peter had folks like that. . . he didn't, not anymore, but if he did, he sure wouldn't be in this fix.

He kicked a rock into the next territory. What was he going to tell Cort's gang? They'd have some hard questions for him when he showed up empty handed— and their decidedly uncivil manners would not encompass an understanding of such niceties as 'sorry' or 'excuse me'.

SOMETIMES life does not work out. No matter what you do, or how you come at it, life simply does not work out. You prepare yourself for– and expect– a box bright and shiny with precious metals and what you get is chunks of rubbish, a load of mud, and boots that squelch. Some days you don't even get the mud which, in a pinch, could be useful to the optimistic miner of life's resources.

Some people will say, as you stand there holding a salt grain worth of expectation and a wheelbarrow full of everything else, that this is somehow your fault. They would have you believe what you put in is in direct, measurable proportion to what you get out. They will say it's about material selection, rocker technique, whether you turned around at noon and spat seven degrees to your left.

That's as may be. They have a point. There is another point: sometimes life plain does not work out.

At this juncture the more socially maladjusted cut a trail to another man's box— unwise and decidedly unhealthy.

As Gideon saw it, a fellow had two options. A: he could accept the lumps life delivered, as all men must occasionally do, or B: he could snatch up the rocks, overturn the rocker and cut a trail downriver before life had wiped the mud off its face. The situation sketching itself out before him forecasted a whole heap of A without much promise for B.

On the one side stood Mrs. Driscoll, broach in one hand and Gideon in the other, shouting her fool head off with a passion intended to draw every living soul like a human whirlpool. On the flip side stood Mr. Reed, pickled up and marching down on them to add his vociferous two cents of accusation to the rising tide. As if that were insufficient to tip life's scales, beyond Driscoll's wagging finger came Aspen with an expression fit to melt the stronger types of metal. Whether he meant to join in or help out was more than Gideon could have said.

At this point Gideon had run out of hands on which to count, which was a shame because there was far more counting up to do. A flock of suited men swooped towards him, with the appearance of seriously aggrieved men everywhere about to pounce upon their prey. Gideon felt pretty sure he hadn't done anything to them but, given the look of them, he was not sure they knew that. Pultrie now, him he had offended, so there was no need to wonder about that man slinking in on the edges of the ruckus.

Teach him to do a good deed, wouldn't it? The only thing missing to make this whole mistaken disaster complete was—

Sheriff Luke Gandy.

Yep, that'd right 'bout do it.

It was unbelievable. It really was.

It's a knack.

Gideon figured he could do with a different sort of knack, because the sheriff was cutting towards him with an obvious eagerness to step smack bang into the affray.

Hey, boyo, take a gander.

Ah. Of course. Like a handful of black pepper thrown into an already overdone stew, those wish-they-were prospector boys choose that moment to make an appearance. Gideon didn't know what burr bunched their blanket, but they headed straight for Peter, presumably to unload whatever grievance currently burdened their minds.

Wadda they want with Peter?

Realization sliced through Gideon like a hot knife through bacon grease.

Dang! Dang, dang, dang!!

He could have kicked himself right there and then for the triple blasted fool he was. What should he have done though? Any reasonable person would have done the same thing in his position.

Yeah, but any other fellah wouldn't a-flopped face first into some other gent's stew.

Gideon may have borrowed Peter's trouble, but he was not about to turn it back on him. Unfortunately, no matter what Gideon did, he was in for a few of life's rougher sorts of bumps.

Ah well, time to kick the rocker over.

Arms were waving, accusations flying, people yelling and, amongst it all, Gideon commenced yelling back. The racket instantly doubled. In the chaos, no one noticed the chair, abandoned by some looky-loo who'd been inexorably pulled in. Nor did anyone expect the burst of energy with which Gideon latched onto said chair and sent it crashing through a window.

The sound of glass shattering to smithereens made every single body jump. Some jumped towards, some away, some flat out straight up. Most importantly, the distraction caused Mrs. Driscoll to lose her hold on Gideon. It almost made her lose her hold on everything right down to her sanity, which some people questioned anyway.

Gideon did not stick around to witness the commotion. There were fighting times and running times and a wise man ought to know the difference.

F that kid was trying to keep low, he was no earthly good at it. Men and women of multiple sizes, ages and volume tossed about in his wake, to-ing, fro-ing and generally stirring themselves into a dither. At the edges of it all a dog ran about, yapping excitedly.

So this was Caswell Crossing. And somewhere in swirling noise Matt would find at least one more Rivers and several Millers– all of whom he intended to have a word with in due time. He had already located his first target amongst the swarm of riled up humanity.

A pounding of feet and shouting of voices followed Gideon as he ducked and dodged his way to. . . well, he didn't rightly know where, but getting there struck as a mighty fine idea. He turned a corner, hit the ground, and rolled under a building. Who knew what poorly trained or overly influenced carpenter had manufactured such spaces, but Gideon was quite sure they were for his own personal convenience and made use of them accordingly.

Barely within the embracing shadows, the mob caught him up and passed him by. He watched them stream past and thought they looked rather like a centipede with an eclectic taste for shoes. Lying there, the dampness seeping into his clothes, he took a moment to consider his most immediate needs. The general idea was to survive the latest turn of events Aspen liked to call 'calamity'.

Pultrie had come back. It was in the nature of wing

rippers everywhere because, to the bully, the insect should never fight back. More to the point, it should never, ever win. Gideon had to see it finished or Peter would spend the rest of his life looking over his shoulder, and Gideon knew how that went.

Unarmed, one handed and not a soul left on his side. With assets like those, what could possibly go wrong?

W HY the concern? The stranger had been everything you could ask for in a passing visitor. Nonetheless, the brothers felt an undeniable anxiety.

"Not in a big hurry, is he?" Ember observed.

"Or doing much to hide his tracks," Lee added.

Neither observation, where accurate, did much to eliminate the tingle of intuition. Not looking over one's shoulder could simply mean not having been caught yet.

Maybe, if they hurried, they could prevent calamity this time around. Or at least scrape Gideon off the wall when it was over.

A T the top of the highest stack of boxes in the Rivers' warehouse, Gideon found a fair sized shipping crate. A friendly nudge and Pultrie would have one big, freefalling mass of dry goods on his hands. Gideon put his shoulder into it. Then he put his back into it. He scrunched down, braced his feet and put his legs into it. In exchange for his labor, the crate took his breath.

Blast!

Gideon could hear Pultrie below, searching. A couple of much smaller boxes caught his attention and he pushed with enthusiasm. Over they went, lids breaking, contents spilling, sides splintering, cans clattering and who knew what bouncing, twanging and tumbling to the siren call of gravity. The avalanche danced with a grace like to a herd of blind, storm crazed cattle and stampeded onto the head of the unsuspecting thug below.

Whilst the cast iron cookware echoed and the curses hit the walls, Gideon launched himself to the comforting embrace of folds on folds of forgiving cloth. He scrambled to his feet, and then very wisely used them to make tracks. Behind him, the herd bawled and bellowed their complaints to a highly unsympathetic audience.

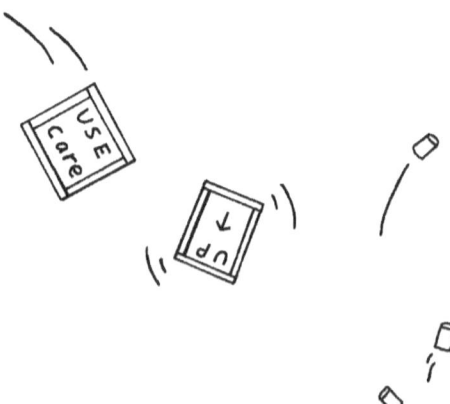

CHAPTER 14
Of Frying Pans & Fire
Gallant Damsel
Scrambled

G IDEON froze. There was nothing fancy about it, nothing thought out or done with deliberate, measured intention. His primal instincts simply kicked in and locked every joint in his body without asking for permission.

Admittedly, common sense suggested one should endeavor to avoid alleyways as they did not boast many redeeming qualities. What this one had offered was privacy, until now. A shame really.

"You know what that was?" a voice inquired.

There had been no mistaking the distinctly metallic click, small yet arresting. Gideon nodded.

"Good," said the voice, "then I don't have to tell you breathing wrong would be a really bad idea, do I?"

The eastern accent, liberally dosed with pure venom, left Gideon in no doubt as to who held the gun at his back.

"You know," Pultrie taunted. "if you were smart, you wouldn't have crossed me. Hands behind your head. Slowly. You wouldn't want any accidents."

Gideon scrabbled to imagine how his adversary stood, and completely failed. If it had been himself holding the gun, the thing might have been harmlessly aimed at the sky or not even loaded. Then again– if he were as wet hornet as Pultrie– it would be loaded and leveled in a very resolute manner.

A broom left by a backdoor suggested possibilities. If he could—

"Up!" Pultrie snapped.

Gideon measured his chances. It didn't take long.

Reluctantly, he did as he was told.

"Both hands. Eh-eh," Pultrie warned. "I did not say talk. I said up and I mean now."

There was no use trying to explain the impossibility of lifting his injured arm that high. Pultrie was not receiving visitors, most particularly rational ones. So Gideon held his peace and did his best. Now, with his left hand full of his right wrist, anything he tried would be unpleasantly painful and awkwardly slow.

This suited Pultrie perfectly. Since there was no longer a deed, there was also no job, no pay packet and no old lady. The critical point being, there no longer existed any impediment to doing whatever he pleased– and what pleased him most was revenge.

"Move," Pultrie ordered, and his tone harbored a malicious eagerness only a man covered with syrupy, greasy, slimy, miasmic nastiness could muster. "Straight ahead. Anything funny and I will not stop to ask questions."

It didn't require book learning for Gideon to see 'here' was a mighty fine place to not be. Amazing how that kept happening. No matter where he went, eventually, it ended up being a good place to leave– often in a hurry.

Presuming he enjoyed breathing, not that breathing anywhere within fifty feet of Pultrie counted as salubrious, exactly how much could a fellow in his position do?

Pultrie willn't shoot 'til he gets what he wants. That there's lev'rage.

Gideon held onto that hope with a passion only a man with a gun to his back could muster.

With his feet moving, and the initial gut clenching shock beginning to fade, his adrenalin gave a sheepish apology and put itself to better use. Namely, compressing existence down to a single moment, **this** moment, until it was more tangible than inconsequentials like sanity or healthy life preserving fear. Those things could get you killed. Whereas, through the eyes of adrenalin, everything became a possibility.

"Move," Pultrie ordered his already moving prisoner, and reinforced the command with a shove from the business end of his revolver.

Gideon stumbled and wondered if he could turn fast enough. He had seen it done once. An irritated gunman had stepped in too close. His prisoner spun around, slapped the gun aside with one hand and delivered a wicked punch with the other. As the gunman staggered, the Colt was neatly twisted away. It was a good move– tidy, quick and effective.

You'll get your fool head blown off.

He was right. With a ganky arm, off side or no, he would likely end up grappling with Pultrie, who was in exactly the right mood to plant him.

That'd save ya from Aspen.

Is this the time?

Not lookin' to be much of-a later.

Thank ya for that. Now stow it an' lemme think.

I am you thinkin'.

Then shutup an' think-a somethin' useful, will ya?

A contingent of haranguers lingered on the street, exchanging heated words, arms waving and gesturing to emphasize their particular point. Several other folks ducked in, out and around as if searching for something.

Isi took it all in and wondered what it was about, but in a town this size– who knew? Almost anything could count for high distraction. Interested as she was, Isi didn't figure her opinion would be highly desired. Besides, she had her own business to attend to.

Eggs. They were not her best friends. Last time she

had gone to buy a dozen, life conspired against her and only four made it through the saloon's kitchen door. Perhaps Gin-Bow would be better off putting in a coop. Then again, if she couldn't handle the eggs, how on earth would she manage the chickens?

Quite suddenly, Isi took an acute interest in the contents of her shopping basket. She toyed with the contents, shifted an apple, nudged the sugar and righted a jar of cherry jam.

That seemed about long enough.

Picking up her skirts, she raced down an alley. At the far end she stopped, clung to the rough-hewn wall, and peered cautiously around, basket still ridiculously clutched in her hands. A broad back filled her vision. One of the men she'd helped frame held a gun to Gideon's back. Isi had been right, her friend was in it up to his ears.

"Move," the man snapped, and his captive stumbled forward.

The idea came in a flash. Could Isi actually do it? She set the basket down and withdrew a few choice items. Gin-Bow would forgive her, given the need. Taking a breath, she imagined what must be done and then forced herself to step into the open.

What happened next defied belief and etched itself indelibly in her memory, where it would forever bring unabashed joy and endless pride.

Her arm came up. She yelled out. Pultrie spun. Slick goo splattered across shocked features and brown shells went flying. Yellow slime clung to Pultrie's matted beard and dribbled down his bemired shirtfront, adding to his disgustingly polychromatic state.

Another egg flew through the air as its mother never had and Gideon tossed himself to the dirt with remarkable determination.

Eggs? For real play?

With no time to spare for the logic of women, he addressed his shoulder to the back of Pultrie's knees. Down they both went in a crashing jumble of limbs.

Gideon swung hard and the blow landed squarely on Pultrie's ear. There was a yell somewhere between a growl and a shriek, then Gideon smacked into the ground, the air exploding from his lungs. He knew there should be pain, but for now adrenalin ruled, shouting and cheering with senseless mad frenzy.

An arm fell across Gideon's chest. He latched onto it for dear life and bit down.

UGH! Molasses!!

His taste buds cringed and threatened horrible repercussions. He had no time for such things though. His entire focus shifted to keeping his teeth in his head. Pultrie rolled on top of him, yanking and pulling in a vain attempt to extricate his arm. He weighed a ton. Fingers began to dig into Gideon's throat, severing his relationship with the air.

Gideon bite down harder, like a piranha with a mouthful of elephant. It couldn't last. It wouldn't last, not one second longer than Gideon's lungs could endure their deprivation. His body grew heavy and, rather quickly, ceased to exist. A hollow echo swelled in his ears and drowned out every other sound in the world. Life centered on teeth and jaw muscles and the fingers on his throat.

Drip.

What the devil?

Egg again. Egg was dripping on Gideon's face. What a peculiar thing to notice at a time like this.

Now or never, I reckon.

Is this you helpin'?

Oh, you'd like my help now? It's me been a-tellin' ya for a coon's age. Did ya listen? Hmmm? No. I keep a-tellin' an' you keep a-tellin' me to shutup. Well, boyo, it's you as got us here an' it's you gonna get us an all night stay in a pine box. Next time ya—

Next time? Next time?! You idjit! What next time!? I swear—

The world came crashing down, cutting off Gideon's argument with himself. Air rushed into his starved lungs. He gasped it in, vision blurred and heart racing.

Reckon that's 'bout a dollar an' two-bits saved.

Huh? What're ya on 'bout?

Dollar twenty-three really. Only who wants to dicker over two cents with a coffin 'twixt ya?

When in blue blazes did ya start a-pricin' coffins?

Seemed likely.

Mister, we gotta work on your notion-a helpin'.

Somewhere, at least a hundred miles away, were Gideon's feet and somewhere, presumably, were his hands. Arms. How many should one body have? Gideon was pretty sure he could count, at least to three. He counted again, wishing he could use his fingers, but that really did drop a loop neatly around the crux of the problem.

"Gideon? Gideon!"

It was the whisper of an echo of a thought from the end of the world's longest canyon.

"Hhnnn?" he said.

He had meant to ask any number of intelligent questions, but his brain was so addled it didn't even reach for the waking-up-in-strange-situations checklist. Until he rounded up a few more brain cells, inarticulate grunting would have to suffice.

"Let go!" a girl's voice pleaded.

Did Gideon know any girls? He didn't think he was the type to go around knowing girls. It wasn't entirely **im**possible, only why would he? Two? Was two the proper number for limbs? Two legs. Two arms. That had a certain rightness about it.

"Let go!!" Isi repeated.

Her urgency finally broke through and, in a fit of coughing and gasped breath, Gideon let loose his cannibalistic hold.

"Come on," Isi urged. "I don't think eggs will work a second time."

She really couldn't believe it had worked the first time. She could not have attacked an armed man with an egg. She could not have knocked Pultrie out cold with his own gun. Despite Isi's shock, no one else stepped up to claim responsibility.

She looped Gideon's arm over her shoulders. Where could she take him? There had to be somewhere safe. Well, there was certainly one place. It was hardly seemly, but it wasn't like she hadn't entertained a male guest before.

Up on the second floor of the saloon, Isi turned the key to her room and locked them in.

"You shouldn't—"

"Don't you tell me what I should or shouldn't do, Gideon Fletcher." Isi sat Gideon down and pushed a cup of tepid tea into his hand. "Drink this. You'll feel better."

Gideon had rarely been mothered. Bullied, cajoled, forced, threatened, and on one occasion intimidated, but rarely mothered.

An' then there were Aspen.

Isi was a far sight easier on the eyes than Aspen Rivers. Being mothered by her didn't seem all that bad. Gideon decided his brain must have been dropkicked. What he needed was to get out of there. Definitely. Yep. Right after he finished his tea.

The ancient armchair cushioned his aching body nicely. He was especially grateful for the wings that cradled his head; his skull had never felt so heavy. Adrenalin was beginning to balance its ledgers.

"Ya ever wanted to do somethin' else?" exhaustion asked, as Gideon stared vacantly around Isi's boudoir.

It wasn't the sort of question a working girl generally tolerated. Not that Isi hadn't thought it out and planned it over and over to the minutest detail, but she had never once told anyone else. Or even said the words aloud.

"Yes. Now, what did that man want with you?" she replied briskly, her voice remarkably steady for a girl who had just faced down a large, angry thug.

Behind his cup, Gideon shrugged. "Beats me."

"Don't you lie to me."

"Right," he sipped again and the herbal tisane, despite being cold, reminded him of companionship and a full belly. "No shoulds, no shouldn'ts an' no lies."

Isi plopped to her knees at Gideon's feet, and planted a sisterly kiss on his cheek.

"And no sass," she added.

Gideon blinked hard and his abused brain made no pretense of holding to the here and now. Isi's kiss had catapulted him back through the years to another perfumed room where his feet dangled over the edge of another gaudy chair. There had been a girl there too. Was that her lemon verbena or Isi's?

"No lies," he heard himself mumble.

"Good. So what's this all about?"

"Say," Gideon wondered, his own curiosity finally catching up with events. "Were you a-followin' me?"

"Looking for you. Who—" A bellow from the ground floor interrupted them and Isi's rosy lips curled with annoyance. "I'd better see what's started Hank hollering this early. I expect you to be right here when I get back."

She poked Gideon playfully and went downstairs.

Gideon did stay put and, as he abandoned himself to the chair and lingering traces of delicate perfume, Connell's words came back to mock him. 'Next time go easy' he had said, 'or better yet, don't have a next time.' Well, there was always a next time and nothing was ever easy.

Of their own accord Gideon's muscles began to call it a day. His shoulder burned and his side ached and there was absolutely nothing he was going to do about it. Ten minutes. What could ten minutes hurt? Peter had probably gotten away and. . .

Great day in the mornin'!

Gideon jumped from his chair, all lethargy forgotten. Looking for him! Isi had been looking for him! He was an idjit, a great big blue blasted idjit! Suppose Gin-Bow had sent her? Suppose he had news?

Gideon ran for the door and wrenched it open with barely enough sense to look before he leapt. The hallway was occupied by no one. Still, if he came crashing down the main stairs, questions would be asked of Isi and that would not do. There was no internal staircase to the kitchen. Gideon would have to use the stairs along the outside of the building and then duck around to the backdoor.

He took the steps three at a time. At the bottom, he grabbed the rail, skidded around with feet flying and took off like a shot. He should have expected what happened next, because there was always a next and nothing was ever easy.

Gideon slammed against something immovable and was, for a wild spinning moment unstoppable, then a hand clamped over his mouth and his feet lost all purchase. He fought and bucked, but whoever had him was entirely serious in their intent. Gideon could not budge himself one lousy bit. Silently, he gave vent to an incredibly vibrant, polychromatic and heartfelt malediction of a dominantly monosyllabic nature. He had to get to Gin-Bow! This was no time to be caught for the love of Paul.

Caught? By whom? And for what? The list of possibilities seemed to be continually growing longer.

It's a knack.

Of all the natural born talents to have there were easier options. Right. Easy. Not for him then.

A wagon lay overturned, one wheel spinning to no purpose. Another stood wedged into an alley never meant to oblige anything nearly so broad. Its front wheels would never be the same. And who knew where its horses had gone, probably quite far away with as much hurry as eight feet could coordinate. A hitch rack lay in pieces, an overturned trough spilled its watery innards, and the doors to the saloon lay clear across the street, hinges and all.

Gandy hadn't even known anyone owned a goat, but there it went, munching away on something that did not wish to be readily identified. A wide swath of the road had been churned to a muddy quagmire by Zeek's horses as they stampeded towards a freedom apparently best reached at top speed.

Much nearer to hand, the town's ancient old man rocked on his crate, unscathed by all, his cackle carrying across the myriad sounds of utter chaos. Somewhere something large and wooden splintered into toothpicks. By the sound of it, a broom would be too big for the job.

"Table?" Aspen guessed.

"Staircase," said Gandy, with the confidence of a professional.

They stood, side by side, in the middle of the road. It was the safest place. Attempts to mitigate the damage had been made, to no effect whatsoever. There was nothing for it but to wait for the fallout to quit falling and pick up the pieces afterwards.

From the balcony of the hotel, a pile of white linen drifted down, to forever lose its bleached dignity. No one noticed. Half the town was too busy brawling to bother with anything as insignificant as clean bedclothes, and the other half was far too busy yelling at the first half.

Another horse snapped its tether, snorted wildly and careened into the distance. Mud flew from its hooves and a thick, earthy spray landed with an organic splat upon Mrs. Driscoll. This did her no great harm, though it did cause her further indignation. Twice she had tried to get up— and twice fate had contrived to plop her back down. There she sat, on her duff, covered in red-brown muck from head to toe. Her wide brimmed hat, with its enormous cluster of preposterously bright silk flowers, had long ago succumbed to the unexpected trials of life and now drooped pathetically over her face. Later she would have fire in her petty soul, a woman on a mission for 'necessary measures', but for now Mrs. Driscoll was a woman in need of a bath and a calming cup of chamomile tea to bolster her sorely bruised dignity.

"Justice?" proposed Gandy.

"Possibly," Aspen acknowledged, with a certain small measure of sympathy trying valiantly to counterbalance a much larger measure of satisfaction.

In front of the café, an outspoken chicken clucked a complaint at all the fuss, whilst herself being a significant contributor. Her crate had crashed to the ground and lay in shattered pieces amongst a pile of its fellows. More chickens ran amuck, adding an addition and addendum to the already voluble noise. Fat bellied birds ran one way, a uselessly helpful dog chased after them, stirring them into greater and greater frenzy, and feathers flew everywhere.

Mathers himself chased chickens and shooed the dog,

cussing both indiscriminately. Chicken soup would never again bring him soothing thoughts of comfort. Just when he nearly had one blasted bird cornered, up burst another, distracting man and beast alike. The biggest malcontent gave out an ear piercing: squaaaawk! Then evaded capture and returned to the very top of the crates, where it resumed its rabble rousing.

Up above it all a hawk circled, judging its chances.

Aspen heard his aunt's voice ring out over the aviary cacophony and then a bonnet launched itself out the mercantile's front door. It held air bound, two small clawed feet peddling madly beneath it, until gravity demanded its rights. The hat hit the ground running, long ribbons streaming out behind, flapping in the self-made breeze.

"Roebucks?" Gandy wondered.

"Mrs. Harmon," Aspen informed him.

"Nice work."

The bonnet drifted left, spun around, cut to the right and swerved blindly— straight into Mathers, who grabbed gamely, but came up with neither bird nor bonnet.

"Lousy aim," Gandy observed.

"Makes good time though," said Aspen.

Some niggling, taunting thing suggested itself; some half recognized point of interest which perhaps really ought to have commanded a greater interest in a much more immediate and pressing fashion.

"Was that—" Aspen finally said, lines of uncertainty creasing his face.

A loud explosion rocked the air and both men ducked as something screamed erratically overhead. It pin-wheeled asymmetrically, a shrill whoom-whoom accompanying each revolution. The involuntary missile arced for a roof, where it went clean through without so much as a pause.

The spectators turned to find the blacksmith's had all

but disappeared behind a great, billowing cloud of black smoke. From out of the soot and cinders, came the goat. Its hair was singed and it was missing whatever it had been carrying by reason of said item having just been blown to smithereens. The impudent creature was followed closely by Smyth, who had given up trying to run it off in favor of having it for supper.

Luke Gandy hooked his thumbs over his gun belt and studied the remains of his town.

"Well. He's done it again."

"Ye-ep," Aspen drawled.

Both men winced as a brawler was knocked cups for teakettle and tipped headlong into the street. The goat caught him, dragged him an impressive distance and then dumped him directly under the feet of the smith, who then hauled the unfortunate up and proceeded to demonstrate exactly how much strength a man who works with iron day after day can put into a right cross. The brawler was left to contemplate the lesson whilst the chickens pitter-pattered over his unconscious body.

"Do you think he plans it?" Gandy wondered.

"No, sir," Aspen answered, with a confidence born of experience.

The sign over the bakery gave up its last hold and fell, swinging wildly on one hook.

CHAPTER 15
Ghost
Culpable To Capable
Reunion
Lay Of The Land
Going To The Mountain
Fit To Be Tied
Repaying A Debt

T HE shack had been abandoned. Some long forgotten builder had made use of the natural curve of the landscape, probably in hopes of gaining a measure of shelter from the wind, which just might have been the only reason the structure still existed.

Pathetic attempts at architecture, however, were not Gideon's concern. Presenting a maximum amount of grief to the man hauling him towards the sorry excuse for human habitation was. He fought for all he was worth, and found it worth not very much.

The door slammed shut with no regard for the resounding crack and Gideon's back hit the wall. Naturally. It was a prerequisite to any decent conversation.

Lately leastways.

"I ought to nail your hide to the wall, boy, and so help me, I might yet."

Gideon's attention flicked to the hands twisted into his shirtfront. His toes barely reached the earthen floor and that was definitely decrepit old wood digging into his shoulder blades. Exactly how much more nailed up did his captor propose to offer?

"You better start talking before I take up doing to you where your brother left off."

'Bout that much.

"He ain't my brother," Gideon protested.

The stranger leaned in closer, brows furrowed. "That is no way to show respect."

"Aw, go soak your shirt!"

"Your brother would kick your sorry carcass from perdition to breakfast for—"

"He ain't my brother!" Gideon repeated, kicking out.

The man dodged, but his grip tightened and his expression darkened.

"You better listen up, and listen good, Andy—"

Gideon flinched. He tried to cover it, but nothing doing. He had flinched and the stranger had seen it. Only. . . muted rays of amber light pierced the gloomy interior causing deep, flickering shadows. The contrast teased and obscured. Gideon squinted at the older man. This was no one to do with Tarlston that Gideon could recall, and he had inculcated those faces upon his memory very well indeed. Apparently, he had moved on to new and different enemies.

Oh, good.

It occurred to Gideon something other than malice lurked in the stranger's face. Irony? Satisfaction?

"How. . . ?" he nearly asked.

"Why shouldn't I know your name? I gave it to you."

Y OU'RE taking this remarkably well," Gandy opinioned.

"I've been feeling culpable long enough," Aspen told him. "It's about time I went back to being capable."

Gandy peered behind Mary's wash barrels. "And what do you plan to do, now that you're feeling so capable?"

"Isn't it obvious?" Aspen paused, one hand on the laundress's doorknob. "Hey, Luke? Didn't you say the thieves left this unlocked?"

"Sure did. Why?"

"It's more than locked now."

Someone had not only locked the door, but jammed the mechanism. Key or not, no one would be getting in that way again. The two men considered on the situation. Neither considered for very long.

"We have a real saint on our hands," the sheriff declared.

"Yeah, only he's dirtier than a coal miner from flirting with the fires below."

The two men flattened themselves against the building as the goat raced by, Mathers in hot pursuit. The dog loped along behind, mostly because everyone else was running so why not him? A chicken took up the rearguard, feet churning frantically. Eventually, the parade traipsed away and disappeared behind the clinic.

"What do you intend to do?" Gandy asked, not missing a beat.

"Get my hands on the little devil and explain to him the joys of having a brother."

"Don't use too many big words; our boy might get confused."

"Oh, I don't think there'll be much chance of that."

GIDEON let out a rush of breath.

"You sure had me worried for a minute there."

"Well, you better get worried all over again," Matt threatened, keeping a double fisted grip on Gideon's shirt. "Stealing? For real play? What were you thinking?"

"I ain't no thief!" Gideon shot back.

"That's not what that mob back there would say, and I'd say they feel pretty strongly about it too."

"I din't do nothin'!"

"Save it," Matt countered. "I've heard it before. Practically every outlaw in history has sung that tune to his grave. You do know you're blowing things all to heck here?"

"I done got Tarlston," Gideon rallied indignantly.

"Yeah, I know. And I know why. One question: self-defense or murder?"

Gideon knew Matt wasn't talking about the letter of the law. He didn't care what a court would say. He wanted to know what had been in Gideon's head and, more importantly, in his heart. What consumed Gideon's heart, soul, body and bone was revenge. He wanted Tarlston dead— then, now and always.

Self-defense or murder?

The unavoidable fact was, he should have pulled the trigger to balance the debts of the past. But when the time had come, he had fired to change the future instead. To keep the Rivers from being planted in shallow graves. To keep Peter from being one more name on the roll call of Tarlston's victims. After that, there hadn't been much time to think. A man had pointed a gun and Gideon had done his best to stay alive.

"Why's ever'body keep askin' me that?" he said irritably. "It don't matter none what I done thought nor wanted. Done's done."

One set of storm gray eyes met the other, two tides locked in opposition. Would Matt approve or condemn? Gideon had intended to kill, to bring about the justice good men deserved, and in the end they hadn't been any part of it. For this, that Gabe kid had idolized him. If only he knew.

"Defense," Gideon grudgingly admitted, and endured a long moment of heavy scrutiny for his trouble.

"Andy," Matt finally said, "avoiding killing doesn't

make a man a coward."

"Reckon," Gideon muttered.

Matt eyeballed his captive and reckoned maybe he didn't. Well, first things first and the first thing Matt needed was a clearer picture of how the cards lay.

"Half that town's after your scalp. What did you do?"

Gideon circled around the conversation. The words 'You do know you're blowing things all to heck here' presented themselves for examination. Exactly how much did Matt know, or think he knew?

"You tell me," Gideon stonewalled.

"I see you haven't forgotten everything I taught you," Matt said, his attitude relaxing, if not his grip. "Come on, let's see if what I've heard matches with what you've done."

"I din't go a-lookin' for nothin'."

"Looking or not, you found it."

"Aw, some half-wit judge pinned me with rustlin'."

"Rustling?" Matt whistled. "Boy, you're lucky you weren't hanged."

"He knowed I din't do nothin'."

"Then why—"

"How'd I know? By the time that judge were done I were staked out to dry. I'm a-tellin' ya, they're worse'n bog mire for not lettin' a man go. Tar'd be more civil."

"The judge?" Matt said, grasping for the conversational thread.

"Those blasted Rivers!" Gideon exclaimed. "Acted like I were some kind-a threat to decent-livin' folks, that confounded judge did. Said as how, 'stead-a jail, he were a-makin' me a ward— which ain't nothin' but a fancified word for pris'ner— and stucked me with 'em."

"For self-defense?"

"No! The judge done lit afore all that. For the beef."

"But you didn't steal the—"

"I know!" Gideon exploded in exasperation. "He knowed it too. They all did."

Like a man drawing two cards and finding them precisely what he needed, the fragments of stories Matt had picked up laid themselves out and finally made perfect sense. Of all the charges for Gideon to be pinned with, and all the situations for him to end up in– how ironic. This was one hand Matt knew exactly how to play.

"How long?" he asked.

"How long what?" Gideon hedged.

"Andy."

"Three years, an' don't you laugh at me."

"You've been railroaded, boy!"

"I know. An' I don't see nothin' so all-fired a-musin' 'bout it neither."

"Don't you?" Matt replied, his reaction reined in to a bubbling chortle that rolled between his words. "Well, you think on it some and you will."

"You gonna keep a-holdin' me here?"

"I'm comfortable."

"Aw, give over!"

"You just keep still a minute," Matt said, holding firm. "I didn't ride all the way out here for a nod and a handshake. You and I have a few things to talk over, son."

M A'AM?"

Eddie turned to greet her newest customer. The stranger had removed his hat and now held it in one hand. He was tidy, dark haired, clean shaven, plainly dressed, and not bad looking. If Eddie was any judge, he knew it too.

"If you're here for trouble," she warned conversationally, "I wouldn't recommend it."

What had given her the hint she did not know, but hint

there was. The man flinched, gave her a quick appraisal
and then seemed to make up his mind. It was just possible
Eddie was about to hear a very interesting story.

ASPEN Rivers?"

Aspen turned and looked into eyes that could have
been blue in one moment or slate gray in the next. He
couldn't decide if they were friendly eyes or very good liars.
He leaned towards the latter.

"Yes?" he said. "May I help you?"

"Actually," the stranger replied, his words in no
particular hurry, "I'd like to help you."

Alarm bells sounded in Aspen's head and red flags
whipped to attention.

"How's that?" he asked, all politeness.

"I believe," the stranger answered in the same ambling
manner that suggested there was no need for anyone to get
upset, "I may have something you want."

Aspen put a hand on his revolver. "Tell me, mister, is
this the hill where you want to die?"

SOMETIMES life plain does not work out. No
matter what a man does or how he comes at it, life plain
does not work out.

Sounds a mite familiar, don't it?

True enough. Gideon had kicked over the rocker box
and cut his trail and life had jeered at him. So much for
spreading out a man's grief.

He tugged at the ropes knotted around his wrists. So
much for talking things over too. Nothing though, not
ropes, nor Matt LaConner, nor the want of a single solitary
provision, was going to get in Gideon's way. He had to get

back to Caswell Crossing. He needed to talk to Gin-Bow. Then, maybe, he would learn the name of a killer.

W HO'S this?"

Aspen let the stranger fend for himself.

"Name's LaConner, Sheriff. Matt LaConner. I'm. . . a friend of Gideon's."

Anyone who had to pause before making a statement, especially one as simple as that, naturally piqued Gandy's interest.

He closed the heavy door to the lock-up and the repeat offender currently smelling up, and stickying up, an entire cell all on his own. There had to be a good story in there somewhere, and someday Gandy would get Gideon to tell it.

The stranger before him was leaner than most. An aura hung about him hinting, no matter how still, he would never truly be at rest. The corners of Gandy's thoughts told him quite clearly, if this man wanted to lie, you would have to be very quick indeed to catch him. Gideon might lie as a matter of necessity become habit, but this man struck as the type who could turn a common falsehood into an elegant masterpiece with a bare minimum of brushstrokes.

"A friend?" Gandy echoed, lowering himself to the edge of his desk.

"Yes, sir," said Matt.

Aspen's expression radiated doubt of any keen friendship and his hand remained quite comfortably on his revolver, as if unholstering it would prove no inconvenience.

"And why do I get the feeling," Gandy inquired blandly, "that you know where our friend has gone?"

"Probably because I'm the one who put him there," Matt answered, equally calmly.

"You always been a lefty?" said Gandy.

"What?"

Gandy nodded towards the gun on Matt's left hip.

"Have you always been a lefty?" he repeated.

"Sure, what does that have to do with anything?"

"How did you come to be way out here?"

"On a horse. Listen, Sheriff—"

"No. You listen, Mr. Matt LaConner, because I am only going to say this once. No games. No gentlemen's parlay. You are going to tell us exactly who you are and what you want or I am going to throw you into the deepest, darkest hole you have ever seen and you will **not** live to see the light of day. Do I make myself understood?"

"I'm Matt LaConner and I swear I'm a friend of Gideon's. I've spent a good long while trying to find him and I'd sure like not to get shot before I have a chance to finish what I came here to do."

"Which is?"

"I'd like to help."

"Are you his friend," Aspen asked, "or his father?"

"Father!" Matt exclaimed. He nearly raised his hands in emphasis and then thought better of making sudden movements. "Great stampeding bison, no. Not his or anyone else's. I'm a card player, a gambler. That's all."

"Then how do you know him?"

"There was a snowstorm. It was bitter cold and blowing something awful, let me tell you. I was caught out, and sick to boot. By the time I stumbled onto a trapper's cabin, I was all in. Would have been done in too if it hadn't been for Gideon and his brother nursing me through. They let me stay the whole winter."

"Keep going," Gandy prompted.

"When I heard what happened at the Harris place, I figured it was about time I looked those boys up. It wasn't easy, but eventually the trail led me here. Now, Andy and I, we've talked things over some and I have to say he won't exactly care for my brand of settling the score between us."

"Precisely what did you have in mind?" asked Aspen, his tone suggesting gunplay was still an option.

"Frankly, I think he ought to remain in your custody."

"How's that?" said Aspen and Gandy together.

"That young man has done some changing since I saw him last," Matt explained, "and not all for the good. What I hear of the Rivers, that's a hand to hold onto. Don't get me wrong, I can't blame Andy– Gideon— for hating Tarlston. What that man did to Harris and his boys, he should have been lynched. If it had been my brother— wait— I'll bet Andy didn't tell you about his brother, did he?"

"Not in so many words," Gandy admitted.

"Well, I will," Matt said, pulling up a chair. "Zebadiah Fletcher, Seb for short, was the elder by six, seven years. Can't tell you what name he was born with. For all we swapped a lot of talk that winter, he never did tell me."

A happy shadow brightened Matt's features.

"When I fell into that cabin, I must have startled the wits clean out of that poor boy, because all he could come up with to introduce himself was J.P. Elder. Just Plain Elder. Can you believe it? Well, I looked right at his scrawny kid brother and said, 'And he's the younger?' Andy Younger he was from then on— at least when I knew him. Anyhow, Seb ended up riding for Harris and he was the type to ride for the brand. Right to the end, from what I gather."

Gandy thought the flicker of remorse that played across Matt's face vouched for his sincerity and he found he wanted to believe this man. Handy trait for a gambler.

"How old was Gideon when you met him?" he asked.

"Hard to say," Matt answered readily, if vaguely. "Neither of them knew themselves. Maybe nine?"

"That's awfully young to be saving a grown man's life,"

said Gandy, tugging at threads, searching for holes.

"You have met him?" Matt replied, brows lifted and point clear.

"Reckon I have," Gandy relented, smiling ever so slightly.

"Andy always was full of spark. He didn't used to be choking on bitterness and dead set on solving his problems with a bullet. Seb wouldn't want that kind of life for him."

"And that's where you come in?"

"As a matter of fact, yes," Matt tried to assure lawman and guardian alike. "I owe him."

"You seem to know an awful lot, if you haven't seen him for as long as you say," Gandy suggested.

"I'll answer anything you like, ask away. But I'll start by telling you a man learns a lot by listening. Plenty of folks are willing to talk and I've had a lot of miles to think about what I've heard."

Aspen and the sheriff held a silent council. Minute signals were exchanged, meanings swapped, and conclusions drawn. It took a matter of seconds.

"Well?" Gandy asked, giving Aspen the lead. After all, it was his foster brother they were discussing, even if Gideon did prefer to think of himself as a prisoner.

Aspen gave a half shrug. "They must have met somewhere, who else says 'great stampeding bison'? And he's not asking for a ransom. So where is Gideon?"

"I thought we should talk first," Matt answered. "I left him at a cabin not far from here."

"Alone?" Aspen said, all attention.

"He's alright. I tied him up."

"Mister, you know those changes you noticed? Well, there have been a few more. You cannot leave that boy anywhere, for any reason, unless you want him gone when you get back. We'd best go find him."

Gandy raised a preemptory hand. "Hold up, Aspen. Do you suppose you could play the bad guy again?"

Aspen hesitated between staying and going, but he had played run and chase long enough. There were smarter, more efficient, ways to catch a man.

"What do you have in mind, Luke?"

"Well, if you'll go along with me on this, I think we can solve two problems with one stone. For a start, we'll need to move our guest over to the lock-up in the courthouse. I suspect we are going to have need of him but, before that, I'm going to need some room in the cells."

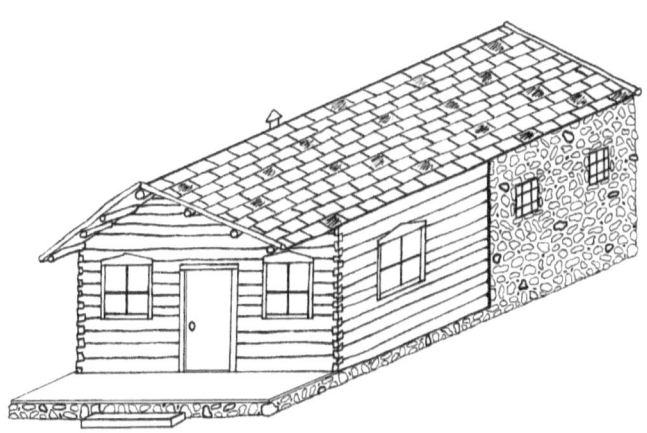

CHAPTER 16
Determined Leap
A Bit Odd
Directions
Multiple Counts
Speaking Of Thieves
Here– Again
What Mark Found
Bitter Pill

L AMPS shimmered. Voices drifted, disconnected and unnamed. Darkness reached into every corner and it did not matter. Gideon knew exactly where he was going.

Really? There's different.

Mind your own.

Hey, I am your business.

I ain't convinced.

Who helped ya with Tarlston?

You.

That mob?

Alright! I get your drift an', if'n ya want, I can quote it right back at ya t'other way 'round. Now, if'n ya don't mind none, I gotta pay a-tention.

The saloon doors stood wide open, spilling yellow light onto the dark street. Behind this patch of brightness, the same pitch challenged vocalist valiantly strove for operatic heights and the tinny piano went on regardless. Gideon had never seen printed music and would not have believed vocalist nor pianist had either.

Something felt. . . not entirely right.

Inching along the side of the blacksmith's, Gideon's hand came away smeared with black soot. Smyth did not seem the type to leave random bits of scrap metal peppered all over the ground and a definite aroma of explosives lingered in the vicinity. If Gideon had to guess, someone had blown up the forge. Whomever had done it, if the smith caught up with them, they would probably end up worse off than the forge.

Gideon studied the alley beside the saloon.

Wait.

There ain't time. We gotta get to Gin-Bow.

The darkness conveyed Gideon across the street, where he tucked into the alley and paused. Why? He had no idea. Nothing out of place reached his ears. Nothing unusual met his searching eyes. There was nothing to explain the tingling sensation dancing across his nerves. Less than twenty feet away lay the future. Possibly redemption, but probably not. Some things were unforgivable. Nevertheless, he had promises to keep and so he stepped out from the crates that hid him.

A shadow mirrored the movement.

"You mind telling me what in tarnation you think you're doing?" it asked.

Gideon spun on his heel, already half launched for the other end of the alley—

– and a second shadow blocked his escape.

Door!

Gideon lunged. Locked! Now what? The lawmen weren't advancing, but they weren't retreating either.

"Come on, Gideon. Time to come in," the reasonable tone suggested Gandy was nothing more than tolerantly amused at a good trick.

Gideon was not amused, tolerantly or otherwise. A few feet, a few blasted feet, separated him from answers. The lawmen had been expecting him.

That don't mean they know nothin'.

He couldn't let them know either. Nearly two years he

had searched, hunted, followed one measly, useless scrap of hint after another. Not for months– **months**— had he heard a thing about the man who murdered his brother. Sure Tarlston had ordered it, but someone else had pulled the trigger. Now, a measly twenty feet away, there might be a lead. All a lawman could do was mess things up.

"Ya gonna tell me ain't nothin' wrong, Sheriff?' Gideon said, measuring Gandy and then Wilson. "Ya gonna tell me how the whole town don't think I done stoled that fancy woman's trinket? With that Driscoll woman a-buglin' the news to heck an' gone? An' Reed a-throwin' in with her?"

"Did I say so? Come in with me and we'll sort this out."

"It don't go down, Sheriff," Gideon replied, shifting his weight to the balls of his feet.

"You will if you try it," Gandy cautioned.

Neither lawman looked likely to budge. Well, if they thought Gideon was going to give up, give in or give over they had a serious stop and think coming. By the time the town had its say and run him up the nearest tree, whatever Gin-Bow might have told him would be so much dust in the wind, one more cold trail.

That's what the rational part of Gideon said, but this was a rather small part and growing smaller with every second. The irrational part said it was really quite simple: there was Seb and there were these men. There could only be one. The other was merely an obstacle to overcome.

THE coffee was hot, fresh and mild. Aspen knew at first sip Wilson had made it. Cup in hand, he helped himself to a seat on the deputy's bed.

"How did Wilson get the black eye?" he asked.

"You know," said the sheriff, pouring himself a mug, "if Gideon's shoulder had been better healed, that boy just might have given us a fine chase."

"I'm surprised he didn't take you both head on."

"Oh, he thought about it," Gandy replied, settling down next to Aspen. He drew up one leg and propped his mug on his knee. "You know those crates outside the saloon? He scaled them like a mountain goat and made a jump for the stairs, nearly had it too. We hauled him down, but I'll tell you, he hit the ground with fists flying and feet kicking. There wasn't much we could do but sit on him until he wore himself out. It was root hog or die from his side of things."

"You're proud of him," said Aspen, mildly surprised.

"I wouldn't say that," Gandy denied quickly.

"But you like his sand."

"That's not the same thing."

"Well, I'll speak with him about Wilson. And your ribs," Aspen said, acknowledging the bruises Gandy hadn't.

"Forget it," the sheriff said generously. "He didn't know what he was doing."

Aspen's ears perked up. "He went odd?"

"I'll say. Clean out of his skull as far as I could tell. I hoped he'd come in but. . ."

"You ever seen anyone else act like that?" Aspen wondered. He'd known Gideon to get that way, but didn't know what to make of it.

Gandy sipped his coffee and nodded. "Met a retired soldier once. He said sometimes something would click inside. Next thing he knew, he'd gone clean through an entire regiment. He didn't much remember doing it, but the other side sure did. What was left of them anyway."

"What's it called?"

"I'd call it nuts, personally. I'd best have a word with Wilson. You want me to send that LaConner fellow over?"

Wilson had drawn the duty of minding their unnamed prisoner over in the courthouse. If it had been the egg shaped one, they would have the entire story by now. This one barely made a peep.

"How did you find him anyway?"

"The prisoner?" Gandy chuckled. "I followed the trail of slime. It'd take a corpse to miss the stench."

"Tell you what," Aspen suggested, getting to his feet and prudently not mentioning how Gandy supposedly wasn't proud. "Why don't I check on Wilson. If he doesn't need anything, I'll invite Mr. LaConner over to the doc's."

"For a few private words, you mean?"

"Yes, sir," Aspen agreed with a nod.

"I'd have to count you a fool to miss the opportunity."

Aspen would have counted himself a great fool indeed. There remained a warehouse of information he did not know about Gideon Fletcher, or Andy Younger, or whoever he had been before that. Aspen would grow old waiting for Gideon to elucidate or elaborate a single detail more than strictly needed. And that simply would not do because, as every older brother knew, what you really needed was leverage.

G ANDY sat under a wide spreading field of shimmering stars. The night was lovely, peaceful, and calming right down to the bones. The sheriff had even blown out the lamp over his door so he could enjoy the night view. Conveniently, this also gave the approaching riders less of a chance to locate a target.

There were three of them: one big fellow with two smaller riders like book ends on either side. Gandy sipped his coffee. Someday he would have to convince Wilson to add another handful of grounds to the pot.

"Luke, you seen our brother?" Fort asked, drawing up level with the jailhouse porch.

"Got the little one inside," Gandy answered, voice low. He tipped his chair against the wall. "You'll want to have a word with the big one."

"Have you seen—"

"Yep. They're both down at Connell's."

The boys glanced at each other. Gandy didn't seem worried but. . .

"You sure?"

"I'm sure," Gandy told them, and the slyness edging his voice reassured them more readily than words could.

"Thanks, Luke," said Fort, and headed for the clinic.

IF the law had a kink in its rope, Gideon figured he was doing something right. He would be danged if he'd turn snitch. That business with the broach may have cost him Peter's friendship, but that was life. People came, people went— sometimes for the good, sometimes not.

But what a man stood for could not come and go. The world could kick him, take his horse, steal his water. It could leave him stranded in a metaphorical desert of desperation, but there had to be a bottom line. What was the point of making it through the desert if you weren't still you when you got to the other side?

No, Peter would get a right thumping when Gideon had the chance, but turning him over to the law was not going to happen. Gideon wasn't that mean.

Gandy slouched against the corridor wall, thumbs hooked over his gun belt. He'd been asking questions and getting no answers. Frankly, this came as no surprise. This was not the mile high, cheeky specimen who had so recently visited his cells. This was a taciturn, grounded and pointedly stubborn prisoner with heels dug in.

"I'd like to be perfectly clear," Gandy explained, for

Gideon's benefit and edification. "I am not locking you up for being stupid and I am not locking you up as protective custody. I am **arresting** you on multiple counts of theft. So many, in fact, I had to buy a new bottle of ink. Aspen will not be along to let you out, though he may be along to sort you out."

Gideon stared out the barred window. The view hadn't changed, but that wasn't the only thing not shifting.

"The way matters stand," Gandy moseyed on, "I have no choice but to arrest you. And the way it looks, you could be in that cell for a good long while."

The sheriff was well aware of Gideon's feelings regarding enclosed spaces. He did not want to spend one single minute locked up. Confinement grated against his very nature. Gandy decided to perform something of a litmus test on his prisoner's mood.

"You want some coffee?" he asked.

"What?" Gideon said, jolted out of his indifferent middle distance.

"Do you want some coffee?" Gandy repeated innocently.

"What's with all the blasted coffee? For the love-a Paul ain't there nothin', one single solitary nothin' else for a man to drink in this miserable, forgotten excuse of-a town? There a shortage on sa's'p'rilla? Ain't nobody never heard-a tea? Nor plain out water? China's got itself a thousand diff'rent kinds-a tea. Every t'other blasted country on this here great green earth's got at least a dozen ways-a makin' whiskey."

Gideon was on his feet, hands gesturing broadly as his tirade steamed on. Gandy stood by and watched the show.

"Even cactus'd give a man a drink!" the boy exclaimed. "But no! Every livin' soul in these deuced, confounded parts is a-drinkin' confounded coffee! **It's bean filth!!** Ya hear what I'm a-sayin'? It's a load-a dried up beans burnt to a crisp an' ground to a stench-a dust a-washed over with water. Only, 'stead-a throwin' out the muck, folks go an' drink it! **Soot water!!** An' they act like they done got themselves the fanciest dang eatable ever put in a rusted up tin cup!"

This was one of the longest speeches Gandy had ever heard Gideon make and it gave a fairly accurate indication of Gideon's state of mind– or crumbling thereof.

"I suppose it's always possible there is some evidence I haven't seen, some witness I haven't heard from." Gandy paused to let the implications sink in. "Would sure be nice to know I'd arrested the right person."

"That's mighty civil," Gideon stonewalled.

"Maybe I could—"

"Don't," Gideon interrupted, with the boldness of a man not behind bars. "I ain't a-sayin' as there's nothin' I could say, but if'n there were, why in great blue blazes would I tell the likes-a you?"

"Because I can help," said Gandy.

Gideon gave a sharp laugh. "Put that in a rocker box an' see what ya get."

"I could do a lot more if you'd be straight with me."

"I know 'bout talkin' to the law. At best it comes to nothin'." Gideon turned back to the window and whispered his next words to a distant past he could have reached out and touched. "At worst it comes to people dead."

"Boy, someday you're going to—"

Gideon was not to learn what he would someday, because just then the bell over the front door rattled its perky jingle. Gandy scowled. This was definitely not a good time, but someone had to deal with the visitors.

"Be right there," he called out.

"No hurry," a man's voice returned, "we've waited this long."

Gandy's feet hiccupped mid-step. Councilman Barker. Caswell Crossing's truant sheriff had finally been caught. Right there in his own office too. Of course, thanks to Gideon, Gandy kind of had to be in his office, didn't he?

"I do b'lieve," his prisoner beamed, "that there's your future a-comin' to catch you up, Sheriff."

Gandy gave an indescribable look that very efficiently promised serious retribution to come.

IT's about time," said Mrs. Driscoll, who had already said a fair piece more.

"You're absolutely right," Reed lent his air to the whirlwind. "Gandy is a servant of the town and ought to pay more heed to what its citizens expect. At least now it's been made so plain he can't afford to ignore it."

"I always said no good would come of the Rivers taking in that thief," Driscoll huffed imperiously. "I, for one, will sleep more soundly in my bed knowing that riffraff is finally behind bars where he belongs."

"Blood will tell," Reed agreed vehemently.

That was all Peter overheard before the two busybodies moved along and he, startled at what he had overheard, stayed put.

LIFE was full of choices, good and bad. Even a fellow behind bars had choices, albeit far fewer than if he stood on the more salubrious side of the bars.

The thing about cells, the interesting thing, was that where they were designed to keep some things in, they also very effectively kept other things out. That must have been what Gandy meant by protective custody because, at the moment, being on the wrong side of the bars was providing

Gideon a fair measure of protection. Where he would not
count himself afraid, he did have the distinct feeling being
anywhere within a hundred yards of Aspen was not a choice
he would be able to live with.

Or through.

Oh good. You're a-helpin' 'gain. There's a treat.

"Why are we here? Give me one good reason why—
we— are here— again."

Aspen's words acted as if even they did not want to be
near themselves and were building up a good steam to give
each other room. Gideon could hear the pressure leaking
through the syllables.

"   " he said.

"Don't."

"—"

On the other side of the bars, Aspen's hand came up,
forestalling any attempt to give the demanded answer.

"Don't even try it. There is nothing you could say, no
excuse you could give, no story you could dream up that
could possibly explain why you and I are **here**. *Again*."

Gideon summed up his odds and opted to stand mute.
He did wonder in a sort of passing way if, having put fuse to
powder and struck the match, if, on reflection, he should
have put himself a skosh farther from the bang.

"I am waiting," Aspen fizzled.

Waiting? There was nothing Gideon wanted to say
about anything. There was nothing he could say about a lot
of things. Added all up, it didn't leave much on the table.
Clearly, what he was expected to say ran along the lines of
carefully constructed demure acquiescence– which he
hadn't a prayer of inventing. It was also not even in the
same general territory as what he actually wanted to say.

It wasn't looking too likely for half-truths, that was for
sure, or even little guppy ones, let alone the whoppers

required to see him or Peter out of this mess.

"You had better answer me, boy, and I mean straight."

Only, first Gideon had to keep Aspen's hands off of his own neck.

"It's a misun'erstandin'," Gideon tried.

"Really?"

That was a 'really' with a lot to say for itself. And its neighbors. It was even carrying a few letters down the line for folks it had never met. It was a 'really' that said 'How dumb do you think I am?' and followed with 'Would you like me to come through these bars?'

How long d'ya fig'r to live?

That had become a clear and present question in Gideon's life. Just then, he didn't figure more than about three seconds. He couldn't say he hadn't done anything— obviously someone had. Apart from Peter's broach, several other items had gone missing. Add this to the list of things temporarily borrowed without consent, and the general result could be described as a state of communal discontent.

No one would circle around to Peter– not perfect Peter— and he, Gideon, was already so mired in suspected criminality a few more accusations wouldn't make any difference. So what if it wasn't true? The town sure didn't care, and Peter would be safe. At least until Gideon caught up with him. So, all said and done, best not to say anything.

Um? Boyo?

What?

Ain't you a-seein' what I'm a-seein'?

What?

Look!

Gideon did. Something about Aspen had changed. There was nothing Gideon could point to and say 'Ah, here it is', but something had definitely changed. This wasn't mother-henning. This was—

The cell key materialized in Aspen's hand.

Dollar twenty-three time.

"I'm-in-for-theft," Gideon babbled out, his tongue struggling to keep up.

"Figured that," said Aspen, bluntly unimpressed.

"That's why I'm here, why we're here."

Aspen caught Gideon's eye. "You aren't a thief."

"It's why I'm here," Gideon repeated lamely.

"For something you didn't do?"

That was a loop looking for a steer and the thought nudged Gideon onto a possibility.

"Din't steel no beef neither but I'm in for that, ain't I?" Aspen fit the key into the lock, prompting Gideon to add, "It's the truth!"

Aspen paused. "Tell me another truth."

"Uhmm," Gideon stammered, at a loss in unexplored territory.

"What did you steal?"

"Can't tell ya."

The key turned, internal mechanisms clicked and—

"I can't tell ya!" Gideon repeated. "You can take me apart without no thought-a never puttin' me back together, but I swear I can't tell ya."

"Why not?" said Aspen.

Clearly this was not a question with a wide range of acceptable answers.

'Cause I ain't got no notion what were stoled seein' as it weren't me what stoled nothin', that's why.

That ain't 'zactly nothin' I can say, now is it?

Ya could tell 'im you're a-protectin' a no-good dirty thief.

The idea of talking to Aspen bobbed to the surface for a fleeting moment, soggy and dismal in its forgotten eddy, and then sank beneath the unforgiving stream of life.

Gideon had to come up with something because his immediate future stood one quarter turn from disaster.

"I ain't a-sayin' nothin' not nohow, not to no one. On a'count-a, if'n I do, there ain't nothin' a-keepin' 'em from doin' whatever the blazes they take 'em a notion to, an' me in no po-sition to do nothin' 'bout nothin'." And then, unaccountably, Gideon's inner voice grabbed the reins and added its own two cents, entirely without his permission. "Ain't pers'nal, an' I wish it weren't so, but a fellah's gotta make do with whatall he's got, 'cause it's 'im as got it to do. Ya hear what I'm a-sayin'?"

Aspen returned the lock to its duty and pocketed the key with a sigh.

"It's me an' trouble," Gideon shrugged. "Telled ya, ain't nothin' ya can do."

"Do you recall your first morning at the ranch, after I hauled you off that mountain?"

"What?" Gideon stalled, unsure where this was leading.

"You heard me," said Aspen, hooking his thumbs into his vest pockets. "Who kept Pa from jumping down your throat?"

"You but—"

"Who fixed your leg after you gashed it open?"

"You but—"

"Who kept Ember from walloping you after you gave him that headache?"

"Did you?"

"And I didn't kill you for losing my best rifle either."

Gideon wanted to say 'So what's your point?' except he wasn't an idiot and Aspen didn't expect him to be. Only. . . only nobody had watched Gideon's back or guarded his secrets for a long time. Even then, there had only been Seb. That's how it had always been– until Tarlston.

A random thought reached up and struck Gideon.

"You backed my play," he blurted out, with a distinct lack of credulity.

"Been doing it all along," Aspen agreed.

"No, no, no," Gideon babbled, one hand waving as if to erase the very idea. "What you been a-doin's called interferin'. What you done did with Rydel– that– that were backin' my play."

"Rydel?" Aspen echoed.

"You done heard me," Gideon insisted. "You had you one-a them words-a yourn with Chase Rydel. Din't ya? That's why he ain't been 'round none. You done did scared 'im off. You went an' done did backed my play after he done cleaned my plow for me."

"Truth?" said Aspen.

"Yeah!"

"Yes, I did. It's my job."

"You ain't my brother," Gideon objected indignantly, impatiently and inimically.

"Nevertheless," Aspen said, clearly pleased with himself, "you owe me."

"What?!"

"Truth for a truth— you owe me."

"You tricked me."

"Easily."

"Now see you here—"

Aspen tipped his head and lifted his brow, his meaning clear. It was not he in a cell. It was not he who had been arrested. Again. Therefore, it was not he in the answer giving position. Though, if Gideon wanted, Aspen could certainly explain a few things.

With some effort, Gideon swallowed his argument.

"Come on, Gov," Aspen coaxed. "Talk to me."

Someone to back his play. What was Gideon supposed

to do with that? Occasionally someone had lent a hand, especially if they could profit from doing so. But having someone to count on– that's what brothers were for and that road led only one direction: straight to the past. For Gideon, time had stopped two years ago. Life had stopped. The only thing that survived was his promise to hunt down every last man who had anything to do with Seb's death. Anything else was just a distraction.

"Truth?" he said, sincerely hoping to be let off.

"Truth."

"I can't tell ya."

"Well, you think on it some and let me know if you change your mind," Aspen replied, turning to leave. "I'll know where to find you."

"Aspen?"

Aspen waited whilst Gideon struggled with his thoughts.

"I. . ."

When this seemed to be the best Gideon could assemble, Aspen lent a hand.

"I know, Gov. You're still back to front. I do wish you'd dig up that grain of intelligence though and try using it. Keeping silent is not helping anyone."

Satisfied?

Shutup.

I'm just a-sayin'.

Shutup-shutup!

"Hasn't he told you?" Gandy asked, appearing in the doorway. "He's in for theft, multiple counts."

Gideon never figured a lawman for much use beyond giving a nickel's worth of metal a place to hang, but he was sure grateful for the interruption.

"And for the damages to the town, of course," the sheriff added.

And suddenly Gideon was un-relieved. "Damages?"

"That's right, you haven't seen the wreckage." Gandy let out a low whistle. "I'd avoid Smyth for a while, if I were you. Mathers too, come to mention."

"How much," Aspen asked, like a man bracing himself for the unpleasant, "do the damages come to?"

"Oh, they haven't finished the tally yet. No, sir, not even close. C'mon, I'll tell you all about it."

"You think on what I said, Gov," Aspen advised.

Gandy threw a broad wink in Gideon's direction and followed Aspen out. Gideon fancied he saw a dozen futures forming in that half second— and none of them good.

P ULL up a pew," said Gandy, pointing to the top step of his porch.

"Haven't you found Gov's picks yet?" Aspen said, rightly guessing Gandy did not wish to stray any farther then he might have to chase.

"Have you?" Gandy countered.

"You're the lawman."

"So? You're the guardian."

"Then I guess we're both outsmarted on that front."

"You almost had him," Gandy offered. "If our boy were going to talk, that would have been the time."

Aspen plucked up a grass stem. "Close doesn't sheer the sheep."

"Don't worry, Peter will be along and I have a feeling he will be far inclined to talk."

"I wish he had come to us sooner."

"I'd lay odds he does too," Gandy agreed, eyes twinkling.

"Or he will by the time you're done with him?"

"That too. Peter's alright, just a little turned around is

all."

"You know, Luke, I'd swear you mean to rescue every poor soul who wonders across your path."

Gandy shrugged. "Simpler is all. I straighten them out first thing, I don't have to hang them later. Saves on paperwork."

"Speaking of which," Aspen said, peering sidelong at Gandy, "the council asked me to be sure you actually attend the next meeting."

"I'll be there," Gandy promised, but it came out more like a complaint and nearly a curse.

The town council had threatened to lock him in his own jail and hold their retched meeting right there if he didn't schedule a time on his own and promise– on pain of his deputies dragging him to the courthouse– to keep the appointment.

"You surely will," Aspen drawled, "because they asked Mathers too. And Smyth."

Gandy winced. Those were two of the toughest men in town, and Aspen was no glance-over either. The sheriff had sort of hoped he might still find some plausible excuse.

"Oh, shut up. Where's LaConner?"

"Talking with the boys." Aspen grinned, but politely refrained from commenting on this obvious attempt to change the subject. "Seems they met up already. They like him. Now that they know what he's up to things are downright friendly. I don't imagine Gov will like that too much. Is Mark back yet?"

"Half an hour ago," Gandy replied, clearly satisfied.

"Oh-ho, and did he—"

"Yes, sir."

"And do you?"

"Yes, sir. There's something else you ought to know."

"Yes?" Aspen asked, curiosity brimming.

"Mark bumped into someone else out there and decided to bring him along."

"Who. . . wait. . . you don't mean?"

"That's right."

"Luke Gandy, you do love your job, don't you?"

"Yes, sir. You still in?"

"Oh, yeah," Aspen agreed wholeheartedly.

PETER had been there for twenty minutes. The facts had not changed. The sheriff's office had not moved. He had just about got it figured out though. He had just about laid his finger right on the crux of the matter. Unfortunately, it took some hard swallowing to get it down.

He had been a fool to let himself become entangled with Cort's gang. Worse, he had stolen from people who had never done him a moment's harm. Granted, Peter hadn't actually done everything that had been reported, but he had been in on it. And now he was not in. He was out. It was Gideon who was locked up and in for it.

He had felt so. . . well, no man likes to admit it, but Peter had felt helpless. Everything had been happening **to** him, and he had simply been reacting. He fingered the bracelet on his wrist: his mother's hair, his father's treasure. From the day they met, they had never looked back, only forward. To him. To their son and the man he would become.

They had taught him about manners and hard work, but no one can teach a boy how to feel like a man. Every boy needs someone, sometimes several someones, to be their guide, but no one can reach inside, pick the boy up, put him on his feet and make him stand his ground. That moment is entirely up to the boy himself.

Out there in the dust, with dynamite exploding all

around, Peter had crossed the line. He had found his moment and there was no going back. Not for him.

The jailhouse door clicked shut ten times louder than usual. What would a cell door sound like when it closed? Peter figured he was about to find out. This was not an answer he especially wanted.

"Sheriff?" he forced himself to say.

The lawman sitting behind the desk set down the rifle he was cleaning. "Peter."

Every thought in Peter's head log jammed tighter than a miser's fist.

"Sheriff, I. . ." he said, took a deep breath and tried again. "Sheriff, I think we should talk."

CHAPTER 17
Curry Comb And A Brush
Uneasy
Prove It
Tic
Evidence Always Snitches
Toc
Fried

ASPEN did not come across as a man interested in talk. His was not the terse sort of saying nothing a man might take as due warning of rough country ahead. There was no sign of anger, or danger, or anything else. This was simply nothing. It was creepy.

"Peter done spilt," Gideon dared to explore. "He done telled me. There ain't no charges on me no more."

"Sheriff Gandy told you to be on your way did he?"

"No, only. . ."

"Yes?"

"Well, if'n you're here, an' I'm out, ain't that the same as let loose?"

"Not exactly," Aspen said. "Inside, please."

"But this's Mary's. What're we a-doin' here?"

"Do you really think you're in the best position to be asking questions?"

"I got me a right," said Gideon.

"As a matter of fact, you don't. That's what prisoner means. Now, inside, please. You have an appointment."

"Huh?"

"It's something gentlemen keep."

"An' you reckon that's got aught to do with me?"

"It does today."

Gideon's instincts screamed half a dozen warnings in

at least three languages. He was pretty sure he did not wish to stick around and discover whatever was about to transpire.

"So you say," he refused, with strong and immediate thoughts of faraway places.

"So I say," Aspen asserted, latching onto his ward with both hands and ushering him into Mary's back room.

His brothers stood waiting, morbid curiosity causing them to wonder what on earth Gideon had been up to and what— exactly— did the other fellow look like. Plain good sense kept them from actually venturing down this path.

In the same blink of time, Gideon noticed the half-barrel in the middle of the floor, the large bar of soap in Fort's hand, and the unified resolve on the brothers' faces.

"I got rights!" he protested, tugging against Aspen's iron grip.

"Really?" Fort replied, idly rubbing the edge of the soap against his jaw, as if actually considering the notion. "And here I thought you had a record."

"And a sentence," Lee added.

"And not much sense," Ember joined in.

"And a standing option for long term imprisonment," Aspen finished, making it sound like a promise.

The boys stepped in, closing their circle around Gideon— who felt pretty sure ganging up on a fellow was against the rules.

PETER tried not to think about the night he had broken into the judge's office. It wasn't such an easy thing to forget whilst sitting on a bench right outside the selfsame office. It was really tricky when you knew every thought you had, every wrong deed you had ever done, was perfectly clear to the lawman sitting beside you. Peter's fingers gripped the edge of the polished bench.

"What about Gov?" he asked.

"He'll be along," Wilson replied uninformatively.

Silence fell again. Peter told himself not to worry. It was hard to hear himself though, what with the sound of the cell door banging shut echoing inside his skull. He had been right about that, it had sounded louder from the inside. He hoped to never, ever, hear that sound again.

"Aren't I being charged with the thefts?" he brought himself to ask.

"Yep," said the deputy.

Another long minute crept by, feeling more like six and a half years. Peter mustered himself to try again.

"I thought. . ."

"Did you?" Wilson countered dryly.

"Yes, sir. I thought Gov would be cleared."

Wilson settled his back against the wall, a man content to wait out eternity.

Peter stared at his wrists. Wilson had handcuffed him. The dense weight of the metal rings pushing against Peter's skin was nothing compared to the implications pushing against his imagination.

"Deputy Wilson?" he asked, trying hard to keep his voice level. A slight tilt of Wilson's head suggested he should proceed. "What's going to happen?"

"I'm just a deputy, son, not the judge."

"Is he a real justice of the peace?"

"Real as they come."

"So. . ."

"So you might want to be on your best behavior."

Peter swallowed. It wasn't easy.

G IDEON'S very best behavior on his very best day

was not likely to be of much help to him. He stood before the same desk confronting the same judge whose acquaintance he had already made on a previous, and well-remembered, occasion.

Their first meeting had put Gideon in mind of a snake on stilts. Politely phrased, the judge was a gray haired gentleman of progressed years, remarkable height and very little mass.

The Rivers— four sons, father, and even Cricket— rode drag, and, off to one side, Gandy held flank. Gideon was one maverick who was not going to be allowed to stray.

"Do you have anything to say for yourself?" the judge asked, all business.

"Would it matter?" Gideon replied, all Gideon.

The judge remained bent over the document before him. His eyes travelled line by line, item by item, infraction to infraction. At last he looked up and set the paper aside.

"Tell me about your Mr. Tarlston."

The image of a gallows jumped to Gideon's mind. Would it always come around to that?

I been a-tellin' ya.

Shutup.

"He's dead," said Gideon, to drown himself out.

"Indeed," said the judge, "and by your own hand. I suppose you'll try to tell me you had no choice?"

"Always a choice," Gideon contradicted.

"And what was yours?"

"Let 'im kill Peter."

"Or you?"

Gideon gave half a shrug that clearly spoke his indifference to this possibility.

"I'm curious," the judge mused, settling back in his chair, "how exactly did you get Tarlston to direct his attention to you instead of Peter?"

In the absence of a gun, Gideon hooked a thumb over his pocket. Should he answer? The deck might already be stacked against him; anything he said could make it worse. Who knew what that sheriff had said? And what about Aspen? Had he spoken to the judge? Aspen wouldn't lie, but he hadn't actually been there either.

Aspen made not a sound, even so, Gideon could feel the weighted silence pressing against him.

Talkin's easier afore they get a rope 'round your neck.

"Mr. Fletcher?" the judge prompted.

Ya gonna let 'im have nothin' but the sheriff's half-a the tale?

"Tarlston wanted me," Gideon finally answered. "I let 'im find me."

"You just stood up and hollered 'Here I am'?" the judge questioned.

"Yep."

"To an armed, vengeful man with nothing to lose?"

"Yep."

"Did you perhaps think this through at all?"

"Why?" Gideon's inner voice piped up. "Thinkin' can get ya killed. Actin' done kept Peter alive."

"But nearly killed you," the judge pointed out, as if there were something in this Gideon should be grasping.

Gideon merely shrugged. Life was full of choices.

The judge regarded him for a long moment.

"You did have a strong motive– that is, reason— to hate Tarlston."

Ah, we're a-fishin' 'gain.

"Let's cut to it," Gideon countered. "I din't hunt Tarlston, but I sure buried 'im. I ain't gonna take no part-a that back. If'n I din't a-done what I did, Peter wouldn't be here. If'n you're gonna hang me for that, best to get a rope an' get it done."

Gideon's tone made it plain, if this was life's idea of justice, he would be happy to give it a black eye on the way to the gallows.

He tugged at the stiff collar around his neck. The Rivers hadn't put him in a real collar, that would have been absurd, but they had picked a crisp, new shirt and secured him into the garment right up to the top button and all the way to the wrists. They'd even strangled him with a ribbon necktie and hitched up every last button on his vest. The hems on his trouser legs sat just so. Those blasted Rivers had even tackled him into a brand new pair of boots. They were polished. They nearly shone.

Least you'll look good in the coffin.

You're a-makin' a habit a that, ya know.

Lately.

Gideon realized the judge was staring at him in a most peculiar way and he wasn't the least sure what it meant. Was he being weighed? Would he be found wanting? He had certainly found himself coming up a smidge short recently. Recently? For nearly two years now.

"I see no reason to pursue the Tarlston matter further. The statements on record align with yours and, as you say, lives were at stake," the judge declared, giving the stack of documents on his desk a tap to square the pages. "So, let us proceed to the present charges, shall we?"

That's all?

You'd laver we went back to ropes an' coffins?

This was a good point, and Gideon took it to heart. All the same, habit was habit.

"What charges?" he challenged.

"Would you care to read them for yourself?" The judge held up the charge sheet and managed to look nothing but helpful. "No? Well, why don't I go ahead and read them aloud then. We open with: Obstruction Of Justice and Withholding Evidence. Neither are good ideas, but things could be worse. Ah, and so they are. Here we have: Breaking And Entering, Aiding And Abetting, and Interfering With An Officer In The Execution Of His Duty. You're going to have a hard time convincing me that one is inaccurate, Mr. Fletcher. And then we have: Assault On An Officer Of The Law, multiple counts, and Attempted Jailbreak, multiple counts. Ah, and Resisting Arrest, also with multiple counts. And I see Deputy Wilson has added a footnote: Being An Unmitigated Nuisance Despite Having Been Repeatedly Warned. Not precisely an official charge but, in your case, there might be sufficient grounds. Now, I ask you again, Mr. Fletcher, do you have anything to say?"

Gideon wasn't sure what all those fancy words meant. What was a fellow supposed to do with 'abetting'? He couldn't recall having gambled recently. And a body would have to hope 'execution' had an alternant, and remarkably less violent, meaning. Adrift in a sea of jargon, he latched on to a charge he could get a loop around and ran with it.

"Don't reckon as it'd make sense to break jail an' not resist arrest," he said, pointing out the obvious flaw in logic. "If'n ya did resist, nat'rally you'd be interferin' some too. Reckon it kind-a piles up on a fellah, don't it?"

"Are you pleading guilty?"

In Gideon's experience it did not pay to admit to anything the other fellow had not out and out proved.

"Nope," he said plain, to avoid confusion.

The judge tapped a narrow wooden plaque on his desk.

"It's Forsythe, in case you've forgotten," he said, in the same annoyingly helpful tones, and then he did a double take. "Dear me, I seem to have missed one. Larceny, it says here. Really?"

Honest doubt tinged Forsythe's features. The only

thing tinging Gideon's features was confusion, in some quantity. He peeked over his shoulder to borrow a hint from Aspen, who merely lifted his chin towards the judge.

Oh, good.

You were spectin' help?

Not really.

"Larceny?" Gideon queried, annoyed at having to admit to ignorance.

"A dignified word for theft," Forsythe explained.

"I ain't stoled nothin'."

Forsythe stared pointedly until Gideon added a reluctant 'Mr. Forsythe'.

"And the other charges?" the official asked.

"Nope. Not them neither."

P ETER listened to the vague sounds of conversation coming from the judge's chambers. The lack of details encouraged his imagination to fill in the blanks and he wished he could shut himself up.

"Deputy Wilson?"

"Yes?"

"How long do you think they'll be?"

The deputy stretched out his legs and crossed his ankles. "Oh. . . hours sometimes."

Hours? Hours to sit there wondering what was being said and what could possibly be said when his turn came?

Peter rubbed one sweaty palm against the other. Suppose Gideon gave the judge a hard time? Mightn't that mean he'd be somewhat shy on patience? Was there any chance Gideon might think of this and keep it short? Were they even still friends enough for Gideon to care about Peter's agony of waiting? Were either of them going to survive long enough for it to matter?

T HINGS were not going well.

"I have seen Deputy Wilson's eye, Mister Fletcher," Judge Forsythe said, putting down his pen and peering over his wire-framed spectacles. "Are you telling me that was not, in any way, your doing?"

They had him there. That was one very black eye and it was all Gideon's doing.

So that's what 'assault' means.

Gideon sincerely wished he could do the same to Gandy, who had brought the matter up in the first place. It was not helping his case in the least– with anyone.

Ya wanted ev'dence.

"Reckon that were me," Gideon had to admit, because there really wasn't much else he could say.

"And why, exactly, did you hit my deputy?" Gandy cross-examined.

As if'n he don't know darn good an' well.

Gideon could clearly see one of those futures Gandy had winked at him and it was coming up mighty fast.

He jabbed a thumb at the over helpful sheriff. "Could he wait outside?"

S ITTING there was killing Peter. Or maybe it was the waiting. Or the not knowing. Or the aggravated voice to which he could not put a name. Surely pacing would be better than sitting. Wilson dropped a restraining hand on his prisoner's arm, but Peter couldn't settle. His fingers tapped against the handcuffs. His toes tapped against the floorboards. His nerves tapped against each other.

"How long has it been?"

Wilson pulled out a pocket watch. "About five minutes

since the last time you asked."

FORSYTHE wasn't sure if he should call Gideon a miscreant, a petty malefactor or a straight up criminal. On that count, he was willing to withhold judgment for the time being. He reached down and slid open a desk drawer.

"Care to explain where my files have gone?"

"No," Gideon answered flatly, and the flat of Aspen's hand smacked him on the back of the head.

"Would you care to try again?" the judge offered, rather generously by his estimation.

"Weren't no theft," Gideon rallied gamely. "Them papers were mine to start with."

Forsythe peered at him. "Are you at all familiar with the term 'incarceration', Mr. Fletcher?"

"Don't seem likely."

"You would be amazed."

Gandy coughed and various abbreviated forms of snigger emanated from the Rivers boys.

"I got me words 'nough," Gideon grumbled, in his own defense.

"Indeed, 'contumacious' and 'incorrigible' being first among them," Forsythe opinioned, picking up his pen. "I might suggest you consider brushing elbows with 'penitence' or possibly 'sagacity' in the near future. In the meantime, I think we can safely add another count of obstruction to the list."

"What's that?" Gideon asked around his pride, leaning forward to read the marks on the judge's paper as if they would somehow grant understanding.

"Obstruction means to prohibit," Forsythe stopped himself and reached for his sub-layman's terminology. "That is to say: butting in so justice cannot be done."

"Scratch that there one off then."

"You have some logical reason why?"

Why? Because of sheep. Simple, heads down pathetic little sheep. What did sheep know about justice? Sure they wanted it, provided someone else acquired it for them, wrapped it up, delivered it special. Then they wanted it. If they had to get up off their knees, leave their green fields, fight tooth and nail and drag it home? Not a chance. That was why. Because someone had to keep an eye on the balance of things and Gideon couldn't come up with one single, solitary reason why it shouldn't be him.

"Lawmen ain't got no claim staked on justice," he replied. And this might have worked if he hadn't followed with, "I ain't never met no tin-star as could find a single ounce-a justice with both hands an' a map."

"The charge stands," Forsythe declared, his words like a gavel. "Mr. Fletcher, on your last visit to this court you were sentenced to three years in the custody of Mr. Rivers."

The judge indicated Amos, who politely nodded his acknowledgement of this fact.

Since you seem to have missed my meaning when I directed you to conduct yourself civilly, and legally, we shall back up and let you have another run at it. I am declaring your time served thus far un-served."

"You ain't serious?"

"It beats the alternative, son. Now quit giving Aspen a hard time, do as the sheriff tells you, and, for mercy's sake, try to stay out of trouble. I do not wish to see you in this office again and, if I do Mr. Fletcher, you will not care for the consequences. Is that understood?"

Gideon considered on this. "S'posin' I say no?"

The half-circle of men around him shifted one step forward and, despite the fact the Rivers therefore took up less actual space, it felt as though they occupied every inch of available space.

"Do you understand me?" Forsythe repeated more firmly.

"I got me no kind-a choice?" Gideon countered, the words sounding not entirely dissimilar to sailors' parlance.

"I would never have it said I am an unfair man," replied Forsythe. "I did indeed intimate there exists an alternative. Should you prefer, you can be remanded into the custody of Sheriff Gandy, who will lock you in a cell for the next three years. Now, what will it be, Mr. Fletcher?"

Gideon didn't really believe Forsythe had a lick of authority to give such an ultimatum. The men ranged around him, however, did at least possess the authority of greater numbers. And size. And strength.

Choices. It was all about choices, and sometimes a man was not presented with anything he would actually want to swallow. The trick at such junctures was to choose the bad choice with the greatest potential to reach into the future and line up the greatest number of prospective good choices for tomorrow.

A ten by ten cell don't fit the bill, boyo.

"Reckon— if'n I gotta give one way or t'other— I'd laver go 'long with Aspen, if'n it's all the same, thanks."

"I see you have added some new words to your vocabulary. I cannot help but wonder if you fully appreciate their meaning. Take him home gentlemen, before I change my mind. Sheriff, bring in the other one, please."

CHAPTER 18
For The Record
A Word
Some Explaining
The Joys of Having A Big Brother
Some More Explaining
Can We Talk
Peter's Debts

PETER sprang to his feet. Gideon was leaving. He wasn't in handcuffs, but he sure didn't look happy. What happened? Why had it taken so long? No one spared Peter much of a glance and there was a noticeable void where words of encouragement should have been.

"Peter?"

Gandy held open the door to the judge's chambers. For all that Peter could hardly sit still five seconds ago, he stood rock still now. Wilson touched him on the back and he must have moved because, of a sudden, he was in the judge's chambers. Sheriff Gandy stood to one side and Peter's guilt filled up the remaining space.

The judge sat behind his massive desk, with its rigid file cabinet sentries, and reviewed a document. Peter wondered if he had even been noticed. Then he wondered, if he hadn't been, maybe he could change his mind and slip out of this. Without doing anything, Gandy radiated the kind of authority one would be wise not to cross. Peter concentrated on breathing.

"Sir?" he managed to choke out.

"Yes?" the judge prompted, still not looking up.

"Gov, he. . . he's not so bad, sir. He doesn't mean any harm. Mostly he was trying to help me."

"Thank you. We don't appear to have your full name on

record."

"Anderson, sir. Peter Thomas Anderson."

"Ah, and would you, by chance, spell it like this?"

The judge held up a scrap of paper. Ridged scribbles zigzagged across it and, shining through, a surname clearly announced itself.

"Yes, sir," Peter agreed weakly.

"I found this right here in my own office. Which is interesting because, other than perhaps Sheriff Gandy, not a soul has any legitimate business up here. Before we become too deeply involved with any specific charge, however, what do you say we have a look at the entire list?"

"Yes, sir," Peter replied, and began to realize what had taken Gideon so long.

COULD you give us a minute?" Aspen told his brothers. "Gov and I need to have a word."

Once again Gideon tagged along, although mostly this was because Aspen had him firmly by the arm. This time Gideon knew precisely where they were headed— the livery. This could have been merely a matter of convenience, as it was near to hand and offered some privacy. It was certainly hard to imagine Aspen starting a dust-up behind a barn. Such conduct would hardly be gentlemanly, but then, you never knew.

"Do you think he'll be alright?" Lee wondered, peering after them.

"Aspen knows what he's doing," Fort assured him.

"I meant Gov."

"So did I," said Fort.

"You made me a promise," Aspen began, the moment the barn obscured them from view.

"There been a few," Gideon hedged. "Which one did ya

have in mind?"

"The one where you were going to play nicely with Deputy Wilson. I don't call a black eye very nice."

"Oh, that one," Gideon said, for want of anything more intelligent.

"Yes, that one, and don't even think about giving me the kind of lip you tried on Judge Forsythe."

"Would it help none if'n I said I weren't 'zactly thinkin' straight at the time?"

"What do you think?"

W HAT do you have to say for yourself?"

Peter forced air into his lungs and held up his head.

"Guilty, sir," he said.

"Of which charges?"

"All of them, sir."

"All of them?"

"Yes, sir."

Forsythe glanced at Gandy, "How refreshing. Would you care to tell me why?"

Peter looked desperately from one official to the other.

"Would it help?"

"It might," the judge allowed.

Peter began to talk. Several minutes went by. The judge asked some questions and Peter talked some more.

"Let me see if I have this straight," Forsythe said, gently rocking his chair. "You have no family?"

"My mother took ill and my father went six months later. He. . . I don't think he had the heart for it anymore, sir. Living, I mean. He tried," Peter clarified hastily, lest anyone think his father a coward. "Only. . . his heart died when she did. His body just didn't get the message for a while."

"And your father, excuse me for being blunt, he left you with no means of support?"

"He left me the cabin and he taught me to work."

Forsythe aimed a piercing frown at the young man before him. He was more than a boy, yet not fully a man grown. He stood at a crossroads. How many times had Forsythe looked over his desk at a young man who had taken a wrong turn?

"I imagine your father taught you not to steal too."

"Yes, sir," Peter admitted, studying his feet.

He wrapped a hand around his wrist and, beneath the unforgiving metal of handcuffs, touched a band of braided walnut hair.

"And the two men who were after you?"

Peter's head snapped up and his eyes went wide. He hadn't mentioned anything about Pultrie or Wilcox. That he found himself broke, friendless, without provisions and generally in a bind, this he had admitted. That he allowed himself to be maneuvered into stealing for Cort's gang, yes that too. He enumerated which thefts belonged to him and which to others. He had even given names and descriptions; he was through light-stepping for the likes of Cort.

"Mr. Anderson?" Judge Forsythe prompted.

Admitting to the thefts, no matter the consequences, had put an end to Peter's trial of conscience, cleared Gideon and hopefully ended Cort's run. But, should he say anything about Pultrie, keeping Gideon's name out of it would be difficult. Admittedly, it would yank the lid right off his own kettle too.

"Peter."

Peter could not stop himself from meeting Sheriff Gandy's gaze. He seriously wished he could have.

D 'YA reckon Aspen'd lend ya the dollar twenty-three?

Mite busy here.

Aspen had twisted Gideon's left arm behind his back and pinned him against the barn. This was no way to hold a discussion, at least not from Gideon's point of view. Possibly Aspen saw things a little differently.

"Do you know what you're going to do?"

"Whyn't you tell me," Gideon answered, unwilling to venture a guess.

"You're going to set things right with Deputy Wilson."

"Like h—"

"Eh-eh," Aspen warned, edging Gideon's arm up a fraction farther, yet his voice remained smooth as honey. "That is not how this works. You see, this is where I do the telling and you do the listening. Right?"

"Sure now, only it don't make no sense me squarin' with Wilson, seein' as I done promised you. An' I already done told ya I din't do it on no kind-a purpose, so I did. Ain't nobody can hold a fellah for breakin' no promise when he din't know he were a-doin' nothin' nohow."

"Gov?" Aspen said, right in Gideon's ear.

"Yeah?" Gideon said, still mashed against the wall.

"I'd like you to think on something, and I'm only going to tell you once, so I'd appreciate it if you'd pay attention. With me so far?"

"Reckon."

"Good. Listen closely. Every action has a reaction. You push one side of a scale, the other goes up. Still with me?"

"Reckon."

Aspen gave Gideon a pat. "Good for you. This means everything you do has a consequence. Now, you made me a promise. Eh-eh, don't interrupt, because this is the good part. This is **me** holding **you** for breaking that promise. I do hope you're still following me, Gov, because, if not, I'm afraid I will have to be more clear."

P ETER waited. What would the judge make of his story? The man had certainly followed every detail with full attention. He had even taken notes.

"And you never figured out what they wanted?"

"No, sir. They kept saying deed, but my pa never had anything I could find."

"And Mr. Fletcher burned a false deed, you say?"

Peter mitigated his first response of 'He blew it clean up.' to a simple 'yes, sir'.

"You see," he explained, "no matter what Pultrie and Wilcox thought they were after, if we could convince them it had been destroyed, they'd pack it in."

Sheriff and judge swapped a clandestine glance. Now they knew where the contents of Forsythe's drawer had gone: up in smoke. Gideon had neatly obliterated every scrap of paper trail that had anything to do with him, his past or his legal history. Peter probably had no idea— Gideon wasn't the information sharing kind.

Forsythe withdrew a rumpled envelope from his suit pocket. There was nothing remarkable about it, except perhaps that he had come by it all.

"Ever been to Kelman's Point, Mr. Anderson?"

A peculiar, breathy whistle, that nevertheless carried quite well, pierced the air. Aspen leaned around the corner of the barn. Down by the courthouse, Lee thumbed towards the upstairs office.

"Somebody's a-wantin' ya," Gideon remarked hopefully.

"Where are they, Gov?" Aspen repeated.

"A gen'l'mun keeps his a-ppointments, ya know."

"That's right. So I suppose I will have to quit being reasonable and just turn you inside out until I find them."

"Waitwaitwaitwait!"

"Yes?"

"Can we talk this over?"

Apparently, they couldn't.

SERENDIPITY had delivered the letter into the hands of the wide traveling Matt LaConner, who had read the missive and, upon learning Peter's name, had given it to Aspen, who read it and gave it to Gandy, who read it and gave it to Forsythe, who read it and gave it to Peter, who had read it and now gave the letter back to Aspen who stood reading it again as if he had not already read it.

"Settles your problems," Aspen declared, handing the much traveled paper back to Peter.

"How's that?"

"According to that letter, you've inherited several proven thoroughbreds and half a stake in your family's estate. You could go east, make a new start."

"East?" Peter echoed.

"Why not? You have folks out there and they say they'd be happy to have you."

Peter thought on this, but could not make the information line up. He didn't own anything. No one in his family owned much of anything. Anf then, like a bug treading through a pool of yesterday's honey, memories began to slog onto the shores of awareness.

"The box," he muttered, and then, realizing he had spoken aloud, went on. "I didn't put it together. I swear. 'Deed' was all they said. We'd been drifting since Ma died.

And they were hers, the papers I mean, not Pa's, so I didn't think about them."

Peter looked at the men around him. A sheriff, a judge, and. . . could Aspen be considered an officer of the court? Either way, they were all listening attentively as he fumbled to connect the dots.

"It happened years ago. Ma hardly talked about it. The family property was to be split between her and an older sister. But their mother didn't approve of my father, so Ma eloped. She took only what was hers. She said Pa was everything, she didn't want anything more. I thought she meant clothes and stuff, but Ma must have meant the papers on the thoroughbreds too."

The truth hit Peter all at once. Pultrie and Wilcox must have been led to believe his mother left with more than stock papers. They must have been told she'd run off with the deed to the estate. Surely his own grandmother wouldn't be vindictive enough to send the likes of them after her own kin? Had she gone completely senile?

"Do you suppose," he asked, needing to hear the words aloud, "this is all some kind of family squabble?"

"Do you still have your ma's things?" Gandy asked.

"Pa kept a box," Peter readily admitted, he had come too far to hold back now. "We used to talk over it some. I don't remember any deed though."

"You searched through it?"

"Nosir, it was Pa's."

"Perhaps you ought to have a good look?"

"There's no deed there, Sheriff. I swear."

"Then I'm afraid you're right, this has all been a misunderstanding. Probably several misunderstandings. One thing is clear though."

"What's that, sir?"

"You could go back east," Gandy explained. "See what's

waiting for you."

Peter stood, completely flummoxed. He stared blankly at Gandy and then at Aspen. Finally his attention settled on the judge still seated placidly behind his desk.

"Would I have to?" he asked.

"Did you have something else in mind?"

"Well, sir, I'd rather stay."

Forsythe leaned forward on his elbows. "And do what?"

"Try to quit being an idiot," Peter answered bluntly, rising to the implied challenge. "I've been digging myself a pretty big hole. My father told me a man, a proper man, squares his debts. I'd like to stay here and pay back what I stole, and the damages to the town too, since that's more my fault than Gideon's."

"Do you have a reliable means of acquiring such a large sum?"

"No, sir," Peter said, shoulders sagging.

He felt utterly transparent, as if there were not a single misdeed or the tiniest of bad thoughts the judge could not see as plainly as if they had been penned in a book and placed before him to read at his perfect leisure.

"Well," Forsythe declared at last, "I don't think we can blame you for the town, that falls elsewhere. The thefts, yes. That the law can and will hold you to. As for the rest, and we cannot ignore there is a rest, you have already pled guilty on all counts. All that remains is for me to determine your sentence."

Peter bit his lower lip, feeling much younger than his years, but refused to look away. Whatever came, he would meet it head on.

"One year," Forsythe pronounced, "and fines to equal the aforesaid property. Every cent, paid by your own hand. I find out anyone else has done satisfied the debt for you and you will find yourself right back here in front of me.

Understood?"

"Yes, sir."

"Good. Now, as for the year, I suppose we could house you with Sheriff Gandy. That is what jails are for and where criminals usually end up." The judge eyed Peter until he was sure his point had settled properly. "Tell me, were I to place you in the custody of Mr. Rivers, that is the senior Mr. Rivers, do you suppose you could work off your time without too much hassle?"

Peter started to breathe again. A whole year with folks like the Rivers? It was more than alright.

"Yes, sir!" he agreed, lightheaded with relief. "I won't give anyone a lick of grief, sir."

"Do try to convey that concept to your friend," Forsythe suggested dryly.

"Yes, sir."

"That one too, if you please. Mr. Anderson, I am under the impression this has been a long day for you. I suggest you remember it, very carefully, because this is what it feels like to stand on the wrong side of the law. I do not recommend adopting the lifestyle."

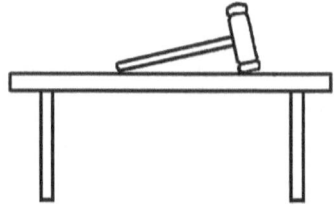

CHAPTER 19
Half Paid-up
Three Feet Deep
Negotiations
Where Credit Is Due
Colossal Pain & A Liar
And The Winner Is

NONE of the Rivers so much as twitched when Matt moseyed up, draped an arm over Gideon's shoulders, and pulled him aside. Naturally, this led Gideon to some mighty uncomfortable suspicions.

"I know you aren't too happy with me right now," Matt began.

"That's one way-a puttin' it," Gideon agreed darkly.

"I pay my debts as I see fit," Matt replied, not the least repentant.

"Well, I don't count nothin' as paid."

"To you, no. This was my debt to your brother. He's not here to twist your arm, so I had to do some twisting of my own. My debt to you, for that I will need a name."

As it turned out, Gideon had more than a name because floor sweepers who don't speak English are invisible and pretty saloon girls who do are more easily suspected of collusion.

"I oughtta put you on my list," Gideon grumbled.

"My shoulders are broad. But I find you out there," Matt warned, pointing to the greater world, "and I will haul your carcass right back here. Listen, Andy. Take a break, regroup. In the meantime, give me a name. I travel, you know that, and I meet a lot of people. I'm sure I don't need to draw you a picture. You're not the only one who wants to see right done by your brother. All I need is a name."

S HERIFF?"

"Hello, Peter."

"Looks like we'll be leaving in the morning," Peter said, inching a little farther into the sheriff's office. "May I ask you something?"

Gandy fiddled with the tip of an uncooperative ink pen and nodded vaguely.

"What about Pultrie, sir?"

"Taken care of," Gandy answered enigmatically.

His deputies were currently seeing to it Pultrie got a good start back to the States. That was one gentleman who would never return willingly.

"Sheriff?" Peter continued, like a man fixed to get the worst over with. "How did you know it was me? I think you knew about Cort too. I know you figured Pultrie and Wilcox weren't anything to do with Gideon. But how?"

Gandy reminded himself he was going to have to buy an extra bag of candy for Mark. It had taken him awhile to catch up with Harvey Wilcox. It had taken him remarkably less time to get the man to talk.

"Your mistake was slipping Haverston's property in with the things you used to frame Pultrie. Then again, it did end up saving you."

"How's that, sir?"

"Blasted pen," Gandy mumbled distractedly. "Guilty conscience. Gave you away, but made you worth saving."

"Oh," said Peter awkwardly.

Curiosity had made him open the little silver snuff box. Once he had, leaving it in Cort's hands had been unthinkable. Clearly it belonged to someone very much in love, like his folks had been. And they were right, some things tallied higher than money.

Gandy rummaged in his desk for another pen and

found one at the very back of the bottom most drawer. He extricated it, examined the tip, and sighed. Maybe with a knife and a plank of wood he could carve his report.

"Sheriff, I. . ." Peter fished about and finally found the words he'd been wanting, "Thank you, Sheriff. I hope I never give you reason to scare me like that again."

It had been wicked in a way, what Gandy had done. Like a man treading water for dear life, only to stand up and discover the water a mere three feet deep, Peter couldn't help feeling a mite small and a touch mud-dumb.

"I hope so too," Gandy replied, staring hard at Peter. "Because next time I will do a whole lot worse than scare you. Go on now. I have to tackle these ledgers before the council does something horrible to me."

Peter took the pen, adjusted it and handed it back.

"Yes, sir," he smiled, and left the sheriff to his work.

Anyone who didn't know better might think Gideon was alone, but he wasn't. Gandy and Connell lounged on the front porch of the jailhouse. Across the way, Mary had brought her rocker outside to work on her sewing. Next door, the blows of the smith's hammer echoed across the approaching twilight suggesting there was someone he would like get his hands on. And, as always, the Rivers loitered nearby.

Perched on the top rail of Zeek's corral, Gideon gave his shoulder a cautious rub. His arm had been lashed up again and Connell had threatened him on pain of pain to leave it the heck alone. Gideon sighed. In the corral, the horses milled about and, by and large, ignored him.

Leastways someone is.

It occurred to Gideon an awful lot of people had taken it into their heads to figure his business was somehow more theirs than his. He had a profoundly clear opinion of this recurring phenomenon.

Gabe Rivers trotted up, a large mason jar cradled in the crook of one arm, and leaned against a lower rail. The little boy lifted out a peach and set the jar on the fence, an implied invitation. One small hand remained on the treasure to protect the jar from the whims of gravity.

"Aspen send ya?" Gideon asked, slipping the button he'd been rubbing like a worry stone out of sight.

"Which one were you thinking?" Gabe inquired.

"Big fellah by the trough."

Why not? It wasn't like anybody actually thought he wasn't thinking about lighting a shuck.

Gabe scanned the available options of colors, shades and markings. "The sorrel with the socks'd be faster."

Gideon plucked out a peach and tipped his head at the big gray. That's the one he would stick with. What was speed against a horse who would stay the miles? And miles there would be.

"Snow's coming," Gabe mused.

"Reckon," Gideon said, though he didn't suppose winter was coming all that fast.

"You'll need a place to hole up, won't ya?"

"Reckon."

"I stay with Aunt Eddie. Don't have any brothers, but I got cousins. Fred's a cousin too, only he says he's more like a brother and I reckon that's alright. He's plenty of fun. The boys are awfully fun too. Don't you think so?"

"Reckon," Gideon said, because he knew what you were supposed to say to a kid who said something like that.

"Do you have a brother?" Gabe asked, taking a long pull from the peach jar. He put it back on the rail and wiped his mouth with a sleeve. "Do ya?"

"No," said Gideon.

He reached for a peach, but the water level had gone down and his hand was too big for the rim. Gabe dangled his fingers in the sticky water until they wrapped around a fat wedge.

"Here," he said, holding out his prize.

Gideon took the slice and shoved the whole thing into his mouth at once.

"That's not what Aspen says," Gabe started up again. "He says you have lots of brothers, only your heart's all banged up like when you get thrown from a real big, mean horse an' you don't know which way's up. Were you thrown? I've never been on a mean horse. Were you?"

Gideon sat on the fence, caught between the past tense and the present. What was he supposed to say? 'I had me a brother. He were the best you'd ever want. An' oh, by the way, he were shot cold an' I ain't done nothin' 'bout it.'? That's not how fairytales went. Maybe Connell was right: why disillusion an innocent little boy?

"Ever'one gets throwed sometime, kid. That's life."

And death.

And death.

"So, you stayin?"

"Huh?" said Gideon, blindsided.

"Are you staying?" Gabe repeated doggedly. "I asked Aunt Eddie, only Aspen said I had better ask you directly. You oughtta stay on account-a I ain't had a chance to show you my marbles. Mine's the best collection in the whole territory. Fred says so. Rodger says his is better, only he doesn't have any steelies. I got four an' won't play 'em for keeps, so he's just mad. So?"

Gideon put some serious thought on the big gray horse. Matt had drifted on, but not before being armed with a name and a direction. Gideon hadn't really wanted to do it, but he did not need book learning to read the signs. Folks would have to simmer down before he'd have a chance to budge, or even breath. And winter was closer than farther. And Peter had gone and landed himself a year of captivity. Gideon supposed he would have to see him clear of that somehow. And there was no denying a man who had to negotiate with a peach jar was a man not entirely healed.

He looked down. Gabe was looking up at him with blue eyes full of stardust and a face full of hope.

Reckon a fellah'd have to be right mean to say no to that.

Regroup, stock your kit. That's what Matt had said. Besides, that gentleman would be easier to track than Lucas Wade.

"S'pose," Gideon allowed, without a great deal of enthusiasm. "'Til spring, anyhow."

Gabe gave an excited whoop, half turned to answer his aunt's hale, and whirled back around to slap a final peach into Gideon's hand.

WHAT an odd pair Gabe and Gideon made— the innocent and the never been innocent. Aspen puzzled on it some and then leaned over to give his aunt a peck on the cheek.

Eddie drew up short. "What was that for?"

Gabe went flying by. Eddie tussled his hair whilst Aspen neatly plucked away the peach jar. Then Eddie took her nephew by his vest and tipped her head back to study his face. The expression she found there was so like his father's, and Eddie knew what it meant. She'd been found out. Aspen knew she sent Matt LaConner to speak with him and, like his father, when it came to saying thank you, Aspen Rivers ran short on words. Somehow kissing his aunt in public came easier.

"You get much sharper and you'll cut yourself, boy," she teased, taking the jar. "And this was a dirty trick."

"I know," Aspen agreed, and headed for the corral.

E VEN Gideon's limited vocabulary was up to the challenge of what to call a man who kissed his aunt in public.

"Nancy," he ribbed, as Aspen sidled up beside him.

"Courtesy. . . Ah, right, you haven't figured that one out yet. Look, Gov—"

"I know, you're sorry for bein' a colossal pain."

"Colossal, good word. Ever figure out efficiency?"

"Shove off."

"I had a very interesting talk with your friend."

"Some friend," Gideon remarked, studying the idly milling horses as if they were the most going concern. "You know don't ya? 'Bout my brother. That's what ya were gonna ask when I gived ya them two questions."

"Yes," Aspen acknowledged simply.

"How?"

"For one thing, I grew up with brothers. When they start feeling bossed, they're pretty quick to tell me I'm not their father. You always said brother."

"Ya done fig'red from that?"

"There were other hints," Aspen admitted.

"Like?"

Deliberately, Aspen kept shut.

"Colossal pain," Gideon repeated.

"So you say."

"Yeah, so I say," Gideon rallied. He fidgeted, searching for a way to say more than he could articulate. "So. . . so you know. . ."

"Why you keep running, yes," Aspen agreed,

acknowledging the surface question, but answering the hidden one too.

"Can't nothin' change what I gotta do. Can't nothin' get in the way neither."

A compact little paint stretched out her neck to nuzzle Gideon's hand and he recalled the peach there with some relief for the distraction. He let the mare have the treat and lick the last of the sugary remains from his fingers. When she gave up, Gideon ran a be-slobbered hand down the leg of his new britches.

Aspen groaned.

"Ya knowed it din't fig'r to last," Gideon offered smugly.

"I knew."

"Hold up!" Gideon exclaimed, his brain finally catching up with his ears. "You an' Matt done talked?"

"Yep," Aspen answered, at his most serene.

"That dirty—! How much did he tell ya?"

"More than he told the others."

"How much did he tell them?"

"More than I'm going to tell you."

"Aw, c'mon! You can't not tell me nothin'!" Gideon persisted, anxiety dripping from every syllable.

"You would do the same in my position."

He's got ya there.

"Nope. If'n I were you, I'd be a gen'l'mun an' wouldn't have me no choice but to tell on a'count-a it bein' the decent thing."

"Let's trade. We'll take every time you've been straight with me– ah, there's a problem. Alright, every time you've told the whole truth to anyone– ah, right. How about you just get used to me keeping this particular advantage?"

"You're right funny, you are," said Gideon who, of the two of them, was the only one not amused.

They went back to watching the horses, one thinking hard and one waiting patiently. A palomino slurged water at the trough. Tails twitched and feet stomped away flies. The sorrel sisters stood side by side and head to tail, the equine equivalent of back to back.

"Who else knows?" Gideon finally asked.

"Only the family."

"Ya mean the boys?" Gideon clarified, searching for the outer limits of the disaster field.

"At the moment."

Oh, boy.

"Wadda ya mean at the moment? Thems is all, right?" Silence met Gideon's probing. "C'mon, it's a simple question."

"I mean the **entire** family," Aspen replied calmly.

"Ya can't do that!" Gideon said, uncalmly.

"Guardian, remember? You have a real gift for saying the things you oughtn't, but you're not so good at saying the things you should. Don't worry, I'll take care of it until you figure it out."

"Sons of–"

"That's one of the oughtn'ts," Aspen interrupted helpfully.

"Least ya didn't tell 'im," Gideon grumbled, lifting his chin at the approaching sheriff. The lack of answer turned statement into question and Gideon spun on Aspen, who stood there smirking. "I thought ya done said family!"

"What do you think he is?"

"I oughtn't to say."

"One wise decision in a row. Careful, you're liable to start a whole new habit."

"Aw, shove off."

"Why don't you shove off?" Aspen suggested. "Peter's waiting. He seems to feel he might be able to endure your company, which only goes to show he's more of a gentleman than you."

"You gonna tell Gandy?" Gideon demanded, refusing to fall for the distraction.

"No."

Gideon eased himself to the ground.

"He already knows," Aspen finished.

"For real play?"

"I said so didn't I? And I do not lie. Now get going before I twist your arm again."

"You got lucky's all. If'n I—"

"Is this you sassing me?"

Gideon tipped his head and hooked a thumb into his pocket, the perfect picture of contemplation.

"Yes," he said. "Yessir, it is."

G ANDY planted his elbows on the top rail of the corral.

"Doesn't look like you got too far with that one," he remarked dryly, tipping his head at the departing Gideon.

"You did alright," Aspen offered amiably.

"Not a bad day's work, if I do say so. Cort and his boys are charged with the thefts as they should have been and Pultrie took the blame for the damages to the town, which is the least of his worries. Peter can keep his name out of the mud and I suspect he will be more inclined to speak up in the future. And Gideon, despite his best efforts, takes the blame for nothing– publicly that is. Think you can hold onto him this time?"

"I'll see what I can do."

"Let me know if you need a hand."

"Thank you, Sheriff, I surely will," Aspen accepted the ribbing with mock sincerity. "You coming to supper?"

"What about Connell?"

"Would I leave him to starve on your porch?"

Gandy gave a sharp whistle, waved Connell over, and turned towards the café.

"How did Wilson like his candy sticks?" Aspen asked, strolling along.

"Alright, I was wrong there," Gandy conceded. "You did get Gideon to apologize."

"Oh," Aspen said, with an artfully absentminded snap of his fingers. "Could you hold onto these?"

The sheriff found himself holding a set of homemade lock picks and decided there was one more angle he could play, even if it did come round-about.

"You know that pretty little filly over to the bakery?" he asked, altogether too innocently. "The one you've been noticing and hoping no one notices you've been noticing?"

"You've noticed?" Aspen said, pulling the rug out from under Gandy's punch line.

"Me and a few others," Gandy acknowledged equitably. "You might like to know there's a little something you have not noticed."

"Yes?" Aspen prompted, and suddenly felt perhaps it was he standing on the rug.

"Well, as I recall, you weren't in much of a state for noticing details, but you know that young lady you bumped into the other morning? The one who was a touch dismayed by your less than gentlemanly condition?"

"No," said Aspen, only it came out as half question and half statement wrapped in dreadful realization and tied with impending embarrassment.

"'Fraid so," Gandy gloated, with no shame whatsoever.

"You sure?"

"Definitely."

And all of Aspen's brothers were in town and, oh look,

there was Gus going into the café. It was just possible Aspen could manufacture some critical pile of paperwork that, where not preventing the coming harassment, might at least grant him a temporary reprieve. Gandy's arm fell across his shoulders and Aspen gave it up. He would have to face it eventually. And eventually he would find a way to get even with Gideon Fletcher.

Writing this book has made my blood sing,
my heart laugh and my soul. . .
at home.

Natalie Jayne seeks out the far and away
places. She particularly enjoys going walkabout
in the remote corners of her own imagination.
Now if only the dang magpies would quit
eating the bread crumbs.

CHICANERY

(Rivers Series #3)

To paraphrase Mark Twain,
"Any person caught 'Loitering With Intent To Find A Plot'
in this narrative will be arrested. Any person caught
searching for a deeper meaning will be banished forthwith."

As the title implies, *Chicanery* follows the tricks and
coups of the Rivers clan. So fetch yourself some coffee,
or beverage of choice, and join 6 rowdy brothers, an uncle
(by adoption), a conniving father, & 1 mighty determined
chicken as they spend an entire winter— all six feet deep
of it— bundled into one cabin. There might be room for
all the boots, hats, and associated bodies, but so many
personalities scrunched up together is begging for trouble.

CHICANERY

BEING dangled by the ankles from a second story
window presents certain inherently annoying
inconveniences. Top of the list is the challenge of getting
your fist anywhere near your tormentor's face. Gravity
simply was not on Gideon's side. But then, neither was
anyone else, a reoccurring state he neatly chalked up to
life's funny little ways.

Life def'nately ain't no lady.

Not on her best day.

"Careful, we don't want him to crack his skull."

That Ember then allowed Gideon to 'slip' a few inches

completely undid any concern his tender words implied. The twins wanted information, specifically the location of one long-dead fish— the little guy was overdue for eviction. They had searched every nook, emptied every crevice and come up with nothing but a nose full of stench. Gideon had been threatened, cajoled and then, with alarming speed and commendable teamwork, he had been presented with a unique opportunity to review his position.

How dead d'ya fig're they'll be if'n they let go?

Not half as much as when I get my hands on 'em.

"I'll pummel ya both!" Gideon hollered, the blood ringing in his ears.

"You really should be more polite," Lee suggested.

"Polite? Ya want polite?" Despite his current desire not to fidget overmuch, Gideon made a valiant effort to haul himself up. "I'll learn you side-winders polite."

"You don't have the manners to spare," said Ember, around the most infuriating giggle Gideon had ever heard.

They gave him another jolt, which not only cut off his creative linguistic endeavors, but returned him to his previous cups for tea kettle position.

"Care to try again?" Lee asked, ever so sweetly.

Gideon promised his tormentors a number of dire consequences, and attached to this a string of vitriolic, voluble, and remarkably vibrant aspersions.

"Gideon Fletcher, that will do!"

Aspen's admonishment preceded the man himself into Gideon's skewed view. Fort followed, the frown on his face aimed at Emberlee. Ember stared back defiantly, enormously pleased with himself. Lee offered a small, sheepish shrug.

"I'll knock you good-for-nothin'. . ."

Gideon pressed on, his temper not one whit dampened

by the arrival of reinforcements. It did not occur to him to wonder if the new arrivals were on his side or Emberlee's. As far as he was concerned, they could take their pick.

"You might try not provoking them," said Aspen, before Gideon could get to the heart of his malediction. "Especially at the moment."

It was good advice, which naturally Gideon did not take. He expanded upon his previous threats, amended a few and improved upon others.

Like two kids at a game of hide-and-seek, Amos and Cricket secreted themselves on the porch and waited to see how the olders would deal with the situation. They peeked out, shooshing and batting at each other to keep quiet.

"Pull him up," Fort directed, ignoring Gideon's acidic stream of displeasure. "No, better yet, hand him down."

"Down?" echoed Gideon, suddenly, and acutely, interested in the men below him.

He let out an inadvertent, but heartfelt yelp as he plunged on a head first date with a rather flat future— and then Fort caught him mid-fall. The ground once again firmly beneath his feet, Gideon did not shake his fist in embarrassed indignation. Ember did not need a show of injured pride. He needed a few things explained to him– in very clear terms. If Lee had any smarts at all, he would keep out of it this time, because Ember Rivers was going to get exactly what he deserved.

Other great stories available through
Two Square Books Publishing

Natalie Jayne
(Fiction / Informative)

Gideon's Way (Rivers Short Story Intro))
Between the Rivers (Rivers Series #1)
Indebted (Rivers Series #2)
Chicanery (Rivers Series #3
Redemption (Rivers Series #4)
Spectacle (Under construction)

Three Cousins (dyslexia, dyspraxia, ADHD)

Robin Rush
(Children's & Young Reader)

The Straw Hat Penny Horse
A Dog, A Grump & A Garden
A Day to Bark About
My Me In The Mirror
Yuck to a Duck

**Want help getting <u>your</u> wholesome,
fun or inspiring story into print?
We would love to hear from you!**

Your story, your rights, your way!

For **ebooks** please go to: smashwords.com

To order print books use:
twosquarebooks.com
contact@twosquarebooks.com

4068 Mother Lode Suite J, Shingle Springs, CA
(upstairs— custom services by appointment)
(530) 748-7756 (11:00 a.m.—7 p.m. only please)

www.ingramcontent.com/pod-product-compliance
Lightning Source LLC
Chambersburg PA
CBHW050901250626
47155CB00001B/50